THE LOVE PENALTY

CAROLYN MILLER

PRAISE FOR CAROLYN MILLER

Praise for *Northwest Ice* and the *Original Six* hockey series

"A delightful, laugh out loud romance that fans of hockey stories will love!" ~ *SUSAN MAY WARREN, USA Today bestselling author*

"With a strong hero and even stronger heroine, *Fire and Ice* combines tough issues with romance and laughter in such a real way. Miller is becoming masterful at both deep plots and well-rounded characters that keep you invested and turning the pages. Even better, she never fails to leave you with a smile and happy sigh when you reach the final page. This latest addition to her hockey romance series only cements that fact. A must read." ~ *SUSAN TUTTLE, best-selling author of Along Came Love series*

"Not only was I entertained by the engaging characters and well-written plot, I also loved the deeper explorations of faith, value, prayer and how women are treated in sports reporting. Hannah and Franklin's chemistry is full of fireworks and they might melt the ice with their can't-resist-any-longer kisses. Needless to say, *Fire & Ice* scores a big win with me!" ~ *CARRIE BOOTH SCHMIDT, Reading is my Superpower blog*

"Fire and Ice starts with a fun premise then digs deeper into the kind of relationships that last throughout this whole series and beyond. Sure to inspire." ~ *ANGELA RUTH STRONG, bestselling author of* Husband Auditions

"He's a hockey player trying to transfer smoothly into his hometown team, and she's a sports reporter trying to keep her job. Between the two, things are heating up on and off the ice in this newest addition to Carolyn Miller's "Original Six Hockey Romance" series! A great read for fans of hockey and romance alike, don't miss out on this Canadian getaway!" ~ *ANGELA K. COUCH, author of* A Rose for the Resistance

"I loved the dialogue and the hero and heroine, the very authentic and real challenges they faced and the unique setting and hockey slant." ~ *RACHEL MCMILLAN, bestselling author*

"A touching romance set on the breathtaking shores of Canada's Lake Muskoka. Sarah and Dan are so vividly drawn they practically leap off the page! Their sweet, slowly evolving friendship deepens into the kind of lasting love Christians long for. A must read!" ~ *MEGHANN WHISTLER, award-winning author of* The Billionaire's Secret

"There is nothing like a wonderful redemption story where someone changes their life and becomes a better version of themselves. It is a good reminder to me that God offers incredible grace to all of us." ~ *GOODREADS review*

"Carolyn Miller keeps on turning out these beautifully written, tender hearted books!... There was humor and brilliant bantering conversations, heart stopping romance, as well as exciting descriptions (and sometimes dangerous passages of play) of hockey games. Well worth the late night/early morning read!" ~ *KAYE'S REVIEWS & NEWS*

"I am emerging out of my book hangover after reading *Checked Impressions* by Carolyn Miller....The romance, humor and themes of identity are so enjoyable and make for a great read!" ~ *BECKY'S BOOKSHELVES*

"Adrenaline, chemistry, romance, and lots of wooing!...You do not have to be a fan of sports or even knowledgeable in hockey and short track to appreciate *Love on Ice.*" ~ *GOODREADS review*

"Carolyn Miller scores another win with *Love on Ice*, the second book in her Original Six Hockey series. I absolutely loved the faith thread in this story. It's message that success does not lie on what we do, but who we are is powerful." ~ *GOODREADS review*

CHAPTER 1

Calgary, Canada
Late January

She didn't fit in here. She'd never belong.

It was funny how a person could feel opposite desires simultaneously. One: the recognition that Sylvie was completely out of her depth, and she wanted to leave. Two: the recognition that something deep within her demanded she stay.

She glanced around the pews filled with good and lovely people. No one else had dressed in all black. No one else wore Doc Martens boots. Sure, some of them had tattoos—she knew Bree's best friend, Holly, had a tattoo of the Olympic rings on her ankle—but for the most part they looked like a style option, rather than a protest against the world. And while she knew that statement made her sound as judgy as everybody else in this building, she couldn't help it. She knew she didn't fit in, and despite Bree's efforts over the years, she'd never belong. Never be good enough. Even now, the walls felt like they were closing in on her, making it hard to breathe.

So that fact made her want to run away. To escape this church building. Further. Like, maybe go back to Ontario. Or possibly Mexico.

But even that feeling was countered by one equally potent, a heavy internal tug that demanded she stay—and not just because the place was filled with hot hockey players. She gulped, and glanced around.

Bree and Mike Vaughan sat in the row in front, surrounded by various family members, including Mike's parents, Bree's folks and her grandmother, Violet. Both Mike and Bree's moms had basically moved in since Christmas, taking turns to help out with the kids, and then Bree and the tiny twins, Madeline and Matthew, born five weeks premature. Even to help poor Mike, who'd been so exhausted that he'd taken time off work for several weeks.

Sylvie swallowed. She understood. It wasn't a slight on her care for little Ethan and Ellison during the last quarter of last year. It was simply all the other things that had needed doing, like cooking, cleaning, washing—things that Mike had wearily said he could pay someone to do, but both mothers had insisted they were needed, as family came first after all. And while Pam Karlsson was lovely, Mrs. Vaughan had made no secret of the fact she didn't like Sylvie, so Sylvie hadn't tried too hard to turn the other cheek. It was like Regina thought that just because Sylvie liked piercings and black attire that made her somehow dangerous around Bree's children. She rolled her eyes as the minister or preacher or whatever he was kept talking.

Another peek across the aisle showed Bree's twin, Brent Karlsson, and his wife Holly, and their two children, sitting listening raptly. Bree's older brother, Dean, was there too with his wife and kids. Nearby were some of Mike's teammates, including Franklin James and his girlfriend Hannah. It wasn't exactly a mystery how so many NHL players happened to be in church on this day. Mike and Bree were so good they seemed to have a hotline to God, who probably could've caused the NHL schedule to shift around or something. But then Bree's babies had been born to allow the timing of their christening to coincide with the start of the mid-season break, which meant more players could attend than was usual in the regular season.

As she peeked across, one of those men glanced across, his eyes touching hers for a long moment before sliding away. Brian or Ryan or something like that. She was fairly certain Bree had mentioned that he was one of Mike's friends, even if he did play for Calgary's biggest rival, Edmonton. Apparently, he was from some online Bible study group that Mike disappeared to most weeks, leaving her and Bree to juggle the babies. Whatever. He seemed way too clean-cut for her. The guy he sat next to, Winnipeg's Luc Blanchard, was more her usual speed, with his sleeve of tatts and resting scowl face. Beyond them sat another of the NHL's no-bull players, Vancouver's Chris Thomas, with his wife Diana and three freckled kids.

Her heart ached as the service continued. All of these rich and beautiful people with their perfect lives, their perfect husbands and perfect wives, their perfect families. What did any of them understand about fractured families and trying to find love? It was like they lived in a rose-scented bubble of obliviousness, and had no idea how others struggled in the real world. And although Bree and Mike were better than most, even they could never really understand what it was to desperately want a family, to feel like there was an anchor in this world. Even before her parents' deaths, Sylvie had always been alone.

The walls were closing in. She couldn't *wait* to leave. A prayer was prayed, she mouthed an Amen, not that she thought God—if he or she even existed—would pay attention to her, then stood and swiftly exited down the long aisle to her rust bucket parked outside.

She huddled in her coat, almost slipping on the icy pavement as she neared her car. Bree had asked for Sylvie to help with preparing the lunch, and knowing Bree had plenty of hands to help with getting the tiny twins and older two into her new mom-van, Sylvie hadn't needed to stay. She *had* needed to get a moment's respite at home—Bree's home, but whatever—before the deluge of visitors hit again. She was so thankful that Bree had insisted Sylvie keep her place in the guest room, even as others—like Mike's mom—had made it plain that she wasn't exactly their first choice in caring for Bree's children.

She'd overheard Regina Vaughan say that once, and Bree's laughing response, "You don't seriously expect me to kick out a friend of mine who specifically moved here to help with the babies, now do you?"

Sylvie had rounded the corner at that time, pretending she hadn't heard. Not for Regina's sake, but for Bree's. Bree had proved a good friend, and sure as heck didn't need more drama in her life, not after complications with Bree's health meant an early caesarean delivery of her twins. It had been a super scary time for them all, and Sylvie had done her best to calm Ethan and little Ellison, who didn't understand why Mommy had gone away to the hospital for several weeks. Bree and the twins had come home nearly two weeks ago, and had wanted the christening service held as soon as possible, and somehow they'd pulled it off. But Sylvie knew her friend was tired, and the fact Bree had reached out to her during Sylvie's hour of need, and done so much for her since, meant she'd do whatever she could to help her now.

She'd just picked up Ethan's toys when the first car pulled in. A glimpse through the large plate glass revealed it wasn't Bree's van, but a sportier vehicle. She sighed. Time to act like she liked people again.

She busied herself in the kitchen, removing the plastic-wrapped trays of hors d'oeuvres that Bree had ordered from a local deli, and placing the trays of kid-friendly meals in the oven to gently warm. She just had to look busy, like the paid help Regina so clearly thought her, which in some ways probably was true. Bree hadn't just paid for Sylvie's moving costs, but had paid her a nice little salary since she'd moved here nearly four months ago to work as the nanny while Bree battled health challenges in the lead up to her delivery. One day that'd change, when Bree decided she didn't need as much help anymore. Or if Regina decided to stay much longer.

The slam of car doors preceded the opening of the front door which she'd left unlocked, trusting that today wouldn't be the day a serial killer chose to visit.

"Yo! Anyone home?"

Brent Karlsson. Bree's twin, and NHL superstar. Sylvie checked her appearance in the mirrored backsplash and tucked loose curls behind her ears. "Back here," she yelled.

A patter of little feet drew an ache to her heart and a smile to her dial as two dark-haired kids raced inside, then skidded to a stop at the sight of her.

"Hi." Sylvie smiled, but the two children only looked at her wide-eyed. She was used to this, as lots of kids seemed to find her appearance unusual.

"Don't mind them," Brent said, his entrance causing both kids to run behind his long jeans-clad legs. "Say hi, guys," he instructed his children.

Two soft "Hi"s met her ears, and she crouched down to their level. "Do you want to go play in the kids' room?" They nodded. "Come on."

She led the way to the room which sometimes doubled as a downstairs guest room, but which today had been set up for the use of the visiting children. Sylvie planned to supervise them, but Bree had been a little iffy on the numbers.

"Don't worry," Sylvie had assured her, "it'll be just like preschool days. You just need to relax and take it easy and not worry about a thing. You know the doctors want you to rest, so if you need to get a break or have a sleep, do so."

"But so many people have taken time out to be here for today."

Sylvie had nodded. A bunch of the hockey players were heading home or off on short vacations after this, which meant the post-church service lunch was their chief time to socialize with Mike and Bree. "And everyone is here because they love you, and want you to be well, and they'll all understand and be completely supportive if you need to rest."

Mike had nodded, thanking Sylvie later, "as we both know she's inclined to take too much on."

"That's what I'm here for," she'd assured.

"You're a Godsend, that's what you are," he'd said. And she'd tried not to roll her eyes.

She now pointed out the toys and games in the room, and returned to the kitchen where Holly Karlsson was pulling out more of the trays in the well-stocked fridge, while Brent fiddled with the sound system.

Holly glanced up at Sylvie. "Thanks for that." Her voice held an Aussie inflection. "It's Sylvie, right? We first met at Bree's hen night years ago."

"Hen night?"

"Bachelorette party?" Holly's nose wrinkled. "You'd think I'd know the North American terms by now, but I still forget. Anyway, it's good to see you again."

"You too." Although she really hoped Holly didn't remember the way Sylvie had once spoken about—and ogled—Holly's now-husband, Brent. That wasn't awkward at all.

"You look a little different." Holly's head tilted.

Try a lot. That's what losing thirty pounds, gaining new ink, and changing her hair did. Those people who talked about a haircut to get over a man had no idea. Her mom's death had proved a catalyst for change, and she was more than happy to do anything to leave the old Sylvie behind. Moving west from Toronto meant a fresh start in lots of ways.

By now others had arrived, including Bree and Mike, Bree being instantly told by her mom to sit down and put her feet up. Sylvie led Ethan and little Ellison to the playroom to play with their cousins, knowing there would be plenty of willing arms for baby cuddles with Maddie and Matt.

Sylvie stayed there, listening to the sounds of others arriving, the conversation and laughter, unable to ignore the fact that once again she felt sidelined, not part of the crowd who already had so much going for them. Which was dumb, especially as this was what she'd signed up for. But there it was.

"Hi."

She turned and faced Diana, the shy-looking woman married to Vancouver's goalie, Chris. Diana held the hands of another two children, while a third child eyed Sylvie, his snub nose wrinkled like he didn't like what he saw.

"Bree said you were looking after the kids in here. Would you mind—?"

"Awesome! Look at all the Lego!" The oldest boy barreled past his mom, straight past Sylvie, as the other woman sighed.

"I'm so sorry. Tanner is a little hyperactive at times—he gets that from his father, would you believe—"

Sylvie had seen the man in games she'd watched with Bree. Oh, she'd believe it.

"—and we'd love the chance to just relax for a moment."

"No problem. There's food heating up now. Any allergies to be aware of?"

A long list of gluten, dairy, and nut intolerances followed, which she met with assurances of the fruit and healthy snacks and gluten-free meat pies that Bree had insisted on.

"Thank you so much." The woman visibly sagged in relief. "I'm Diana, by the way. Diana Thomas. Chris's wife."

"Sylvie Miles."

"Thank you, Sylvie. You've been helping Bree out with the kids, haven't you?"

"For a while now, yeah."

Diana smiled. "You're a real blessing to her and Mike."

Sylvie tensed. All these references to God and blessing and stuff were making her feel itchy inside. "Just doing what I can. Now go, have fun. I'll look after..."

"Faith and Jack," Diana supplied, gently pushing them toward Sylvie. Jack screwed up his nose and went to sit beside his brother, while his sister lingered by Sylvie's side.

"Come on, Faith." Sylvie held out her hand. "Do you like dolls? Ellison is only little but she has a few."

Faith shook her head. "I like cars."

"A girl after my own heart, then." She waved off Diana who wisely escaped without a sound. Some parents made their departures unnecessarily hard. "Okay, Ethan has plenty of cars he won't mind us playing with."

That hope was soon lost as Jack and Tanner soon got into an argument, forcing Sylvie to intervene, before it disrupted the others. "Come on boys, put the cars down."

"But I had it first," yelled Tanner.

"Jack, if he had it first then we can't snatch it from—"

"See?" Tanner yanked his arm away from his brother, holding the car up high. "You can't have it."

Jack started crying, the high-pitched wail soon bringing his father in.

"Man, I knew it had to be you two." Chris glanced at Sylvie, shaking his head. "Are you supposed to be in charge here?"

Defensiveness rose as part of her wanted to shrivel under his narrowed gaze. Another part wanted to point out that his kids were ultimately his responsibility. "Yes."

"I'm real sorry about them." He sighed. "Tanner has ADHD, and Jack bounces off his behavior."

"Diana explained. They'll probably settle once they eat. Which reminds me, do you mind waiting here a moment while I go get the kids' food trays?"

"Sure." He beckoned over another guest with the physique of a hockey player, leaving her to hurry to the kitchen while they continued their conversation. She wasn't sure how much actual supervision was going on, but she'd take this chance. A retrieval of trays from the oven, a quick rearrange, then she was halted by Holly again.

"Are they behaving?" Holly asked. "We heard screaming before."

"Not yours, but Chris Thomas's kids."

They were joined by Hannah Wade, Franklin James's girlfriend, who Sylvie had gotten to know last year. But perhaps not just Franklin's girlfriend anymore, judging from the sparkly rock on her finger.

"When did this happen?" Sylvie demanded, pointing at the ring.

"New Year's Eve."

"Congratulations!" Holly hugged her.

"Thanks. We're hoping to get married at Franklin's family ranch this summer, provided his sister can coordinate it around a movie being shot there."

"Three Creek Ranch," Sylvie explained to Holly. "There's an old western town that's been used for lots of movies and TV shows, including *As The Heart Draws*."

"Ainsley Beckett is in that one, isn't she?" Holly asked. "Between the kids and my studies, I don't watch a lot of TV these days, but I've seen a few episodes. She's really pretty."

Hannah nodded. "It's beautiful there. Especially in summer." She smiled at Holly. "It's funny talking to you today after doing that interview two weeks ago. If I'd known there'd be so many of you here today I would've begged for a camera crew."

Because Hannah had recently earned a new role as a correspondent for ESPN. ESP-flipping-N. Envy soared. The big lives of these women—Holly was a Winter Olympics short-track skating gold medalist, as well as studying to be a doctor, Bree had said—made Sylvie feel so small.

"I think Bree and Mike are happy to keep things on the down-low today," Sylvie offered.

"But there's nothing stopping you from doing some interviews on your phone, right?" Holly said.

The two chatted on, leaving Sylvie to carry her trays of now-appropriately cooled kids' food to the room. Around her the conversations continued, the men and women with lives more important than hers offering a smile or ignoring her as she moved past. It was hard not to feel less-than, sometimes. To feel like she was a cog in the wheel of someone else's big life.

Mike caught her attention from where he was talking with a couple of teammates she'd met here before. "Thanks for all you're doing."

"No problem."

"Seriously, Bree and I appreciate you."

She shrugged. "It's what you pay me for."

She noticed the way his teammate eyed her spiderweb clips in her hairdo then trickled down her attire of black shirtdress, fishnets and Docs, his lip curled and dismissive, like he thought her a weirdly-dressed waitress. The fact that she clearly wasn't memorable to anyone here drew new resolve to put her extra sassy boots on. She offered the plate to him and fake-smiled. "Let me guess: you're eyeing me like that because you're secretly wanting one of these little pastries, am I right?"

"Uh..."

"They're for the kids, but I can understand a grown man feeling like he needs something a little more basic sometimes."

A quick glance at Mike revealed his usual laid-back good humor had fallen away, replaced with a slight frown. Hmm. Maybe that last comment had too much bite in it. Still, it didn't stop her from snatching the tray away, just as his big doofus of a teammate reached to grab a pastry.

"Oops, I just remembered. They're for the kids. And you wouldn't want to deprive a child now, would you?"

She pivoted and strode away, almost crashing into Franklin, who did his own quickstep to avoid her.

"Hey, sorry, Sylvie. Here, you want me to take that?" he offered.

"Um, sure. Thank you." Finally, one of the guys here was taking thoughtfulness beyond mere words. "If you could take that inside the kids' room, I'll go get the rest of the trays."

"Better hurry. If Chris sees this, he's likely to eat it all."

"Truth." See, she had time for someone like Franklin. Hannah had really lucked out with him. But was it any wonder he loved Hannah when she was so pretty, talented, and thanks to her TV sports reporter job, famous? Sylvie's heart dipped, and she avoided eyes as she returned to the kitchen to grab the next tray.

By the time she returned to the kids' room, Franklin had joined the man crew, who were talking hockey playoff predictions, now they were over halfway through the season.

Chris broke off his conversation to eye her. "You're back, huh?"

"As you can see."

"'bout time. I'm starved."

"Then go eat," she snarked.

Franklin cleared his throat as Chris scowled at her then stalked off. "Hey, Sylvie, have you met Luc and Ryan?"

Not formally, no. But as she was feeling pretty ticked off with the world she couldn't be bothered explaining that Mike had talked about them often, and so settled for a nod. Besides, if this was some not-so-secret way to set her up, then no thanks. She wasn't that pathetically desperate.

The mullet man crossed his tattooed arms over his barrel chest and nodded. But his friend… Um, okay, hello.

She obviously hadn't got a thorough look in the church before, because now she saw him better, his scruff and sparkling dark hazel eyes, and yes, his muscles, mightn't be exactly Brent Karlsson caliber, but were still quite enough to tempt her. "Hey."

He smiled, his eyes on hers, not on her hair or her legs or her chest or anywhere they shouldn't be. He held out a hand. She grasped it. Her breath hitched. Heat lay there, so much that she'd love to feel his hand in hers, to snuggle up with him on this freezing January day.

Then a child screamed.

THAT MAGICAL MOMENT of connection snapped as Sylvie dropped Ryan's hand and raced into the room, separating two kids who were obviously hockey wannabes judging from the WrestleMania moves and threats not unlike what Ryan had seen and heard on the rink. Or what he and his brother had done on occasion.

But when Chris's eldest son started laying into Sylvie instead of his brother, Ryan moved with Franklin and Luc as one unit to separate the fighting kids, Franklin and Luc a wall against Tanner's flailing kicks, while Ryan grabbed the smaller one, Jack, and drew him away. But not before one of Jack's fists found Sylvie's face.

She gasped, and grabbed her cheek.

"Oh man, are you okay?" Ryan asked her.

She peered at him, then glanced at Jack, who stood open-mouthed at what he'd done, even while his older brother still raged. "It's okay, Jack. I know you didn't mean it."

He started wailing, and she moved to her knees in front of the kid. "Hey. Don't cry. It's all okay." She glanced up at Ryan. "Help me stop him crying," she muttered. "We can't let this ruin Bree's big day."

But the tears quickly drew Chris and Diana back to the room, their slumped shoulders saying this wasn't the first time something like this had happened. Ryan could feel the tension between them as Chris muttered, "See? I knew we shouldn't have brought them," to his wife.

Diana pressed her lips together, spoke softly to Sylvie who simply shook her head and assured her she was fine and smiled. But Ryan could tell it wasn't a real smile, as it only went up half one side of her face, like she really was injured.

Chris spoke in an undertone to his sons, which instantly shut down all tantrums, and he and Diana took their children from the room.

"Are you okay?" Ryan asked Sylvie again. "I can go get some ice."

"I'll be fine."

"You sure?" Franklin asked. "You look like you might be getting a nice shiner there. Speaking from experience."

"Honestly, I'll be happy as soon as we can all settle down." She offered a gritted-teeth-looking smile. "And I'm *really* happy to be here on my own. I don't want Mike or Bree feeling like they need to worry about the kids."

Luc shrugged. "If you're sure." Franklin cut Ryan a look, then followed Luc from the room.

But Ryan didn't want to leave. Not yet, anyway. The fact she wanted to downplay things, he suspected as much for Diana's sake as Bree's, drew a sense of admiration. He'd noticed the way she'd been working here over lunch, doing her job without fuss. And that, as much as her cool hair, pierced nose and eyebrow, vibrant painted nails, and the tatts dancing around her neck, intrigued him.

She was obviously Bree's friend, and he knew Mike had been glad she'd come to help out Bree when the pregnancy had taken its toll on her health. Then, when Bree had needed the emergency caesarean, Mike had often said how thankful he was that Sylvie had been there to keep the other kids calm. Mike had needed time off from captain duties, the whole experience so unsettling Calgary's team that they'd lost several games in a row, the most recent in the latest Battle of Alberta, when Ryan's team had thumped Calgary by five goals. To see so many people, including Mike's teammates, come out in support of their twins' christening today was special, to see them attend church was awesome, and he'd prayed they'd heard the pastor's message about God's grace and love for all.

But surely the fact that Sylvie had attended, that she'd bowed her head during the prayers—yeah, he'd peeked—meant, unlike what Mike had implied before in the group chat, that Sylvie now believed in God, too. Which was…good.

"You're still here," she said now.

"Are you sure I can't get you anything?" he asked. "If you ice that bruise now, it mightn't show as much tomorrow."

"You concerned about my looks?"

"You look good to me." Such an understatement. But then, he'd never met anyone with her striking blend of dark chocolate eyes, purple dipped hair, pale skin, and unique style.

The narrowed gaze softened a fraction, and she shrugged. "I can't leave the kids again, so if you really want to help, you could find one of Mike's ice packs in the freezer."

"Back in a moment."

Her lips curved up briefly, and he hurried from the room, passing various grandparents and family members, including Bree's brother Brent, who was talking with Mike's sister Callie. So many people, he was getting kind of overwhelmed. But he'd only be here another hour or so before he'd need to drive back north. God had pulled a miracle to have so many of the online Bible crew gather here today.

He found the ice pack, reassured Mike who was sitting with a clearly exhausted Bree, but who refused to go to bed as her mom and grandmother suggested, instead insisting on entertaining their guests.

"But honey," Mike began, as Ryan hastened his escape. Nope. He had no interest in getting in the middle of domestic drama.

He returned to the kids' room, pausing to allow Mike's mom to bustle in before him. "And where is my favorite Miss Ellison?"

Sylvie's upturned lips flattened, her expression growing stiff.

"Here you go." He offered her the ice pack, and she gingerly held it to her face.

A glance at Mike's mom showed her slight shake of the head, but whether it was at Sylvie's injury or something else he didn't know. He waited, wondering if he should stay or leave, but then Luc called him, so after a last check on Sylvie, which she waved off, he left.

He tried to join in the conversation, but the incident before had him tense. Some might call it dumb for a pro hockey player to not like confrontation, but he'd always preferred to avoid making waves. He'd learned from his first professional team to keep his head down, thanks to a coach who was rumored to have psychopathic tendencies, and had kept quiet ever since. Some might know Ryan was a Christian, but he wasn't in your face about it. About the most significant thing he'd ever done was to join the others in the online Bible study groups in last year's video. That video had gone viral as pro hockey players took a stand against violence and abuse affecting women, after Hannah had been subjected to trolls. Some of his teammates had been stunned to learn Ryan had a voice and knew how to use it.

But he'd always preferred to observe than speak, and it felt like there'd been plenty not being said in the room before. Which made him wonder what the undercurrents were about. He vaguely remembered Mike once saying something about how his mom had had issues with Sylvie in the past, but he couldn't remember the details. And really, if someone wanted to judge someone on their ink or the color of their hair, then he didn't care to know them too much.

He noticed Mike's mom carrying Mike's little girl out, just as Brent called for attention. Then Mike and Bree thanked everyone for coming, especially thanking those who had traveled great distances to be there. This was said with a look at Mike's sister, Callie, who apparently had come from Germany.

"I hope you all know how much we've appreciated your support in recent weeks and months, with everything from delicious meals being dropped off, to offers of babysitting, and your emotional and practical support. I," Mike cleared his throat, "I honestly don't know how I could've survived if it wasn't for God, and for all of you helping out." He faced Bree, pressing a kiss to her hand as he studied her with a look of deep emotion. "I love you so much, Bree. I'm so glad you're on the mend now, honey."

Bree clasped Mike's hand, looking up at him with a look of love that twisted Ryan's heart. His all-in focus on hockey meant he'd never really had a girlfriend, let alone someone who could make him look like that. He peeked across to where Sylvie had entered, on the outskirts of the room, holding Ethan's hand. Ethan weaved his way to his mom's side, resting his head on her lap.

Mike drew a hand over his son's tousled curls. "I thank God for my family, every day, and I know now we can't take our families for granted for one second."

Ryan noticed how Sylvie's lips rolled in on themselves, her shoulders slumping.

Bree waved a hand, which was not unusual, Ryan knew, as

she often had something to say. "I wanted to add my thanks for all your help and support, especially to Sylvie, who has made such a difference in coming to stay here for the past few months. You truly have proved a Godsend, my friend."

Sylvie nodded, shrugged, waving off the thanks like she was embarrassed.

"Well, once again, thanks for coming," Mike said, "and I know many of you have to get going soon, that you've got vacations to get to, but I hope you know how grateful we are that you decided to join with us today. And hey, seeing none of us have games tomorrow, please make sure you enjoy some of the twins' special cake, as they sure won't be eating any of it."

"Happy to oblige," Kurt Matthews, Calgary's goaltender, said, to laughter.

A little commotion in the corner drew Ryan's attention to Mike's parents, who were whispering loudly to each other.

"Mom?" Mike asked. "Did you have something to say?"

"Why, yes, I did." She glanced at Mike and Bree, then at Bree's parents, who were holding the twins in their arms, then back at her husband, who gave a small nod. She smiled. "We're so proud of you both, of you all, and we decided we'd surprise you with some news of our own."

Ryan crossed his arms, shooting raised eyebrows at Luc, who gave a shrug. He peeked at Sylvie, who wore her own furrowed brow.

"Now the twins are here, and we're both retired, and our daughter Callie has finally returned from her work in Germany, we have decided that we do not want to live so far from our family. And that's why," Mrs. Vaughan glanced at her husband, then at her son, "that's why we've sold up in Toronto and are moving here permanently."

Bree blinked, as Mike grinned. "Are you serious?"

"Sure are, Son." His dad clasped him in a bear hug. "There's no point in us being over there when you are all over here."

"And we know you need more help, Breanna," Mrs. Vaughan said.

"But I have Sylvie."

"But she isn't really family, is she?"

Ouch. Ryan cast Sylvie a look, just in time to catch a flicker of emotion before her face blanked and she glanced down at her Doc Martens boots, biting her lip.

"We didn't want to say anything until we closed on the deal, especially with all that's been going on here, but know you'll have us nearby, anytime of day. And soon, your own on-call doctor, with Callie, when her service in the army is up."

"Mom." Mike's older sister wrinkled her nose at Mike, who nodded, like they'd shared similar silent conversations before.

"Wow. That's great news." Mike appeared delighted even as his wife appeared stunned. Clearly this was news to them. And to Sylvie. "Okay, then. Well, everyone, please have some cake, and enjoy the afternoon. For as long as you can, anyway."

Ryan glanced at his TAG Heuer. Winced. He and Luc really needed to leave now if they were going to get to the airport in time to make Luc's flight.

Luc moved beside him. "We need to hustle."

For sure. Yesterday's game against Nashville was their last for ten days, and while Ryan wasn't heading to his apartment in Edmonton, he had planned to catch up with his family in Red Deer. And as that drive was at least an hour and a half, on top of getting Luc to his flight, they needed to get to the airport pronto.

He wished Brent and Franklin good luck in next weekend's All-Star game, then joined others in thanking Mike and Bree for their hospitality. Mike backslapped him. "Thanks so much for coming, man. It really means a lot to us."

"Wouldn't have missed this for the world." Ryan bent and kissed Bree's cheek. "You take care of yourself, okay? Sounds like you'll have plenty of helpers now."

Her brow wrinkled. "That's for sure."

Ryan glanced around for Sylvie, but she was nowhere to be seen. So, he sent up a silent prayer for her, fist-bumped Brent and Franklin, and gestured for Luc to follow him out to his Lexus LC.

Some things obviously just weren't meant to be.

CHAPTER 2

Red Deer, Alberta

"Excuse me, Miss, but have you got anything by Jane Austen?"

Sylvie pasted on a smile. "Have you tried the classics section?" She pointed in the general direction for where it might be. She hoped.

Her smile fell away, as the customer left without acknowledgment, let alone a word of thanks. Maybe she was still getting used to things here, but she'd forgotten what working in retail could be like. It sure was different from when she was working with Bree, where appreciation had flowed.

Regret gnawed, as she slowly picked up a stack of books to replace on the shelves.

Two days. She'd lasted only two days before circumstances forced her hand and she'd told Bree she needed to quit. The following day she'd moved here, after finding a cheap apartment and a job opening in this bookstore, misgiving chasing her every step of the way.

She'd upset Bree. The one person in her life who'd given her a chance, who'd proved faithful through the years, and Sylvie had gone and upset her. Something Sylvie had no wish to do. She cringed. How she hated being that person, that failure of a friend. She *had* tried, but Mike's mom had made her intentions obvious. Why else would the woman have insisted on moving halfway across the country from Toronto to Cowtown, making Sylvie's time here pointless? And while Sylvie might love Bree and her kids, Mike's mom had made it plain that family came first, not friends.

The only way to keep the peace had seen Sylvie murmur to Bree that she'd need to leave. That she had family commitments of her own in Red Deer. Which wasn't exactly true. Technically, her grandparents lived here, but she hadn't gone to see them yet, more focused on getting settled with her accommodation and job than finding the emotional fortitude to speak to the grandparents who had basically disowned her years ago. She couldn't believe how conservative some people still were these days, but knowing some folk would judge her, she'd rocked up to the job interview here with long sleeves, piercings-free, less made-up than normal, still dressed in black sans her usual skulls and quirkiness.

The bookstore owner had been a little skeptical about Sylvie's vast array of jobs in recent years, and maybe she'd caught a whiff of Sylvie's general vibe as she'd suggested that she might be better off working in one of the comic book stores, which was a little insulting, to be honest. And while the thing that had swung the job in Sylvie's favor was the fact that she'd at least had some experience working in a bookstore before—back when she was a teen, but whatever—Sylvie thought it was more the fact that an NHL captain's wife had written her a glowing reference that had got her the job. At least, that was what she'd figured from the way Marie had studied her hastily put-together CV, before saying, "Are you telling me you know Mike Vaughan? Calgary's Mike Vaughan?"

"Yes. His wife and I have been friends for years. I've been caring for their kids."

"And why'd you leave?"

"They have family nearby to care for them now."

And that was the stone-cold truth.

Bree and Mike had family. People who loved them. People who wanted them nearby. Sylvie did not. Maybe one day she'd find courage enough to talk with her grandparents, but that day was not this day. She pressed her lips together. And maybe one day she'd find the courage to return to Bree and fully explain the situation. Fully explain about her past, too. But she couldn't right now. Bree was already too fragile, and Sylvie wasn't much better. But at least Bree had told her she was always welcome to return. That was something, at least. Something that showed the generous nature of her friend, her huge heart for others, that was so opposite to the tight knot that substituted for Sylvie's own.

She replaced books, glancing across the store, hoping Marie would see just what a useful employee Sylvie could be, that today's trial should lead to a permanent position. She returned to Marie at the front desk. The store was fairly quiet, with only a few browsers that she'd already checked on.

"So, is it true that Bree Vaughan nearly died?" Marie asked.

Sylvie swallowed the first words begging to spill. Telling her new boss to mind her own business wasn't likely to go down well. "I'm not sure what you've heard," she hedged.

Marie shrugged. "I can't say that I've heard too much—we tend to support the Oilers around here—but I heard rumors that she was very unwell."

Well, that wasn't exactly news. It was no secret that Mike had taken several weeks off "for personal reasons" due to the twins' emergency delivery. "She's on the mend now, and as I said before, she's got a good support system around her."

"Hmm." Marie frowned at her, like she didn't understand why Sylvie, as a self-confessed good friend of Bree's, was here in Red Deer, and not 150 kilometers south.

Sylvie wasn't about to explain to Marie the ins and outs of the dynamic that she shared with Regina Vaughan. She could barely explain it to herself, which was why her departure from Bree's had proved so tricky. Besides, she needed this job, so playing meek and mild had to be the name of the game.

"Well, I guess that's good to hear," Marie finally said.

"You guess?" Heat roared at the dismissiveness of those two words. How dare she? "This is my friend who nearly *died*. Surely it shouldn't matter what team her husband plays for." Oh, look whose mouth had decided not to listen to her brain.

"Excuse me?"

"Nothing," Sylvie muttered. She picked up another stack of books. "I'll go re-shelve these ones too."

"You do that."

Great. She'd gone and ticked off her boss—on her first day. This was no way to find a new start. But—she shoved a Nora Roberts novel firmly into the shelf—failing to keep her mouth closed might've contributed to the reason she had so many jobs listed on her CV. She was going to have to try a lot harder to keep her head down and big mouth shut if she was going to have any chance of keeping this job and afford the dumpster of a rental that she now called home.

Her shoulders slumped. How had her life changed so dramatically in such a short time? Just over a month ago, she'd been happily ensconced in Bree's guest room of her luxury home, taking care of Bree's gorgeous kids while having a friend to talk to, even if Bree had been tired a lot of the time. Sylvie had felt valued, and appreciated, like she finally had a toehold in that mythical dream called a family. Then Bree and Mike's real family had come, and everything had changed.

Family came first. Family always *should* come first. But sometimes, when people put their family first, it came at the cost of further marginalizing those who didn't have one. Yet to point this out would only make Sylvie look selfish, and as she knew darn well she was pretty selfish she sure as heck had no desire to draw more attention to it. Besides, deep down she suspected Regina was just as scared about Bree as Bree's own mother had been, and that it was fear that sharpened Regina's comments until Sylvie felt like she had a million needles stabbing her soul. Porcupines had nothing on her.

But how was a girl to overlook Regina's constant sighs, and murmurs to Mike and Pam of her concern about the type of influence Sylvie was, let alone the interruptions to the routines Sylvie had already established with little Ethan and Ellison? They'd been getting so confused, being put down for their usual afternoon nap, then being expected to stay awake because their grandmother thought that meant they'd sleep better at night? The household had seen a teetering of routines and expectations, both spoken and unspoken, moments when she was talked to then talked at, so that trying to find a balance was so hard. And Mike had been so stressed he hadn't noticed his mother's constant sniping, and Sylvie hadn't wanted to add to his stress, so she'd let herself be considered the bad guy. It was a mess, and the only solution she'd seen was to escape, let Regina win, and try to salve her pride ninety minutes north, in the place that had kicked the stuffing out of her and her mom, years ago. "You sure know how to win at life," she muttered to herself now.

She glanced at the spine of the next book, one that would need to be replaced on the high shelf. The fantasy book looked good, but she couldn't afford non-essentials, even with the staff discount. Maybe she should see if there was a local library she could visit. She found the movable stairs and rolled them into position so she could reach the high shelf, then realized her knee-length silver-web-stitched black skirt—as business professional-like as she had—meant she'd need to shimmy it up an inch or three to climb the steps. This accomplished, she replaced the book, then took a moment to glance around.

The front door opened, and from her high perch she could see the new arrival was a man in a baseball cap, overcoat collar popped as he moved through the vestibule. Hmm. Now he was shrugging out of the jacket warranted by outside's early February minuses, and she blinked. Rubbed her eyes. No way.

He spoke to Marie, too far away for her to hear, but it looked like he'd dismissed her offer to help, content to browse. Which meant any minute now he might draw near. And while part of her would love the chance to meet him again, another part shrank back. He was Mike's friend. Mike, who wasn't Sylvie's biggest fan at the moment, seeing she'd "left him in the lurch" as he'd said on Tuesday. But explaining to him that it was his own mother who had basically needled Sylvie right out of Bree's house was not what he needed to hear. So she'd left, knowing he was disappointed in her. So, who knew what he might've said to his friends about the fickle, untrustworthiness of Bree's Goth-dressed friend?

Uncertainty made her hesitate, and she saw the way he turned down the aisle where her ladder was. She swiveled to face the books, glad for her leggings-under-a-skirt today and that her attire was a subtler version of her usual style. Maybe he wouldn't recognize her. He probably wouldn't recognize her, nor remember that moment when they'd clasped hands back at Bree's house four days ago. She pulled out a book at random, holding it in a way that she hoped made it look like she was scanning the back cover, but which could double as a retrieving-or-replacing-or-covering-her-face prop as needed. No way did she want Ryan thinking she'd followed him here. Neither would she do a thing to make him think he held one iota of interest.

Ryan moved through the store, grateful to have escaped the clutches of Marie. In, then out. Get the book for his dad's birthday then escape without having to talk to any superfans like the woman who'd known his family since he was in Peewee. Especially if she was going to drop her daughter's name into the conversation. His dad and brother had often laughed about the fact that Mom's friend could barely talk to Ryan without mentioning Olivia, and the fact she was such a good teacher, and *so* sweet and yada, yada, yada. He'd tried to be the nice guy and have a conversation or two with Olivia, but she barely spoke, all blushes and embarrassment and stuff he didn't know how to deal with. He certainly didn't need any more of that in his life. He already indulged in that too much himself.

And yes, he knew that avoiding Marie didn't exactly make him a nice human, but this week was his only real break until April, when they might squeeze in a few days off before playoffs began. And Edmonton was tracking well to make the playoffs this year, which meant every second this week had to count, so he could maximize rest, relaxation, and rejuvenation. Hence, after the christening for Mike's twins, he'd reveled in coming home to his family in Red Deer, away from the Edmonton apartment he shared with Mats Hansen, his teammate, and back to his roots. Back to feeling like introverted him might finally get a chance to relax and not feel like he needed to perform for others all the time. Being "on" so much was exhausting.

He veered down the aisle Marie had mentioned, checking the names listed on book spines in alphabetical order. Drewe, Drummond, Druzinski…

A muffled cough drew his attention up. Then further up. To

see a woman with purple hair and pale skin holding a book atop a set of rolling stairs, wearing a store lanyard. Standing very, very still.

His heart thudded. No way. He took a step back, noticed how she angled herself away, as if she didn't want to be seen by him, and that movement drew his suspicions. *Was* it her? It must be; nobody else around here looked like that, and why else wouldn't a sales assistant want to help a potential customer? Unless she was like one of those restocking agents in a grocery store, who always acted offended when someone mistook them for actually working there. Or maybe that was just him over-thinking things. Whatever, her move was shady enough for him to clear his throat, and say, "Hey, I don't suppose you know where the military fiction is?"

There was a long pause, then a faint, "Nope."

Huh. Some assistant Sylvie was. If indeed she actually worked here. Maybe she was just a customer, although she was dressed like she was working, and not browsing, and without any of those skulls and things that had led him in past days to do some internet searching to find out more about this woman who so intrigued him. "Excuse me?"

He waited, but she still didn't turn to look at him. Which made him ask again more loudly, "Excuse me."

He heard a sigh, then, "Yes?"

He crossed his arms, mouth twitching. If this really was her, he couldn't understand why she didn't want to act like an adult and actually face him. Same went for if it wasn't. And hey, while he wanted to fly under the radar, it was a blow to his ego to have her ignore him if she really was whom he hoped. So he tried one more time. "Do you work here?"

A louder sigh, this time accompanied by slumped shoulders. "Yes."

"Then could you please turn around and face me? I could really do with some help."

"Excuse me." Marie's voice came from behind him. "Is there a problem?"

Ryan closed his eyes. See? This was now exactly what he hadn't wanted to happen. Things were escalating into drama he really didn't need.

"Sylvie—"

Bingo. So it *was* her.

"—what are you doing up there? Surely you've had time enough to put that book away by now. Come down at once."

The slump in Sylvie's shoulders became more pronounced. And as much as he, too, wanted to know the answer to that question—and more, like what on earth was she doing in Red Deer and not Calgary—he couldn't help but notice the way she looked at Marie, almost like she was scared. Which drew protectiveness, as he offered her a half-smile then turned to face Marie who instantly smiled.

"Ryan, I'm so sorry for my new assistant. It's her first day on the job, and she's still learning how we do things around here. If there's anything I can help you with, I'd be very happy to oblige."

"Thanks Marie, but I needed to talk to Sylvie."

"Oh!" Marie's eyes rounded. "I didn't realize that you two knew each other."

"We met through Mike and Bree Vaughan." He side-eyed Sylvie, catching the way she tensed. Why exactly was she here? Her actions so far hadn't screamed jersey chaser or crazed fan stalker. Quite the opposite. Which made a nice change.

"I see."

Judging from the way Marie was eyeing him, no she didn't. And because she knew his mom he didn't want Marie getting crazy ideas and passing them on before he'd had a chance to explain. "We're friends."

He caught the start of surprise from the woman still standing on the steps, as Marie's gaze drifted to her then back to him. "Well, Sylvie did mention that she knew them, so I guess this confirms that."

He fought the inclination to frown. One of the perks of being a little bit famous was people believing you over less well-known types. Which sometimes had its benefits, but other times, kind of sucked. "We'll be fine, thanks," he said as firmly as he could.

Marie seemed to get the hint and nodded, and moved away. Leaving him to pivot to face Sylvie again. He smirked. "Did you seriously try to ignore me before?"

Her dark gaze stole into him, with that same intensity as back in Mike's house. Then she shrugged. "I'm not a groupie, if that's what you're asking."

"Yeah, I figured that from the way you tried to pretend I wasn't here."

She exhaled loudly.

"Hey, are you ever planning to come down so we can talk like normal people?"

"Speak for yourself, buddy," she muttered.

His lips twitched, and he waited, hands on hips as she slowly moved, that tight skirt doing her plenty of favors as she slowly descended.

"Sylvie!"

At Marie's call, Sylvie pivoted, her high-heel-booted foot slipped, and she spun to face him, her eyes wide with panic, arms flailing. "Oh!"

"Whoa." He braced and caught her, then staggered back.

Sylvie was flush against his chest, her face an inch away, her wide eyes finding his.

His arms tightened. "You okay?"

She nodded, and somehow in that moment, as her chin dipped and her arms slipped around his shoulders, somehow, somehow, his mouth lowered and brushed hers.

Then, as she sighed, his eyes closed, and her lips firmed, and he sank into wonder—

"Sylvie!"

Sylvie jerked away, untangling herself, tugging her skirt down, even though he'd certainly had nothing to do with *that*. But it was apparent from Marie's open mouth she wouldn't believe anything he said, as it looked awfully like a place that a spectacular kiss like that could take them to. And now, it seemed several other customers had appeared, the youngest of which was holding up a phone.

Whoa. Talk about a mess.

He covered his culprit mouth with his hand. "Um, sorry about that," he murmured to his partner in kissing crime.

"Don't be," Sylvie muttered. "You'll do better next time."

Laughter sputtered from him, but judging from the way Marie—and everyone else— was staring at them, he needed to talk fast, and somehow explain that the most amazing kiss of his life had been an accident.

Like, for real. He'd neither experienced such a kiss, nor intended to kiss her, so, "It wasn't what it looked like."

Marie cleared her throat. "I feel I must point out that I do not appreciate my employees canoodling while on the clock."

Canoodling? Is that what older folk called it?

"It *was* an accident," Sylvie muttered.

"And yet your lips somehow landed on his, is that what I'm supposed to believe?"

"She tripped, and I caught her—"

"How you choose to conduct yourself in your own time, Mr. Guillemette, is none of my business—"

But simply saying that suggested she'd judge him nonetheless.

"—but I will *not* allow my employees to conduct themselves in such a manner, especially in public where children may see."

What?

"Is that understood?"

"Yes," Sylvie murmured.

He stared at Marie, who seemed to be getting a massive power trip out of this. "Yes, ma'am."

Her head jerked, then her gaze narrowed at Sylvie. "You need to get to the back room and start unboxing that new shipment that arrived this morning."

Sylvie's lips pressed together, and she nodded, her gaze sliding to Ryan before she turned on her heel and walked away. Leaving him facing the smirks and shaken heads of the other customers, which drew heat up his neck to his cheeks, and hastened his exit, his dad still present-less, as part of him wondered if he just should have chased Sylvie and somehow explained things better—and learned exactly why she was here too.

He hurried to his car, already ruing what he knew the social media optics would be. Why—? How—? Man. That past ten minutes had been insane.

By the time he'd driven halfway home his phone was buzzing with notifications he glimpsed while waiting at the red lights. Images. The two of them tangled in each other's arms. Then apart, with him looking like a doofus, Sylvie looking like a boss, and Sylvie's boss looking like an old-time schoolmarm with her finger pointed at them, like they were naughty children.

Teammates were sending emojis. Fire. Laughing faces. And some vegetable and fruit combos he didn't want explained. Then his own brother called. "Ryanator."

He loved his family, but kind of hated how his car had some automatic speaker mode which always sent his family's calls straight through. "What?"

"How long until you're home?"

"Two minutes? Why, does Mom need something from the store?"

"Not the store. He'll be home in two," Jacob shouted to someone else.

Ryan clenched his teeth. He had a pretty good idea what his mom wanted. And he bet her good friend Marie had already called and filled her in on her version of things.

So much for a relaxing time back home this week.

Even if that had been the absolute best kiss of his life.

He drove to the outskirts of town then into the street he'd grown up on, thankful for the millionth time that his parents had a property large enough for the private drive and frozen pond where he'd first learned to skate. Not technically big enough to be called a farm, but big enough for privacy and all the things a kid might need. His parents' cars were still here, his brother's too, so he knew he was in for a treat. That's what a lifetime of focus on hockey led to. No girlfriends, no experience, save for a desperate New Year's kiss too many years ago with a girl whose name he couldn't even remember. He was Mr. Hockey, Mr. Clean-Cut, Mr. No-Time-For-a-Relationship. It was no surprise that people were making a big deal out of this.

He parked, but didn't exit, knowing the Inquisition awaited. He propped his head on the steering wheel. *Lord, I need some help here. You know that wasn't intentional.* Even if a tiny part of him protested that wasn't entirely true.

A tap on the window jerked him upright.

Jake. Smirking at him. Before thumbing at him to go inside.

He just loved how his older factory worker of a brother seemed to delight in bossing around his NHL-playing little brother.

By now his phone was chiming the arrival of other texts and messages, including one from Luc and one from Franklin. He switched off his phone, shoved it in his pocket, then braved the short dash through the slush to inside.

"Is that you, Jakey?" his mom called.

"Yep," Ryan said, just like he had growing up.

"That better be the last lie you tell." Jake followed him into the kitchen. "She's already plenty ticked."

"Awesome."

Ryan went inside and found his mom bent over a cake, frosting it perfectly for his dad's birthday tomorrow. "You're back," she said, without looking up.

When they'd been really little, he and Jake had often wondered if his mom really did have eyes in the back of her head, like the stories she'd told about her Ukrainian grandmother. Mom had always possessed the ears of a bat, so maybe she could discern his footsteps instead of Jake's heavier tread.

"Hey, Mom."

She finished the last intricate swirl of blue frosting, then straightened, her hands clasping the counter edge. "I'm disappointed, Ryan."

"Mom, if you're talking about any pictures you've seen, I can explain."

"Can you? Because I really didn't like Marie calling to tell me something my own son should have."

"Mom, there's nothing to explain. It was an accident."

"An accident? Are you trying to tell me your lips accidentally met this, this Sylvia person's?"

"Sylvie," he mumbled. "Look, I barely know her."

"And you think that makes it better? You just go about hugging and kissing random women in public places now, do you?"

He loved his mom, and while he might be used to her flying off the handle, he'd never understood if it was a personality thing or a woman thing. Maybe it was just a mom thing. "You know I don't do that."

"Then please explain."

He sank onto a stool at the kitchen counter, rolling his eyes at his brother who stood, arms folded, leaning against the wooden cabinets in the corner, that stupid smirk still on his face like he was enjoying the show.

"Look, I met her on Sunday at Mike's baby christening, and was surprised to see her at the bookstore today—"

"She's a groupie," Jake said.

"No, she isn't." He really hoped not, anyway. "She's just moved here—"

"Yep. Solid gold puck bunny."

"Do not talk like that." Mom pointed at Jake, while her eyes remained fixed on Ryan. "You know I've never liked that kind of talk."

"Sorry, Ma."

"Keep going," his mom commanded Ryan, her eyes like lasers that cut steel.

"Honestly, we were talking, then she slipped off the stepladder she was on, and I caught her. End of story."

"So did you or did you not kiss her?"

His cheeks grew hot. "Mom."

She exhaled. "Marie called and said it was getting very hot and heavy—"

"It wasn't!"

"—and you know we've raised you to respect women, and not go giving anyone ideas unless you mean to turn those ideas into reality." Her eyes narrowed. "So did you kiss her?"

Honestly, his mom should be employed by the Canadian Security Intelligence Service. She was better than water torture at getting the truth. He swallowed. "Yes."

She exhaled heavily, her shoulders rounding. "When are you going to bring her around?"

"Mom, we're not dating."

"You kissed the girl. You just admitted it. You are not a man with loose lips, now are you, Son?"

"No."

"And yet there are now photos of you kissing a near stranger."

"I didn't know we were being filmed—"

"That shouldn't make any difference!" Her lips pursed, her disappointment plain.

Sometimes it was hard to believe he was twenty-eight years old. His mom could still take his measure with a glance, and make him feel really small. "I'm really sorry. I never meant any of this to happen."

She sighed heavily. "When do we meet her?"

"What?"

"Everyone is going to be asking at church what she is like, so I need to say I've met her."

"No, you don't. You can just tell them to mind their own business."

In the background Jake was silently laughing.

"You can stop laughing, Jacob," Mom said, without a glance behind. "Especially when this is your fault."

"My fault? How?"

"If you'd gotten your father the book he'd wanted then your brother wouldn't have had to go into town, and none of this would've happened."

Ryan crossed his arms and nodded. "True."

His mom clicked her fingers at him. "But that does not excuse your behavior. What do you know about this girl? Is she a Christian? Is she good enough for my son? What's her family like? Are you sure she's not going to take you for a ride?"

He didn't know too much about Sylvie, apart from the fact that she'd willingly helped Bree, was good with kids, and he loved her desert-dry sense of humor. Oh, and that she was an excellent kisser. "Mom, there really is nothing going on between us."

"And yet there is now, because you kissed her."

He fought not to roll his eyes. Clearly his mom wasn't giving up on this any time soon. "Look, she's a nice girl, a friend of Bree's, great with kids, she was at the christening service on Sunday, and she's got a cool style about her."

"Purple hair." His mom sniffed.

If she thought that was bad, wait until she saw the skulls and other Goth-like things. "Come on, Ma. Is purple hair really any different to blonde or brown? I really don't think hair color affects a person's character."

"And what do you know about her character?"

Not enough. He probably should message Mike and find out if he knew why their nanny had suddenly upped sticks and moved to Red Deer.

"Exactly." She sniffed again. "You need to sort this out, Son."

"I know."

"Then get to it. Time is a'wasting. Especially if she's coming here tomorrow."

"Mom, she's not coming."

"What's her name again?"

"Sylvie."

His mom shook her head. "I'm going to be praying for that girl. You better warn her."

"You do that. And maybe pray that Marie doesn't fire her."

"She wanted to fire her? Over one little kiss with my son? Oy."

Exactly.

"Next time Marie talks to me, I'll give her a piece of my mind."

Ryan kissed his mom on the cheek. "Love you, Mom."

"And I love you. And if you're going back to see her, tell her I want to meet her."

"Aren't you worried she might be a gold digger?"

"Hmph. You are not stupid. I trust you."

His mom might be prone to high emotion, but he'd always known she had his back.

Ryan moved down the hall to his old bedroom he used whenever he stayed here, still filled with Gretzky posters, and a few embarrassing ones of Edmonton's current captain that he really should take down. Thank God nobody ever came in here. He plugged in his phone to recharge, wincing at the notifications demanding attention.

"So what are you going to do?" Jake asked from the doorway.

He exhaled, put his hands behind his head, and turned and faced his brother. "I guess I'm gonna have to go back and find her and explain."

CHAPTER 3

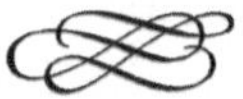

$\mathcal{A}$ floorboard creak drew her gaze up from where she was unboxing books. "You."

"Hey."

Ryan stood in the storeroom's doorway, shuffling his feet, his gaze touching then sliding away from hers. But he'd come back? Most guys she'd known were all about kissing—or more—then running as far away as they could once they got what they wanted. But she sensed Ryan didn't do that. He seemed far more clean-cut, even if that facial scruff he wore was sexy.

She straightened. "Come to finish the job, huh?" Why she felt so instantly comfortable with him that Ms. Snark had returned had nothing to do with that slide of lips on hers before. Nothing.

His cheeks reddened, as he lifted a hand to rub the back of his head. "Do you mean you want me to leave so you don't get into trouble again? Or...something else?" His gaze trickled to her mouth.

Drying hers. He felt the same way too? Like that accidental kiss had cracked open a world of glittering, technicolor possibilities, so that perhaps she didn't have to live in this gray no-man's-land world anymore.

Which was stupid. God—if he or she was real—certainly hadn't gone about serving up life on a golden platter to Sylvie. Or her family. Instead, that seemed reserved for the likes of Bree and Mike, and this man here. They were each one of the chosen few. A golden child. She was scratched and worn, any sheen sure to be rubbed off and revealed as brass or painted gold.

"Is there something I can help you with?"

He blinked, took a step closer. "I, uh, I don't know if I apologized properly before, but I really didn't mean to get you into trouble."

"And yet you're here again."

His lips twitched. "As you can see."

Oh, this man was dangerous. She'd always been a sucker for a man with good looks and banter. "How'd you manage to sneak past Marie?"

"I didn't sneak. I told her I needed that book I didn't get earlier."

"What book?"

He shrugged. "Something my dad said he mentioned. Military crime fiction from World War Two."

"Sounds rather niche."

"That's my family. We do..." Again his gaze lowered to her mouth then back. "Niche."

She was pretty sure if she was one of those heroines on the covers of the store's historical novels—hysericals, as she liked to describe them to Bree—that she'd need a fan or a fainting couch or something. This man was hot. And making her feel very warm indeed. Call her stupid, but the man seemed to like her or something.

She took a step forward, eyes fixed on him. "So, how niche do you like?"

As soon as the words escaped, she inwardly flinched. She was acting exactly like the brazen hussy her grandmother had once accused her of. But direct had always been her style. And she *really* wanted to know this man's kiss again.

His throat rippled as he swallowed. "Pretty, uh, niche."

Her lips curved.

"I think."

Those words halted her walk. Her head tilted. "You think?"

"I, uh—"

"Ryan?"

He winced at Marie's call from beyond the room. "Give me a moment," he murmured.

She nodded, returning to the table where she'd been working before, telling herself to calm down as snatches of conversation trickled from outside.

"…this aisle here."

"Thanks."

Footsteps indicated Marie's return, and Sylvie hurried her movements in the hopes she looked efficient and like she knew what she was doing.

"How are you doing in here?" Marie asked her.

Aw, that was nice. "Fine, thanks. How are you?"

Marie's forehead crinkled. "I don't mean how are you. As if I cared."

Whoa. There went Marie's coffee that Sylvie was about to offer to buy.

Marie sighed. "Why are you unboxing that one? I didn't tell you to do that one."

"You said do the boxes. You didn't say not to do all of them."

Marie's exhale was louder this time, edged with frustration. "Yes, but surely you should've realized that unboxed books need to be put on display, otherwise they get dust on them."

"Actually, no. I didn't realize that. But thank you for pointing that out," she added, softening her tone, throwing in a smile she hoped might be enough for Marie to overlook the bite in her words.

Perhaps Marie didn't like Sylvie's smile, or she'd been too quick with her words again, because her frown only deepened. "I know this is a trial, but I really don't feel like this is working out."

"But—"

"I'm sorry," Marie said, with a glitter in her eyes that suggested she really wasn't. "I don't like how you talk to me—"

"I'm sor—"

"—nor how you interrupt all the time. I really think you have a problem with authority."

Only when the authority was petty or mean. She kept her mouth closed for that. There was still a chance she could salvage things. "Marie, I'm truly sorry if I have done—that I have given that impression, and—"

"I bet you are," Marie interrupted.

See? Double standards. She wouldn't point that out either. "Please, give me a second chance. I'll do anything. I really need this job."

Marie sniffed. "Surely your famous friends should be able to help you out."

"I don't know what you mean."

"Isn't that what you wrote on your CV?"

"If you mean Bree and Mike, they're in Calgary, not here."

"Then maybe that's where you should return."

Wow. "I'm sorry, Marie, but I really don't understand the hostility. What have I actually done wrong?"

"As I said before, this is a trial, and I'm afraid you're not fit to work here."

"I am, actually." Sylvie's chin tilted, her eyes narrowing. "You just don't like me."

"I don't like your attitude."

Well, that wasn't about to change. Sylvie shrugged, aiming for casual even though her insides were shaking. "You do you, then." She tossed the scissors on the table where they bounced and clattered to the floor.

"Pick them up," Marie ordered.

Maybe it was petty, but she wasn't going to let this woman boss her around a second longer. "Hey, you've just made it clear I don't work here anymore."

"Get your stuff and leave."

Hot and cold shivers rolled over her as she collected her bag, her coat, and exited the room, eyes straight ahead. She no longer cared where Ryan was. That flirty moment from before seemed a lifetime ago. She moved to the front exit where Ryan finally caught up to her. "Are you leaving?"

"I've been asked to leave, yes." Which was kind of humiliating. The first time in a decade that she'd been fired. First time *ever* she hadn't even lasted a day. She'd always managed to quit before, knowing she had another job to walk into. And yet now…

Panic roared. She had no job. A crappy apartment for which she'd outlaid most of her savings to afford this month's rent. And now no way to meet next month's.

"Let me get this book, and we'll talk."

She shook her head. "I'm not staying here a second longer than necessary." Even now she could feel Marie's death-glare searing her spine.

He held the door open for her as she exited, then moved beside her in the cold air. "Is your car here?"

Her chin dipped. Her little Mazda. The secondhand one she'd bought in Toronto when she'd gotten the preschool job where she'd first met Bree.

"The Ontario plates, right?"

"Yes."

"Hey, get in mine." He remotely unlocked it.

"So you can kidnap me?"

"So we can talk. But only if you want."

She peeked at him, past a shield of hair, but he'd already turned away, was going back inside, was speaking to Marie, as if he didn't care he'd just left his expensive vehicle accessible to anyone to get in. And as tempted as she was to go home and lick her wounds in private, another part of her desperately wanted to know what he wanted to say. To have the chance to explain herself, to someone who seemed kind, who might even be able to help make things right with Mike and Bree one day, seemed an opportunity too good to pass up. So, she trudged through the snow, almost slipping on ice, as she moved to his sporty red Lexus, and got in.

Half a minute later he was there too.

"Hey, what's happened?"

She couldn't look at him. Why she still sat in his beautiful car was a mystery. Why was he going to so much trouble for someone he barely knew? The man was so wrong for her. Actually, she was so wrong for him. Everything, from his thoughtfulness to his expensive vehicle to his spotless car interior proved him the complete opposite to her.

She cleared her throat. "Marie feels I'm not suitable for the position." Story of her life. She never fit in anywhere. As wanted as frost. She was pretty sure her mother's maiden name should've been Moroz, not Melnyk.

"I heard some of what Marie said before. She and my mom have always had a weird dynamic, and Mom has said Marie's wanted me to go out with her daughter, so maybe she's upset about before."

She huffed out a breath. "I can't believe she'd get so upset about an accident like that."

"Mmm."

She snuck a look at him. He was staring out the windshield

like he had his doubts about whether it was accidental too. But it *had* been. Sylvie had fallen, he'd caught her, and somehow their faces had met in that beautiful moment she wanted to explore more of. Her heart sank. But maybe he no longer wanted to…

"Come on. Let me make it up to you and buy you dinner."

"You don't need to do that."

"I kinda feel like I do."

Her heart teased to know if he meant more than feeling bad about her situation. But she wasn't going to act like some jersey chaser. In the short months she'd lived with Bree and Mike, she'd seen and heard about women chasing hockey players and doing stuff even she could never imagine. And the fact she'd once acted like that too brought shame—and a resolve to not act like that again.

She grasped the door handle. "I should go."

"Please." He shifted in his dark gray leather seat and faced her. "I feel bad about what's happened, and I really want to make it up to you."

"You shouldn't feel bad. I have a big mouth sometimes, and I'm pretty sure I managed to get fired all by myself. And if it wasn't today, it would've been one day soon."

"I don't believe it."

Yeah, because he seemed to have a sunny-side up view of the world, while she ate disappointment and rejection for breakfast. Her time at Bree's had been the one golden exception to that rule.

"Besides, I don't need food." Even though she hadn't eaten anything but a Pop-Tart this morning. Once-curvy girls soon learned the art of staying slim was being okay with constant hunger.

But as if her ears had picked up on that last word, and transmitted signals to her brain which finally made its way to her insides, her stomach growled.

He snickered. "Yeah, you sound like you need dinner."

She shook her head. "Nope. What I need is a job."

He winced. "I'm really sorry this didn't work out. Maybe we can talk over options over a meal. You don't have to eat anything if you don't want. I'll need to eat, though."

He really wanted to help her? A desperate part of her jumped at his offer. Was this man the sweetest in history or what? Still, she'd play it cool to the end. She exhaled heavily. "Twist my arm, why don't you?"

"Is that a yes?"

"Maybe."

"Please?"

"Why do you care anyway?"

He shrugged, his cheeks pinking. "I..." He bit his lip, ran a hand through his hair that she suspected might be his tell for anxiety.

That thought softened her heart a little more. She liked a man who could be vulnerable around her. And she got that sometimes she could appear intimidating, and she didn't want to make this poor man any more nervous, especially when he was going out of his way to be so nice to her. Which meant there was only one thing to say. "It's okay. I understand."

His head tipped. "Understand...?"

"That you loved our kiss and want another one, right?"

He blinked.

She bit back a smile. So that wasn't her merely projecting her own desire. She clicked her seatbelt in. "Fine, then. Feed me."

His eyes widened. But no, she wasn't implying a need for his kiss but food. Especially now she'd been reminded she was starving.

He cleared his throat. "What do you want to eat?"

"Anything, anywhere."

"Low maintenance, huh?"

"Do I look like a car?"

"Nope. You look…"

~

WORDS FAILED HIM. He wasn't exactly sure what had just happened. He'd never been in this situation before. Never sat in a car with a woman he so desperately wanted to kiss before. There was something about the way she looked at him, eyes dark and filled with sparkling tease, that made him want to risk everything and dive into the mysteries within. Which he knew his brother would die laughing about if he ever expressed those words out loud, but Ryan couldn't deny this connection that seemed to hum loudly between them.

"I look…?" she prompted.

"Great," he said lamely. "Beautiful. But also kind of scary."

Her lips curved in that half-smile thing she did, then she shrugged, as if his words weren't new, and she heard them all the time. Which maybe she did. But he sure didn't say them all the time. He'd hadn't had a girlfriend even in pre-NHL days, and while his brother and teammates had tried to set him up a few times, he'd never met a girl with whom he felt such an instant connection.

He wanted to have dinner with her. More, he wanted to know everything about Sylvie, who she was, why she was here, what she thought. She fascinated him. Yet, some part of him urged caution, and not just because of what his mom had said before about whether Sylvie was a Christian or not. He sensed his attraction could be dangerous, and needed brakes, even though it felt like they were already sliding to inevitability.

He drove, the engine roar as it started one of his favorite things. He slid a look at her. Her mouth tipped up. She glanced across. "Nice car."

"I like it. It does the job."

She snorted. "Yeah, my car does the job. Comparing my car to this car," she stroked the dashboard, "is like comparing a railway handcar to Tokyo's bullet train."

He laughed, and turned onto Gaetz Avenue and drove to an Italian place which had booths where they could get a little privacy, at least. They knew him there, and knew he didn't like people in his face or asking for photographs or anything.

Fortunately, the early evening hour meant Giorgio's had just opened, and he could get the booth he wanted, right up the back near the kitchen entrance, which meant the only people who could really see them were the staff.

"Hey, George."

"Mr. Guillemette," the owner greeted them with a smile.

Ryan rolled his eyes. He'd gone to school with George before his career had taken him away, but George never failed to treat him like a prince.

George turned to Sylvie, glanced back at Ryan with a smirk, then handed them menus. "Please take as long as you need." He winked at Ryan, leading to that all-too-familiar burn in his skin.

Sylvie arched a dark eyebrow at Ryan as George departed. "Mr. Guillemette?"

He shrugged. "What can I say? Some people seem to think I'm a celebrity."

"Might have something to do with your choice of wheels."

He sipped his water. "And then there are others like George who take pleasure in reminding me I'm not that different to who I was before."

"You drove a Lexus as a teenager, huh?"

Call him weird but he liked how she surprised him with saying stuff like that. Her blend of tease, sass, and snark was unlike anyone he'd met before. Like she didn't try to hide who she was or use politeness as a weapon to get people onside. It still kind of amazed him how sweet-as-pie Bree and sarcastic-prone Sylvie had become friends, but that opposite thing must work in friendships too.

Too? He internally rolled his eyes. This wasn't a relationship, he told himself firmly. *Not yet,* a voice whispered in the back of his head.

George returned to take their orders, which reminded him to stay focused, so he ordered his usual, while Sylvie got the loaded Caesar salad.

"So," he said as George departed again.

"So." She sat back against the padded chair, her lips tilting.

He studied her, his eyes tracing her features, the almond shape to her eyes, the dark eyelashes and brows, the freckles that her makeup no longer hid. He liked the fact she wasn't wearing as much makeup as before, like she didn't need to shield herself with him, but there was something different about her. That's right. "Hey, where are all your skulls and things?"

Her lip curled for a second. "I didn't figure Marie would appreciate it today."

"I think you figured right."

"Not that it matters now."

Because she'd lost her job. Because of him. He exhaled, just as George returned with their drinks. "Thanks, George."

"No problem."

"Look," Ryan continued once George had left, "I'm really sorry about that."

"You don't need to keep apologizing." Her lips twisted. "Like I said, I think it was more my big mouth than anything else that saw her fire me."

"So, what will you do?"

She sipped her lemonade. "Look for another job. It was the best I could get at short notice."

"There were other options?"

Her nose wrinkled. "A few."

Hmm. He guessed by that response those options weren't too good. "So, is there anything I can help with regarding that?"

"What are you? A knight in shining armor?" She shook her head. "I really don't know why you're bothering with me."

He searched for the right words as she glanced at the waiters passing by. It felt too soon to explain this intrigue he felt about her. "Look, I know you say I'm not responsible, but I still feel like that contributed to what happened today. And I know that you're Bree's friend, so I feel like I owe it to them to make sure you're okay."

Her lips flatlined, and she glanced down.

"Is everything okay with them?" he asked. "I gotta admit I was surprised when I saw that you were here and not there anymore. Can I ask what that was about?"

Her shoulders slumped slightly. "They had family there, and didn't need me anymore."

"But I thought you were helping with their kids."

"I was. But there were too many of us there, and you know that saying about too many cooks? It's the same when it comes to looking after kids. Everyone has their own ideas about the right ways to do things, and it was getting a little tense, so I left them to it. Family comes first, right?"

Judging from the way her face shadowed, it hadn't been her preference, but rather something she'd felt obliged to do. Maybe he should contact Mike and get his point of view.

"I bet they miss you."

"The kids have their grandparents there now, so I think they'll be fine."

"But I thought Bree was your friend."

"And she is. But she's been overwhelmed with everything, and I was just adding to the overwhelm by being there, which is why it was better for everyone for me to leave."

From her tight expression, she hadn't wanted that to be the

case. He reached across the table and touched her hand. "Hey, I'm really sorry that didn't work out."

"Thanks."

"Mike and Bree are such good people, and it's been really tough seeing them go through this."

"I know."

He bet she did. From what Mike had said, and even Bree's words on Sunday, Sylvie had been there every step of the way through the emergency surgery and the weeks of hospitalization. Now the fact she'd felt she needed to move on seemed a little unfair. His heart snagged on the injustice.

George returned with their meals, and even as Ryan ate, he kept digesting this new piece of information. How could Mike let her go after all Sylvie had done for them? Shouldn't he have fought a little harder to keep his wife's friend nearby? Family might be important, but he knew from experience they could have the tendency to meddle in a way that didn't always allow for personal peace. He ate, and kept sneaking peeks at her, trying to figure her out.

She caught his look. "This is really good, thank you."

"You're welcome. Like I said, I needed to eat, so I'm glad this worked out."

"You're glad I needed a sympathy meal?"

"I didn't mean that."

Her lips twitched, and he realized she'd been teasing again. Huh. It was fun learning this woman, with her mix of vulnerability and cheek. He'd never met anyone like her.

"So, why did you choose to come to Red Deer?"

Her face closed. She glanced down. "I, um, have some grandparents nearby."

She did? "Cool." But judging from the lack of animation she didn't want to say anything more. Okay, he'd try again. "Tell me about the spiders and stuff. Are you a recovering arachnophobe?"

Another tweak of lips. "No. I just like them." She shrugged. "I saw a cool spider handbag at a market in Toronto and it was so different I had to buy it. Then people started giving me cool earrings and it kind of became my thing. Now I like not looking like everyone else."

"So, it's not based on a deep love of Spiderman or anything?"

"Please."

He guessed from that eye roll they wouldn't be watching any Marvel movies together anytime soon.

"Okay, so this might make me sound ignorant, but does all the black mean you're a Goth?"

She snickered, and once again he realized he'd put his foot in things.

"I'll take that as a no."

"Look, I'm not a Goth, or an emo, or anything really. I just like to dress this way. I don't want to be like everyone else."

"You're an individual."

"Yes, I am." She placed her fork down, slouched back in her seat and studied him. "And you? What are you, apart from a famous hockey player and a nice guy?"

A Christian. But something within hesitated to say that aloud. Besides, she knew that anyway. "I'm not that famous." Not compared to Mike, or Brent Karlsson, or some of the other team captains and major endorsement-earning players out there. His agent had once offered him a deal to be the spokesman for a shed building company. He'd turned it down. His family might own a property on the edge of town but he wasn't a farmer by any means, and hadn't felt like he had any real right to promote a rural building company. If he was going to put his name to anything, he wanted it to be because he legitimately believed in the product, not just for a paycheck.

"But you *are* a nice guy."

Her words, so direct, punched through his insecurities to find a soft spot within. He liked that this unique woman who made few apologies for her life could appreciate the fact he was genuine. It felt so long since he'd met a woman he liked who seemed to like *him*, and not just see his dollar value. And he'd pretty much never met one who was so unapologetic about who she was and what she liked, and didn't play polite games like she was hard to get. "I try to be."

Her mouth curved higher, both sides now, and his pulse increased. He stretched out his hand, tangled his fingers with hers, and he was half-surprised she let him. But as he smiled, and caught the softening in her gaze too, his heart seemed to expand to double its size. Attraction throbbed between them, and he felt like he could spend forever wanting to know the mysteries in her eyes.

"So, tell me more about you, Mr. Guillemette. Apart from the fact you have a nice taste in cars."

"I didn't figure you for a motorhead."

"What did you figure me for?" she asked, her smile provocative.

Trouble. The word shimmied in the air between them.

"You don't need to answer that. But you do need to tell me more about you. Go on. Spill."

"There's not much to tell. I've pretty much lived and breathed hockey since I was a kid, and never had much time for other things."

"Other things like…?"

Would it make him seem lame to admit to never having a girlfriend? "Hobbies," he said instead. "I like fishing, and golf, hiking, and camping in the summer—"

Her nose wrinkled. Guess that was another way they were opposites.

"—and watching movies when I can, but nothing too niche."

Her smile flashed at his use of her word from before.

"I have friends," he continued, "but I'm closest to my family."

Her eyes cooled.

"How about you? Tell me about your family."

She shook her head. "There's not much to tell."

From the way her hand tensed and her eyes dropped, that wasn't exactly true.

But before he could ask, a cleared throat drew his attention up. George. Great. He slid his hand from hers.

"Is there anything else I can help you with?"

George could leave. That might help bring back that mood from before. "Want anything else?" Ryan asked Sylvie.

Her gaze returned to his, before dipping to his mouth then back, her eyebrow lifting a little.

Whew. In that case, "Just the check, thanks."

"Of course, sir."

Ryan arched an eyebrow at him, which scored him a smirk before George turned away.

"You want to go, huh?" he asked Sylvie.

"I should probably get back and figure out what to do about my next job."

Her job. He mentally slapped himself. That's right. That's what he should be focused on, rather than thinking about how soft her lips might be.

He paid, leaving a nice tip, and managed to escape the restaurant without anyone stopping him for conversation. Keeping his head ducked down probably helped with that.

He opened her car door, then escaped the cold himself, thankful for all the mod-cons that meant winter's icy clutches had no say in here. The confined space and darkness cocooned them in quiet intimacy, his gaze on hers, hers on him, and if they hadn't been parked where anyone might see them, with the strobing headlights of cars passing, then he might've been persuaded to further investigate what had happened "accidentally" at the bookstore before.

He exhaled. "I should get you home."

Her twitch of lips made him hastily add, "Your home, I mean."

"I know what you meant."

His mouth was dry. Talking with her felt like stepping through landmines, like any moment he might say something that could blow this—him—into smithereens. The headiness of desire was blurring his thoughts.

A horn drew fresh awareness that kissing on Red Deer's main street wasn't the best way to go flying under the radar, so he started the car and drove back to the bookstore.

He motioned to the radio. "Want to pick something to listen to?" It would be another way to find out more about this woman.

She skipped through the stations, past the country that was usually his jam, before settling on a song that sounded straight from eighties UK.

"What's this?" he asked.

"Lullaby, by The Cure."

He listened to the sweeping orchestral sounds, the whispered lyrics unsettling. "Not a Goth, huh?"

"I like their music."

His phone rang. He glanced at the in-dash screen and saw it was his mom. His heart tensed as the call automatically opened, as it always did. He really needed to figure out those auto-settings.

"Mom." He glanced at Sylvie, mouthing a "Sorry."

She shook her head, half-smiled.

"I'm in the car, you're on speaker, and there's someone here."

"Who?"

He winced. "The bookstore girl?"

Sylvie turned to face him more fully now, her smirk twisting his heart. Nope, he hadn't wanted her to know he'd been talking about her to his mom. "What is it, Mom?"

"She's there? Listening?"

Sylvie pointed to herself then to the door. He shook his head and mouthed "Stay." "Yes, she's here Mom, and can hear you."

"I'm glad."

Huh?

"I'm afraid I might have put my foot in things, and I want her to know I'm really sorry about what's happened with Marie."

"Wait, what do you know about Marie?"

His mother sighed. "I don't think she appreciated it when I called her about what happened before. And I didn't want her to take it out on your friend."

"Sylvie." Ryan gestured for her to talk.

"Hi there," Sylvie piped up.

"Oh, Sylvie. That's such a pretty name. I'm sorry about all this."

"That's okay. I didn't want to work there anyway."

"What? Do you mean she fired you?"

Ryan pulled up outside the bookstore. "She did."

"Sylvie, I feel so bad."

"It's not your fault, Mrs. Guillemette."

"I want to make it up to you. I know, you should come to our place tomorrow for my husband's birthday."

"I couldn't—"

"You can. And you better. Between us all, we'll find you another job."

"You better say yes," Ryan murmured. "She won't quit until you do."

"I heard that, Ryan."

"I know you did, Mom. See you at home."

"But I want to meet her."

"Bye Mom."

He ended the call. Caught Sylvie's little smile. "What?"

"Your mom sounds sweet."

"She is. She can also be a fierce Mama bear."

"You're lucky to have a mom who cares like that."

He remembered what she'd said before, about there being not much to tell about her family, and his heart grew sore for her. "I am. But hey, you don't need to go if you don't want to."

"She sounds like she'd be mad at you if I didn't."

There was that. "Are you saying you want to come?"

For the first time that evening, uncertainty washed across her face. "I don't have to if you don't want."

But he did want. He wanted to see her tomorrow, and the next day, and have her enter his world, so she'd get to know him and he could know her more fully. "I want."

"Looks like I'll be coming home with you after all."

His throat held a rock he needed to swallow. "I can pick you up."

"I'm sure you can."

He laughed, and her smile glimmered then fell away.

"Thanks for dinner," she murmured.

"You're welcome." *Anytime*, he wanted to add, but didn't say. He'd be heading to Edmonton on Sunday afternoon, and once the season resumed, if she remained living here then "anytime" couldn't exactly work. "Hey, I should get your phone number."

They swapped numbers, and then she lifted her phone and snapped a photo of him.

"What are you doing?"

"I like to have photos of my friends."

She thought they were friends? "Then I suppose I should get one of you, too."

He took it, then studied the photo. Her face held an insouciant tilt, her eyes burning into his, her lips slightly parted. His heart thudded again, and he peeked up.

To see her lean forward, then kiss his cheek, her voice wispy thin as she murmured, "See you tomorrow."

"I'll text you the time, and you can text me your address, okay?"

"Sure. See you."

He didn't want her to leave, but there were undercurrents here he wasn't sure he could swim against, so settled for a simple "Bye" as she exited, slouching in his leather seat until her car's lights lit and she drove away.

He didn't exactly know how that had escalated so quickly, but he wasn't sorry. Wasn't sorry at all. And to think he'd now see her tomorrow?

His father's birthday would be something to remember.

CHAPTER 4

Job hunting was the worst.

Sylvie scrolled through the long list of available jobs, her heart sinking a little more each minute. She didn't much fancy driving a furniture van, or working as a park laborer dealing with trash or planting trees. And while she'd had experience working retail, working in the dead of winter as a food counter attendant and unpacking store supplies in freezers felt a little too cold for her liking. She could work at a fast-food restaurant or as a sandwich artist or at Starbucks, but they all felt like jobs she'd done years ago. She'd studied and gained qualifications in childcare, and while that was an area that would probably pay better than some jobs listed here, again, it felt like that season in her life was done. Caring for Bree's kids wasn't the same, that opportunity coming at a moment when her life was desperate and in transition anyway. And while she was tempted by the remote camp housekeeping attendant, the thought of twenty days away at a time seemed a little steep, and the pay wasn't exactly stellar.

Still, beggars couldn't be choosers, and so she sighed and clicked on the link for the head cashier at an indoor playground and day care. Bree's reference, and that of her former boss back in TO, would likely come in handy again.

Her phone flashed with a message. Ryan. Her pulse leaped. She told it to settle down.

Just because he was a nice guy didn't mean he'd hang around. The nice ones never did. As soon as they glimpsed the real her, they always ran away. And while she sensed something about him was different, and she'd never been invited this early on to meet the guy's family—and being invited by the guy's mom to meet had occurred precisely never—her nerves had meant the only distraction to offer was the drudgery of scrolling through jobs, and editing and re-editing her CV to suit each one.

She eyed his message again: *Looking forward to tonight. Pick you up at 5?*

Feeling strong enough?

He sent back a smiley face and a strong-arm emoji. She'd take that as a yes, then.

After texting him her address and getting a thumbs-up in response, she returned to her job hunting. But her eyes kept straying to her phone. She tapped open her photos, and gazed at the sneaky pic she'd taken last night. She'd wondered if he'd object, or think her just like one of the crazy stalker fans, but his wanting her photo seemed to make things even.

She zoomed in on his picture. The darkness obscured most of his features, but the angle of his jaw, the curve of his cheek, his lips drew her to ponder. He was so handsome. Gut-level handsome, yet with none of the hard arrogance of the usual kind of guys she'd been attracted to in the past. For all his hockey toughness Ryan possessed a softness to him, something revealed in his manner toward her, with none of the cocky swagger some of Mike's teammates possessed when they'd tried to flirt with her in the past.

Ryan wasn't like that. He seemed genuine and good. She

might've spent a little too long last night searching through the internet to learn more about the man whose arms she'd fallen into, and everything she'd seen and read suggested he was exactly who he said he was. No girlfriends. No scandals. Barely a blip—until yesterday, at least.

Still, she knew all about that particular bookstore incident, and how cameras could capture something that wasn't real. What she'd wanted to know was what to expect about tonight. So the pictures of his family—especially his mom—had drawn her greatest perusal.

His mom looked nice, yet her photos revealed an intensity she'd shown in yesterday's phone call to her son. Ryan shared her hazel eyes, direct gaze, and light brown, almost dark blonde hair. He got the softer features from his dad, whose picture she'd also seen. She still couldn't believe she was attending his birthday tonight. Which reminded her.

She grabbed her phone and tapped out, *Does your dad like wine?*

He's a burgundy fan. But don't worry about a present.

But he clearly wasn't opposed to gift-getting, not considering all the trouble Ryan had gone to get him a book yesterday. Which meant she really should make an effort and not show up empty-handed.

Her muted phone flashed with an incoming call. Her stomach knotted. Bree. She answered it. "Hi."

"Oh, thank goodness you're answering. Are you okay?"

"Yes. How about you? How are you feeling?"

"I'm fine. But, uh," her voice lowered, "maybe getting a little tired of feeling smothered with all the love."

"Sucks to be you, huh?"

Bree's chuckle didn't hold too much amusement. "Are you sure you can't come back?"

"You've got your mom and parents-in-law there. You don't need me as well."

"The kids miss you," Bree said softly.

Way to go to turn the knife. "How are the twins doing?"

"Would you believe I got three hours sleep last night? That's some kind of record."

"You need to rest as much as you can."

"I'm doing my best, but..."

"But what?" She winced. She didn't want to have to ask. She suspected she knew what Bree would say.

"It's not as easy as when you were here," Bree said.

Sylvie's eyes closed.

"And I don't mean to sound selfish," Bree continued, "especially when I want you to be free to do what you need to do. But I just wanted you to know that I miss you."

Her throat closed. She coughed to clear it. "I miss you too."

"Are you sure you can't come back?"

Not while Mike's mom was there. "I'm sure. Things will settle down soon. It takes a while for people to figure out new routines."

Her words echoed in her ears, and she propped her head in her hand. Maybe she had been a little hasty...

"Hey, how did the bookstore interview work out?" Bree asked.

How'd she—? Oh, the reference. Marie must've called. "Um, it's been interesting," she hedged, hurriedly adding, "I'm really grateful for your reference."

"You know I'll do whatever to help if I can."

Sylvie nodded, her heart knotting. "I know."

"Now keep in touch, okay? You know if there's anything I can do, I'd be more than happy to help."

"Thanks, Bree."

"And don't go doing anything I wouldn't do, okay?"

"Can't promise that," she said, before saying goodbye amid Bree's laughter.

So maybe Bree hadn't seen the pictures online about Sylvie

and Ryan. Which was good. She suspected if Mike saw them that he'd be going after Ryan and telling him he could do a lot better than Sylvie. Which was true, but didn't mean anyone needed to be saying so.

She pushed back from the table, got up and refilled her water bottle, catching her reflection in the mirror. She owned a face that she'd overheard others describe as "resting mean-girl face", which she knew was code for something worse. But unlike Bree, life had hardened Sylvie to expect the worst, to assume good things didn't last. That it was best to get in early and get what she could before life kicked her in the teeth again.

And there had been so much kicking.

Her phone vibrated with another notification, and she opened her inbox to see an email from one of the companies she'd contacted mere hours ago. *Thank you for your interest, but unfortunately that position has already been filled.*

Her heart sank. See? Rejection. It was everywhere.

And while a girl might like to dream and imagine a cute hockey-playing nice guy might actually like her, he wouldn't once he knew all that she'd done. He'd be just like all the others, rejecting her, kicking her to the curb, just like Marie.

Good people might like to think they were tolerant, but their actions often proved just how narrow-minded they could be. An image of Mike's mom flashed before her, and she shook her head, willing it to rattle free from her brain. Nope. She wasn't going to waste a second longer on those who pretended to be Jesus followers while wearing prejudice like a crown.

"ARE YOU SURE ABOUT THIS?" she asked Ryan when he pulled up outside her apartment at five o'clock on the dot.

"One hundred percent."

His grin made her insides gooey, and if she didn't have a heart to protect she might've smiled back fully.

But because she did, she only offered her usual tweaked lips, before settling into an expression Victoria Beckham would be happy to wear.

She was glad he was driving, even though it meant he got to see her dingy apartment, as then she had extra time to subtly check him out. His strong forearms that the long sleeve tee couldn't hide. The way his facial scruff seemed more carefully shaved than yesterday. The way his eyes lit whenever he glanced at her. His scent of Cool Water. Oh, there was a lot to like about this man.

"So, how was your day? Any news on the job hunt?"

Ah, that. "It could've been better." She'd received another phone call rejecting her just before five, right when she'd been getting her glow on before Ryan collected her. Awesome timing.

His nose wrinkled. "I'm sure the right one will appear one day."

She tensed, then relaxed. For a moment, he had sounded like all those Hallmark movies that promised Mr. Right would appear one day. Maybe he would, for Ms. Right. The only problem was that she would forever be Ms. Wrong.

Nerves doubled, tripled, at the thought of meeting his family. Was he actually insane? Or was his mom? Tonight's encounter suddenly seemed incredibly foolish.

"So, uh, how about you?"

He slowed, his gaze fixed out the front. "I caught up with some friends, watched some of the All-Star skills contest with my dad."

"Brent was in that, right?"

"Yeah. A few other friends I know as well, including Jason McHale."

"McHale's your captain, right?"

"Yeah." His jaw throbbed. "I head back to Edmonton on Sunday."

"Okay." She appreciated the heads-up, the fact he thought to mention this, suggesting he saw as limited a future as she did. Because if it was one thing to sort-of kiss a man, it was quite another to meet his family, and quite another again to successfully turn that into a relationship. See? She knew this wouldn't work.

She was tempted to ask him to pull over and let her out, when she realized eating with his folks would be a guaranteed better meal than if she stayed home. And while she knew this thing with Ryan would end soon, she probably didn't need to shut things down quite so quickly.

"You okay?" He glanced across at her. "You don't need to be nervous. Mom doesn't bite. Too hard."

"You're funny."

"Thanks."

She almost smiled at his humor. There was something so wholesome about it, like he'd never met a slammed door or a raised fist in his life. She'd never understood how people could expect life to automatically work out well.

"So, what exactly have you told them about me?" She had to ask, as much for her own curiosity, as to change the morbid direction of her thoughts.

"You heard Mom yesterday. She feels bad about what happened, and wants to make it up to you."

"Inviting me to your dad's birthday dinner feels a little excessive, I gotta say."

"Mom doesn't do things by halves."

Okay, now the nerves she'd denied really had set in. He slowed and turned onto a road that led to a house lit up in the twilight. It looked like a farmhouse, with two dormer windows poking out from under triangle roofs, and a classic porch like something from the show *As The Heart Draws* that Bree enjoyed watching. French doors on one side led to a fire pit and Muskoka chairs, while hanging baskets awaited spring flowers. Her heart panged. Someone who had grown up here would never understand her life.

"Ready?"

She half-expected his mom to walk onto the porch, dusting her hands in a *Little House on the Prairie*-type apron. Instead, the white French doors remained closed, although the soft glow from inside said welcome.

Ryan opened her car door, then she followed him, feeling a strange desire to hold his hand. She'd liked the feel of his hand in hers last night. She'd felt protected.

He opened the red front door, then gestured for her to step inside. "Mom?"

Sylvie slowly exhaled. The yellow walls and blue-and-white tile floor screamed friendly country hospitality, and golden timber bookshelves were filled with photographs of Ryan as a kid and what her online search had revealed was likely his brother. A black wood-burning stove emitted welcome heat, and a nearby sign boasted "Love lives in this house. Always has, always will." Her throat grew tight.

Movement drew her attention to a woman nearby, the same woman she'd seen on the photos online. Sylvie smiled, glad that she'd once again forgone the usual look of heavy eye makeup and left the skulls and spiders at home. She still rocked dangling panther earrings, though.

"Mom, this is Sylvie." Ryan touched Sylvie's back, encouraging her to step forward. "Sylvie, this is my mom, Heather."

"Sylvie. Welcome to our home." The words were accompanied by a smile and a quick sweep up and down Sylvie's attire.

Sylvie's chin tilted. She'd worn black jeans, a red-checked shirt, and her black denim jacket. Red wasn't her usual color, but she hadn't wanted to freak out his parents too much, so had gone for the most conservative look she owned. Well, apart from yesterday's business-like shirt and skirt ensemble. But hey, if it made her look like she'd fit in on this small farm, then she wasn't above that either. "Thank you for having me. You have a lovely home."

"We like it. Now, put your boots there." Heather pointed to a nearby rack holding everything from scuffed slippers to several pairs of rubber boots.

Sylvie obeyed, tugging off her Docs, glad she'd traded her usual holey socks for a new pair. This woman carried authority like she was used to getting her own way.

"Now, let's get a better look at you."

She studied Sylvie, taking in her nose stud and eyebrow piercing with a nod, then peering at her earrings. "How old are you?"

"I beg your pardon?"

Heather's head tilted to Ryan. "My son is twenty-eight. I just want to know if those are panthers or another animal."

"Like what?"

Heather's eyes narrowed. "A cougar."

Sylvie blinked. "Are you asking if I'm a cougar?"

"You don't look like one, I'll grant you that."

Wow. Sylvie's jaw dropped, but when she glanced at Ryan, he'd covered his face with both hands and was shaking his head, while another man who had appeared beside him—presumably his brother, judging from the similar facial features—was silently laughing, clutching his sides.

Her earlier indignation faded. This woman was simply direct to a fault. Which meant she should be too. "I'm not a cougar. I'm twenty-nine, but I don't think a year's difference means I've reached cougar status yet, do you?"

Heather's head tilted. "Are you a gold digger?"

Sylvie's mouth fell open.

"Mom! You need to stop," Ryan pleaded. "Sylvie is my friend, that's all."

"A friend you've kissed," his mom snapped, her eyes still lasered on Sylvie.

Sylvie inched back and glanced at Ryan. Was it any wonder the man didn't date when he had a mom like this? "I don't think I want to stay—"

"Do you like my son?" Heather asked.

"Yes." The word spilled before she could stop it.

"Are you a Christian?"

"Mom!"

"Well, if she's not, then it's best you know because this won't work out. So, Sylvie, are you?"

She'd been going to church with Bree and Mike since she'd moved west. It wasn't like she was attending a mosque now, was it? "Yes."

"Just as well. It never works out when people are unevenly yoked, now does it?"

Sylvie frowned, but nodded, like she understood anyway.

"What's that look for?" Heather asked her now.

"Heather, I appreciate you might have concerns, but—"

"I looked you up on Facebook."

Sylvie's mouth dried. So, two had played that game. She'd managed to clean up most of the posts, but Heather would've seen—

"Those pictures online suggest you normally dress like a punk or Goth."

"Do you have a problem with that?"

"No. I'm just trying to understand the woman who is trying to get with my son."

"Mom!"

Sylvie's eyes narrowed. "If you have a problem with me, I'd rather you just come out and say it. I don't want to stand here and be abused."

"Am I abusing, or is this simply me asking questions?"

"Mom, please." Ryan shot Sylvie an apologetic look. "I'll take you back—"

"No, you won't. Not yet, anyway. If you like this woman,"

Heather stabbed a finger in Sylvie's direction, "then you need to know if she can handle us. And she needs to know that too. And whether she can handle all the stuff that will be said about her in the media."

"So this was a test?" Sylvie asked, her own eyes narrowing. "Forgive me for thinking this was a chance to get to know you, and for believing you when you said you might actually want to help me find a new job."

Sylvie froze, ruing her truth-spilling tendency as Heather placed a hand on her hip.

A peek at Ryan showed his own shocked expression, and her heart plummeted. She so should've kept her mouth shut, played the meek girl game, let this woman's words wash over her and pretend it didn't matter. Even if it did.

Heather's scrutiny was intense, then she turned to Ryan and nodded. "I like this one."

What?

His eyes widened, then he looked at Sylvie, and inched closer. "Just as well. Because I like her too."

RYAN PEEKED at the woman seated beside him at the dinner table, who thankfully hadn't decided to leave, even after the worst grilling he'd seen his mom give any person. Ever. Although he'd not been witness to what she'd said to Marie, the "frenemy" whose actions had caused the bulk of the dinner's conversation, after the earlier tension had dropped a hundred knots with his mom's acceptance of his "bookstore friend".

Sylvie glanced at him, lips tweaking upwards briefly, before she returned to listening to his dad talk about ice fishing at nearby Sylvan Lake.

"I've never tried ice fishing," she admitted, when his father's spiel finally wound down to a pause.

"Your dad never took you?"

She hesitated for half a second. "No." Then grasped her water glass—his mom had never believed in drinking empty calories during the season—and finished it in one long swallow.

His mom exchanged looks with Ryan, as if to say, *huh, here's something for you to find out about.* He nodded, but he didn't need his mom's encouragement. That hesitation had clued him in really fast.

Although how much he dared to ask would depend on how the rest of tonight's conversation went. He was pretty sure his lack of defense before, when Mom was in attack-mode, meant Sylvie's opinion of him had sunk low. But he could barely say a word, his mom's actions so foreign to what he'd expected. Except, now he thought on it, he probably should have expected her to act that way. He'd had questions to face last night, after arriving back at his folks' with Sylvie's lipstick on his cheek. Him bringing home a girl-who-was-a-friend was new territory for them all. It felt like a miracle Sylvie had stayed this long.

"Well," Dad put his fork down on the side of his plate, "if you want to go sometime, I reckon I know someone here who'd be happy to take you."

Ryan swallowed a piece of brisket. "If you're talking about me, then I'm not around much this month." He faced Sylvie. "I'm heading back on Sunday, then it's road trips for most of the month."

"What are you doing tomorrow, Son?"

Wow. Way to go to put him on the spot. Put like that, it now seemed impossible to admit he'd kind of been hoping to see what Sylvie was planning for her Saturday, and spend at least part of the day with her. "It's your birthday weekend, so I'm doing whatever you want." Although he had a funny feeling what that was now going to involve.

His dad smiled at Sylvie, confirming Ryan's suspicions. She

—bless her—was calmly eating her mashed potatoes like she had no clue what his dad was about to say.

"Sylvie, would you like to go ice fishing with us tomorrow?"

Sylvie straightened. Glanced at Ryan. "Um…"

"Look, I know you have job hunting to do, but if you wanted to try it out, it's pretty fun."

"It is?"

His mom nodded. "I thought exactly the same when Pete first mentioned it to me."

"We try to do it every year around Dad's birthday, which is nice as it often coincides with the mid-season break." Ryan shrugged. "But there's absolutely no pressure to go if you don't want to."

Sylvie's lips twisted. "Would it shock you to know I've never actually been fishing?"

"What?"

"That's a yes, then."

His mom laughed. Caught his gaze. Mouthed "She's a keeper."

Gnarly knots inside loosened. Mom sure was a surprise packet today.

"Then we better remedy that as soon as possible." Dad turned to Ryan. "Sylvan Lake, tomorrow. I've already got the hut set up in the usual spot."

"So you're definitely going?" Sylvie asked Ryan.

Wait—she actually wanted to go?

"Yeah, I'll be there in the morning, and then we always watch the All-Star game, which will be on after lunch. And it'd be great to have you come too. But only if you want." He could still spend the day with her, get to know her more, even if it was in front of the rest of his family. He'd almost be prepared to blow off the All-Star game, but maybe, seeing she was Bree's friend and presumably used to hockey, she'd be okay with watching that. Because he couldn't admit that spending time alone with her was what he wanted. Not when his parents and brother were looking at him. He and Sylvie might be able to steal some time alone later. "And only if you feel like you don't need to be doing your job hunting."

Sylvie nodded, as his mom rubbed her hands together. "That's right. A new job. Tell me what you are qualified in."

He wasn't sure if this was Mom trying to be helpful or some kind of sneaky way to find out more about Sylvie. He wouldn't put that past her.

"I'm trained in childcare, which is how I first met Bree Vaughan. Bree Karlsson, she was back then."

"Brent Karlsson's sister?" Jake asked.

"Yep. I, uh, continued in that for a while after she moved to Calgary, then retrained in aged care and did some administrative and aide work on a temporary basis in various Ontario facilities for a while."

"Aide work, you say?" Mom asked.

Sylvie nodded. "Then I left that when Bree asked me to come care for her kids last year. I was there about four months, then I came here."

"And did I hear that you had family around here?"

Ryan bit back a sigh. He loved his mom, but sometimes wished she didn't feel it was necessary to prove just how much he'd shared with her.

"My grandparents."

"And how are they?" his mom asked.

Sylvie glanced at the table, then met his mom's gaze. "I don't know. I haven't spoken to them in ten years."

"Huh."

Jake's utterance was the only sound rimming the table.

"And yet you've moved here," Ryan's father said.

Sylvie's chin notched a fraction higher. "It was time."

"What about your folks back home?" his mom asked.

Again, Sylvie hesitated, then said quietly, "My parents have both passed."

He saw how Sylvie stiffened at his family's murmurs of sympathy, and knew he had to turn things around and get them focused on the important thing. "So, what kinds of jobs are you interested in?"

Her nose wrinkled. "I have good references for my childcare work, so I suppose something in that field."

"How would you feel about doing aged care again?"

Ryan eyeballed his mom. No. She wouldn't…

Sylvie shrugged. "If a job was available, and the money right, then sure. Why not?"

His mother nodded, her gaze flicking from Sylvie to Ryan then back again. "Did Ryan mention I work at an aged-care facility in town?"

"No, he did not."

"Hmm. I'll see if there are any leads."

"I'd appreciate that. Thank you."

"You're welcome."

His mom eyed him, and he obeyed her unspoken command to help clear plates and load the dishwasher while she prepped the birthday cake for dessert. As expected, their time in the kitchen also consisted of a whispered conversation, where Mom reminded him to be careful.

The evening continued with cake and candles, presents, which included Sylvie's gift to Dad of a bottle of red, then goodbyes.

"See you tomorrow?" Dad asked her.

Sylvie glanced at Ryan, and he nodded and smiled. "Um, sure. If you don't mind."

"I'm asking you to come, so I don't mind at all. I want you there."

"Thank you." Her face softened a fraction, like she couldn't believe her ears. "What do I need to bring or wear?"

"Your warmest clothes," Mom said. "And we'll supply the

rest."

"Okay, then."

His mom smiled, and opened her arms. "Welcome to the family, Sylvie." She drew a clearly-startled Sylvie in with a big hug. "See you tomorrow."

"Thank you for a lovely evening."

"You're more than welcome." Mom pointed to Ryan. "Don't keep her up too late. Tomorrow will be a big day."

"I'm not thirteen, Mom," he grumbled.

"Twenty-eight, wasn't it?" Sylvie murmured with tilted lips.

Jake snickered, and after putting on boots and coats, Ryan and Sylvie hurried through the snow to Ryan's vehicle. "Wow."

"Wow is right," she said.

He started the engine, putting a hand on the back of her headrest as he reversed, then paused, glancing at her. "I don't know whether to say 'You're welcome' or apologize."

"Your mom is intense."

He winced. "I've never seen her be so scary. I get that she's protective, but that was next level."

She half-shrugged. "To be honest, I can't blame her. If I had a son in the NHL, I'd be doing all I could to protect him too."

"I don't need protecting," he said, as he drove through the gates and onto the road.

"Your mom seems to think you do."

Ouch. Was there anything more emasculating than that? The town's streetlights pooled gold onto clumps of fresh-fallen snow.

"But it's okay," she continued. "I can understand why she'd be cautious. Especially with someone like me."

"What do you mean?"

"I'm not exactly a Bree Karlsson-type girl. I don't have the perfect family background, or the sweet happy personality that makes moms warm to me."

"My mom likes you."

She exhaled. "Your mom is fierce. In a good way."

"She's one of a kind, that's for sure." She'd always been that way. Always his number one advocate. "My mom has Ukrainian heritage, and she also lives up to my dad's family name. Guillemette in French means determined protector." Something he'd always tried to be, both on the ice and with his family and friends. "But hey, if being with us all again tomorrow is too much, then please know you don't have to come."

He peeked across. Saw her bite her lip. Then she sighed.

"You know, I wasn't joking before. I've never gone fishing, ice or otherwise, and I've never felt like I was welcomed into a family like yours before, either. I mean, Bree and Mike were nice, but I don't know, I guess I always felt like I was there as a guest or that I had a job to do. It wasn't the same as being welcomed for my sake. And it's been so long since I felt like I was accepted into a family, that I," her voice trembled, then she cleared it, "I don't know if I can tell you just how much I appreciate that."

His heart panged at what she didn't say. "If my mom likes you, you're in."

"In?"

He pulled up outside her apartment. Quit the engine. Unclipped his seatbelt. "I'll walk you inside."

"You don't have to."

"Actually, I do." His lips tweaked. "This'll probably make me sound even more like a Mama's boy, but she'd whup my backside if I didn't treat you as a gentleman should."

"I don't think you're a Mama's boy," she murmured.

She didn't? "Then what do you think?"

"I think you're a gentleman." Her gaze dipped to his lips, lingering there for a moment, before lifting.

Right now, with his pulse rushing in his ears, he sure didn't feel like one. "What else do you think?" he dared.

She moistened her lower lip, her smile briefly flashing in the glow thrown by the streetlight, as she leaned forward. "This."

Then she reached across the car's console and clasped his face and kissed him.

His eyes closed, his hands reaching to draw her head nearer, as surprise faded and he sank into bliss. Her mouth was warmly insistent against his, heating his senses, drawing his need. He'd experienced so few kisses in his life that he felt compelled to rush, and only when the corners of the car's middle console started digging into his side did he realize this wasn't perhaps the best place to kiss like this.

He drew back, breathing heavily, as her heavy-lidded gaze held him prisoner. "I like you," she murmured.

"And I like you." And he really liked kissing her like this. He leaned close and captured her mouth with his again, and fell back into heaven.

Her hands slipped from his jaw, sliding through his hair, then tugged him closer still, until that pesky console demanded they take this somewhere else.

He pulled back. The car's windows had fogged up. "We should go inside."

Her eyebrow arched.

"I mean, we should get you inside. Nothing else." Nothing else would happen, could happen. Even if her kisses felt like a drug, a powerful elixir that could make him lose all reason and self-control.

"I'd really like something else to happen," she murmured.

So would he. He blinked at that realization, as common sense slowly trickled back to his brain. He exhaled heavily. "Come on. It's getting late." He opened the car door before he could hesitate a second longer. Sure enough, the rush of frigid night air chased away any thought of lingering.

He walked her to her door, and after a tame kiss said good-night. Once she was safely inside, he hurried back and slumped across the steering wheel. Whoa. What had just happened?

CHAPTER 5

She barely slept that night. Thinking about Ryan. His kisses that stole her senses. His family who, after that initial mishap, had literally opened their arms and welcomed her in. She was so hungry for that. *So* hungry. Hungry to feel accepted, to feel like she might finally belong. Could it really be possible?

Everything about the night had proved eye-opening. The hammering Heather had given her, which strangely, she did understand. She hadn't lied to Ryan about that. Why wouldn't a mother want what was best for her son? It seemed such a miracle that Heather had flicked to warm—or at least accepting—after Sylvie's own moment of directness. Their home, their sweet home, that she longed to live in. Even the revelation that Heather had Ukrainian heritage, like Sylvie did, too. And then there'd been Ryan's kiss.

Did Ryan have any idea that he could ignite her senses with that long-lashed look most women would call a smolder? She bet he had no idea he did that, or the effect it had on mere mortals like her. And she'd be willing to bet her life that he had no clue about the feelings he churned inside of her when his mouth met hers. It seemed impossible that he hadn't perfected the art of kissing with a thousand women before. Then there had been the moment in the car, when she'd wanted to climb across and prove just how much he was starting to mean to her, to give him all of her so he'd never want to leave her.

She was glad she hadn't, though, knowing that it was always after she'd offered everything that other guys had dropped her. But she sensed Ryan wouldn't demand that of her, that he'd not want to explore that kind of thing until they were in a committed relationship, or even engaged. She shuddered. Imagine marrying someone you'd never experienced that level of intimacy with. Bree had once said she'd be waiting until marriage to be truly physical, which had shocked her. How could a couple know they were truly compatible if they didn't try-before-you-buy, so to speak?

She wondered if Ryan had done that, and if so, who the lucky girl was. Then wondered if he hadn't, and if she'd be the one lucky enough to teach him all she knew…

Her stomach swooped, and she dragged her mind back to more fundamental things. Like whether he considered they were even in a relationship or not. He had to, right? Kissing like that, for a guy like him anyway, had to mean they were boyfriend and girlfriend now. Everything his family had said seemed to suggest they considered that they were. Ryan didn't do casual flings. Didn't do hookups. So him kissing her *had* to mean he wanted her. Didn't it?

But because he was different to the usual guys she'd dated, she'd likely have to treat him differently to what she'd done. There was no point scaring him off by being too forward too quickly. Better to start slow, to give him a taste of what could be, instead of laying it all out straightaway like she'd done before.

She pulled the blanket over her ears. She really had to snatch what sleep she could, before the ice fishing expedition tomorrow, today—she no longer knew. She rolled onto her side. The clock's lit numbers said two. Today, then.

She closed her eyes, rolled the other way, tugged the blanket around her shoulders. Why were the Guillemette family so quick to accept her? Others—Mike's mom came to mind—had proved to not be so willing to understand. Maybe Ryan's family really did live up to their last name.

She didn't understand them, but knew one thing. She wouldn't do anything to wreck this chance.

By THE TIME Ryan called for her at nine she'd managed to snatch a few hours of rest. If she had any chance of making this relationship work then she'd need to learn he liked to be on time, and work on her poor timing to allow for that. She opened the door. "Hi."

"Hello." His eyes darkened as he leaned down as if to kiss her, but she ducked away, so he kissed her cheek instead.

When she next looked at him, he seemed confused, so she smiled to assure him. "Shall we go?"

"Uh, sure. Got everything you need?"

She lifted her bag, and shut the door. "Let's do this."

Playing hard to get wasn't her usual game, but this man deserved better than her usual routine. And she didn't want to get distracted by him coming in, and realizing just how gross her place was. Her apartment had a funky smell and wasn't pretty, especially compared to the perfect home he'd grown up in. Love didn't live here, although mold and mice certainly did. Besides, if she was going to make this work that meant not giving him ideas that she was any more uninhibited than what he already believed, which meant trying things differently to what she'd always done in the past. She huddled in her thickest winter coat as she hurried to his vehicle.

Inside the car, she met his next attempt to kiss her with a

quick peck before easing back. She traced a hand down his cheek. "Good morning."

His brow furrowed. "Is everything okay?"

"Yep! I can't wait. Your family was so nice to me yesterday, so I don't want to make us late."

His mouth tweaked, his gaze heavy. "I'm pretty sure they'd understand."

"I don't want them to think I'm that kind of girl."

"What kind of girl?"

"The kind of girl who might lead you astray."

"Whoa." He turned to face her more fully. "I don't even know where to begin with that kind of statement. But first, as far as I'm concerned, you're not that kind of girl at all."

Bless him. That was because he didn't really know her.

"And second, what should matter is what you mean to me, not what other people think."

"And what's that?"

"Like I said yesterday. I like you. And I know that I'm heading back to Edmonton real soon, but I still want to know where this can go."

He did? She smiled.

His face softened, as he leaned close. "And third, even though I loved kissing you last night, I'm not the kind of guy who lets his emotions get away from him. So, I'm not about to be led astray, which means you don't need to worry about me."

But she might lead herself astray. She willed her smile not to falter.

This man was so good, and spending time with him might help her become a better person. But history—and Bree—had told Sylvie that she relied on a man to make her feel better, and she knew that tumbling into love with someone gave them the power to break you.

So, while she wanted this man and all that his family repre-sented, she'd need to guard her heart for when it didn't work out. Because life didn't work out for her. And despite her best efforts, history had taught her that sooner or later she'd fail.

THE THIRTY-MINUTE RIDE to Sylvan Lake passed in further conversation about music preferences, favorite movies, and him sharing about his many years fishing with his dad. The picture he painted enticed her to want more, tantalizing her with the possibility that if she behaved she could finally get a chance with what so many others considered normal. Which was why she continued to evade his questions about her own family background. He wouldn't want to know about all that.

They arrived at the lake, and her heart thrilled at the pretty scene. Bree would likely think she was insane, as fishing had always held as much appeal as running a marathon in Africa. But the fact this was something Ryan loved to do made it an easy yes.

The iced-over lake had a number of huts and tents, and she could see tracks from where vehicles had driven onto the lake.

"How do people know it's safe to drive on?"

"People measure the ice. Four inches is safe to walk on, twelve inches is safe for a small car, and fifteen inches is safe for a big car or pickup." He shot her a smile. "Haven't you seen ice fishing before?"

"I've seen it, but never known anyone who has actually done it."

He nodded. "The best thing to do is to pay attention to what other fishermen are doing. Some lakes have underwater currents that can decrease the ice thickness in some spots, so if nobody has gone there then that's probably for a good reason."

"I need to copy others. Got it." Just like she was trying to channel good-girl Bree. "What else?"

"Some people say you should keep your seatbelt off when

driving, and lower the window slightly so if the car breaks through the ice you can escape more easily."

Her jaw sagged. "Are you serious?"

"We're not going to fall through." He pointed to the tracks ahead. "See the tire marks? We'll be okay. Besides, I'd never let anything happen to you."

"But wouldn't the number of vehicles weaken the ice?"

"Not when it's already several meters thick." He slowed his car. "We can park here if you want, and sled our supplies across, but it means walking several miles."

Walking miles in these cold temperatures? No thanks.

"Sylvie, you can trust me."

That look of earnest entreaty drew her nod. "I know."

He grinned. "So, we're doing this?"

"Yes." She powered down her window half an inch and released her seatbelt. "Don't let me drown today."

"I won't let you drown any day. You're safe with me, Sylvie."

And somehow she knew that she was.

BREE—OR anyone else who had known her in her Toronto days —would die of laughter if they could see Sylvie now. Seated on a plastic chair, huddled over a small hole, draped in a thousand layers, hands mittened against the cold, as she clutched a bendy fishing rod she was pretty sure Ryan's dad had described as a spinning something.

Spinning totally fit. It was a spin out to be doing something like this. But it felt pretty good too. She mightn't have caught any fish in the past two hours, but she'd learned more than she ever thought possible as the Guillemette men described every piece of gear, from fluorocarbon line to steel leaders to propane-powered augers.

"Heather always complains this type is too noisy when it drills the holes in the ice, but I've had this one for years, and if it ain't broke, then why switch it?" Pete pointed to Ryan. "This one keeps threatening to buy me an electrical one, but I say it's too expensive."

"Yeah, Ryan is hardly struggling," Jake said with a roll of his eyes.

Ryan shrugged. "I don't think you'd even use it if I did buy you one." He glanced at Sylvie, smiled. "He gets a little senti-mental. Thinks the old ways are the best."

"Pfft." His dad shook his head, but it was easy to see the way he loved his sons, and how they loved him.

Yearning thickened to be part of this family, to feel that kind of love. For so long she'd felt like she was on the outer. Too strange or weird or broken for others to accept. Sure, Bree had tried, but Sylvie had sometimes sensed she wanted to fix her, like she didn't think Sylvie was enough as herself.

And maybe she was a little broken and scarred, but nobody liked feeling pitied. And while she knew that Bree would rather use an auger on her brain than have intentionally caused Sylvie to feel that way, it had happened nonetheless. Sylvie always felt less-than when around Bree and her perfect family. The fact this family were making efforts to include her felt like a gift she'd do anything to avoid wrecking. So, she'd taken Ryan's earlier comment about copying others literally.

She'd copy what Bree used to say and do, pretending to be the nice Christian girl without the past like she imagined they wanted her to be. Pretending she wasn't a mess of scars and issues and could relax as easily as they did here. Every so often she'd slip into ease, like a patch of warm water when she'd swum in the lakes back in Ontario. But it never lasted too long. She didn't want to mess things up, so she watched and tried to follow the cues of a family who didn't seem to have a care in the world. Another savage longing rose. Oh, how she wanted to belong here.

Conversation flowed, along with snacks and hot coffee from

a thermos, too. Heather held out a round container of cookies, insisting Sylvie try one. She did, biting into walnut-shaped deliciousness with a moan. "That's so good."

"Mom, you know I'm not supposed to eat food like this."

"You choose what you do with that mouth of yours, Son."

Sylvie met his glance, biting back a smile as he pinked.

"It's a traditional recipe handed down on my side of the family," Heather explained. "I'm proud of my Ukrainian heritage, and always wanted my sons to do traditional dance at the local Ukrainian dance club, but they refused."

Sylvie snorted, peeked at Ryan. "You would've looked so cute in those little red ballet shoes."

"Right?" Jake said. "It's weird he preferred skates, but whatever."

"How do you know about those shoes?" Heather asked her.

"My mom's family is Ukrainian too, and I remember seeing pictures when she was a girl of her dressed in a traditional outfit with red ballet shoes."

This instantly led to rapid-fire questions about potential connections, which fell sadly short, as Sylvie had to explain she'd never really known any of that, as her mom had left her heritage when she'd married her dad and moved east. More like Mom had abandoned her culture when Mom's parents had rejected her, but whatever. These good people didn't need to know everything.

"I think I can see Mallory and Derek over there." Heather blew on her gloved hands. "We'll be back soon. Keep an eye on our lines."

"Sure thing," Ryan said, and they departed, Jake too.

Sylvie peeked over her shoulder, catching Ryan's smile. Her chest fluttered. He really had a great smile. And oh, she loved how easygoing he was with his family, how obliging he could be. He was one thousand percent a nice guy.

"Who are Mallory and Derek?"

"Longtime friends. There's a community of fisherfolk who ice fish at this lake each year, who rent huts or bring their own, like we do."

"Committed to the cause, huh?"

"Not every day is as beautiful as this one." He pointed to the clear skies. "So if it's already set up, then it makes it easier to want to come, and makes it worthwhile."

Pete Guillemette had explained they had permits to stay until the spring breakup, which usually happened at the end of March. She didn't want to imagine what would happen if someone mistimed their departure, and got stuck in the middle of the lake.

"How are you doing?" Ryan asked her, drawing his toque down to his eyebrows.

"I don't know if fishing is my forte, but it's been fun."

"It has?"

"You don't need to act surprised. I'm not just about spiders and stuff."

He touched her hair. "You know, I kinda miss the spiders."

She desperately wanted to lean into his hand, to steal his kiss, but who knew what his folks might see? The cold, clear skies meant visibility on the lake was good. Too good. And while she could suggest returning to the hut for some alone time, she was trying to be like Bree. And she'd never suggest a thing like that. Mind you, she could pretty much guarantee Bree had never gone ice fishing, either…

"The spiders will return." One day. Just not while she was trying to impress his folks. Which might actually mean never. Huh. She gestured to the hole in the ice. "I'm not sure if the fish will, though."

Clumsy her had managed to drop her rod in the hole, which had meant a desperate snatch before Ryan had scooped it out for her. Jake had told her the fish wouldn't be back, and it seemed he was right. She'd not had a nibble since.

"You can always try somewhere else," Ryan said. "Or I can give you some tips on how to hold the fishing rod, if you like."

Oh, she liked. "Is this your way of helping me or helping yourself to keep warm?"

"Look, I'm simply wanting you to enjoy the experience, and not feel like it's a waste of time."

"It's not a waste of time. I've loved hanging out with your family."

"Just my family?" His eyebrow rose.

"Yep. Just them. I haven't enjoyed spending time with you at all."

His lips stretched into a grin. "Is that so?"

"Very so."

He moved closer, so his breath warmed her skin. "I could try to change your mind."

"You could try, but there are no guarantees."

His chuckle rumbled through his chest, as he shifted behind her, his arms stretched along hers as she held the rod in suddenly unsteady hands.

"See? You do need me. You won't catch anything if you're shaking."

"I'm not shaking."

"What do you call it then?"

Her mind blanked.

He laughed softly. "Can I ask why you're suddenly trembling?"

"It might have something to do with the company," she muttered.

"Might it?"

His face pressed into her cheek with a kiss, and she almost lost the rod again, glad he was there to snatch it back.

"Whoa." He grasped it, handing it to her with a smile. "Do you want this? Can I trust you?"

She nodded, words failing her. Oh, she wanted. She'd do

everything in her power to prove to this man and his family that she could be trusted. And hope that, just like this iced-over lake, time with this family might help cover the treacherous waters of her life.

ALL THROUGH THE morning he felt twitchy, wanting her to himself, yet delighting at how she was getting on with his folks. For someone who hadn't fished before, and whose nerves about being on ice had been made very plain, Sylvie had done well. She hadn't caught anything, but ice fishing wasn't just about catching fish. It was about spending time with each other, sharing about their lives, relaxing. He'd noticed how she was starting to relax around them more. She wasn't quite the same edgy girl he'd met in Calgary, or even at the bookstore. It was like her walls were coming down. A brick or two, at least.

Dad caught some pike so he was happy, but the day was cut short because of the All-Star game, which meant leaving at midday to get back in time to watch it.

Yesterday, they'd watched the skills contest, and he'd tried not to be jealous as he watched his friends compete. Like San Jose's alternate captain Jai Mullins in the fastest skater contest. Brent Karlsson going four-for-four in the accuracy shooting, before being knocked out for top spot by Ryan's captain, Jason McHale. Toronto's Dan Walton, in his first All-Star appearance, winning the hardest shot. Montreal's Beau Nash owning the goaltenders' contest.

He was glad for his friends, they certainly deserved their shot, but sometimes it was like he was watching them with way more than just thousands of miles and a TV screen between them. They seemed top-tier, while he was firmly on the shelf below. Or even the one below that. Not quite an also-ran, but it sometimes felt like he was running close to that.

He was pretty sure some of his own teammates thought that. He might play as part of the second defense pairing, and on the penalty kill sometimes, but his lack of voice in the locker room meant he'd never earned attention like Mats Hansen and Viktor Malenski had. Ryan had heard sports commentators describe him as a solid asset, but without any of the playmaking abilities that people heralded in elite players like Brent and Jason. And he was mostly okay with that. So what that he didn't have Sidney Crosby talent? Stubbornness could take a man a long way. And the desire to prove the critics wrong. It helped when others like Luc and Chris Thomas weren't shy about teasing their All-Star friends in the group chat.

He'd joined in a bit yesterday, but hadn't wanted to respond to any of their comments about Sylvie. Trying to put an explanation in the chat made things too real, and this all had such an unreal quality he wanted to stay in the bubble for as long as he could.

He glanced at her, sitting on the couch in his parents' living room, as the NHL All-Star game blared on the big screen. Only about half a meter of empty space separated them. but it might as well be half a mile the way he yearned to have her close again. Like when he'd wrapped his arms around her in his pathetically obvious attempt to show her how to hold the fishing rod.

That had only fueled desire for more. He wanted her closer, but the fact his parents and brother sat nearby didn't allow for the kind of snuggling he wanted. Having kissed her, merely holding her was like drops of water to a dying man. But as that wasn't going to happen—he'd never hear the end of it if he blew off the All-Star game for a girl—he'd have to settle for sitting beside her. Feeling caged, like a lion, feeling tense, like his nerves might explode through his skin. Now he'd had a taste of her, he just wanted more.

Still, kissing Sylvie wasn't going to happen right now, so he'd have to settle for something else. He managed to subtly inch over, to grasp Sylvie's hand, entangle her fingers with his.

Others might not agree, but he thought there was something intimate about holding her hand, feeling the fragile bones beneath soft skin. Hearing her soft hitch of breath as he thumbed her palm. Her sleeve had tugged up, and he released her hand to trace the tattoos lining the soft white inside flesh of her arm. She was watching him, her lips parted, like this was affecting her as much as him.

His phone flashed a message. He glanced at it. Put it away. He'd normally watch All-Star games with the others in the Bible study group, leaving comments in their group chat, like he'd done yesterday during the skills competition. But he didn't want that today. Wanted only this today.

"Who was that?" his mom asked.

"Luc." He glanced at Sylvie. "Luc Blanchard. He was at Mike's on Sunday."

She nodded. "I know him. Plays for Winnipeg."

"How is he?" his mom asked.

"Fine." He guessed. They didn't live in each other's pockets.

The on-ice action changed, Vancouver's Zac Parotti charging down the ice as Brent Karlsson paired with Ryan's captain Jason McHale to stop him. Brent's one-armed stick move stole the puck, and the momentum shifted, as pressure now mounted against the other goalie, before Brent slap-shot the puck into the upper corner of the net.

"Nice."

"Karlsson's slick," Ryan's dad said.

Smooth, professional, never wasting a movement. They might play different positions, but Detroit's alternate captain was everything Ryan aspired to be.

He peeked at Sylvie. She was watching the screen. "You know him, too."

"I've met him a few times. He married the Aussie skater." Her nose wrinkled. "Bree's best friend."

There was a slight edge to her voice that he didn't understand. Did she not like Holly or something? "I've only met her a few times but Holly seems nice."

"For an overachiever."

"Huh?"

Maybe she caught his confusion, because she turned to him with wide eyes. "I didn't mean it to sound like that. But it's hard to not feel pretty small when around people like that. She's got a gold medal, and now is studying to be a doctor. I swear, if I lived in Tennessee then she'd live in Elevensee, at least."

He snickered, but her words stole inside. Comparison was a game he was all too familiar with as well. He squeezed her hand. "Good thing you live in Alberta, then."

Her gaze found his, and for the first time in his life, he didn't care what was happening on the All-Star game. He just wanted to drink her in, instead.

Drink in the pale skin that her hair color and dark brows only accentuated. Drink in the way she seemed to see him, to know him, to understand him in a way few others had. Drink in the way her mobile mouth twisted and pursed. He couldn't wait to dive back into her mouth's pillowy softness…

"You two watching this or what?" Jake said.

His brother's comment swung Ryan's attention back to the screen, and he sank into his seat. Then sensed Sylvie's gaze on him, which made him wish he was braver and maybe didn't love hockey quite so much so he could just get up and leave and take her with him. Then they could kiss, and—

"Anyone want anything else to eat?" his mom asked.

"Fine thanks," he mumbled, which seemed to be the mood for the room.

The coverage switched to a commercial break, and his mother did another round of beverage requests, which Sylvie offered to help with. He helped too—he didn't want to leave her on her own with his mom just yet. Mom might've behaved today, but he still couldn't quite get the memory of her interrogation yesterday out of his mind.

"Got plans tomorrow?" Mom asked Sylvie. "You'd be welcome to join us at church."

"Oh." Sylvie bit her lip, glanced at Ryan, and he nodded. She winced, then glanced back at his mom. "Thanks for the offer, but I, uh, had already made plans."

"With Ryan here?" Bless his mom for getting in other people's business.

"No."

"You could have lunch together," Mom suggested.

"Thanks Mom, but I'm able to ask that myself."

Mom poured the new rounds of coffees. "Just trying to help."

He caught her wink at Sylvie, and the way the corners of Sylvie's lips tipped up for a moment.

Then Sylvie glanced at him. "I, uh, didn't want to assume—"

"If you've got plans, that's okay with me." Even if knowing she hadn't wanted to make plans with him was a little disappointing.

But hey, he could understand that she might need a break from the Guillemette clan. He loved his family, but too much time with them drove even him insane.

Maybe he wore his disappointment too well, or that Sylvie felt she now owed him an explanation, for she looked at him, her unease obvious as she sighed. "I, uh, wondered about going to see my grandparents."

"Good for you," his mom said, not even having the decency to pretend she wasn't listening.

Sylvie's lips twisted again. "We'll see."

"Let me know if you want company," Ryan offered. Hey, she'd met his family, so they were at that place already. And from everything she'd said before, her family was fraught with challenges, so she might appreciate a supportive face.

"Thanks, but not yet."

"Well, maybe we could do lunch," he murmured, as his mom returned to the living room with his father's coffee.

"Maybe."

"Just message me when you're done and I'll make it work."

She wet her bottom lip, and if she hadn't been holding a cup of coffee, he would've swept her up in a swoony embrace like on one of those cheesy romance movies his mom liked to pretend she didn't watch. He'd have to save that for later.

"Game's about to start again," his dad called.

Ryan gestured her inside. "Shall we?"

"Sure."

They resumed their seats, and the game continued, but after he'd finished his coffee he still felt too far away from her. But he wasn't going to make an obvious play, like man spreading until their knees bumped, or the old stretch-the-arm-along-the-back-of-her-chair thing. He mightn't have Brent Karlsson's smooth moves, but he wasn't that lame.

Still, he wondered how to draw closer, whether she'd welcome his nearness in front of his family like this. This was all so new to all of them.

"You warm enough there, Sylvie?" his mom asked. "Use the blanket if you like."

"Thanks." Sylvie released his hand and removed the pink and gray blanket folded on the couch's back, shifting closer as she placed it over her knees. "You want some?" she asked, holding up a corner.

"Sure."

Her invitation gave him permission to finally inch closer, to feel the heat of her body closer to his. He caught Jake's smirk, but didn't react, keeping his eyes on the screen, where Beau

Nash, Montreal's goalie, was facing another Zac Parotti sniping threat.

Beau kicked out, and the puck went flying safely to Franklin James, whose stellar season had seen him called up for the first time. Franklin shot to McHale who tic-tac-toed with Brent to where the puck slammed into the opposition's armor.

The room gave a collective hiss, and Ryan's phone flashed again. He glanced at it. Luc. Again. *You watching this or are you dead?*

Honestly. Friends could be so annoying sometime. He tapped back *good game.*

That all you got? Luc demanded. *Let me guess. You're with her.*

Nope. Not gonna respond.

His phone started buzzing. But he wasn't going to play. He switched it off. Luc would demand to know why he hadn't responded earlier, and he didn't have the energy to explain it was because he'd rather hold hands with a girl. And something within didn't really want to have to go into any explanations with Mike yet, either. That seemed fraught with difficulty. How could he explain how Mike and Bree's nanny had left them and come here? It would make him look like a nanny-stealer.

So, it was best to ignore them. To pretend this was his world, at least for a few more hours. A world where he and Sylvie were an item, she fit in with his family, and they could escape all the craziness and do simple things like ice fish and watch hockey together and share meals.

This was the world he wanted. And that stubbornness thing? Yeah, nobody was going to stop him.

CHAPTER 6

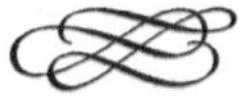

"How did you enjoy today?" Ryan asked her, when he drove her home later that night.

"It was certainly one of the more interesting days I've had."

"So, does ice fishing score a yay or nay?"

"I think..." She wouldn't want to do it ever again, except with Ryan and his family, "it could be a yay."

His smile flashed as he glanced at her. "Could be?"

"I didn't catch any fish."

"Which means you need to go again and keep going until you do."

"Maybe."

"Definitely."

She bit back a smile. He really seemed to like her. His family did, too. She still couldn't quite get over the contrast between yesterday's machine-gun of a welcome to today's hugs and warm invitations for more.

"So, your grandparents, huh?"

"Yeah." That. Her nose wrinkled. She supposed she should actually do it to ensure she hadn't lied. It had been more of a tactic to avoid feeling obliged to go to church than from any real wish to see the people who'd judged and disowned her all those years ago. But perhaps it was the sweetness of family, of the positivity this family believed, that made her think it might just be possible for her grandparents coming to accept her, and things possibly working out well in her life too.

Families didn't have to stay fractured forever. There was a chance that her grandparents might've forgiven her mom by now, and by extension, forgiven Sylvie too. Some families could be sweet. Others could be weird. Or just downright dysfunctional.

"That offer is still open, you know," Ryan said, as he slowed to turn into her street. "If you want company when you meet them, I can come."

Her heart thumped. Maybe they would forgive her if they could see her life was turning out okay. "I thought you had church."

"I could go to the early service, then join you after that. What time are you meeting them?"

Good question. She probably should've figured that out before blurting any of this aloud. "Um, nine, ten? I hadn't really decided."

"Hmm."

"But it's okay," she rushed to add. "You don't want to get involved in my family's drama. Maybe we could meet later for lunch instead."

He nodded. With relief, she thought.

"What time do you need to head to Edmonton?"

"I want to get there before dark, so I'd need to leave by three." His lips curved. "Which leaves plenty of time for lunch."

Or other things, his smile seemed to say.

Her heart skittered. She didn't want to behave like the girl she'd always been, but another part of her did too. She'd found magic in his lips, and there was something intoxicating about being sought by a man like this. And yet the hesitations still lay there. He was so good, and clean, and she…was not.

He parked, and before she could try to explain anything, he'd turned and captured her face in his hands. Then he was kissing her, and she was sinking into pleasure, as his hand wrapped around the back of her neck, and she leaned into him, deepening the kiss.

His breath hitched, and he pulled back, studying her from under heavy eyelids. "Sylvie, I…"

She winced. She'd gone too far, too fast, and now he regretted it, and—

He swooped back in for more. This time it was his lips demanding more, and she savored his nearness, his desire, his whispers of "Sylvie" that somehow meant so much more than all those men who could barely remember her name.

Ryan wanted her—she could tell from the way his hands caressed her back, as if he was trying to get her nearer—but he respected her enough to not push.

Finally, she dragged her mouth from his, thanks to a need to breathe. "Ryan, you…" Words failed her.

"I?"

Kissed too well. Made her heart soar. Dared her to believe this could be real. "I really like you," she murmured.

"I really like you," he breathed, as his mouth slipped to her cheek, then to her ear. She jerked away.

He straightened, his face shadowed by the lack of street-lights. "Too much?"

Not enough. If he grazed her ear with his lips again she'd do things she'd promised herself she wouldn't do. And definitely wouldn't have a chance of clinging to any good-girl facade he might think she owned. "I think I should go inside."

"I'll walk you in."

"Thanks." She might know some jiu-jitsu defense moves, but she appreciated the company of a tall strong man nonetheless.

Some of her neighbors seemed a little creepy, always peering out when she got home.

They walked, hand in hand, inside, then up the stairs to her apartment. He placed a hand on the doorway as she fiddled with her key, trying to unlock the door.

"Need help?"

"I'm fine. Thanks," she added.

Finally, the door opened with a rush, so much that she almost fell inside.

He reached out to steady her. "Whoa."

She wasn't sure if the "Whoa" was from her near-fall or the smell that rose to meet her. The stale garbage smell that no amount of deodorizing spray or incense candles banished. "It's weird they didn't advertise that this apartment came with its own garbage aroma."

"Has something died?" he asked.

"Probably." A mouse or three. A rat. Maybe a raccoon.

"Can you call the janitor or maintenance or the landlord to fix it?"

She bit back a sigh. Another thing to do. "I'll call on Monday."

"You don't have to stay here," he said, frowning as he looked around.

"Actually," her nose wrinkled, "my finances say that I do."

He rubbed a hand over his chin. "Have you heard anything more about any of your job applications?"

"Nope." She should check again soon, though. She'd been swallowed up in impossible fairytale-land to care too much today.

"Look, I'm sure there are other apartments out there. You don't need to stay in a dive like this."

"I looked, and this was the only furnished one available that I could afford and move into straight away."

"I don't want you to feel unsafe," he said, his face tilting until his forehead touched hers.

"I'm safe." She hoped. "It's just not very nice."

He chewed his lip, and to stop him worrying, she pressed to her toes and kissed him.

It seemed to work, as his arms instantly slid around hers, and they were soon indulging in the deep, long heady kisses that the car's console always interrupted before. Now they were flush against each other, she was melting into him, when a harsh bark of laughter from outside pulled them apart.

"We shouldn't kiss like that here," he muttered, his eyes intense.

They probably shouldn't kiss like that anywhere. Not if he didn't want to explore certain, ahem, consequences.

She blinked at herself, then pushed him away, both hands on his chest. "You need to go home." Now. Before she caved.

"So, I'll see you for lunch tomorrow?"

"Only if you promise to behave."

His lips curved on one side. "Now that's a promise I can't promise."

Amusement spurted, and she stepped inside, waiting as he kissed her one last time then walked away, but not before giving her a final wave as he passed into the stairwell.

She blew him a kiss, her heart sore as she closed the door. Locked it securely. Then closed her eyes as the pounding in her chest refused to go away. This man. Oh, this man. What was she going to do with him? The heady attraction was begging her to call him back, bring him inside, and see just where their kisses could take them.

And she knew if she did that, there'd be no way that she could show her face with his family again. There'd be no way she could ever finally find a place to belong.

It was a good thing he was leaving. She might find time to

figure out what to do. Her spirits sank. Like what to do when he asked about her supposed visit to her grandparents tomorrow.

SUNDAY MORNING, she dragged herself from bed, wincing at the too-cold floors. She'd need to light some more smell-masking candles, but she didn't want to waste the nice ones Bree had given her for Christmas. Those candles were a little too nice, and Sylvie might've seen the price tag, and been amazed that something that would literally be burned could cost so much. Still, the violet and patchouli scent was heavenly, and heaven probably knew she needed more of that in her life, instead of the environment she was pretty sure came from the other place.

Weird. She frowned as the kettle boiled. Maybe it was the talk of church yesterday, but she hadn't thought about heaven or hell all week. Not since last Sunday's christening service, when Sylvie's shortcomings had been made plain at that place she only attended to appease Bree.

Guilt gnawed. She should probably check in with her again, make sure the kids were okay. She'd made the best decision she could at that moment, but while Bree had said Ethan and Ellison missed her, she hoped they didn't miss her too much.

She made her tea, hurried back to bed, as her phone bleeped a message.

Her heart raced. Ryan?

She snatched it up. Smiled. It *was* him. Asking once again if she wanted company in visiting her grandparents. Aww, he was so sweet, so kind and considerate. *Thank you, but the answer is still no. But the answer is still yes for lunch, if that's still on offer.* She tensed. Was that too forward?

His message came a few seconds later. *Of course it is.*

She fist-pumped herself. Then he texted back, offering to collect her at twelve.

Can't wait! Oh, look at her, using excited punctuation like a Bree.

Me either. See you then. Smiley face.

Oh, she could like a man who used emojis. Once upon a time she might've thought it lame, might've teased Bree and Mike for doing it. Now she understood. If she was bolder, and not trying to rein things in and act cool, then she might've sent a heart. Or a blown-kiss emoji. But because she was trying to be cool she didn't.

She shivered, pulling the blankets around her shoulders. Talk about cool.

Her teeth chattering reminded her she needed to actually call her grandparents, and see if they were open to seeing her. Tea sloshed uneasily in her stomach. Who knew if they'd want to see her? It had been so long. She didn't even know if the phone number she'd last been given for them was still the right one.

Her fingers tensed. She *really* didn't want to do this. But knowing Ryan would be asking her at lunch meant she needed to make the effort. So she sighed, and pressed the numbers.

She put her phone on speaker mode, and the sounds of a call connecting filled her ears. Then, "I'm sorry," an automated voice said. "The number you have called has been disconnected."

What?

Then came a series of phone-call-ending bleeps.

Huh. Maybe she'd dialed wrong. She tried again, checking the numbers carefully this time. "I'm sorry. The number you have called has been disconnected."

She frowned. This was the number she'd been given, right?

A third attempt revealed the same result, leaving her chewing her lip, her heart sinking. They must've moved. So, if they weren't there, then where were they? Her chest grew tight. She couldn't very well ask her mom. That was impossible. But would they even want to see her—presuming they were still alive?

She exhaled unsteadily. No. Thinking about the alternative was impossible. She couldn't be too late. So, in that case, if not there, then where?

She tapped open her website browser and typed in Red Deer's aged care facilities. A list of a dozen places popped up, none of which sounded familiar. Mind you, it'd been several years since her mom had given her the number, so the facility might've merged or changed its name. Which left only one course of action.

She tapped on the first name that popped up.

"Hello, this is Golden Pines. How may I direct your call?"

Sylvie cleared her throat. "I, uh, would like to speak to somebody there."

"May I ask who?"

She closed her eyes. "I'd like to speak with Esther or John Melnyk, if they're staying there, please."

There was a pause, then the woman's voice was considerably cooler as she replied, "I'm afraid we don't have anyone here by that name."

"Oh, but—"

There were no buts about it as the woman hung up.

She exhaled. Okay, so if they didn't live there, maybe they'd moved and she should try calling the next facility listed on Google.

So she did, a place called Aspen Lodge, only to receive a variation on the same answer. She tried a third time, earning the same result. Huh. Who knew old people were able to keep anonymous so well? The hedging continued, even when she prefaced her query with words she'd never thought would come from her mouth, "I'm their granddaughter."

Nope. Nobody would play. Which left her feeling adrift, with a sense of secondary abandonment. Why she was even bothering to track down people who'd made it clear they wanted nothing more to do with her? If it wasn't for Ryan she wouldn't even try. And she kind of hated the fact that now she'd tried, it bothered her that she didn't know where they were. Old people didn't just disappear, did they? Unless they really had died…

She chewed her thumbnail. There had to be records somewhere that would indicate whether they had died. Newspaper reports, maybe. But the thought of chasing these down and expending so much emotional energy on a couple who had made it clear they had no wish for contact with her made her pause. She *could* do that. But maybe one day when the need for a job wasn't so pressing.

She rolled onto her stomach, dragging the blanket over her shoulders as she tapped her phone's screen to bring up the jobs list from before. Ugh. But she needed money, stat. And while she'd loved the past two days with Ryan, that was hardly the way an independent woman should live. She had zero desire for anyone to think she saw him in any sugar daddy role. Experience had taught her that nobody could be trusted, not long term.

Another shiver wracked her body, forcing her to return under the covers. A shaft of wintry light stole around the too-short blinds onto her face, forcing her to shift. The furnishings didn't seem designed for minus temperatures, the blinds' length no doubt encouraging more of the cold to steal past too. She needed to get out of here. If she found a job that paid enough she could afford to move from this dump. And maybe one day find out exactly what had happened with her grandparents.

RYAN MET her at twelve on the dot, and she was thankful to forget the unfun of missing grandparents and applying to jobs she didn't want as she lost herself in his kiss hello.

"Church was that good, huh?" she asked, placing her hands on his chest.

"It was okay." His eyes darkened. "Seeing you is better."

His next kiss seemed to prove that, and she had to drag her mouth from his as she pointed to the door. "We should go eat."

"I like this, though," he protested.

So did she. Too much. She pushed him away. "You promised lunch. I didn't figure you for a liar."

"Fine, then," he grumbled.

On the way to the restaurant he asked about her visit to her grandparents. She hedged, saying they hadn't been available. Which was technically true, maybe. They certainly hadn't been in any of the places she'd tried, and she'd tried them all. Where could they be?

"Hey," he covered her hand with his. "I'm sure you'll get the chance to meet them soon."

"Maybe."

"Definitely." He gently squeezed her hand.

Oh, bless him for thinking all families were like his, where people actually liked each other and wanted to stay connected. Hunger grew for those kinds of relationships. To just once feel like she was wanted.

She peeked across, caught his smile, which instantly soothed the worries inside. At least Ryan liked her.

They ate, and talked about his upcoming schedule, and she did her best to sidestep his questions about her work situation, admitting only that she'd sent off more applications. "So I guess we'll see what happens."

"Well, if there's anything I can do to help, let me know."

Yeah, unless he had a magic lamp with a genie she didn't think that would work.

"I'll be praying for you when I'm gone."

His words tugged at today's well of emotion. It was something like what Bree and Mike used to say to her, too. "I," she had to clear her throat. "I appreciate it."

"Any time." He squeezed her hand.

Their meal soon finished, he paid, then drove her to a park she supposed would be scenic in summer, but now just seemed a collection of gray-brown leafless trees and clumps of snow. He'd pointed out the wooden buildings he said housed the Norwegian Laft Hus Society, displaying the legacy of local settlers of Norwegian heritage, then mentioned the nearby Museum and Art Gallery. And as tempting as it was to dive back into kisses, she sensed his need to talk, the fact he was not-so-subtly watching the clock, and she knew he had to go soon.

"When can I see you again?" he murmured.

"Whenever you like. You know where I'll be."

"Can you come to Edmonton? We're flying to Vegas tomorrow for our road trip, then we'll be back next Sunday. You could come visit, we could hang out. You could watch us take on Detroit on Tuesday the following week."

"Detroit?"

He nodded.

And possibly see Bree's brother Brent? Possibly have to offer explanations why she was here and not in Calgary? "We'll see. A lot depends on whether I find a new job or not."

"Is it bad for me to wish you'd find one after Valentine's Day?" he murmured, as he nuzzled her neck.

Her breath snagged. Celebrating a day like that together suggested he was thinking of this *way* more seriously than she had dared hope. "It's very bad," she said instead.

He chuckled softly, then kissed her again, his lips searing yet tender, so that she soon forgot all about anything else.

It was only when he returned her home, with a gentle kiss goodbye and promise that he'd call as soon as he arrived in E-town tonight, that she could finally breathe again. And realized that maybe, just maybe, she could afford to give her limp hopes much-longed-for air.

THE BLACKFALDS INTERCHANGE passed over Highway 2, the small industrial area soon giving way to farmland and lakes as he headed north. Ryan had always liked this drive, passing the stretches of lakes, ranches and farms and small towns that led home, whichever direction he took. It was why he preferred to drive, to get time to himself, to think, to order his thoughts by speaking them aloud. He might like his teammates, one of which was his housemate, but he appreciated this time to himself. Even if his thoughts puckered his brain.

This past week seemed to have changed everything. He'd thought he was simply heading to a christening before spending time with his family, but somehow that had turned into so much more. He liked Sylvie. A lot. And yeah, he bet some might think he'd rushed too hard and too quick into things, but he couldn't help how he felt. And the more he thought about her, the more he wanted to help her. It seemed wrong that she was forced to live in that gross apartment while he was heading to someplace new and clean, with all the mod-cons, half of which he didn't use. He kind of hated the discrepancy between them.

He wished he knew her better to suggest something like, oh, staying with his folks, instead of something that a rat might turn up its nose at. But he knew it was too soon, that four days wasn't long enough to suggest anything so dramatic. He'd almost wondered if he should investigate a different apartment, before his mouth had slipped and he'd suggested she come visit him in Edmonton instead. Which actually made a lot more sense. Edmonton would definitely have more jobs that could suit her. Then they could see each other all the time, and instead of being the teammate always going stag he could bring her to team events, like a normal guy on the team.

Some of the others had always thought him weird. He'd heard the nicknames, and just because he was more introverted than some, that he preferred fishing to nightclubs, he didn't think that was fair. He liked people. Mostly. Especially when they didn't get in his face. It was just unfortunate that the nature of pro hockey meant many days away, which meant sharing rooms with guys who sometimes thought his quietness and values strange.

But hey, if he got his energy from being away from people then that was okay. Even Jason McHale, king of hockey as he was so often proclaimed, had described himself more than once as an introvert. It didn't make him wrong. Just meant he wasn't the same. He wished more people would understand that.

Sylvie seemed to understand that. She seemed to realize he wasn't a showboat. And still liked him anyway. Which drew new affection for her, and made the miles increasing between them seem too far.

His phone rang. He glanced at the car's screen. Luc. He was about to stab it off when the stupid automatic-answering thing clicked into action again. He bit back a sigh. "Hey."

"Dude."

So, the fact that Luc hadn't jumped into saying whatever he thought needed saying meant this was going to be one of *those* conversations. Still, the guy had called him. So Ryan took pleasure in not breaking down and asking first.

"What are you up to?" Luc eventually said.

"Driving north to E-town. You?"

"Just hangin'. Thought I'd give you a call. See if you actually were alive or had some person messaging on your behalf and screening your calls."

Ryan winced as he slowed for traffic turning off at Lochinvar. "If I was screening, do you think I'd take your call?" he tried to joke.

"I don't know anymore, man. Why don't you tell me?"

Wow. Ryan glanced at the screen's red End Call button, tempted to press it now. But that would just fuel Luc's suspicions. "I had a big weekend with the family for my dad's birthday."

"Uh huh." That tone said Luc wasn't buying.

"It was my dad's *birthday*," he emphasized, rolling his eyes. "We went ice fishing yesterday, watched the game, it was good."

"Right."

He wouldn't bite. He'd keep his cool. That was part of his role on the ice, be the protector who others relied on to make sure things happened as they should. So if Luc thought he could call up and offer his big opinions to Ryan free of charge, then Ryan was going to make him work for it.

"You still there?" Luc asked.

Billboards flashed past. "Yep. Like I said, I'm driving, so I need to concentrate."

"Because you haven't driven that road a million times before."

He gritted his teeth to stop the exclamation of "was there something you wanted?" from spilling out.

Luc sighed. "Fine. Be like this. What's this picture with you and a girl?"

And there it was. Luc was getting to the point at last. Ryan's fingers gripped the wheel. "Nothing you need to worry about, that's for sure."

"Really? I don't know if you've talked with Mike lately, but Mike is worried, and if Mike's worried, then there's usually something to worry about."

"Well, he's wrong."

The words sounded so bald and bold said like that.

"Ryan, I don't know what's going on with you, but you're acting weird."

"Am I?"

"Yeah, you are. You're not talking to us, and I'm getting worried that you might be getting mixed up with someone and getting too deep too fast. Especially when there's this pic of you and her—"

"It was nothing. She fell off a ladder, I caught her, that was all. Some kid videoed it and tried to make it look like more than it was but it was an accident."

"So, the rumors that you and her are actually a thing are just rumors?"

There were already rumors about them? Man. "I don't know what you've heard, but you know you should never believe what you hear, and only half of what you see."

"Yeah, which is why I'm calling you. What's going on?"

"Nothing."

"Come on. Get real. For as long as I've known you, you've always been part of the All-Star Messenger chats. Then this year you weren't. The same year you get yourself snapped in a picture with a girl who looks a lot like the one we met at Mike's last weekend."

"So?" He winced. Clearly his rebuttal skills left a lot to be desired.

"So, Mike doesn't think she's a Christian, and you know better than to get mixed up with someone who's not a believer. So, is there something going on?" Luc pressed.

He gritted his teeth. What right did Luc have to push him on this?

"The fact you're not denying it says there is," Luc continued.

"I *am* denying it," Ryan snapped.

"Yeah. That thing about not believing what you hear? It's ringing pretty true right now."

"Then why are you still on the phone?" He stabbed the button to end the call.

Exhaled. Ground his teeth. Clearly that was not the way to go to downplay suspicions.

Suspicions? He rolled his eyes at himself. But still, he remembered the conversations from last year, when people had been way too quick to dismiss Sylvie just because she had a different vibe to the usual Christian girl. Why his friends had to judge her—and now judge him—he had no idea. Where was the support? Where was the grace? Where was the understanding? Nope. This world seemed to be filled with prejudice and discrimination, people too quick to judge others when they had no clue. No clue at all.

He shook his head, turned up the music to really loud, and drowned his thoughts as he drove the rest of the way, the lights of Edmonton beckoning in the approaching darkness.

CHAPTER 7

"**W**ould you like fries with that?"

Sylvie tried not to roll her eyes as the teenage kid shoved his hands in his back pockets and offered a sneer. "If I wanted fries, I would've ordered fries, lady. And did I?"

Judging from the way he eyed her, that wasn't a rhetorical question. "No."

"So just get me what I ordered, okay?"

She bit back the words that longed to escape, punching in the order on the machine as she'd been trained yesterday. How desperate was this franchise for staff that they had called Monday afternoon and offered her a job with an immediate start? But then, she recognized desperation, being familiar with it herself.

Still, most of the staff here were nice, patient with helping a newbie out, a status she'd earned considering it'd been ten years since she'd last done this kind of work. Dave, her supervisor, was younger than her, and while he'd looked her over in a creepy way, and had given a few arrogant boss-man better-than-you vibes, she'd managed to hold her tongue. So far, anyway.

She gave the kid the order total, which drew his instant complaint about prices going up. She willed her lips to remain clamped as she eyed him, waiting, then he finally tapped his card and paid.

"Excuse me a moment," she said to the next customer in line, then went to gather the punk's order. She had a set amount of time to do this, as Dave watched the clock with eagle-eyed precision, and she'd already learned that movements deemed too slow saw docked pay. And if she was forced to work here, then every cent mattered. She collected the burger and chocolate shake, placed them on a tray, and pushed it in his direction.

His lip curled higher. "I said I wanted this takeout."

"Then take it out," she longed to say. "Do we look like a five-star eating establishment?" she asked instead.

Yeah, that comment was probably not much better.

His eyes narrowed, and for a second, she thought he might flip the tray at her, but then he grabbed his stuff and slouched off, complaining about the rude staff here.

Her cheeks heated as she resumed her place on the register, aware that her supervisor's folded arms meant he'd probably heard everything. Which was awesome.

Maybe this job would prove to be her second shortest, after last week's bookstore fiasco. But at least that had possessed the silver lining that was Ryan.

Her heart fluttered, but she forced herself to concentrate. Take orders and payments, collect the ordered food, and when she got a spare moment she could clean up the plastic-shrouded family eating establishment, or so Dave had informed her, like he thought that was a privilege.

So she did, until her feet ached and her hair stank of the deep fryers, and her mind was numbing into apathy. She appreciated the job, and the fact it came with benefits, but could understand why Dave had been surprised at her application, saying most people who worked here were younger. She'd tried to joke it off, saying something to the effect that beggars couldn't be choosy, and he'd shrugged, saying at least she had some experience in customer service. She hadn't needed to show Bree's references here, which was something at least. She was sure this guy would be pumping her for any and all information about Bree, or more particularly, Mike Vaughan, seeing as Dave was a huge hockey fan. She had no wish to open the door to all that.

She bit back another smile as a customer came in who obviously knew Dave and started joshing about Edmonton's hockey team. What would any of them say if they knew one of their star defensemen was now calling her each night? They probably wouldn't believe it. Especially seeing she wasn't the usual thin, blonde, model or designer type that online research had revealed was the type of partner usually preferred in both Edmonton's team and across the NHL.

Whatever. That didn't matter. Not if Ryan preferred a dyed-hair woman with Goth-style tendencies. Even if her hair and makeup had once more needed to be tamed to suit the "family" atmosphere here.

"Sylvie, people are waiting," Dave snapped, pointing at the people hovering near the counter.

She hurried to her register. Bent her lips upward. "Hello, how may I help you today?"

Later, after her shift had finally ended, she retrieved her phone and saw she had several missed calls. One was from Bree, which she'd save until she returned home. Several were unknown numbers, which was probably from her job hunts. Nothing from Ryan, but then he was training today in Vegas, before tonight's game which she planned to watch. It started at eight, which she figured gave her enough time to go home, shower off this awful grease, eat, then watch the game in her

PJs. He'd said he'd try and call after the game, which she hoped wouldn't go too late, seeing as Dave had rostered her onto a six AM shift tomorrow, something she couldn't very well say no to, not on her first week, anyway.

She listened to the messages as she drove home. Sure enough, there were rejections from a toy store cashier job, and another from a downtown pizza joint. At least they bothered to call back, unlike some others from last week's job search efforts who had not yet responded, although she'd since seen their jobs had been deleted online. Not responding to a genuine applicant sure was classy.

She'd just pulled up outside her apartment when the final unknown caller's message came on her phone's speaker. "Hi Sylvie, this is Heather."

Who?

"I hope you don't mind, but Ryan gave me your number."

Oh, his mom.

"I wondered if you were free tonight and would like to come here and watch his game with us."

Her chest tightened. Really?

"Anyway, if you'd like to, please give me a call so we'll know to save you some dinner—Ryan mentioned you were working. You know where we live now, but here is the address just in case you've forgotten."

She read out an address, but Sylvie didn't need it. They truly wanted her company? Weariness floated away. Oh, who cared about PJs and an early night? Between this invitation, and Ryan's talk of Valentine's Day, surely that had to mean he saw her as his girlfriend. Right?

She glanced at her phone, saw Heather had also left the address as a message. The fact she'd gone to so much effort suggested she really did want Sylvie there.

Her palms slicked. But no. It would be okay. They only wanted to get to know her more, and going there would mean a chance to eat well for a change, instead of the meager rations she'd allowed herself. There was a reason she'd agreed to work at a fast-food restaurant that offered a small burger or salad as part of its incentivization for long shifts.

The memory of that greasy burger paled as she contemplated what Heather might have on offer. So she snatched up her phone and pressed the voicemail's number. "Um, hi, Heather, this is Sylvie. I just got off work and—"

"You got my message! I'm so glad. I do hope this means you can join us?"

"Um, sure. I'd like that. Thank you."

"Wonderful!"

"And if…if it's still okay I'd like to come for dinner, too."

"Of *course* it's okay. We're eating soon, but I'll set a plate aside and you can have it when you get here."

"Thank you. I, um, have to clean up, so I can probably be there in an hour."

"You take as long as you need. We'll see you when we see you, honey."

Honey? Her eyes filled. "Thanks."

She ended the call, sitting in the darkness. For as long as she could remember she'd never been anyone's "honey." Her family had other words they preferred to use, none of which she cared to remember. And while Heather was obviously calling her this because of Sylvie's relationship to Ryan, she was greedy to take the endearment for herself. To think she might be liked. That she might fit in. Somewhere. Finally.

She hurried inside, did her best to have a quicker-than-normal shower, but the smell of grease still seemed to cling to her skin and hair. It meant she had to wash it twice then wait a little longer for the product to saturate the lengths, then take time to do her makeup.

Finally, she was ready, and stepped out onto the dim stairwell. She clutched her phone in one hand, as shadows and creaks filled the space. She wasn't normally so nervy, but this was the first time she'd been out after dark on her own. And given the too-long stares of her next-door neighbor, she missed the company of someone whose presence made her feel safe.

Ten minutes later she'd pulled into the Guillemettes' driveway. She glanced at her phone. Maybe she should send him a text.

Good luck tonight. She sent an emoji of praying hands. He'd like that.

His message came quickly, almost like he'd been waiting. *Thanks. Hey, did Mom call?*

Yes. I'm sitting outside their place now, trying to find the courage to go in.

You got this. He sent a muscled arm emoji.

So do you, she typed back. *Talk after?*

Can't wait.

The front door opened, spilling warm light as Heather's body was silhouetted in the doorway. "Sylvie? Come in." She gestured her inside, then closed the door, keeping the cold out.

Time to do this. She exited, hurrying up the path to the door that was slightly ajar. But before she could knock, Heather pulled it open, drawing her inside, then shutting the door.

"Put your coat and shoes there," Heather gestured to the coat and boot racks that she remembered from her last visit, "and come inside. From now on, I want you to consider this as your home, okay? So, no knocking or wondering about whether we want you here. We want you here, okay?" Heather emphasized that with opened arms, which Sylvie obeyed, stepping into her hug like she was her child.

Heather squeezed her, then released, pointing to the kitchen. Sylvie waved at Pete as she followed instructions to take a plate as Heather pulled a slab of homemade lasagna from the oven.

"We want you to feel right at home, so cut yourself a slice, then help yourself to the bowl of salad," Heather directed.

Sylvie obeyed, sneaking peeks at this generous-hearted woman. Why had she opened up her heart and home so much?

"Stop looking at me like that," Heather said.

"Like what?"

"Like that." Heather chuckled. "Look, I will admit that I was a little surprised that you said yes to coming tonight, but I'm really grateful too. Sometimes it's hard to see my son traveling around the world, like he doesn't need me anymore. So if I can spend some time with someone he cares about, then it's like I'm getting another little insight into his world. Pete says it makes me like a stalker mom, but I only do it because I care."

Oh. Her heart sank. So, Sylvie wasn't here for her own sake, but because Heather hoped Sylvie might spill the beans on her son. "Um, okay."

Heather's brow creased. "I'm not sure I said that correctly. I certainly didn't mean to suggest we don't want you here."

"It's okay." Coldness washed across her chest.

But before she could spiral and indulge in a pity party, Heather said, "So Ryan mentioned you have a new job."

"Yes." She hadn't mentioned to Ryan which specific company that job was with. There was no reason for their video calls to involve his look of pity. So there was definitely no reason to tell Heather anything too precise. "It's in hospitality, so we're seeing how it goes."

"Well, I'm glad for your sake. The other day when you mentioned you needed one, I was going to—but never mind. You're sorted now. Now, do you want to eat here, or in front of the TV? We don't mind either way. Pete's got the pregame show on already, so you'd be eating with noise on."

Which meant she'd not be forced to face too many more of Heather's questions. "A TV dinner is what I'd planned to do tonight, anyway, so I'm happy with that."

"Great. Well, got everything you need?" She pushed a

napkin-wrapped knife and fork at her. "Water okay, or would you prefer juice?"

"Water please." If she continued working in—and therefore eating—fast food she probably should cut calories where she could.

Heather poured her a glass of water from the fridge, then passed it to Sylvie. "You go sit inside. I'm going to fix Pete something extra too."

Sylvie obeyed, and took a seat on the couch she'd shared with Ryan several days ago. How bizarre to be back at his parents' place so soon, but without him. It was like being on parade, but in a bikini, with no place to hide.

She asked about Pete's day and cut into the lasagna, its reheat obviously helping it hold its shape, nodding as he shared.

"Mmm, this is delicious."

"You like that, then?" Heather asked, joining them.

"It's the best thing I've eaten in days."

Heather smiled, and the chit-chat continued, Sylvie learning that Heather worked in an administration role in Red Deer. She missed the details, as the pregame show had switched to coverage of Edmonton's team, including the defense pairings.

"There's our boy," Heather said, smiling as the screen showed footage of Ryan engaged in his most recent games.

"He looks pumped," Ryan's dad said, as the footage shifted to show the on-ice warm-up.

Sylvie's heart twisted. So, this was what it was like to have family who were proud of their child. She felt so close she could almost taste it.

The camera zoomed into a close-up, and her heart snagged again. It was funny to think that the man looking so focused and determined had been the one kissing her until her lips ached just two days ago. Clearly, Ryan put great intention into all he did. She smiled.

"And now we're going to cross to Hannah Wade for some on-ice interviews. Take it away, Hannah."

A new picture showed Hannah Wade smiling as she began a to-camera spiel then moved to speak to Jason McHale. "And how are you feeling after the recent All Star win?"

He nodded, serious as ever. "It's always a fun time, for a really good cause, but it's great to be getting back into the season again."

The interview continued, and Sylvie watched, amazed that only months ago she'd been there watching this now-poised sports reporter almost unravel in Bree's home. She didn't know what had drawn ESPN's attention, whether it was the quality of Hannah's work, her connections, or her video of hockey players talking about the importance of protecting women that had gone viral. Maybe the Big Man Upstairs had something to do with it, like Bree and Hannah credited.

"It's so good she's back on air again," Heather said. "I was shocked by what had happened at her last station."

"It's good that they recognize talent," her husband said with a nod.

"Have you met her?" Heather asked Sylvie.

"A few times," she said. "She became friends with Bree, and hung out a bit with her and Mike last year."

"She's engaged to Franklin James, right?"

Sylvie nodded. "Which is why she has a clause in her contract meaning she doesn't report on Calgary's games, so she can't be accused of bias."

"Hmph. I can't see how she wouldn't be biased against other teams," Pete grumbled.

"I don't know the ins and outs of it. Only that her agent and legal representatives managed to come to some arrangement so she can keep doing what she's trained to do."

"Just as well," Heather said. "Ryan and Franklin used to play together, years and years ago, and he always seemed like a nice boy. Lovely family, too. He's got a few sisters on that ranch where they make movies."

"Some families have all the luck," Sylvie said without thinking.

Heather peered at her, and Sylvie had to quickly fake a smile and act like she was joking, while shoving another piece of food inside to prevent another answer. Act nice, remember? Nobody ever wanted to see the real Sylvie. Real Sylvie never got invited back to cozy family meals.

Fortunately, the anthems were starting, and all attention returned to the screen.

Sylvie slowly exhaled. She needed to pretend she was normal, not give away clues to her past. She couldn't afford to do anything to mess this up.

The game soon started, and there was a noticeable increase in focus as Ryan's line came on. She placed her finished plate on the coffee table, her stomach tense, and she watched him skate, scooping up the puck then passing it on. He was a smooth skater, with crisp passing, or so the announcer said.

"…and here's Guillemette with a clean pass to McHale, who shoots at goal but is stopped by the big body that is Jacques Paviour, here in his first stint for Las Vegas. He's certainly been bringing the razzle dazzle tonight, hasn't he, Bryan?"

"Absolutely," the other announcer agreed. "I hear their front office is being inundated with requests for Paviour's jersey after they sold out in a matter of days."

"Quite the welcome to town. Now the stoppage of play is done, and they're skating to the blue line, and once again Guillemette is in the thick of things. He passes to Viktor Malenski who shoots, but again, it's close but no cigar, as Paviour collects the puck and sends it to the other side."

The game continued, her heart lifting then dropping depending on what happened on the ice. It was funny having watched games before with Bree, and seeing how invested she was. She'd never really understood that level of investment until now. But it was like the hits on Ryan seemed to physically impact her, and something violent rose within when he was thumped into the boards. How dare that pipsqueak do that to her man!

Heather glanced at her, and Sylvie offered a small smile, and unclenched her hands. "I forget how violent this game gets at times."

"I spend most of the game praying," Heather confessed.

Sylvie nodded, and pointed to the plate. "Thank you for dinner. That was delicious."

"Lasagna is always easy. I used to make it all the time when the boys were growing up, and even after all this time I still haven't got used to making smaller portions so there's always lots left over."

"In other words, you're welcome anytime." Pete winked at her.

Again, their kindness threatened to overwhelm her, and all she could manage was a murmured "Thank you." Although how many times she could take advantage of their hospitality like this she'd have to see.

It was special to be here, with her maybe-boyfriend's parents, but it made it feel so much more real than what she thought. Ryan might like kissing her, but everything had happened so fast, that it felt too quick to be having a define-the-relationship talk. But then, he had been the one to mention Valentine's Day…

The first period ended, and she sank back in her chair as the between-game commentators talked. Her phone flashed with a message, which reminded her: Bree. "Excuse me for a moment." She picked up her plate and took it to the kitchen.

She listened to Bree's message. Then sent her a message. Mike was playing away in Boston, where he'd played for years before being traded to Calgary. A quick check of the score saw that Calgary was now in the lead in the dying minutes of the third period.

You doing okay? Sylvie texted.

I am bc he's winning, Bree's response came a few seconds later. *Correction: they won!*

Sylvie sent a GIF of fireworks, appropriate for the return of Calgary's captain after several weeks off caring for his wife and kids. *He deserves it. So do you,* she added.

I'm so relieved, Bree messaged back. *Hey, I miss you.*

Guilt strummed again. She didn't think Bree would have time to miss her, not with all the people in her life, but maybe Sylvie had sold herself short. *We can talk tomorrow night, if you're free,* she replied.

What about tonight?

Sylvie winced. How to explain exactly where she was and why…? *Mike probably wants to call you soon, and I don't want you to stay up too late. If not tomorrow we can do another day that suits better.*

Let's do tomorrow then, Bree typed. *Talk then.*

Tell Mike congrats from me, Sylvie typed.

Bree sent a heart, and Sylvie sent back a kiss emoji.

"The second period is starting," Pete called.

"Be right out," she said.

First, however, she needed to find the bathroom.

Make yourself at home, Heather had said, so she wandered down the hallway to where she thought she remembered the toilet was located. The doors down here were closed, probably as this part of the house didn't need to be heated, but she thought it was just past the corner around here… She tried a door handle, really hoping it wasn't a room that Jake would suddenly pop out from, even though Heather had said he had his own place. A flick of the light switch revealed the family bathroom. Which meant this door should probably be—

Oh. The light in here revealed a different room, a bedroom.

Judging from the hockey paraphernalia, this was Ryan's old room.

A queen-sized bed centered the room, a neat desk lined with trophies and ribbons sat near the window, while a closet took the other wall. Several posters of hockey heroes, including one of—aww, bless him—his now-captain, Jason McHale, hung on the walls. She smiled at that, knowing he'd be stupidly embarrassed to know anyone had seen this. But she loved this insight into the boy who'd dreamed, the boy who'd grown up in a family home that hadn't changed much. It pointed to everything sweet and good, fueling fresh hunger for the same. Temptation beckoned to look through his clothes, to try and find more clues about the man she liked to kiss. But no. She turned off the light, closed the door. She shouldn't trespass in his private things. That would only make her weirder, and she'd never forgive herself if Heather busted her coming out of Ryan's room.

She did her business, then washed her hands, and joined the others back in the living room. "Find everything okay?" Heather asked.

"Mm-hmm." Her heart hitched. Heather hadn't seen her accidentally go into Ryan's room, had she? She'd better explain. "I, um, might've taken some detours on my way to finding the bathroom."

Heather nodded. "Other guests have done the same. We tend to keep the doors down that end of the house closed to save on heating bills."

The game had resumed, and she was glad when an Edmonton goal stole the focus. But still her heart kept tumbling over the new information. She'd seen some of Ryan's photos from his childhood on the Guillemette walls, but this, seeing his idols—idols he now played alongside—seemed to crack open the mystery of this man even more.

A man who was focused. One who was strong. Who loved his family. Had a sentimental streak. One who might be quiet but who let his actions do much of his talking. She touched her lips and smiled. Is that what his kisses had been saying?

"Looks like Calgary's won with Mike Vaughan back in the driver's seat," Pete commented, as sports news scrolled along the bottom of the TV screen.

"That was Bree on the phone before," Sylvie confessed. "She's pretty relieved that Mike played so strong after everything that's gone on."

"They've been in my prayers," Heather said. "When Ryan first asked us to pray back around Christmas time, I don't think any of us realized how challenging things would be."

"No."

Challenging had proved so true. It had been Sylvie's first Christmas since Mom's death. And while she'd been relieved to be away, and glad to be focused on something else, the amount of focus caring for Bree's family in the midst of their crisis meant she'd never had the chance to grieve. So that was yet another layer of emotion simmering below all the other regrets.

"You know her well?" Heather asked.

"She's been one of my best friends for years," Sylvie admitted.

"That's right. You were looking after her kids until her family came."

"And family comes first," Sylvie murmured, her attention drifting to the screen.

Her lips flattened. Family always should come first, anyway.

THE DULL DRONE of the air conditioner played background in his hotel room. Ryan threw his duffel on the bed nearest the window, ready to grab what sleep he could before their flight to Anaheim the next day. Nights like this were rare, a chance to sleep where they'd played instead of immediately hopping on a plane. It meant they could relax a little more tonight than usual, like if they were playing back-to-backs, or the more standard road trip where they played every second day, like they would after next week's home game was followed by a Valentine's Day road trip.

That thought propelled his thoughts to Sylvie, and once Mats had left, Ryan called her.

"Hey there. I hope it's not too late."

"It's fine. I'm glad you called."

"I said I would, but by the time we got back to the hotel I didn't think it'd be this late. And I'm not even one of the ones who had to stay behind and do all the media and stuff."

"Do you wish you were?" she asked him.

"Not at all. I'm really happy McHale and the others are seen as the big stars, and I just have to show up for my shifts. I don't know how people like Brent and Mike and Franklin manage with the spotlight on them all the time." He couldn't imagine anything worse.

"Congratulations on your win. You played great."

"It was nice to get back into things, feeling like we were clicking again," he admitted, rolling his shoulders. "So, you watched the game with my folks. Was that good? Did Mom behave?"

"They were great. Fed me lasagna, which was delicious."

He groaned. "Man, I miss Mom's lasagna."

His roommate returned, and Ryan pointed to his phone, which drew a nod before Mats pointed to the bathroom. Ryan nodded, and Mats disappeared. Good, he'd have more time to talk alone.

"So, how was work?" he asked. She gave a faint sigh. "That good, huh?"

"It's a job. It means money. And there are benefits, so I'm trying to look on the bright side."

"There's always a bright side," he encouraged.

"Yeah, some just aren't always easy to see at times, you know what I mean?"

"I know." Which was why he'd always been grateful for the online Bible study group. Those guys were good at bolstering his spirits. He'd missed it this week, thanks to his games, but maybe he could check out the chat again. Some people were life givers, while others sucked the energy faster from a room than a hockey player drinking Gatorade. He'd always endeavored to be the kind of man who encouraged others, but sometimes circumstances could wear a man down. And it was necessary to be with people who encouraged him. Like Sylvie did.

"So, about that job of yours. Do you think you can get a day off to come see me play next week?"

"Are you going to be asking me this every time you play?"

He smiled at the tease in her voice. "Maybe."

"I don't know too many jobs that allow for that."

"Then maybe you need one in Edmonton, and not Red Deer."

Her breath hitched, and he suddenly heard what that sounded like, which rushed him to say, "Look, I don't mean to overstep or rush you, but I want to see where this can go. I," he swallowed, then said in a low voice, in case his roomie could hear, "I...I'm not used to relationships, and I'm probably saying this all wrong, but I like you, and it's a heck of a lot easier to have a relationship when you live near."

"Some might consider Red Deer near Edmonton," she said, after a moment.

"Not near enough."

"It's not exactly Boston and Toronto, like when Bree was interested in Mike."

Nor two separate continents—hemispheres—like when Detroit-based Brent was connecting with Holly, whose home base was in Australia, when she wasn't flying around the world for skating competitions.

"I miss you," he said, his voice husky.

"I miss you too," she said.

He lay back on his bed, closed his eyes. "So, was that a yes?"

There was another pause, then she said, "A yes to seeing you next week, or moving to Edmonton?"

His eyes snapped open. "Would you do that?"

"See you next week?" She sighed. "I suppose I could try to fit that in."

He smiled, his pulse beating faster at the thought. Two days apart already felt way too long. "What about the other?"

"Move there? I..." She hesitated.

"You?" he prompted, when she didn't say anything.

"Look, I can't guarantee anything. I don't want to put a downer on anything but it does seem like a rush. You and I didn't know each other two weeks ago, and now you're talking about me moving there? What if... what if things don't work out? I'd hate to think I'd give up everything just to be stuck in a city on my own. Especially if you were there, hating me," she added in a softer voice.

"Sylvie, I could never hate you," he said. "And yeah, I know it seems fast, but I don't think we should have a relationship according to somebody else's time frame."

She was silent for a long time.

"What are you thinking?"

"You called this a relationship," she said, her voice small.

"Because that's what this is. I like you, you like me, and maybe I am too new or dumb at this, but I figured if that was the case, then we could continue to see each other and not see anyone else." He smiled. "But that's only if we see each other sometimes."

"Do you mean you only want to have a relationship with me if I'm in Edmonton?"

"No." He hadn't said that, had he? "I just mean it's easier if we're nearby."

"Of course it is."

But she hadn't yet agreed. Which meant—what? Was she treating this more casually than he was? Had he just dived in too deep too fast, like Luc had said? "Sylvie?"

"Sorry, I'm just a little stunned. I wasn't sure how you thought about this thing between us, so to now hear you talk like this I'm a little stunned. But delighted."

"Delighted, huh?" he said in a low voice, hoping she'd think that sounded sexy.

"Very delighted," she murmured, in a similar low tone. "Very, very delighted."

His heart danced. "Look, I know it's late, and I'm probably still running off adrenaline, but I want you to know I'm serious about you."

"I'm starting to understand that."

Just starting to understand? Man, hadn't his kisses given that away? He closed his eyes again. "We don't need to talk about you moving to Edmonton just yet if you don't want to, but I think it could work out, and if you're not loving your job, there would be plenty more opportunities in E-town."

"I'll think about it," she promised.

"Okay, well, I better let you go get some rest."

She sighed. "Yeah, I have a six AM start tomorrow."

"Six? What kind of job means you have to start at that ungodly hour?"

She paused. "Um, that's just the nature of certain jobs in hospitality. The customer has to be fed when the customer wants. Not everyone gets the luxury of sleeping in until ten," she teased.

"More like seven than ten, but okay, I take your point. I hope you have a good day tomorrow."

"Thanks. You too."

"Sweet dreams," he said, opening his eyes to see his roomie smirking at him.

"Sweet dreams," she murmured. And the call ended.

Mats studied him, hands on hips, shaking his head. "New girlfriend, huh?"

Was Sylvie his girlfriend? Judging from that conversation, it had firmed into serious territory, so, "Yeah, it's new."

"Did I hear you say you want her to move to live with you?"

"Not with me, just be in Edmonton."

"Huh."

"What?"

His teammate shrugged. "I just always thought you were a saint, but now you're talking about moving in with a girl."

"Moving in with—? Dude, no. I meant moving to the same city, just so I can see her more often. That's all. Nothing else."

"Whoa. Don't lose your cool. I'm just surprised, that's all. How long have you been together for?"

Was it really less than two weeks they'd known each other? Put like that it did seem way too fast to be talking about moving closer. "I, uh, can't really remember."

"Sure you can't." His roomie's arctic-ice eyes narrowed. "You really like this girl, huh?"

"Yes."

"Well, you be careful, Romeo. Too many girls out there can make a guy think she's all that, when all they're really looking for is their next meal ticket."

"She's not like that."

"If you say so."

"I do," he snapped.

Mats tossed his blonde hair. "You're weird."

"If it makes you feel any better, the feeling is mutual, dude."

His teammate grinned, and threw a cushion at Ryan's head.

He sighed. Looked like he was going to have to shine some Jesus light a little harder.

CHAPTER 8

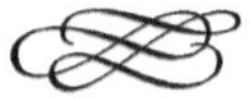

Six AM was an ungodly hour in February in Alberta. Even more awful when she looked at the clock and realized she was supposed to start work in fifteen minutes. After scrambling into her work clothes and speeding to work and getting stuck behind the world's slowest snowplow, she got there ten minutes late, only to have a crossed-arms Dave scowl at her, as she pulled her apron over her uniform and hurried to the front counter.

"I'm so sorry. I overslept, then there was a snowplow, and—"

"Right." His skepticism could shred leaves.

"There was!" Her fingers were shaking as she signed into the register. "Look, it'll never happen again."

"Sure, it won't."

She peeked at him. Did he mean her oversleeping or the snowplow?

"Your first week, Sylvie." He sighed, shaking his head, like he was an aged grandfather and not half a decade younger than her. "What kind of person is late on her first week?"

The kind who'd stayed up way too late talking to her

boyfriend. Her *boyfriend*! The knowledge of their new relationship status took away much of the sting of her lateness. Maybe God really was real, and she and Ryan could actually make this work, and—

"Are you even listening to me?" Dave yelled.

Looked like someone had got out of the wrong side of the bed. "I'm really sorry. I'm just so tired." At that moment a loud yawn ripped from her. How mortifying. Now probably wasn't the best time to ask to leave early next Tuesday.

"Am I boring you?"

"No! I'm one hundred percent focused. Oh, and look, here are customers wanting some delicious breakfast this morning. Hello!" She pasted on perkiness, like what she'd seen from Bree before. If only a smidge of Bree's real cheer could infect Sylvie then maybe she and Ryan could work out, and she wouldn't have to work here anymore, and life could have a happy ending, after all. "Welcome. What can I get for you today?"

The two tradesmen dressed in high-visibility clothing eyed her, then studied the menu board above her head. "We'll get two breakfast sandwiches and large coffees to go, thanks."

"Would you like fries with that?"

"You're serving fries at this hour? Then, sure."

She stabbed the button, but it wouldn't work. Then she realized. "Oh, sorry. We're only serving hash browns at this time of day."

"Then we'll get two of them, too."

Did he mean two of them, for two? Like, four? Her brain synapses were misfiring, she was so tired. "Sorry, did you mean two each, or a total of two?"

The man shook his head. "I said two. Did I say four? No."

"I was just checking."

The man blew out a breath. "You really need better staff here," he called to Dave.

Dave muttered something she didn't hear, which was probably just as well, and she took their money and focused very hard on making the correct change. But she couldn't laugh off their scorn. She knew she was on thin ice, that any second her facade might crack and she could plunge deep through the ice and drown her "hospitality" career.

Of course, she managed to spill the man's coins, which only led to more curses. So awesome. Not.

The morning trade picked up, preventing Dave's talking to her, and she was grateful. It was enough to attempt to ignore the man's contempt when he spoke to his staff, and the way he seemed to undress her with his eyes. Her lateness this morning meant she got light-headed near ten o'clock, when she realized she hadn't eaten any breakfast. How ironic to be surrounded by food yet starving.

Then wooziness and gnawing pain demanded she eat something, so in her bathroom break she bought a breakfast burger, and swallowed it down in the back room, where Dave wouldn't see her and complain. He sure wasn't happy with her today.

She visited the bathroom, and was exiting, wiping away the crumbs from her top as the door opened. Dave.

"Why are you here?"

"Bathroom?" Sherlock Holmes Dave wasn't.

"You've been eating, haven't you?" He pointed to her mouth. "You have sauce on your face."

What? The employee bathroom had only one tiny, dimly lit mirror, so she hadn't had time to check. She hurried back, wincing as she wiped at her face, "I, uh, promise you that I did pay for it—"

"It's a bathroom break, not a breakfast break, Sylvie."

"But I paid for it—"

"Yeah, you certainly will."

"No, I mean I already have. I put it through the system—"

"Am I accusing you of stealing?"

"No." Except it had kind of sounded like he was looking for a way to make her pay…

"I have to say I'm really disappointed in you. I didn't pick you as someone who sneaked around." He again switched into grandpa mode and sighed, like he was three times her age. "I thought you wanted this job."

She had. But now…

"But now it seems you no longer do." Perhaps her lack of denial was why his eyes narrowed and his scowl became more pronounced. "Whatever. It doesn't change the fact that we have policies in this company, policies that employees all around the world follow, and you have stepped out of line and broken one of our fundamental rules."

She tried very hard to not roll her eyes. "I'm sorry."

He shook his head. "Do you know what the punishment is for employees who break that rule?"

Probably not a pay rise. "Let me guess: you release them from their duties. Right?"

"You're smarter than you look."

Wow. Good to know. How could the highs of the past twelve hours have descended so fast? She started unhooking her apron.

"But *my* punishment is that I need to keep you on until your shift ends, as we don't have staff here who can take over." He nodded to her apron. "So you can leave that on for another three hours."

Three more hours of this pain? No, thanks. But sudden awareness of her finances—she really shouldn't have bought that burger for all kinds of reasons—made her pause. "Will I be paid for today if I do so?"

"Yes," he gritted out.

Then okay. She nodded, resuming her spot out the front, her mind in a daze, her welcomes less bright, her heart heavy, as she sank into the rhythms of a decade ago when she'd last done this kind of work. Her movements were robotic, scarcely seeing the customers as they arrived. Her stomach twisted. What was she going to do? She didn't want to fight for a job she had zero interest in keeping, with a manager younger and far snarkier than her. Ryan—his whole family—would think she was flaky, unable to hold a job for even two days. Maybe she should get out of Dodge and move to Edmonton, and see if she could find a job there…

"Sylvie?"

The haze she was in snapped as her attention suddenly sharpened at the new customer. No. A thousand times, no.

"Sylvie?" Heather asked again. "I certainly didn't expect to see you today, when I called in for my usual coffee."

Sylvie's lips twisted. Because there was a reason she hadn't told Ryan or his parents about working here.

"Are you okay? You don't seem yourself."

That's because she barely knew herself anymore. And to now have this new humiliation on top of everything else?

This day was now officially up there with the worst.

THE HUM of the plane and nearby conversations died as Ryan slipped on his noise-canceling headphones, and switched on the Northwest Ice playlist. He and his friends had compiled a bunch of songs they enjoyed, a mix of Christian and secular music, with everything from worship ballads like those written by Sarah Walton, to the energetic rev-up before games, or workout songs perfect for running or while doing weights.

He tapped open his phone and scrolled to where he'd last opened their chat. The chat had moved on with comments about Mike's recent win, and he joined the conversation there with a simple *Congrats*.

He knew several of the others had games today, and might not be able to join in, but he had some time to kill, and he'd rather do this than play poker like some of his teammates always did.

A moment later, Mike's name appeared. *Thanks, Ryan.*

Chris: *And the Ryanator is back!*

Jai: *Missed you, bro. You doing okay?*

I'm fine, he tapped back. *Enjoyed the break with family for Dad's birthday, but good to be back playing again.*

Chris: *Nice to see you guys crushed Las Vegas.*

Luc: *Always good to see a desert town lose to a real team.*

Jai: *Them's fighting words!*

Ryan smiled. Jai was alternate captain at San Jose, another place for which certain diehards struggled to understand why they had an ice hockey team. But money always talked loudest, and had seen numbers of franchises move from their traditional cold heartlands to cities with warmer, more moneyed climes. But occasionally it went the other way, like when the Atlanta franchise moved north to Winnipeg, and became Luc's team.

Luc: *Legit truth.*

Franklin James joined the chat.

Jai: *Awesome goal, FJ!*

Franklin: *Always nice to beat my old team.*

Chris: *We play Boston tomorrow.*

Ryan added his response. *Hopefully Mike and Franklin demoralized Boston enough so Chris's team can now win.*

Luc: *That's gold.*

Jai: *Fist-bumping that.*

Chris: *Rude.*

Franklin: *Did our best to help you out, Chris.*

Chris's GIF of Clint Eastwood looking grumpy caused an avalanche of laughing face emojis.

Ryan smiled. He'd missed these guys with their tease and banter.

Jai: *So, who's playing who next?*
Ryan: *We're at Anaheim.*
Mike: *Devils.*
Chris: *Bind them up, in Jesus's name.*
Franklin: *Amen.*
Luc: *Philadelphia for us.*
Jai: *Still got another week off then we got you, Luc.*
Luc: *Dinner?*
Jai: *Playing Mike the next day, so probs can't.*
Luc: *Shame.*
Mike: *Dinner?*
Jai: *Will try to. Hope to see Bree and kids too. How are they?*
Mike: *Doing okay now. My parents have moved nearby, so that's helping.*

Ryan chewed his lip. He really should ask Mike about the situation with Sylvie. But mentioning her name in this chat seemed a guarantee for tease and mockery he wasn't sure he could cope with yet. Mats was one thing. These guys were like his brothers. Except, maybe more so, as they understood the NHL pressures in a way Jake never could.

Jai: *What happened to your babysitter?*

Ryan's breath hitched. So apparently news of him and Sylvie wasn't as widely known as he'd expected.

Luc: *Why don't you ask Ryan?*

Ryan winced, sorely tempted to leave the chat. He had a funny feeling that any second now this was going to explode...

Mike: *Sylvie said she had to take care of family stuff in Red Deer.*
Jai: *Aren't you from that way @Ryan?*

Ryan took a swig of water. Whatever he said now had to allay suspicions, yet still be the truth. He slowly tapped out *I've seen her a few times.*

Luc: *Is that what we're calling it now?* This was followed with a kissing emoji. A second later, Luc posted the image of Ryan looking like a fool with a short-skirted Sylvie in his arms.

Seriously? Luc had posted this? Ryan exited the app, muting his notifications.

No. What would the others think? He didn't want to read their tease. It felt way too soon to have anyone comment on something that had felt special.

He exhaled, the music in the background a song about running, and yet waiting for God's call. That's how he felt. Vulnerable. Exposed. Open to attack.

He scrubbed a hand over his face, thinking about how the other guys had introduced the women in their lives. Some, like Dan Walton, had kept their interest in a girl on the down-low. Others, like Franklin and Hannah Wade, had had their interactions scrutinized by all and sundry almost from day one. But knowing Mike had held reservations about Sylvie last year, he really didn't want to get into a situation where he was forced to defend his choice of girlfriend to his friends. Even if Ryan remained curious to know more about why she'd left.

The plane landed, and the next minutes were taken up with collecting bags and getting on the bus that was taking them to their hotel. They were fortunate to have rooms to themselves on this trip, which meant when he got to his room he could see his missed calls and decide whether to answer them. And the fact Mike's number was there suggested he should answer it.

He listened to his voicemail, nose wrinkling as Mike's message came through, terse and to the point.

"Ryan, we need to talk. Call me."

He really didn't want to. Like, really didn't. But he hadn't got to this stage of his career by avoiding all hard things, so he manned up and hit reply to Mike's call.

But God seemed to be smiling on him, as Mike's phone went to voice message, which meant Ryan could leave a quick "Hey, it's Ryan, just returning your call" type message and call it done.

But it wasn't done. He knew it. Mike knew it. Luc knew it. Who knew how much the others had guessed the truth about him and Sylvie, although he bet Luc's comments and pic had scored all kinds of jokes and memes in the group chat. But he wouldn't look there. Couldn't look there. He wanted to live in this bubble a little longer.

So he tapped out a quick message to her, and prayed that she was doing okay.

CHAPTER 9

er phone buzzed, and Sylvie glanced at it. Smiled.

"Is that from him?" Heather asked.

"Are you always this direct?" Sylvie wanted to ask. But didn't. She'd never do anything to upset the woman who had basically saved her.

Maybe Someone upstairs had noticed Sylvie needed a break, because, as Heather had explained, she basically had never stopped inside this local non-fine-dining establishment before, and would normally be inclined to simply do drive through. But apparently Heather's nearby meeting had meant she needed to stop and use the restrooms before getting a coffee, which is when she'd recognized Sylvie and her plight. She'd promised to return when Sylvie's shift had finished, and had kept her word, taking her to a small café that felt light years from the personal hell that was Mr. Grumpy meals at Dave & Slaves, Incorporated.

Ryan's mom had bought her a coffee and croissant, then after—once again—expressing her surprise to see Sylvie working there ("When you said you were in hospitality I didn't expect it to be there") then insisted Sylvie spill the tea. So she had.

"I was late, and Dave has standards, and I didn't meet them."

"I'm so sorry. You've not had a good run with jobs recently, have you?"

Sylvie pressed her lips together. The only time she'd had what others might consider a good run with work had been when she'd worked with Bree. Firstly, when Bree had been the assistant manager at the childcare center in Toronto, then more recently when she'd cared for Bree's children. Still, she didn't want to appear pathetic or incapable. Or be pitied.

"So, what will you do next?" Heather asked her.

"I don't know. I keep applying, but only seem to be getting rejections, and it's getting harder to not take things personally."

Heather nodded, sipping her tea, her forehead wrinkling.

See? This was why she hadn't wanted Ryan's parents to know exactly where she worked. It was humbling to know they knew she'd needed to resort to work for such a boss.

"I wonder…" Heather bit her lip. "Would you excuse me for a moment?"

"Sure."

Heather rose, and made a phone call, leaving Sylvie free to look over Ryan's message, his words stirring warmth and affection.

Miss you. Wish you were here with me.

He'd snapped a picture of some palm trees and blue sky, with the Disneyland sign in the background. She'd known he was going to Anaheim, but hadn't realized he was going there. She texted back. *Wish I was there too.*

She wondered if he'd respond, maybe with another invitation to see him next week in Edmonton. Which she was at least free to take him up on now. Hope flickered. Maybe she could follow him there, find a job, make him see that she really was worth pursuing, and keeping around…

Heather returned, holding her phone and a half-smile. Uh oh. Why was she looking like that?

"Well." Heather's smile broadened.

"Well?"

Heather exhaled. "Did I hear you once say that you'd had experience in an aged care facility?"

"Yes."

"Would you tell me more about what you did?"

"Sure. It wasn't too technical, but I trained in some admin work, and as a health care aide. It meant that I could work in various capacities as a temporary assistant."

"So you were working for an agency?"

Sylvie nodded. "I ended up having three or four different facilities that I worked for. It was good. I liked to feel like I was busy, and useful, and valued."

"More so than working in the fast-food industry?"

"I was busy there, but I don't think I was valued."

"Would you like to work in health care again?"

"If the right position became available, I'd take it tomorrow."

"Well, I don't know if you remember, but I work at an aged care facility here in town, and it just so happens that we've been looking for a health care aide for some time. We need someone who can assist our residents in areas such as personal care, social support, and participating in recreation and leisure activities. It goes without saying that person needs to be able to cooperate as part of a team."

Hope flickered. "I can do all that."

"I'm guessing from your previous experience that you have a current health care aide certificate?"

She nodded.

"Are you enrolled in the Alberta Health Care Aide directory?"

"Yes. I came here to work with Bree, but I always like to have a backup plan."

"Good. Now, do you speak French?"

"A little bit."

"Computer skills? No, of course. If you worked in administration then you would've had that."

Sylvie nodded. "It's been a little while, but I can pick it up again."

"Have you had a criminal record check?"

"I got one before I took the position with Bree. It included a vulnerable sector check too, because I was working with children."

"She asked you to do that?"

"I thought it best."

Heather's raised eyebrows demanded further explanation.

"Some of Mike's family members were a little apprehensive about a woman like me having responsibility for their grandchildren." Oh, way to go with not spilling names.

"A woman like you?"

In for a penny… "In case you haven't noticed, I'm not like Bree. I, uh, dye my hair, and have tattoos."

Heather leaned across the table. "So do I."

Sylvie's eyes widened. "You do?"

"Please." She touched her light brown bob. "You don't think my hair is this color naturally, do you?"

It wasn't? Okay. But, "You have tattoos?"

Heather tugged back her sleeve, and undid the watch clasp, to show a tiny cross and heart. "I got a heart and cross to remind me that my life is about loving others and serving God."

For some reason that made Sylvie's eyes water. She blinked back emotion.

"How about you?"

"I don't know how many I have." And giving the reasons why she got them was something she could never easily explain to this woman. Explain that the reason she'd decorated her arms and neck with tiny inked versions of birds, bats, and flowers was to symbolize everything from hope to good luck? That she'd got the feather which represented freedom at the base of her skull to celebrate when her mother's boyfriend had died? That the reason she had a spider tattooed behind her ear wasn't linked to drugs or a prison term, but because she wanted to remind herself—and others—that she could be strong, that she'd overcome and the cycle of life could bring renewal. She'd thought that when she'd moved west to live with Bree, that this was her new chance. But certain events in recent weeks hadn't exactly lived up to that. Even if some others had.

"I find that some of the people I work with are less liberated, shall we say, in their understanding, so I save the awkwardness by covering it up." Heather smiled kindly. "Which is what I advise for anyone who chooses to work there."

"So, are you saying there is a job I could apply for?"

Heather nodded. "A job that needs filling immediately."

"Are you for real?"

"I wouldn't be mentioning this if I wasn't." Her head tilted. "I was going to mention it last week but didn't want you to think I was overstepping."

Sylvie's heart expanded. "As far as I'm concerned you can overstep anytime you like."

Heather smiled. "I just needed to check with some people that that was okay, but I have their blessing. So if you're interested, you could come back with me and see if the role is something you would like to do."

Gratitude flowed, hot and thick. "I don't know what to say."

"You could say yes?"

Sylvie could do better than that. She pushed from her seat and moved to the other side, and wrapped Heather in a hug. "Thank you. Thank you so much."

"You're more than welcome, sweetheart."

Tears pricked Sylvie's eyes, but she blinked them away.

She couldn't wait to tell Ryan what a great mom he had.

～

"AND THEY'VE OFFERED me a job there!" The video call showed Sylvie's excitement lighting her face in a way he'd never seen before. "I couldn't believe it."

Ryan smiled. He could believe it. When his mom had called earlier, he'd been an instant "Yes, it was totally okay" for his mom to mention to his girlfriend about a job where she worked. Sure, it wasn't Edmonton, but at least she wouldn't have to move back to Calgary. Red Deer meant Sylvie would still be close enough that she could travel to see him, and he to see her, something he'd tried to explain to his mom, to which she'd agreed. "Sounds awesome."

"It really looks perfect."

"Like an answer to prayer, huh?"

She nodded. "A prayer I didn't know I'd been praying."

See? He really wished Luc and Mike could hear her talk like this. She obviously was a Christian if she was talking about praying. "I'm really glad for you." God bless his mom for thinking of this.

She smiled, and his chest creased with a pang of longing.

"I wish you were here with me," he said.

"So you could have company on the scary rides at Disneyland?"

"And hold your hand? Sure." And maybe hug her too.

"Did you go to Disneyland?" she asked.

"No. There's never enough time for that. We train, maybe visit the beach if there's spare time."

"Have you been to Disneyland?"

He nodded. "A few times. You?"

"Never."

"Well, obviously that is something that will need to be rectified once the season is done."

"Obviously it is." Her eyes danced as she smiled.

He liked that they could exchange banter, that they could talk about a future. It seemed far better than focusing on their mere weeks together, like Luc or Mats did. He bet Mike would be the same.

Their game of phone tag had continued, with Mike leaving another message for Ryan to call, which Ryan hadn't responded to yet. He'd wanted—needed—another opportunity to talk with Sylvie before he did that. Not so much for confirmation that what they were doing was the right thing, but it did seem sometimes there were forces at work against them. He'd been so grateful for his mom's call earlier today. If his mother was wanting Sylvie to work there then he couldn't ask for a better recommendation. These others had no clue about Sylvie. Not really.

"So, if you didn't go to Disneyland, what did you do all day?"

"Would you hate me if I said we visited the beach?"

"Maybe." She smiled. "Do you know how cold it was today?"

"I've got some idea. Which is why I was more than happy to soak in every last ray."

"That's it. We're adding a beachside hotel to our Disneyland getaway."

"For sure."

This talk about their future was helping bring clarity to other things. He didn't care if it was made in jest; he suddenly really did want to see and do these things with her. "Anything else on your bucket list?"

"Plenty of things." She smiled. "How about you?"

"On our trip here, or bucket list items in general?"

"Either, or."

"Well," he said slowly, "on my bucket list is having a certain somebody come visit me next time I'm playing in the Big E."

"Is that so?"

He nodded.

"And who might that certain somebody be?"

"Somebody who might be wearing spiderweb earrings."

She touched the metal webs dangling from her ears. "I hope you mean me."

"You know I mean you." He exhaled. "So, do you think that's possible? For you to come see me?"

She winced. "It depends on what's happening with this new job."

"I might be able to talk to the manager."

"And have her come too?"

"Or not."

Her lips parted. "You'd seriously tell your mom to stay away?"

"I'd tell her that I want to see you for Valentine's Day. I think she'd understand."

"I thought you were traveling that day."

"Our plane leaves at midday. We could still have breakfast together."

"Only if I'm staying there."

"Which you could. I can get a hotel room." Her eyes widened, so he hastily added, "For you to stay in, as I'd be in my apartment. If your shifts can work out you might be able to start later that day so we could have breakfast together."

"It'd be awesome to see you."

"Then we better pray and hope a certain supervisor can understand a certain somebody needs time off to see me play."

He was pretty sure his mom would agree. She'd been excited to have this opportunity to "help poor Sylvie" as she put it. He hadn't pressed for details about why the other job hadn't worked out, but figured Sylvie would tell him herself. Although she hadn't yet, which meant he probably should ask…

"So, the other job was a bust?"

The light in her face drained away. "You know, it may surprise you that I've been accused of being sarcastic a time or two in my life."

"No-o-o. Really?"

Her grin flashed, faded. "My supervisor was sarcasm personified, and it didn't make things easy."

"I'm sorry you experienced that."

"Thanks. I guess I never knew how unpleasant it can be to work with someone when you can't trust what they say. I don't want to be like that."

"I don't think you're like that," he said softly. "I trust you."

Her lips pressed together and she blinked a few times like she was trying not to cry.

"Hey, it's okay."

She sniffled. "I hate getting emotional. It's just that I haven't had too many people say such things to me, and now both you and your mom have said similar things now. It's just so nice to hear."

"We don't say things we don't mean."

She nodded, her gaze lowered.

"And hey, I'm sure we're not the only ones who think that. Bree wouldn't have invited you to come and look after her children if she didn't trust you, now would she?"

"She's been a good friend."

"Have you spoken with her recently?"

"I was planning to, but so much has happened today. I haven't had a chance to call her yet."

"I'm sure she'll be glad when you do," he encouraged gently.

Another nod, then her head tilted. "Is this your subtle way of you getting me off this call to you?"

"If I had my way I'd never stop talking to you."

She exhaled.

"What's that sigh for?"

"You can't just say things like that, Ryan. You'll make a girl think you really like her."

"I'll let you in on a secret." Her eyebrows rose as he leaned closer to the screen. "I really like you."

Her smile blossomed. "I'll let you in one too."

"Yeah? What's that?"

"I really like you too."

His chest squeezed. "How many days until Valentine's?"

Her nose wrinkled. "A week."

"That long?"

"But if I come see you play the day before..." Her eyebrows wiggled.

"If?"

"*When* I come see you the day before..."

"Six days." He sighed. "Unless you come see me earlier?" he suggested hopefully.

"Mm, there is that thing called a new job I should probably go to."

"Fine. When do you start work there?"

"I'm going in for a half day tomorrow, then a full day on Friday, then I think your mom said she'd give me some more half days on the weekend and next week."

"So you driving to Edmonton could work?"

"If a certain someone talks to his mom, then it might work out really well."

"I sure hope so. It seems too long since I've seen you."

"It's been three days."

"Exactly. Way too long."

Her lips flicked up. "You don't mean to sound desperate, do you?"

He smiled, but the truth was her kisses were like a drug he wanted more of. Which meant planning her visit to come see him had to involve the perfect plan and execution. He needed to book her hotel room, secure tickets to the game, plan a post-game dinner, organize for them to share breakfast together. This had to be the best Valentine's Day ever, even if they could only spend part of it together.

Which meant he needed to call his mom and make sure she

understood her new protégé needed time off to allow this to happen.

And meant he had to talk to some of his teammates to learn about all kinds of things—like where to secure a reservation for a romantic dinner—that he now really needed to know.

Now that Sylvie was his girlfriend.

CHAPTER 10

The signs to Edmonton's international airport flashed past as she drove the last half hour to the Oilers arena. She smiled, her heart skipping in anticipation. Finally she'd see him. Nine days apart was about nine days too long. And sure, she'd seen him on TV and on FaceTime, but that wasn't the same as in person. She'd watch the game, they'd have a meal, she'd spend the night, and steal some precious time together on Valentine's Day, maybe at a café overlooking River Valley, before he had to leave for his flight, and she'd return for the two PM start of her afternoon shift. Could anything be more perfect?

She pumped up the music, the Shania Twain song echoing in her heart. What a difference a week could make. Last Tuesday had seen her working in a crazy place of frustration and disappointment. The past five days, however, had been filled with satisfaction. Finally, she was feeling useful. Finally, she was seeing her people skills put to the test. Caring for older people wasn't that different to caring for the very young. Both age groups demanded considerate attention, support with personal care, compassion and respect. Maybe Heather had eased the way, but the shifts she'd given Sylvie seemed to be with the loveliest people.

Heather had advised that Sylvie's role at the aged care facility would initially be on a casual basis, where she'd be called in for shifts as needed, but that was okay. Sylvie's previous experience meant she was used to working collaboratively in this kind of environment, and the other employees she'd met seemed nice too. Most people who chose to work in this profession were, and while there were some horror stories out there, everyone at Aspen Lodge seemed to be doing their utmost to help the residents here feel cared for in body, spirit, and soul.

It was a little bit unusual to have some of the residents speak so openly about their faith. But past experience had shown that older people were more cognizant about the fact that life didn't continue forever. Part of her role, she was learning, was to be a listening ear, to let people talk, to share. And as they did, she was reminded that working with people like this was a privilege. So many of the elderly might be visitor-less, their relatives too busy or too far away to visit often, which meant many of their stories would be lost unless people like herself were paid to pay attention.

She'd met a retired professional hockey player, an astrophysicist, war veterans, teachers. Every so often she asked about her own grandparents, but nobody recognized their names. But that was okay. Now she was in this environment, surely she had to have a better chance of finding out about them. She'd driven past their old house last Thursday. Seen a young woman drive in, so she'd stopped, and asked, and learned that they'd bought the house from a couple only two months ago, and their name hadn't been Melnyk. Next door, where Mom had said her grandparents' best friends the Thompsons lived, looked like a young family lived there now, so that had proved a dead end, too. Whatever. She'd find them one day. Someone, somewhere, knew something.

Edmonton's city skyline drew into view, the high-rises drawing fresh excitement. She'd be at the arena soon. Ryan had sent her a parking permit, which Heather said would allow Sylvie to access the special family parking and suite used by sponsors, family, and girlfriends. She'd been to Calgary's family room with Bree a few times, and knew a little of what to expect. But this was a different space, with different people, and she hoped they'd accept her, even as she'd tried to look her best but not too weird.

Her hair was cut, the color new, more a magenta than the blue-purple of before. She'd gone for a subtle cat eye look with her makeup, and splashed out on a new manicure. It wasn't every day a girl got to wake up to Valentine's Day with the man she lo–iked.

"Calm down," she muttered, as the traffic slowed. It was still too early for big statements like that. Even if tomorrow was Valentine's Day. And he'd seemed very insistent on making sure she'd packed something nice to wear to dinner tonight.

So while she'd opted for jeans and a low-cut top under the jersey he'd sent to her, she had a little black dress she hoped might knock his socks off. And anything else he wished to part with, too.

She shivered. It had been so long since they'd last kissed, surely he'd want to take things to the next level. She'd never waited this long for a guy to prove his love before. Although, looking back, she wasn't sure how many had ever really loved her. Certainly none of the recent guys in living memory had actually said it to her. The last who'd said it—whether he meant it or not—had been a French chef back when she'd been teaching preschool. Her chest twinged. Back when Bree had given a mini-sermon about what real love looked like. Like she thought Sylvie had no clue.

She knew what real love looked like. It meant not abandoning your kids. Not using fists to make a point. Not giving up when life got hard. Not choosing drugs over feeding your daughter. Real love meant the opposite. Real love meant giving yourself to someone, body, soul, and mind. It meant doing whatever it took to make sure they'd never leave you. And she was prepared to do whatever she could to prove to Ryan that what she felt for him was more than mere really liking.

Even if it meant doing something that Bree would probably not approve.

～

"This way, Miss."

Sylvie swallowed a smile as the attendant led the way past roped-off crowds. There was no point letting the envious fans know she was as amazed to be here as they seemed to think about her too. Yes, she didn't look the part of the other Edmonton girlfriends, with their skinny bodies and long blonde manes, but perhaps she could start a new trend, where women of all shapes and hair colorings could be welcomed.

"Miss, the man at the door will just need your name."

"Thank you."

She tried to look cool and unemotional, like she did this all the time, even while she took in all the details. The arena still had that new look and feel, and the people on this suite level seemed to feel it too.

"Sylvie Miles," she said, when the doorman asked her name.

"Ah, Mr. Guillemette's guest."

She nodded. Surely her jersey should have given that away.

The doorman smiled. "Welcome." He handed her a laminated card in a pouch on a lanyard, not unlike the one she used at Aspen Lodge. "You can show this and that will get you everywhere you need to go."

"Thank you."

He opened the door, and she stepped inside a fancy suite.

Beautiful people, a few sponsors, and what looked like corporate types glanced at her. Most looked instantly away, but some gave her the thorough look-over.

One, a honey blonde, whom she recognized as the girlfriend of Jason McHale, spoke to a platinum blonde then moved toward her. "You're Ryan's girlfriend, yes?" She smiled. "I'm Ashley. He asked Jase if we could look after you."

Some of her nerves eased. So he *had* mentioned her. The fact he'd done that felt...special. "I'm Sylvie."

"Welcome. We're glad you could come." She pointed to the bar, the food. "Help yourself to a drink, something to eat, then come join us to watch the game."

"Thanks."

She was conscious of some stares as she moved to the bar and collected a glass of champagne. It wasn't her normal drink of choice, but then, neither was being in an official box as an official girlfriend, so she might as well celebrate this special occasion.

She collected a small box of chicken salad—she hadn't had time to eat dinner since her shift and it would be at least three hours until she could eat with Ryan—and moved to where the bevy of blondes sat. Ashley rose, then introduced her, the long list of women's names impossible to remember. Sylvie offered a small smile and sat at the end, in a seat that looked spare. The woman next to her glanced up, then continued talking to her friend on the other side, her shoulders angling as if to say this was a private conversation.

Okay, then. Whatever. She'd always admired how Bree made the effort to include the team's girlfriends, something that stemmed from a place deeper than simply because she was the captain's wife. But not everyone had that natural warmth and sense of hospitality, she supposed. Sylvie knew she herself sure didn't, and she was used to being misjudged and excluded, so whatever. At least the lack of conversation allowed time for her to focus on her food, and to watch the warm-ups on the ice below. She ate the tender smoked chicken, wondering if Ryan knew she was here yet, if he'd look for her, be relieved to see her, or if that would add pressure.

The arena filled with laser-like colors and images on the jumbotron that seemed almost sci-fi movie-like, as the count-down to the game started ticking.

Finally, the cliquey bubble next to her burst, as her seat neighbor turned. "Hi. Sylvia, was it?"

"Sylvie. And sorry, I can't remember your name, or who you belong to."

"Belong to? Please." She rolled her eyes. "Lacy. And I'm with Will Santana." She pointed to the goalie.

"Gotcha. And what do you do?"

Lacy's lips curved. "Whatever I like."

Sylvie nodded. Clearly this wasn't the start of a beautiful friendship.

"You?"

"I work at an aged care facility."

Lacy made a dismissive gesture. "No, I mean, did I hear you're here with Ryan?" A mild cuss word dropped from her pink shiny mouth. "Jen and I were just saying that you don't look like the normal type of girl Saint Ryan would be expected to pick."

A physical slap couldn't have hurt harder. How was she to respond to that? "Gee, thanks."

She'd known she wouldn't fit in. Had known that people would think she and Ryan an odd match. But, as the women beside her whispered and giggled and murmured words that rhymed with "witch", Sylvie reminded herself that she wasn't here for them. She was here for the man wearing number twenty-nine. And she'd show him later tonight just how much they belonged together.

RYAN'S BREATH was rasping by the time the siren for the second intermission blared. Detroit was a physical side, and Brent Karlsson was so fiercely competitive it wasn't any wonder he was racing up the ladder as one of the league's top goal scorers. Ryan glanced up to where the team's girlfriends sat, saw the dark-haired woman at the end focused on the ice, while the blondes next to her talked to each other. He lifted a hand, and she waved back. His heart sang. It still felt surreal to have a girlfriend here. To have a girlfriend, period. He moved to the side, catching Brent's nod, before Brent swiveled to glance up at the suite where Sylvie sat, then looked back at Ryan, his gaze unreadable, his mouth guard hanging loose.

Ryan nodded back, and joined his team in the tunnel, then forced himself to refocus as their coach gave instructions about how to overcome the one-goal deficit in the last period. It wasn't hard. They all knew what to do. But trying to contain big, physical bodies like Brent and his sidekick Doug Lehtonen wasn't easy, both of whom were known as true power forwards. Ryan, on the second defense pairing, didn't have to face him as much as Mats and Viktor did, but still had to work to contain them while on the penalty kill.

He retaped his stick, then the final period began, and he watched from the side, as Detroit came out strong, force he felt when it was time for his shift on the ice and Lehtonen thumped him into the boards.

He bit back a word, pain throbbing through his ribs, but when the trainer assessed Ryan he pronounced him okay. He returned just as the announcer's voice boomed, "And he shoots, and scores."

The light might've flashed for Brent's goal, but visiting team goals never earned the fanfare a home goal did.

McHale scored soon after, then the game finished, with

Edmonton one goal down. As usual, nobody wanted Ryan for media or anything much, apart from some choice words from the defense coach. He nodded, acknowledging it was fair—he should've been aware—and he waved off the trainer's concerns. He had places to be. His insides tensed in anticipation as he showered, dressed, and collected his things, before a voice stopped him in the player's tunnel.

"Guillemette."

He turned, saw Brent, with Lehtonen behind him. "Karlsson." He nodded to Lehtonen as Brent fist-bumped him. It was funny how these friendships worked. Guys he'd grown up playing with, like Franklin James, might be all intense business on the ice but when the final siren blew, they were back to being friends. On-ice Brent was fiercely competitive, but off the ice he was way more relaxed, like the guy Ryan remembered from the Original Six Bible study group, before the group had needed to split thanks to time zones. Now he didn't see Brent nearly as much, the twins' christening being the first time in months.

"Good game at All-Star," Ryan offered now.

Brent shrugged. "It's a bit of fun." He peered at Doug Lehtonen. "You hanging, or…?"

Uh oh. Seemed Brent wanted a private word.

Doug shrugged. "The bus has a few minutes before we go to the hotel."

"You're staying the night?" Some road-tripping teams stayed; most flew to their next destination immediately after a game to reduce the hassle the next day.

"Vancouver is next, so we're stopping here."

Ryan's stomach tensed. Awesome. "Where are you staying?"

Brent mentioned the name of a hotel downtown. Ryan swallowed a word. He'd fully expected Detroit would fly on for the ninety-minute flight and not stay. He should've realized it probably wasn't best to book Sylvie a room in one of the city's hotels used by NHL teams.

Nerves ratcheted up his spine. Maybe he should cancel her room. Except she'd probably already checked in by now, and if he didn't leave soon, she would probably already be on her way there… He checked his phone. She'd left a message to say *Good game. Hope you're okay after that hit.*

"You okay, man?" Brent asked.

"Yep." He pocketed his phone.

"So, seeing we're here, want to meet for dinner?"

"I, uh, have plans."

Brent nodded, his eyes narrowing slightly.

Doug Lehtonen laughed and shook his head at Ryan. "Congrats."

"What for?"

"It's not every day that the great Karlsermeister gets blown off."

Ryan glanced back at Brent. "I'm not blowing you off—"

"He's got plans," Brent said, eyes fixed on Ryan. "With family?"

Why did he feel like he was getting the third degree? "With a girl."

"Do I know her?"

Seeing Sylvie was one of Bree's best friends and Brent was Bree's twin brother, "Quite possibly."

"What's her name?" Doug asked.

Ryan's chin jerked higher. "Sylvie."

"Huh." Brent's eyes narrowed further.

That was all he had? Well, good. He didn't need Brent stirring things further by offering his usual opinions that he seemed to think were carved in gold. "And I'm running late."

"And you don't want to be late, not when it's Valentine's Day tomorrow." Doug winked.

Nausea sloshed through Ryan's gut. "So, anyway, good to see you, man." He leaned in for a chest bump with Brent then fist-tapped Doug.

"See you around," Doug said.

Ryan offered a tight smile. Yeah, not if he could help it. And definitely not tonight. Not when he had plans he really didn't want Brent or any of his Christian friends judging.

BY THE TIME he reached the family and friends suite, it was nearly empty. He checked his phone to discover several new messages from Sylvie asking where he was, then saying she'd gone ahead to the hotel to check in. He winced, wishing he could come up with a reasonable excuse as to why she shouldn't stay there, but nothing sprang to mind. Say, "Hey, I think we should go somewhere else, because Brent's team is staying there and I feel like Brent is a spy for Mike and Bree?" Yeah, that wasn't going to fly.

He hurried to the arena parking garage, his mind straining to think of any other place he could book for a romantic dinner at short notice. Heck, at this late stage, it didn't even have to be romantic. Just needed to be somewhere other than where Brent was guaranteed to be. Ryan liked the guy, but Brent owned an intensity that scared him a little too. And the more he thought about it, the more he was convinced that Brent was judging him as hard as any pure-hearted never-sinned Christian might do. Which totally wasn't what Jesus was about.

"Get a grip," he said aloud, as he drove downtown. He shouldn't be thinking about Brent, or anyone else. He should be thinking about that sweet woman who'd come all this way and was probably waiting for him, wondering why he was taking so long, when he'd said he'd be finished as quickly as possible. He liked so much about her, liked her sweet nature that she hid behind the tough girl persona. She was like nobody else he'd ever met. And there was something about her that made him want to help however he could...

He drove to the hotel parking garage, relieved not to see a

bus filled with hockey players, and hurried inside the lobby. *What room number are you?* he texted her. He could go there, they could get room service, if necessary.

Loud laughter bounced off the walls from near the check-in desk. He grimaced. He recognized that laughter. Doug was here. Which meant Brent wouldn't be far away.

I'm in 702.

See you soon, he typed back.

Except when he got in the elevator, he realized he needed a hotel key-card to access the accommodation levels. He swallowed a word, sighed, and exited back into the lobby, slinking to a section of oversized couches and lined with bookshelves where he hoped he wouldn't be spotted. *Change of plan,* he messaged again. *I can't access your floor. Will need to meet downstairs in the library foyer off the main lobby area.*

Be there soon, she typed back.

He blew out a breath, peeking around the couches, hoping this wouldn't be the day when some member of the public finally recognized him. He'd been used to flying under the radar in public awareness, knowing the figure he cut while dressed in civvies was far different to the intimidating one he presented under all the hockey gear. The beard had helped, too.

He tapped his foot, wondering where they should eat, where Brent was in the building, what was taking her so long. It wasn't like they were going to do anything but eat together. And kiss a little. Or a lot. But why did that have to be a problem for anyone? It was his life. Not theirs.

"Ryan?"

He glanced up. Swallowed. Stared.

He slowly rose, then moved toward her. The black lace dress was cut low and revealed lots of pale skin and plentiful curves he'd struggle to not dream about. "You," he had to clear his throat, "you look amazing."

Sylvie half-smiled, and gestured to her dress. "It's not too much?"

Maybe. He'd always been a hockey-mad good Christian boy but that dress was making him think of other things. "I like it," he said hoarsely. "A lot." Too much.

Her face lit, and he could tell she was relieved, which softened his heart toward her more. It was funny to think this woman who presented a tough chick persona needed his validation, but there it was.

"I love the new hair color." It was different to before, less purple, more red.

"Thanks." She touched it, the lift of her arm bulging her curves a little more. "I needed something a little more toned down for the old folks."

Then she shouldn't do that move in front of the old men. "You look fantastic."

In two strides he had her in his arms, and suddenly he didn't care who else might see, as he wrapped her in his arms and kissed her. Kissed her thoroughly, kissed her deep. "I missed you," he said softly.

"I missed you more," she said, smiling up at him, then touching his mouth and wiping at it. "I branded you with my lipstick."

She'd branded herself onto his heart.

Right now, room service was sounding really good.

She stepped back slightly. "So, uh, do you want to eat, or do something else?"

Desire stirred at the suggestive lift to her eyebrow. But tempted as he was, he'd have to eat soon or he'd get hangry. "We should eat."

She tucked herself close to his side, her curves pressing into him. He swallowed. A glance down revealed more of that beautiful pale skin. He jerked his eyes away. Then met the tilted gaze of Brent, standing across the room, his hands on his hips, Doug beside him.

Doug whistled, then gave a thumbs-up. Brent only nodded.

Beside him, Sylvie froze. "Is that Bree's brother?"

Sure was. "Their team is staying here too." He glanced at her. "I didn't know."

Her face looked worried. "Are we eating here?" she murmured.

"I booked a table at the restaurant, but now…" His voice trailed away as Brent and Doug approached. "Hey. Long time no see."

"Sylvie, huh?" Doug's gaze traveled down her then back up, fisting Ryan's hands. "Guillemette mentioned you."

"Sylvie." Brent's voice was tight.

"Hi Brent." Her voice was cool. "Good goal tonight."

He nodded, accepting her praise as if it was his due. "I didn't expect to see you here."

Her clasp of Ryan's hand tightened. "Ryan invited me."

Brent glanced at Ryan, then back at her. Unlike Doug, his gaze didn't dip to her neckline, but Ryan still wished he'd thought to tell her to put on a coat.

"Are you cold?" Ryan murmured to her.

She glanced at him, a crease in her brow. "Um, maybe a little."

He shrugged from his jacket, and placed it around her, which instantly seemed to draw Doug's gaze up, his gaze finding Ryan's narrowed one. Didn't the dude have his own girlfriend or something?

"So," Brent finally spoke again. "How long have you two been a thing?"

"A few weeks," Sylvie said.

"Uh huh." Brent eyed Ryan. "Dude, can I speak to you a moment please?"

No. He really didn't want to.

But Brent was giving him no choice, using his extra height, and a sudden smile for Sylvie she didn't seem fooled by, as she shrugged while Brent hustled him away.

"What's your problem?" Ryan demanded in a hushed voice. "We have a dinner reservation, and—"

"Dude, what are you doing?"

"What do you mean? She's my girlfriend, we're having dinner—"

"At a hotel?" Brent raised a skeptical brow. "I don't know if I've lived too hard or if you're just naive, but a woman doesn't dress like that unless she's got plans for later, if you know what I mean."

"How would you know?"

Brent's face shadowed. "I know. I've been there, done that, so believe me I know. And I know she's not the sweet Christian girl you need."

"Don't go judging people you don't know."

"I don't know? Excuse me, how long have you known her for?"

Um…

"A few weeks? I met her years ago, and I know Bree has known her for years. And I've had both Mike and Bree tell me lately they're concerned about her."

"I don't care. They're wrong."

Brent studied him then sighed. "I hate saying this, but how many times have we talked about this kind of thing in the Bible study group? You need a Christian girlfriend."

"She is," Ryan hissed.

"Is she?" Brent's face wore skepticism. "Bree and Mike aren't convinced."

"She goes to church." Well, she'd said she had. He'd seen her there. Then he remembered, "And she prays."

"But has she asked God to forgive all her sins and made that commitment to follow Jesus?"

"I don't know."

"Well, you should."

"Right. Yeah, because that's a simple conversation." He swallowed a curse word. "That's what you did with Holly, right?"

"That was different."

Sure it was. Ryan folded his arms.

"I knew she was a Christian when she first stayed with my family years before we met again at Bree's wedding, and her actions showed her faith in God over years. You've known this girl only weeks." Brent shook his head. "Look, how long have I known you for?"

The sudden shift in topic left him reeling. "I don't know. I think I joined Josiah's Bible group three, maybe four years ago?"

"So you weren't around when I got caught up with a girl called Chloe." Brent's face tightened. "I couldn't see it at the time, but she was only into me for the status, for my money, and —"

"Sylvie's not like that."

"Because she kisses good, or dresses like that?" Brent waved a hand at Sylvie, but his eyes remained on Ryan.

"You're as judgy as the rest."

"Am I? Or am I a guy who has lived that kind of life, allowing myself to get caught in someone else's web, and who was unable to see the truth for myself?" Brent exhaled, then added in a quieter voice, "Look, I couldn't see it at the time, but Bree and Mike could. So if they think something is not quite legit with your girlfriend, then I think you need to trust them. What do you really know about her anyway?"

CHAPTER 11

Fire roared through Sylvie's chest as she caught some of Brent's words. How dare Brent judge her? How dare his friend assault her with his eyes? Maybe instead of judging her and telling off Ryan he should be telling off his friend, Doug. Who surely couldn't be a Christian, not from the slimy things that he'd been saying.

"Are you finished with my boyfriend?" she asked Brent, hooking her arm through Ryan's. "He promised me dinner, and it's getting late."

"Think about it," Brent said to Ryan. "I'm only saying this because I care."

Her fingers tensed. Sure he did.

Brent glanced at her. "Sylvie."

She didn't bother saying anything back, only narrowing her gaze.

"I'll be praying." Brent pointed at Ryan, then turned and ushered Doug away.

She was tense, but that was nothing compared to what poor Ryan was feeling. He was actually trembling. "Are you okay?" she asked.

He shook his head, then seemed to catch himself and nod. "Yeah. That wasn't what I planned tonight."

No kidding. "I'm sorry he ambushed you."

He sighed. "I'm sorry if you heard any of that."

Pretend she didn't, or go with the truth? The only way to salvage tonight was to move on, to let it stay in the past. "I'm really hungry. Do you mind if we go eat?"

"Yeah." He scrubbed a hand over his face. "I booked for dinner in the restaurant, but I really don't want to see them again tonight."

Neither did she. "We can get room service and eat in my room if that makes it easier."

"Yeah." He frowned. "We could."

That didn't sound like he wanted to. "Or we can run the risk of eating down here." *Please say no, please say no…*

He shook his head. "I'm really sorry about this. I didn't think…I don't want our time tonight spoiled by the stupid things he said."

She rubbed his back. "Please don't worry about it. I'm not worried." She pushed to his front, looping her hands around his neck as she smiled. "Do I look worried?"

The storm in his hazel eyes eased, as his gaze swooped to her mouth. "You look so beautiful."

"Then kiss me," she murmured. "Who cares what anyone else thinks?"

"Exactly." His eyes darkened, then he drew close and pressed his lips against hers, in a hungry, urgent kiss that made her briefly wonder if he really meant it, or was trying to prove something in case Brent passed by.

But she soon couldn't care less, as her own desire roared, and her hands slipped to the back of his shoulders as she pressed closer. Finally, she broke away, with a shaky, "I think we should call room service."

"I think you're right."

She held his hand, and drew him to the elevators, where they had to pretend to not be handsy as an older well-dressed couple eyed them in the brushed gold mirror. But Sylvie's glimpse of her own swollen lips and mussed hair and smudged lipstick were obvious tells, and she angled away, leaning against Ryan as they silently counted the floors until they reached hers.

Then she drew him along the hall to the room, to the beautiful room he'd chosen for her, for where they could take this relationship to the next level. Finally, she'd prove all the critics wrong. She'd prove they were right together. His mom obviously thought so, so who cared what self-righteous jerks like Brent thought?

"I should call the restaurant and cancel our reservation," Ryan muttered.

"You could ask them if they can send the food up here instead," she suggested.

He brightened. "That could work."

Her lips curved. "Great."

She opened her door, and drew him inside, as he seemed to hesitate. "Come on. I won't bite."

"Are you sure?" he asked, half-smiling.

"I only bite if you're mean. And you'll never be mean to me, will you?"

"Never," he breathed, before his lips found hers.

He backed her inside, all the way past the bed to the curtained window, and their kisses soon grew even more heated. She drew away, her breath shuddery. "Why Ryan, anyone would think you're hungry for something more than food."

He exhaled. "Maybe I am."

She cursed herself silently at the way he seemed to cool, as he pushed a hand through his hair, and wondered aloud where the room service menus were.

The next moment was filled with food selection and ordering, then they returned to the window, this time with the curtain apart as they gazed out to the dark street below, her back to his front, his arms around her.

It didn't take long though, before his lips started to nuzzle her cheek, then fall to her neck, as he whispered her name.

She shrugged off his jacket and turned and did all she could to give him an eyeful, as she backed him this time closer to the bed. Her hands slipped to his T-shirt, and she tugged it free from the waistband of his jeans.

"What are you doing?" he murmured, his voice sounding sleepy.

"I just want to kiss you better," she said, her fingers sliding along his warm skin.

He gulped, but whether that was because she'd found his injury, or because he'd reacted to her touch like she did with his, she didn't know. All she did know was that she was even more hungry for him now, and she'd be really grateful if the servers decided to delay delivering their food.

She tugged up his shirt then bent to see the bruise purpling his side, just under a tattoo of an eagle. "I like your eagle," she murmured. Then her lips met his skin.

"Sylvie." His voice sounded thick, breathy, far away. "Sylvie." His hands were in her hair.

She tightened her clasp around his waist, feathering kisses, then—

"Stop." He wrenched free from her arms, pushing her away. "I...I can't do this."

"Do what?" She pouted. "I was only trying to kiss you better."

"Really?" His heavy-lidded gaze met hers. "Is that all you were trying to do?"

Well, no. But if a kiss led to something more, then she wasn't about to stop it. "Hey, I don't mean to make you feel uncomfortable. We can go slower, if you want."

"Slower?" he repeated.

"As slow as you want."

His hands slid down her arms to hold her hands. "Wait. Did you think I came to your room to have sex with you?"

"Well, yeah. That's what most men mean when they pay for a hotel room for me."

He blinked. "You mean you've done this before?"

"Had sex or had a guy pay for a hotel room?"

His eyes widened. "Either." His voice sounded strangled.

"Well, of course. Why, haven't you done this before?" Her heart skipped a beat. Imagine if she could teach him everything she knew…

He staggered backward, falling onto the bed. But his expression wasn't exactly an invitation for her to join him. Neither was the way he scrambled off it, onto the other side, both hands covering his mouth as he shook his head. "I can't believe it."

"Believe what?" Wait. He wasn't seriously about to leave her, was he? She needed to amp up her charms and make him stay. "Ryan," she used her sultriest tone, "I don't know what's happened to upset you, but—"

Suddenly she did know. It was what stupid Brent had said before. Anger spiked. She drew nearer. "But you shouldn't let other people's prejudice get in the way of what you want to do."

She drew nearer, saw the way he retreated. She had to act fast. She reached up to unhook the back of her dress, saw how his gaze fell to her chest then instantly back up. So she still had some cards left to play. She smiled, leaving the hook where it was. "Come on. You just need to relax. We can eat together, then you can leave. Who can argue with that?"

"Just eating, right?"

"Just food," she promised. But she'd be looking for any chance to shimmy in and steal a kiss. And if that should lead to other things, then the night might be redeemed at last.

But for that to happen, she probably needed to tamp down the seductress vibe. So she picked up his jersey from where she'd folded it on the back of the chair before and slipped it on. "Is this better?"

He exhaled. Swallowed. "I like it."

"Me too." Her heart tensed with misgiving. What was wrong with him? She tried to turn the conversation to more neutral things, like the game, and what the team doctor had said about his injury.

His replies were a little slow, indicating he'd clearly been bothered by before, so she did her best to seem safe and non-vixen-like, and convince him he should stay. The fact he stayed had to indicate he liked her, right? He'd just been a little freaked out by her coming on a little strong. But the fact a guy might be a virgin at his age made her heart a little more tender to him, and twisted her feelings deeper. She'd never had to convince a guy to sleep with her. She'd never had a guy be so shy about such normal things. He was so sweet, so innocent, so good, and she wouldn't jeopardize this moment for anything.

Fortunately, the food soon arrived. Ryan tipped the delivery person, being careful to not look the man in the eye, although she was pretty sure from the way the staff member glanced at her, then at his number on the jersey, it might've given things away. She wasn't going to point that out to Ryan, though.

They sat at the small round table near the window and ate: steak and vegetables for him, chicken smothered in cream sauce for her, a large salad to share.

He must've been hungry because he barely talked, and she couldn't help but feel like the evening was fizzling in a way she'd never imagined. Maybe he was just tired, and this was just his usual post-game letdown. He wasn't as talkative as some, she knew that. But this reluctance to talk at all seemed unusual.

So she finally dared ask him. "Are you okay? Did you like your food?"

He bit his lip, nodded. "You?"

"It was wonderful, thank you." She reached across the table and touched his hand.

He flinched.

"Ryan, what's wrong?"

He shook his head, pushed back from the table, then stood, moving to the mirrored closet, his hands clasped on top of his head.

Her stomach grew tight. But it had nothing to do with the food she'd consumed.

When he turned back to her, his face was pale, strained. "Are you…?" He winced.

"Am I what?"

He heaved out a breath, scrubbed his face with his hands. "I can't believe I'm asking this."

"Asking what?" Her nerves threatened to bolt.

"Are you…are you a Christian?"

She blinked. "Um…"

"And no, I don't mean are you someone calling yourself a Christian because you're not a Hindu or a Muslim or a tree worshipping pagan or something. I mean have you ever committed your life to Jesus? Have you asked God to forgive you for your sins and prayed a prayer or done any of those things?"

"Are you for real?"

He dragged his fingers down his jaw. "One hundred percent."

"I…I don't even know how to answer that question."

He winced. "It's a simple yes or no answer, Sylvie. Have you?"

"Prayed a prayer? Of course I've prayed." Who hadn't?

Relief filled his features. "See? I knew they were wrong."

"Who was wrong?" The words spilled.

"Brent, earlier, was giving me this huge long spiel that Mike and some of the others have questioned whether you were a real Christian or not."

"A *real* Christian?"

He paused, his frown reforming. "Sylvie, don't hate me for asking this, but has Bree talked to you about what being a real Christian means?"

Probably. "Um, yeah."

"So you know it's not about whether you believe God is real or not, but actually want to live like Jesus wants us to."

"Yeah."

His smile poked out, and she finally felt like there was a chance this ship hadn't yet sailed, that she might have a chance to tug it back to shore. She just needed to convince him that they weren't so different. "I've been going to church with them each week."

He nodded. "I know, but it's not actually about whether you go to church or not. I guess the real question is, have you asked God for forgiveness for your sins and prayed that prayer and asked Jesus to be the Lord of your life?"

She froze, her heart pounding. No.

"Have you?" he pressed.

"Why? Is this a deal breaker?"

His eyes widened, and she realized she'd gone too far. "Come on, Ryan. You know we're good together."

His face pained. "I know. I love being with you, but this..." He shook his head.

"What do you mean 'this'?"

"You, me," he gestured between them. "I...I can't have a future with someone who doesn't share my beliefs."

"But I do. I believe in God. I even believe in Jesus. Like, he really lived, right? I mean, if I'm completely honest, I don't know that I really agree about sins, because that's such an old-fashioned concept, isn't it? But I'm a nice person, or I try to be. And surely that has to count for something."

His shoulders slumped. His face fell.

"What?"

"So you haven't prayed that prayer then."

"Look, I'm a good person, Ryan. I mean," she gestured to her dress, "I get that maybe this was a little over the top, but you know me. I'm not like that usually. It's just that I wanted tonight to be special," her eyes filled, "and now it feels all spoiled, and—"

"Hey," he stepped closer, stroked her hair, "don't cry."

She blinked back stupid tears. "I just don't understand what's happening. One minute everything was going so well, and now…"

He drew her close, and she wrapped her arms around him, hearing his hiss of breath. She eased back on squeezing him on that side.

She laid her head against his chest, hearing the solid beat of his heart. The fact he still wanted to hug her meant maybe they still had a chance to work this out.

Then he pulled away. Looked at her seriously. "Sylvie, I've been really stupid."

What? No. *No, no.* "No, you haven't," she assured. "It's all okay. We'll be okay, I promise."

He pressed his lips together, then he dropped his hands. "I…I don't think we can be okay."

"What do you mean?"

"I mean, I don't think God wants us to be together."

"What?" Her voice squeaked. "What does God have to do with anything?"

"Everything." His whole face, voice, posture, sagged. "And the fact you don't recognize that hurts so much."

"But what do I need to do? I'll do anything, Ryan. I want to be with you. I belong with you."

His chin quivered, and she caught the glistening in his eyes. "You need to get right with God. And I can't help you with that."

"Why not?"

"Because I'll never know if you're doing that for me or because you really want a relationship with Him for yourself."

His exhale was shaky. "You can't keep falling into relationships wanting people to fix you."

"What? I don't want to be fixed. There's nothing wrong with me."

His look said he disagreed.

"Are you serious? You can't judge me. You're not perfect."

"I know that. And tonight I've realized just how far I fall short. But Sylvie, I know the broken pieces inside me are being healed by God. I want that for you too."

"So help me. Talk to me," she begged.

"Talk to Bree. You need to talk to her. To someone. Anyone. And I'll be praying that God shows you that He is real and wants a relationship with you too. But I just can't—I don't think I'm strong enough or that it would be healthy for me—"

No. *No.* She played the last card she had. "Ryan, I love you."

He drew in a shaky breath. "I'm so sorry, Sylvie. This is all my mistake. I should never have gotten involved, should never let you believe—oh, man." His voice caught. "I hope one day you'll forgive me, but—"

He turned. She rushed to him, wrapped her arms around him. "No. You can't leave me. I love you. I want you. Please, Ryan, don't go."

"I have to." His voice sounded strangled, whisper-thin. "I'm so sorry that I've hurt you. I'll be praying for you—"

"Are you serious? Are you breaking up with me because of what stupid Brent said?"

"He's not stupid. He's my friend. Oh man. I can't believe I never saw it before."

"Saw what? What is wrong with me? Why don't you love me?" Her voice broke on a heaving sob. "If you want me to become a Christian, then fine, I'll do it. I'll do anything to please you."

"And that's why I can't do this," he said brokenly. "You need to want God for yourself. Not because you want me."

She was falling into an abyss, all her hopes and dreams pulverized into tiny atoms, unable to be grasped or seen. "You don't want me?"

He sighed heavily. "I want you—"

Hope flickered.

"But I can't have you."

"Yes, you can." She clung tighter. "You can have all of me. Whatever you want, I'm yours."

He slowly removed himself from her arms, then when she tried to draw near again, pushed her back, grasping her hands tight in both of his as he held her half a meter away. "I want you to want God. That's what I want more than anything."

He released her hands, then walked to the door, as her heart screamed *no, no, no.*

He paused, hand grasping the door handle, not looking at her. "The room's paid for, and breakfast and dinner too. I'm so sorry."

And he exited, and she collapsed on the bed, and cried. She was so, *so* sorry, too.

HE WAS DEAD INSIDE.

Ryan stumbled to the elevator and jabbed a button, hoping against hope that nobody would see him. He probably should've gone down the fire escape, but he'd heard awful stories of people getting lost and trapped and dying in those things. Although the way he felt now, maybe that would be for the best...

He closed his eyes. He deserved to die. That look on her face, her tears he'd heard through the door. He was like the world's most gullible fool, the biggest idiot on the planet. How had he let his hormones lead him into such a big mistake?

The door opened into the lobby, he exited, head down so he

wouldn't be recognized. The last thing he wanted was for someone to say—

"Ryan?"

Nope. How he wished he could pretend he wasn't him. He peeked across. Doug Lehtonen's eyes widened. "Dude. What happened to you?"

"Gotta go," he muttered, picking up his pace. He had to leave, to get out of here. Which was the way to the parking garage?

"Whoa." Doug placed a hand on his shoulder, the momentum jerking Ryan to a stop.

All at once his rage and disappointment at himself thickened and flared, and he pivoted and swung a fist at Doug's face.

Doug swore, swerving, and Ryan missed, finding his collarbone instead. He spilled a word his mom wouldn't be proud of, and shook out his fist as several other Detroit players rushed to their teammate's aid.

"What the"—expletive—"was that for?" Doug coughed out, wincing.

Others were shoving him, yammering in his ear, forcing Ryan to brace.

"Ryan?"

He glanced across. Sure enough, the man he *really* hadn't wanted to see was there.

"Hey," Brent shooed the others away, leaving Ryan standing there with Brent and a grimacing Doug. "What happened?"

"I'm sorry," Ryan muttered to Doug. "I wasn't expecting someone to grab me."

"Why'd you do that?" Brent frowned at Doug.

"He looked like he was about to cry, man."

Awesome. "I'm getting out of here." Ryan headed to the exit. He didn't care if it was minus sixty outside, he had to get away. Now.

"No, you don't." Brent moved to block his way. Given the

dude had almost half a foot of height on him, he couldn't easily escape.

"Get out of my way."

"And if I don't? You gonna hit me too?"

Ryan slumped. "I can't deal with this right now."

"Deal with what?" Brent pushed.

"You. Him." He pointed at Doug, who instantly protested. Or God.

God.

His heart crumpled, like it might cave in. How could Ryan have fallen so far away?

He shouldered past, praying the tears would stay away. No way would anyone here respect him ever again if they caught him crying. He scrubbed his face, heading to the cooler air of the parking garage. Behind him he vaguely heard Brent say something to Doug, then the sound of footsteps chasing him as he neared his car.

"Dude," Brent's voice, "it's just me and you. I don't care where we go, but you're talking to me about what's happened, okay?"

He had a feeling saying it wasn't okay wasn't going to be an option.

"Where's your car? Can you even drive?"

Ryan tossed him a scowl, met Brent's smirk. "You're a real jerk."

"I know. So, give me the keys."

He tugged them from his back pocket and threw them at Brent, who caught them and pressed the button. The rear lights on his Lexus flashed, and Brent whistled. "Nice ride."

Wait until he drove it. "It's an older make, but I like it."

Brent opened the driver's door, complained about the seat, then readjusted it. The engine gave a throaty rumble. "Whoa."

"It's a V-8."

"Sweet. This is so much nicer than what I drive these days."

"Yeah, right."

"I mean it. Holly's all about safety, safety, safety, which means I'm stuck with Jeeps for now."

"Poor you."

"Yeah. But what's a man to do when the company insists on providing me with one?"

"Sure must be hard with all those freebies and endorsements you have to suffer with."

"You've got no idea."

"Obviously."

Brent chuckled. "Funny. Holly has said the same. Now, where to?"

"I don't even know what you want to do, so I don't care."

"Great. Let's take this baby for a joyride."

Brent was a bit jerky at first, forcing Ryan to brace against the doors, but then he got the swing of it, especially as Ryan slowly relaxed and pointed out other key components.

"I think I'm gonna have to get me one of these. They make driving fun again."

"Look at you ready with the advertising campaign," Ryan muttered.

"You know it."

A red light forced Brent to stop at the intersection, then he glanced at Ryan. "What are your cops like?"

"It's a forty zone," Ryan warned. "That's forty kilometers an hour. And I really don't want to get booked."

"I won't get booked," Brent said confidently.

It'd be just Ryan's luck to have Brent's charmed life fail tonight. "Whatever."

The tires squealed as Brent peeled out, hitting forty before instantly having to slow, thanks to a delivery van. "That was fun."

"Great. So let's go home."

"Yeah, let's." Brent glanced at him. "Which way?"

But going home meant facing Mats. And he really didn't have it in him to talk to anyone else. Already he felt exhausted, physically, mentally, emotionally. "You've had your fun, now turn around and go back to the hotel."

"Nope. We're talking, so it's at your place, or a diner, or in the car. But I'm not getting out until you've agreed."

"Is this what you call caring, huh?"

"How are you liking it?"

Ryan swore.

Brent laughed. "That good, huh? So something is working then." He pointed to a sign near the riverfront of River Valley's giant parkland. "Can we park there?"

"Sure." They'd likely get cold pretty quick, but that'd provide a good reason for Brent to leave faster. "Aren't you worried about your flight tomorrow?"

"You're not."

Huh.

"Anyway, I'm the alternate captain, so I don't get into trouble anymore."

If he ever had. Some people had golden ticket lives. Brent's talents and status as face of the franchise meant he'd always scored a free pass.

"Besides," Brent jerked the car into park and killed the engine, leaving the heating running. "Some things are more important than sleep." He turned to face Ryan. "And you have obviously got some things to get off your chest. So, spill."

Ryan shook his head, the distraction of the past ten minutes fading as emotion clamped his throat again.

"Okay, don't spill, and we'll play the 'Nod if Brent is right' game. Okay?"

"No."

Brent laughed. "Let me guess. You went and spoke to your girl about God. Am I right?"

Ryan exhaled.

"Nod if I'm right."

"Fine, you're right."

"Was this before or after she tried to put the moves on you?"

"How did—?"

"I told you, man. I've been there. I've had that happen to me too." He paused. "It's not fun."

Ryan blinked hard against the fresh emotion caused by the compassion lacing Brent's voice.

Snow-draped trees glistened as a few park lights cut through the darkness. Already he could feel the cold creeping against the window.

"You know who helped me?" Brent said after a while.

"Who?"

"Mike. And Bree, but mostly Mike, as there was stuff I couldn't really admit to my sister, and I'm sure she wouldn't like to know about me."

Curiosity gnawed. "Did you ever—"

"No, but it got close." Brent's exhale fogged a little with the cold. "I didn't realize at the time, but Chloe was needy, she wanted to be seen with me for her social media, and didn't care about me at all." His chuckle held no amusement. "When I ended things with her, she trashed my apartment."

"Wow."

"Yeah. Says it all, huh?"

That was different to what had just happened with Sylvie. "I feel like I broke her," he admitted in the dark. Her stricken look would haunt him all his days.

"You didn't break her," Brent said. "She's been broken a long time. That's what Mike and Bree were trying to help her with. Give her a fresh start over here, get some new friends." He punched Ryan's arm. "They just didn't count on her finding certain new friends so fast, eh?"

Ryan shook his head. "Man. I was such an idiot."

"Nah. You're just human. We're all allowed to make mistakes."

"Yeah, some of us. Others, like Mike, however…"

Brent snorted. "Please. He's not perfect. He spent way too long listening to a friend tell him he couldn't date his sister. What kind of man lets that stop him?"

"You?"

Brent's grin flashed in the dim light. "Told you I'm not perfect."

"Yeah, but that's obvious. What kind of person drags a man outside when it's minus ten?"

"You're not outside, so quit complaining."

"You really need to work on your people skills," he muttered.

"So some say. Anyway, tell me what happened after she tried to have her way with you."

Ryan almost laughed at that expression spilling from Brent's mouth. Almost. "I did what you said, and asked if she'd prayed the prayer, and stuff."

"And she said no."

He sighed. "She didn't say she had, which is—"

"A no."

He shook his head. "I'm an idiot."

"You got blinded by lust."

Ryan winced.

"Can you see why I said what I did?"

He grunted assent.

"Friends speak up when something isn't right. And I knew you didn't wanna hear it, and heaven knows that Sylvie didn't wanna hear it, but if you want a future with a woman, then you both have to be on the same page. And that means both being believers."

Ryan leaned his head against the padded headrest. "I don't know how many times we've talked about this stuff at Bible study."

"Talk is talk, but sooner or later you have to walk the walk. And there are plenty of people who say one thing but don't live like it. Call me judgy—wait, you've already done that tonight—but there are plenty of Christians who don't do what Jesus says either."

"I thought it was Paul who said don't be yoked with unbelievers."

"Look at you, you Bible scholar. Pastor Josiah would be proud."

Ryan's lips tweaked up then instantly flattened. "I told her she needed to talk to Bree about finding God."

"Good call." Brent tapped his fingers on the steering wheel. "If she looks to you to find a relationship with God then there's a chance she'll always rely on you, not God, to sustain her."

"But what if she's turned away from God now because of what I've done?"

"Please. Do you really think God would let a little speed bump like this get in the way of His plans for her?"

Put like that, well, "No." Although calling the depths of his devastation "a little speed bump" seemed pretty rude.

"Ryan, I know this isn't easy."

Yeah, he knew that now.

"But giving your relationship to God is always worth it. And just because you have all these frayed emotions right now doesn't mean that God can't heal it or that God can't fix things. But you've gotta reach a point where you're okay, either way. That if this isn't a relationship that God wants for you, a relationship that He wants to salvage, then you've gotta trust Him that He's got something better. *Someone* better. And we always want God's best for us, don't we? Or at least we *should* want what He wants more than our own desires."

Ryan's exhale was shaky.

"I don't know if you remember what happened with me and Holly, but she got concussed after a skating event, and was in a pretty bad way for a while. It got to a point where I was praying for God's will to be done with her and me. And she got healed, and things between us got restored, but in that moment when everything seemed darkest, and it felt like she was rejecting me, I had to keep trusting God that He knew what He was doing." His hand gripped Ryan's arm. "God knows what He's doing, with you, and with Sylvie. So trust Him."

Emotion roared again, and he could only nod.

"I'm gonna pray, okay?"

Ryan closed his eyes, as Brent prayed for comfort, healing, and for Sylvie's salvation, and for God's will to happen. Ryan Amen-ed, cleared his throat, wiped his nose on his sleeve, and Brent headed home. Or at least back to the hotel.

"Do you think you can manage to drive home from here?" Brent said when they were back in the hotel's drop-off zone.

"I can, seeing you didn't crash it."

Brent laughed, and got out. They exchanged hugs. "Hey, do you think it's any coincidence that I just so happened to be here tonight?"

No. But saying that would make Brent's already swollen head twice its size. "G'night. And thanks."

"I'll be praying for you, dude. And for her. And don't forget you need to talk to Mike."

"Sure." One day. "Crush Chris in Vancouver, okay?"

Brent rubbed his hands together. "That's the plan."

Ryan nodded, his smile fading as he drove the short distance to his shared apartment, Brent's words roiling through his ears. He'd talk to Mike, soon. When he didn't feel quite so fragile. But first he had to have a big talk to the Man with the ultimate Plan.

God.

CHAPTER 12

She must've fallen asleep close to dawn. Curled up on the big bed, her clothes askew, her hair a mess, her makeup smeared with snot and tears. All the tears might've been cried out, but her heart still writhed in pain that twisted through her dreams.

Memories of Ryan, his care, his attention, his affection merged with bizarre dreams which involved everything from flashes of *Star Wars*-like lasers in arenas to *Indiana Jones*-esque precarious rope bridges to bizarre images of zombie horses. She had no idea where the zombie horses came from, or what they might signify. But the rope bridge sequence with its snapping lines before she fell into the rapids a quarter mile below was easy to explain. She might've tried to cling to the broken pieces of the bridge, but there was no way to climb to safety. She'd irrevocably broken things, and now she floated face down in freezing currents. She might as well be dead.

"Miss? Excuse me, Miss?"

She was floating. The words sounded so far away.

"Miss? Can you hear me?"

She opened an eye. Then yelped.

The face above her shrieked too. "You *are* alive."

"What?" She slowly pushed up from the bed, blinking against the light peeking past the block-out curtains. So strange, so unfamiliar. She propped her head in her hands and peeked at the woman wearing a cleaner's uniform. "Where am I?"

The woman explained she was at a hotel in downtown Edmonton.

Then the wispy dreams dissolved as the pain from yesterday rushed over her again. Ryan had rejected her. Brent Karlsson had judged her like trash, like the scrunched-up paper poking over the clear plastic bag in the cleaner's cart. Discarded. Unwanted. Unused.

"Do you need a doctor?"

A heart specialist, maybe. Someone who knew how to mend holes in hearts. "N-no."

"Has someone hurt you?"

"Yes."

The cleaner frowned. "Do I need to call security or the police?"

"What?" She'd kill for ibuprofen right now. The headache thumping behind her left eyelid might do her in.

"Miss, wait there while I call the hotel security."

This woman wasn't making sense. "Why would you do that?"

"Pardon me, but it seems you are on drugs."

"What? I don't use drugs." She hadn't used them in years. Maybe recreationally, once upon a time. But not on purpose. And not last night. Or any night in the past year. "I'm fine. Just really tired." And heartsore. Heartbroken.

"You do not seem well."

The compassion in the woman's voice stirred her emotions again. "My boyfriend broke up with me last night."

"Oh, I'm so sorry." The cleaner offered clumsy pats on her shoulder. "But I hate to tell you, you are past checkout time."

"Past checkout—? What time was that?"

"Eleven. It's nearly twelve now, and we need to clean this room for the next guest."

"What?" None of this was making sense.

Then clarity came with lightning speed. "Oh no." She sat upright, her head swimming, then bent to retrieve her clothes. "My shift starts at two."

Which meant she had to leave now. As it was, she'd be struggling to get changed and get there in time. She grabbed her clothes and rushed to the bathroom. "Give me two minutes then I'll be out of here."

She turned the bathroom light on, startling at her appearance in the mirror. A dunk of her face under the water sparked some alertness to her brain, then she scrubbed off the makeup with a face towel, dragged off the special dress, and pulled on the light blue uniform not too dissimilar to what the cleaner wore.

Oh, Cinderella had well and truly left the building.

Her hair could be brushed in the car, and she could be makeup-free today, although the bags under the red-lined eyes sure needed disguising. But again that would have to be a rush job in the car. Her stomach's rumble reminded her that she'd missed breakfast. Her heart quivered. The Valentine's Day breakfast she was supposed to share with Ryan. That certainly hadn't happened.

She returned, spying the leftover chocolate brownie from last night's dessert, and quickly wrapped it up in a paper napkin. That might as well serve as her breakfast. Brownies, the breakfast of champions.

A minute later she'd stuffed her remaining clothes in her bag, was tempted to leave the jersey behind, but figured his mom might like it, so she stuffed that in too. Then with hurried thanks, she raced out to the carpeted hallway, got an elevator and placed her keycard in the express checkout box as she hurried to the parking garage.

She hoped Ryan had paid. She vaguely remembered he'd said he had. Whatever. The room had been booked in his name, anyway. Her heart broke a little more, at the naive idiot who had checked in yesterday, imagining this as a fairytale, where she and he were as good as married and this was normal.

But the past fourteen hours had showed just how non-normal this had been, and that any hope of finding a prince had been simply a fool's game of smoke and mirrors.

She merged onto Gateway Boulevard then headed south, eyes on the clock. No way would she be late today. She needed this job more than ever, and she might still have a chance of keeping it, even if Heather had already found out about Ryan breaking up with her. She pressed the accelerator, glad the conditions weren't too slippery today, as she stayed at the maximum speed. This time of day there was less traffic, and she might have a chance of making it on time.

She glanced across at her handbag, pulled out her hairbrush and began brushing her hair, then swept it up into a short pony-tail with an elastic. A quick jerk of the wheel steadied the car back into its lane. Then it was time for makeup. No fancy cat eye today, just basic foundation to cover the purple shadows and a couple of new stress pimples. She clutched the wheel harder, as she squeezed a tiny circle of liquid foundation onto her finger, then dabbed it under her eyes. Some might think that purple shadows complemented her general Goth vibe, but she wasn't a fan unless it looked intentional, and not tired. She peered at the rearview mirror, resulting in another jerk of the wheel, which sent the brownie tumbling off the front passenger seat. Darn. She was tempted to reach across to pick it up, when she noticed the blue and red lights flashing behind her.

No. That couldn't be for her, could it?

But when the police vehicle drew in behind her, then flashed its headlights, new tears sparked as she slowed and pulled to the side.

Cars sped past her, every one of them holding passengers whose necks swiveled to watch the poor loser who'd been caught doing whatever it was she'd done. She hadn't been speeding. Did she have a taillight out? She'd updated her insurance and registration—hadn't she? Oh, why was the man taking so long?

She'd been watching the clock, and had calculated that with normal travel times she only had ten minutes' grace before she needed to sign in for work. She couldn't afford a delay. Impatience prickled within. Finally, a stocky Alberta highway patrolman exited his vehicle and moved to hers, indicating she lower the window.

"Miss."

She nodded. Found a wobbly smile. Hoped she looked like she was a nice person, and not the pathetic scumbag that Ryan and Brent seemed to think her.

"You in a hurry?" He gestured to the brush and makeup on the passenger seat.

"I'm late for work, but I didn't think I was speeding."

"You weren't. You were just a little erratic." He peered to look at her. "Is everything okay, Miss?"

Her lip trembled, and more stupid tears appeared. "My boyfriend broke up with me last night."

His brow puckered. "Have you been drinking or using drugs?"

"No." Although, now she thought about it, "Actually, I did have a glass of champagne at the game last night."

"The game?"

"The hockey game. Edmonton versus—"

"Detroit, I know. I watched it at home. So, you were there?" His eyebrows drifted north, as if wondering how someone dressed in the humble clothes of an aged care aide could possibly afford the tickets to such a game.

She could only nod.

"That Karlsson goal was something else, eh?"

Her chest tightened. "Someone needs to shut that man down. Permanently."

The officer chuckled, like he thought she was making a joke. But no. She wasn't.

"I'll need you to blow into this." He produced a Breathalyzer, and she breathed into it.

The result was negative, although if he'd had a test for her hatred for Brent it could score maximum top reading. She glanced at the clock. She'd lost all margin and now had no more time to lose. Relief filled her as he returned.

"Okay, looks like you're in the clear, but I want you to take it easy. Okay?"

"Yes, sir."

He indicated for her to merge back into the traffic, but everything was blurry, and she nearly collected a vehicle as she attempted to do so. She caught his shake of head in the rearview mirror, and was relieved the lights didn't flash again as she moved back into the lane.

He eventually passed her, then she saw he'd U-turned and was chasing down a vehicle going in the opposite direction. Thank goodness. She appreciated good highway safety as much as the next person, but it should be focused on the real criminals, not on people simply running late for work. Her speed crept up until she was back at top speed again, but this time there were no distractions, nothing except the desire to get to Aspen Lodge on time and prove she wasn't flaky.

She just needed to get through today. Prove she could be trusted, was reliable, even if some people didn't believe her. She wouldn't have this job, unless Heather had believed in her.

How she hoped Ryan hadn't yet told his mom.

~

HE WAS EXHAUSTED. Talking to Brent, then getting home in the wee smalls had left precious few hours for sleep. But even when he'd closed his eyes, he'd only managed to rest his eyeballs, not his brain. His mind kept ticking, thinking, reliving, wondering, regrets spiking up like shards of broken glass that stabbed his soul.

He might've prayed with Brent—or at least had Brent pray with him—but it didn't stop the guilt, the memories, the—God forgive him—desires from wrestling with his thoughts and dreams.

It was humbling having nearly cried with Brent. Humbling having to admit he was wrong. He was glad for his usual habit of noise-canceling headphones and eyes closed as he feigned sleep on the team's plane. If there was some way of avoiding conversation for the next, oh, six-to-eight weeks he'd be a very happy man.

As it was, he hadn't been able to avoid talking with Mats this morning. The dude had his own Valentine's Day deal with his girlfriend, and had wondered aloud about Ryan when he'd slept in. "Dude, you're gonna be late for your hot breakfast date."

No, he wasn't. But trying to explain that wouldn't be easy, especially when Mats had made no bones about his less-than-Biblical standards when it came to dating.

Not that Ryan could talk. Not anymore. He'd proved just as susceptible as anyone else, fooled by a woman's face and curves. Such a fool. *God, forgive me.*

But, like Brent had said last night, at least it hadn't tipped into the other zone. Kissing and making out like he'd done with Sylvie proved how easily he could slide into wanting more.

He glanced at his phone, checked the message Brent had sent this morning. *Praying for you.*

Mike had sent one too. *Let me know when you're free to talk.*

Ryan winced. It sounded like Brent had messaged Mike, like a little kid gossiping from grade school. But he instantly rebuked that thought, knowing that any communication from Brent to Mike concerning Ryan had come from a place of wanting Ryan's best. Even if Ryan barely knew what he wanted anymore.

He didn't want to interrupt Mike's day off with Bree and his family. Nobody needed Ryan's special brand of drama after being away for an east coast road trip, and he bet Bree wouldn't appreciate knowing just how awkward things had gotten between her friend and him. How could she have even wanted to have Sylvie care for her kids when she obviously wasn't a Christian?

His gut wrenched with misgiving. Should he have gone through the three-step plan to salvation? All he could feel was the need to get out of there, so he had. It wasn't like her salvation was wholly resting on his shoulders. He wasn't responsible for her salvation. That was God's job. But he upped his prayers that she might find the freedom that faith in God and following Jesus might do.

AFTER DEPLANING and settling into their St Louis hotel he had a wedge of time before the team dinner. Luc had called, and Ryan knew he had to touch base after their last messed up phone call. Funny how the scales had fallen from his eyes and he could see exactly what Luc had meant when he'd tried to warn him before. He hated when Luc was right. Still, he had to try. Even if he was relieved that the schedule meant Winnipeg had a game starting shortly, which meant Luc was unlikely to answer

—

"Ryanator."

Ryan closed his eyes. Darn. "I thought you'd be all focused on your game against San Jose."

"Is that why you called now?" Luc asked, way too insightfully.

"I called because I had a moment free. But hey, if you don't want to talk—"

"Stop acting all defensive."

"I'm not—" Ryan broke off as Luc laughed. "You're real funny."

"That's me. So, don't waste a phone call. How you doing?"

"Why?" He frowned. "What have you heard?"

"Is there something to hear?" Luc countered.

Man, the guy might be built like a brick, but he was a lot savvier than people gave him credit for.

"Let me guess," Luc continued. "You and she are no longer a thing."

"Why do you say that?"

"Because why else would you be calling me on the most romantic day of the year?"

"I thought you might be sad about not getting any roses," Ryan mocked.

"What makes you think I didn't get any?"

He had?

"Never fear. This stud is rose-less for another year."

"We need to find you a woman called Rose, huh?"

"Not looking, nor needing a rose or a woman," Luc said.

Yeah, but just because a guy wasn't looking didn't mean she might not come dancing past anyway. He couldn't wait to see what kind of woman would tame the broad-shouldered lumberjack some people called a beast.

"I'm *very* happy as I am, thanks," Luc said, obviously to somebody else, judging from the jeers and laughter in the background.

That made one of them.

Ryan rubbed tired eyes. He was so weary. This conversation

was making his head swim. He shouldn't have called. What he'd give for those footloose, fancy-free days…

"So, you doing okay?"

"Are you asking me now or someone else?" Ryan groused.

"Judging from that tone I'm going to go with option a, is not doing too well. Dude, what's happened?" he asked in a softer voice.

He really didn't want to get into this again. "I just thought you might be glad to know that person you tried to warn me about, well, yeah, that didn't work out."

There was a moment of silence. Then, "what happened?"

"Nothing." Then everything. "Look, let's just say that you were right and it would never have worked out."

"Wow. I'm sorry."

"Yeah, you don't have to pretend. I know you didn't like her, so I hope you're happy now."

"Ryan, I'm not happy. I can tell you're not happy, so I really am sorry this is hard right now."

Ryan's lips pressed together, and he glanced out the window, catching a glimpse of the huge arch over the Mississippi.

"You're my brother, man, and we take care of each other, yeah?"

Man, he hated how talking about relationships made him want to cry like a little girl.

"How long until we play each other?"

Ryan tapped on his phone screen and flicked through the schedule. "Just before Easter, at the end of March."

"Your place or mine?"

"Yours." The calendar said it was a road trip. He'd play Dan Walton in Toronto, then fly to Ottawa then Winnipeg before coming home.

"Steak's on me, then."

"You got it."

"Now I gotta go. Go crush Jai's team."

"Go Jai," Ryan taunted.

"That's it. It's gonna be the smallest, toughest, itty bittiest piece of steak for you."

Ryan finally smiled. Thank God for friends.

CHAPTER 13

S ylvie was fragile, like a painted glass vase with a giant crack running through it. She was holding her emotions in but only just, as any second she could so easily break. She just had to get through the next five hours then go lick her wounds at home. And keep doing her best to avoid Heather, which wasn't too hard considering the demands of the residents. Fake smile, fake good cheer, head down as exhaustion threatened to overwhelm her. She'd already managed to stumble through an hour, going through the motions with Mr. Jenner, thankful for once that the grumpy man's preferred mode of communication consisted of grunts and scowls, before tackling helping Mrs. Wallis-Smith, who continued ignoring Sylvie, like she thought Sylvie was beneath her, which might have something to do with her dementia, but whatever.

"Sylvie?" She froze as Heather approached. "I missed you earlier."

There was a good reason for that. Avoiding Heather had been the name of the game today. Who knew if Ryan had spoken to his mom already about her? Shame clung close—how could she have thrown herself at him?—and she faked busyness.

"I'm really sorry. I need to speak to Mrs. Androvsky. She's waiting for a shower."

"Don't forget you're always welcome to dinner."

Her heart clenched. She nodded, pushing out a tight smile.

"And I'd love to hear all about the game and last night."

No, she really wouldn't.

She pushed the cart to the elderly woman's room, past a string of trailing hearts decorating Mrs. Androvsky's door, who unlike some, was definitely excited about Valentine's Day. Valentine's Day. What a joke that she was working here today of all days.

"Ah, Sylvie!" Mrs. Androvsky's face brightened. "I'm so happy to see you."

Sylvie's throat filled and she did her best to make her smile seem real. The woman was sweet. "How—" She cleared her throat to avoid the frogginess. "How are you today, Mrs. A?"

Mrs. Androvsky's smile said it all as she pointed to the red rose-filled vase atop her movable bed table. "I have such thoughtful children, don't I?"

"Yes."

"They even have perfume! Go on, have a sniff."

Sylvie obeyed, leaning down to take a gentle whiff of the roses. "Very nice."

"Now, how about you? Have you got plans with a young man?"

She compressed her lips, shook her head.

"Why are you looking so blue?"

Sylvie shrugged, her smile small. "I'm sorry."

"Is it a boy?"

What kind of man allowed himself to be persuaded to dump a girl? Someone who wasn't a man, that's who. "I'd rather not talk about it."

"Come on. Do you know how dull life can be cooped up in a

place like this? It does my heart good to know that other people are out there, living, doing things I can no longer do."

For a moment, Sylvie had a mental image of Mrs. Androvsky pulling the same moves as she'd tried in Edmonton, and she nearly smiled. The thing was, this woman was so persistent she probably would've got her man, and would be sitting here, with an engagement ring and all.

"That's more like it." Mrs. Androvsky approved. "Now tell me, what's his name?"

"Who?"

"Don't play coy with me. I don't have enough time to buy green bananas let alone have someone be coy with me. Now, what's his name?"

"Ryan."

"Hmm. Now that's a nice name. Is he handsome?"

She nodded. Gut-clenching handsome.

"But not in his actions, I'm guessing from that expression."

"He…he dumped me last night."

"The day before Valentine's? Oh, that's *terrible*."

Yes. It was. "So now you know. Happy now?"

"No. I'm very sorry, my dear. I would never take comfort in someone else's pain."

Sylvie gritted her teeth. She'd take a fair bit of comfort in knowing Brent Karlsson was in pain right about now.

Mrs. Androvsky patted the bed, but it wasn't protocol to sit there, so Sylvie sat on the nearby chair instead. "You're a good girl."

She shook her head. No, she wasn't. Never had been. And judging from last night's moves, despite her efforts to be good, she never would be.

"Now don't be like that. Your Mr. Right will come along one day."

Maybe. Her eyes watered. But she'd really thought she'd already met him. And regardless, she'd wanted that one. *Still* wanted that one, despite everything. He'd been misled by Brent, that was all. Her heart ached. But as much as she craved sympathy, she also had a job to do, and she couldn't afford to give Heather a reason to fire her like she probably would if she saw Sylvie sitting down on the job. She pushed to her feet. "Come on. Let's get you showered."

She made it through the rest of the shift, thankful for the busyness which distracted her from the most humiliating experience of her life, thankful to grab drive-through as she finally, finally made it to her crummy apartment that night. It was cold and smelled even worse after being shut up for nearly two days. She wished she could live somewhere else, be somewhere else. Anywhere.

For a moment, her cozy room at Bree's flickered through her mind, back where she'd felt like she had a purpose, and had felt loved and accepted. Until she hadn't. But no. She couldn't.

A scurrying sound came from the corner. She cringed. Ugh. But no. She couldn't go back. She wasn't wanted. Wasn't wanted anywhere. Not really.

She showered, doing her best to scrub off the sweat and tears and pain of the past twenty-four hours, but still grief clung to her, like sadness contaminated her very pores. She'd given Ryan her heart, and he'd rejected her. Exactly like the long list of men who'd done the same. Men who had taken advantage of her, men she'd taken advantage of, it all worked out the same. Nobody wanted her. She never fitted in.

She hurried across the ice-cold floor and went to bed, closing her eyes, willing the pervading exhaustion to help her to sleep. But grief still tickled her memories, forcing her to relive those awful moments again and again. When she had literally thrown herself at him. When he'd literally pushed her away. When she vamped to get his attention. When he didn't want her heart. When he'd been persuaded by his friend to give her up. Ryan didn't want her. Nobody wanted her. Not really.

Emotions tumbled and twisted, memories blurring with those from further back, zeroing in on all those times she'd been judged and found wanting. The names she'd heard whispered by Christians and others who judged her clothes and her hair and her actions, those who didn't bother looking past that to realize she just wanted somebody to love her. How could Brent have warned Ryan away from her? He was as bad as all the others. Worse, because he and his little perfect wife had even pretended to be nice to her. So, she was good enough to look after their kids at Bree's but not good enough for Ryan? What kind of sick, twisted logic was that? What kind of man thought he had the right to tell his friends what to do, like he was Mr. Darcy or whoever, in one of those old movies Bree liked to watch.

Beneath this thought lay another: what kind of man allowed his friend to persuade him? But no, she shook that off. Ryan *had* liked her. Had wanted her. He wasn't at fault here. That was all Brent's fault. Oh, she hated—*hated*—Brent Karlsson with a passion.

THE ALARM WOKE her too early. She switched it off, heavy eyelids begging for more sleep. But no. The daily drudgery awaited.

Another shower to wake up, an apple for breakfast, then she was scraping ice off her windshield as she readied for work. She drove there, bracing inside, rehearsing what she should say about Tuesday night in any possible encounters with Heather.

"The game was good." That was true.

"We had dinner." Then tears.

"He left."

"I haven't spoken to him since I returned." Also true. "He was busy with travel and has a game tonight."

That hadn't stopped him calling her before the breakup, but Heather didn't need to know that.

By the time she pulled in she was almost confident she could pull it off.

She signed in, relieved when Heather wasn't in her office when she tiptoed past, and retrieved her supplies for her day of caring for the elderly. Bathing, washing, listening, helping clean up. At least a few of these people valued her. To some degree, at least. And at least it provided escape from the endless recriminations circling her mind like birds of prey.

Focus on her job, on the elderly. Caring for those without family, like her. How weird that with all the scores of people here, none of them knew her grandparents. Her enquiries had made no headway. Nobody here seemed to know John or Esther. So where were they?

During her lunch break she noticed her phone held several new messages. Nothing from Ryan. Her eyes blurred. Nope, he'd made himself very clear. Instead, one was from an insurance thing she owed. The other two were from Bree. *Hey, thinking of you.* And, *I hope everything is okay. Call me when you get a chance.*

Yeah, that wasn't going to be any time soon. It was nice that Bree cared, but Sylvie wasn't about to speak to her. Who knew what she might crack and say?

But later, when her shift was done, she discovered a missed call from Bree, which twisted her heart in knots. What did Bree want to say? It must be important if she'd reached out so many times. She listened to her voice message.

"Hi there. It's just me. Hey, I'm worried about you. Can you give me a call?"

She pressed her lips together. Nope. Not today. Not tonight. Tonight she had a date with the biggest bucket of ice cream she could find.

. . .

THE REST of the week passed with more of the same, working her shifts, taking extra shifts where she could, avoiding Heather, avoiding Bree's calls, as she tried to ignore Ryan's rejection. Distraction helped soothe the gnawing ache inside. That, and tiredness. She got home each day, exhausted, too weary to do much more than shower and sleep. She was too tired to bother responding to the guy in his thirties next door who'd made some comment that sounded like an invitation for more than sharing pizza. And while a tiny part of her was tempted to find validation in some other man's arms, to prove to herself that she was wanted, the memory of that look in Ryan's eyes when he said, "I want you" held her back. It was all she could do to survive the rest of the week without splintering too much.

Whether Heather thought that everything was still okay, or whether Ryan had told her the truth, Sylvie still didn't know. She was grateful to not have to go into explanations. It was hard enough fending off Bree's text messages.

But at nighttime she couldn't help but continue to imagine what she could have done better. Imagined what she should have said. Ryan and Bree might talk about God wanting her, but if he did, then surely he would've given her a sign or something?

Which meant God didn't. He was far away. Which left her pretending by day that everything was okay, and sobbing at night, wondering what was wrong with her. Her heart had cracked open. And it felt like the slightest whiff of criticism and she'd break.

"SYLVIE?"

She paused in the hall and dredged up a fake smile for Heather. "Hi."

"How are you doing? You should come to dinner. I can't believe it's been a week already since you went to Edmonton. I feel like we never get the chance to talk."

There was a five-foot-ten-inches-tall reason for that. Who knew what he'd said to his mom about her? "I'm really sorry. I need to speak to Mrs. Androvsky. She's waiting for a shower."

"Don't be a stranger."

Yeah, no guarantees with that. She'd have to somehow remain estranged with the woman who'd given her this job. Even though it was starting to hurt her heart at the pathetic excuses as to why she couldn't join them for dinner on hockey game days.

But there were limits even to her pretending, and she knew they'd tumble to the truth, and she had no desire to be in their firing line. It felt like dicing with danger simply working in the same place as Heather did. One false step and she'd plunge to her death. Or at least to joblessness. Again.

THE PHONE RANG AGAIN. Bree. Again. Frustration with her friend made her snatch it up. "Hello?"

She closed her eyes. Ungritted her teeth. Bree's kindness in her daily check-ins didn't deserve this. None of this was Bree's fault. Try her mother-in-law's. Her brother's. Her heart twinged. Ryan's.

"Hey, Sylvie. It's been a while. I wanted to check on you, make sure you're okay."

"I'm okay." That was an exaggeration, but she was alive, at least.

"Really?"

"Yep," she lied. Quick, change the subject. "How are you?"

"Okay. It's been a little crazy here, and I don't know if I'm allowed to admit this but I kind of miss the days when life was simpler, and there were less people around."

"Have you got someone staying with you?"

"My brother—"

Sylvie's hands clenched.

"—Dean and Laura and the kids popped in from Vancouver —"

Oh. Her fingers relaxed.

"—and we had some fun catching up with my big bro. But I'm so tired again."

"Are you resting?"

Bree laughed. "You sound like Mike's mom."

Ugh. "Is she still there?"

Bree's sigh was soft. "I really don't want to sound ungrateful, because I do value all her help, but I'm looking forward to feeling like I have my house to myself again."

Which would only happen once Bree made those feelings plain.

"I know I should say something to her," Bree said, as if Sylvie had spoken her thoughts aloud, "but I feel so bad, especially knowing that they moved here to help with this."

"Can you talk about it with Mike?"

"I've tried to. He's been so busy back on the team, trying to prove himself there, that I really don't want to add any more stress right now."

"Didn't you used to have a book about boundaries? I seem to remember you quoting that at me a time or two."

"Did I? Wow. Well, I hope that didn't come across as rude when I did that."

Sylvie paused. No. Bree's comment had come from concern. Just like Sylvie's had just now. Her heart softened.

"See? I knew I needed to speak to you. I should read that again, shouldn't I?"

"Probably."

"I'll do that. I feel so awful sounding ungrateful, but I'm trying to figure things out and it's hard when I can't always bounce ideas off Mike."

Was this her subtle way of asking Sylvie to return?

"Anyway, that's enough about me. I want to know more about you, and how you're doing."

"Like I said before, I'm fine."

"Are you though? Really? See, a few days ago Brent sent me a message, saying he'd seen you in Edmonton—"

Sylvie's heart fisted and she rolled her eyes. Oh, she bet he had.

"—and anyway, he asked me to pray for you."

"What?"

"Yeah, weird, I know. But my bro and I have always had a special twin-thing and I felt like it was important, which is why I've been trying to talk to you recently, and why I'm so glad you finally answered."

"I'm sorry," Sylvie said, her voice small.

"So, is everything okay?"

She dragged in a deep breath. But Bree didn't need Sylvie's troubles adding to the weight of her life. "I'm okay. Work is pretty busy right now."

"Which is what I figured when you didn't call me straightaway."

Sylvie's eyes filled. Bree was way too generous and kind-hearted.

"Anyway, I don't know anything more than that, but wanted you to know that I'm here if ever you want to talk. Or visit. I miss you, you know."

"I miss you, too."

"The kids miss you as well. Ethan has a birthday soon, and he's adamant that you have to come."

"I'll be there."

"Actually, that's in April, so that's way too far away. I'm gonna pull the new-mother-of-twins card and say I'd really love to see you soon. Like this weekend. Or next. You can stay over as long as you like."

Sylvie swiped moisture from her eyes. "Weren't you just saying you were tired from having houseguests?"

"You're not a houseguest, though, Sylvie. You're my friend."

Sylvie's heart squeezed.

"Please? I know I'm starting to sound desperate, but I'd love to see you, catch up on your news."

No, she wouldn't. Bree might be her friend, but she would still judge her, and—

"Let me know when you can, then. And know I'll be praying for you. Okay?"

Emotion roared. And all she could do was whisper, "Okay."

IT HAD BEEN a while since all the guys had managed to join in for their online video Bible study. Ryan hadn't wanted to miss it, knowing Luc would likely have things to say if he did. But there was safety in numbers, and because he was known as one of the quieter members, people never expected him to say much. He was counting on that tonight, at least.

Josiah Abrahams, the pastor who had started this online Bible study years ago when he and Jai Mullins had recognized a need for Christian men to connect across the pro hockey league, welcomed everyone, readying for today's topic.

John, chapter four. About the woman at the well. The judgment she'd received. The fact she'd wanted to know about the true way to worship God.

His gut clenched. Wasn't that what Sylvie had wanted to know? And he'd rejected her? Said he wasn't "strong enough" or whatever? It all seemed like such a mess. He was still a mess. Games had kept him busy and focused, but in his downtime, he still found it all too easy to descend into the whirlpool of guilt and regrets.

Ryan ducked his head, as the conversation circled around him.

"Got any thoughts there, Ryan?" Josiah asked.

So many. None that should be shared aloud. "Not at the moment."

He caught how Luc's head tilted, his eyes narrowing, like he was calculating just what thoughts Ryan might be withholding.

Ryan dipped his head again.

"Okay, then. How about you, Chris?"

Chris offered his opinion, but Ryan didn't really hear him. It was enough that he was here, he was holding it together. He hadn't discussed anything with anyone apart from Luc since Brent's "intervention" and he'd like to keep it that way.

Another peek up showed Franklin seated next to Mike. Mike, the one person Ryan might expect to interfere, was propping his chin up on one hand.

"You okay, Mikey?" Luc asked.

"I'm just tired."

"All those kids, huh?"

Mike dipped his chin, his expression tight. He'd probably heard similar things. Some people seemed to think anything more than two kids being excessive in this day and age. He didn't blame Mike for being over such insensitivity.

Ryan's heart softened. "Is there anything we can do?"

Mike shook his head, his expression grim. "Apart from praying for the babies to sleep through, no, not really."

"How is Bree?" Jai asked. "Allie wants to know."

"She's really tired, which makes me feel bad, because she then insists I sleep in the guest wing so their crying doesn't wake me."

"Remind me what happened to the babysitter you had?" Chris asked.

Ryan's heart froze. Plenty.

"She, uh, decided to move when my parents moved nearby."

"Too many cooks, huh?"

"Something like that, I think."

"Maybe you need to get her to come back," Josiah said.

"Maybe."

Franklin nodded. "Yeah, she was funny."

"In a good way?" Jai asked.

"Really dry wit. She and Hannah got on well." Franklin nudged Mike's shoulder. "You should get her to come back, like a surprise for Bree. I think Bree would get a kick out of that."

Mike's brow furrowed, then he pursed his lips, head tilting as he looked at the screen. Was he looking at Ryan? "I'll think about it."

"Don't just think," Josiah urged. "Love means taking action."

Like rejecting the woman who'd tried to prove her love by action in a very different way.

"Call her and see if she can help Bree again."

Was this where he was supposed to say "No, she has a job in Red Deer"? He kept his lips sealed.

"We'll be praying for you, Bree, and the babies, don't you worry about that."

"Thanks, Jo."

Josiah nodded. "Anyone else?"

Various other prayer requests were thrown in, and relief stole in. He'd managed to get to the end, and any second he could finally sign off, and—

"How about you, Ryan?" Luc asked. "Got anything you need prayer about?"

"Yeah, you've been really quiet tonight," Chris said. "What's going on, dude?"

"Nothing." Anymore.

"You sure? Because that sure doesn't look like the face of nothing going on."

"It's been a big week with road trips. I'm tired."

"We play you on Saturday next week, don't we?" Mike said.

Franklin nodded. "Yeah, we should catch up."

"Sure." There wouldn't be much time for that. Calgary games meant they'd be getting on that plane as soon as the game was done. In other words, there should be a good chance of avoiding any time for a talk, so, "sounds good."

Josiah finished, and was about to sign off, when he paused. "Hey, Mike, before I forget, remind me of the name of the woman who was helping Bree out before."

"Sylvie. Sylvie Miles."

Ryan's heart stuttered. He rolled his lips inwards. Lips that had kissed her, wanted her, rejected her…

"Why?" Luc asked.

Josiah's hands steepled. "I just have a sense that we should be praying for her."

"You mean for her to go back and help Bree?" Jai asked.

"Hmm, more than that. Now I think about it, if I remember correctly, she's the woman you once had some reservations about before, am I right, Mike?"

Mike nodded. "I don't know where she stands with God."

Again, Ryan kept his mouth closed. He had more of an idea these days.

"Well, in that case, I think she'd benefit from us all praying that she finds a relationship with God. Just like the woman at the well."

The woman who'd wanted to know about getting a right relationship with God.

"Wouldn't you all agree?"

His heart tumbled amid the sounds of assent, and he forced himself to nod as he scrambled mentally. These guys were all going to pray for the woman he'd fallen for? The one he struggled to forget? The one who'd carved her name on his soul, just as her kiss had branded his skin?

Some might look at his muscles and on-ice hits and defense

and call him tough and strong. Some might think him bold and brave. But right now, part of him kind of just wanted to cry.

Instead, he blinked away emotion, and bowed his head and prayed that God would use someone, somewhere, to reveal more of His love for her. And that God would heal his heart and help his head get above water again.

"Well, Missy, I think that's enough about me. I want to hear about you."

No, he didn't. Sylvie cleaned up the remains of Clifford's lunch. Clifford was in his mid-seventies, and unlike many of the patients here, interested to the point of fanatical about her life. He said it was because he hadn't met many women with interesting tattoos. She suspected it was more a case that he'd liked her sass, not that she'd managed much of that lately.

Last week's prolonged downer after her dumping from Ryan and run-in with the policeman, coupled with her lack of sleep and continued caginess with Heather had made her both jumpy and morose. After a much better sleep last night, Sylvie had managed to do her usual makeup and hair styling, and Clifford seemed as intrigued as any little kid with her spider decorations. Even if her makeup could only go so far to hide the pain.

"Tell me why you look sad," Clifford invited.

"I'm not sad." More like numb. That was what happened when a heart got broken.

"I know someone who can help with that."

She bit back a sigh. She bet she knew who. It was almost

creepy the number of times people tried to speak to her about God. Almost like all the Christians in this province had a spiritual antenna and thought she needed to hear about Jesus. Still, she'd play along. "Who?"

"Ah, don't go getting too far ahead of yourself. This man doesn't just fix hearts, he fixes eyes too."

Huh. So, it wasn't yet another lame attempt by a faithful zealot to introduce her to Jesus. "I thought medical professionals trained as specialists."

"This one does both. Probably more." He sighed. "I just wish I met him when I was younger."

Was Clifford gay? This might be a faith-based center, but they were accepting of everyone here. Her lips twisted. Which was obviously how she'd managed to get a job here.

"You're looking at me funny."

"I'm sorry. I can't help it. I'm still a little weary from last week."

"Your big drive."

She nodded, conscious that like many of the residents, he thought anything above thirty minutes was a long drive these days. Not that driving was the reason she remained weary. "So, what was it you were saying about this doctor and him healing eyes?"

"That's right." He pointed to the chair. "Settle yourself there. This might take a while."

She obeyed. Honestly, it was amazing that part of her paid role meant actively listening to the stories these older people shared. It felt like a privilege to hear them share about their experiences. "So, was it you who had a sore eye or someone else?"

"It was me." He coughed. "Back when I was a younger man, I used to have a really weepy eye." He pointed to his left eye. "The doctors didn't know what was wrong with me and I used to have to wear sunglasses sometimes to hide it because it got so bad."

"I'm sorry."

"Yeah. It certainly didn't make the girls think I was a catch." He winked. "Lucky for me, I've always had an abundance of charm."

Her lips tweaked. "That is apparent."

"See? I knew you were a good sort, able to recognize that too. Anyway, one day I was going for a walk, and my eye was weeping badly again. So I finally prayed and said 'Hey Jesus, I need to talk to the Father about fixing this eye, and I'm told I need to go through the Son. And that's You. So, I'm confessing my sin and asking you to take it away'."

"Okay." She refrained from rolling her own eyes. She might've known he'd try and bash her over the head with more of this God stuff. "And this relates to your eye how?"

"Next day my weeping eye was dry and back to normal. And I've never had a problem with it since."

Her own eyes widened, her skin tingling. "Really?"

He nodded. "Really. It had nothing to do with me, but every-thing to do with Him." He pointed to the ceiling. "And no, I don't mean Bernard on the second floor. I mean God. So I'm telling you, little lady, if you have a burden there is somebody nearby who is willing and able to take that burden away."

"I'm not burdened."

"Pshaw. Anyone can see you are. Even Artie next door can, and he's blind."

"I don't think God would want to waste a miracle on me."

"Please. He'd love nothing better. You need to ask Him."

She shook her head. "I've prayed in the past, and it didn't work for me."

"How do you know?"

"Because it didn't happen."

"Maybe it wasn't what God thought was best for you."

"Healing my mom of cancer?" she shot back.

"Oh, Sylvie." The deep grooves in his face softened. "I didn't know."

She pressed her lips together. "I…I don't advertise it. You weren't to know."

"How old were you when that happened?"

She shook her head.

"You don't have to tell me if you don't want."

Good.

"But if you ever want to talk, well," his lips tweaked wryly, "you'll know where I'll be."

She nodded, getting up to pretend to straighten some of the potted plants on his windowsill.

"What was her name?" he asked softly.

"Janet."

"How old were you?"

"I was nine when she first got diagnosed," she whispered. "My dad had gone to jail the year before." Which was when her mom had hooked up with vileness. She swallowed. For years she hadn't dared think his name let alone speak it aloud. No way was she going to sully this kind man's ears with what that awful piece of human excrement had done. "Mom's cancer came and went over the next twenty years." Just like her boyfriends. And Sylvie's. "It wasn't easy," she said carefully.

"I'm so sorry."

She shrugged. "It happened. Life moved on."

Except…had it ever, really?

For so long that part of her life had been boxed up and shut away in the furthest, darkest corner of her mind. If she could distract herself from thinking about those days, then it was a good day. She had no emotional energy to unpack that box and face the reality of what that part of her life had been like. People like Bree and Clifford and Ryan and Heather had no idea. Zero. Zilch. The only people who did understand were equally broken, and she had no wish to be the trigger that took someone back to the blackest, most awful time of their life. She had no wish to go there, either.

"You know, not all weepy eyes are on the outside," Clifford said softly.

Oh, she knew.

"You should ask the Great Physician to heal you. He wants to, I know that."

"Thanks Clifford, but I don't think I'm ready for that yet." She'd heard it all from Bree before, telling Sylvie she should ask God to prove himself as being real. So yeah. She'd tried it. It hadn't worked. So that was that.

"How ready do you want to be?" he asked.

"Excuse me?"

"How ready do you want to be?" he asked again. "You maybe haven't heard of the kid who left his father's mansion and blew all his money on parties, drugs, and goodness knows what else."

No, she'd known a few people like that. Even if what she'd lived in was the opposite to a mansion. "Is this another one of your stories?"

"You betcha." He pointed to the chair.

She stifled a sigh and sat again.

"Anyway, this kid spent all his dad's money and had to get a job. Trouble was he didn't really have any great qualifications, so he bounced from job to job till the only one he could find was looking after hogs. So, he was stuck looking after the hogs, even eating their food, and sleeping where they were. He didn't like hogs. Nobody else liked hogs, so they didn't like him much, neither. And nobody else liked being around him because he smelled bad. And it got bad, really bad."

The way this story kept tangling, she wasn't sure if maybe it was real, and not just a metaphor.

"And then one day he decided he'd had enough of living like this. He knew his father still had his mansion, and all he needed to do was to swallow his pride and go there. He figured he had nothing to lose, even though he knew he wasn't clean or smelled good or anything. But the point is he went."

"Then what happened?" she asked, intrigued despite herself.

"Well, all this time, the father was missing his son, and he kept looking out the window, waiting and waiting, hoping and praying that the boy would come home. And then one day, as he was looking out the window, he saw a tiny figure in the distance. His heart started racing, and he hurried downstairs and raced out the door, hoping that this person was his missing son."

She blinked back moisture, looking away to avoid being busted for having emotions. She was tired, that was all. Clifford could tell a good story.

"And when he finally got there it was just to discover that it *was* his son. And he was so happy he hugged him, not caring about how sweaty or dirty he was. Didn't matter he smelled or had hog mess under his fingernails, he was just so happy to have his son home."

"Well, that's a nice story."

"I'm not finished."

"Okay. So what happened next?"

"See, all this time, the son had been rehearsing a story, convinced he wasn't good enough, and that his father would never accept him, especially considering he'd wasted all of his dad's money and done all the things that had made him ashamed. So, when he actually saw his father, he fell to his knees and said 'Hey, Dad, I'm sorry, I'm not worthy. Instead of treating me like your son, I'm willing to work for you and be your servant'."

"And what did the dad say?"

"He hugged him harder, gave him a ring, and new clothes, and told his servants to prepare a party."

"That's awesome."

"And it's real. And that party is something everyone is invited to."

Again, the story seemed to blur between fact and fiction. "Everyone?"

Clifford nodded. "All we have to do is recognize that we weren't born to live with hogs, but in a mansion with a father who loves us."

Now the pieces clicked into place. "You mean God again, don't you?"

He grasped her hand. "You're God's precious daughter. You don't have to live with the hogs."

She pressed her lips together and looked out the window, exhaling shakily.

It was weird how many times in recent days she'd heard similar things. But it didn't mean God was trying to talk to her. She found a smile, pasted it on. "I like your story, Clifford, but I don't think that's true for everyone."

"Why not?"

She shrugged. "I've met people who believe like you do, and they don't want anything to do with people like me."

He nodded. "Yep, just like in this story. I forgot to add that bit."

"What do you mean?"

"Well, when the father wanted to celebrate his son's return, his other son got mad and asked why didn't his dad have a party for him."

"And what did the dad say?"

"He just said I've always had room for you here, what's mine is yours for you to share. But the most important thing is that my lost child has returned."

"So his brother wasn't happy."

Clifford winced. "I've always wondered if it's because the older son wished he'd gone and partied, but had always been too chicken to find out."

"Sure sounds like a real party when it means you're living with hogs."

"See, that's the thing the older son forgot. He kept being focused on the sin, when the father was focused on his son. As Christians, we're not supposed to focus on the actions of the younger son, we're supposed to remember it's about the restored relationship. That's where the father was focused. He loved his son so much, he just wanted him home. But people can be too quick to judge on the stuff that doesn't matter."

She nodded. Like the hogs. Like her hair. Her clothes. She held up her tattooed arm. "They see this and think it means I'm a sinner."

"Well, you are, aren't you?"

"Excuse me?"

"Or are you the only perfect person who's lived since Jesus walked the planet two thousand years ago?"

Huh. When you put it like that... "Look, I know I'm not perfect. But that's beside the point. Even if I did want to join the 'party' there are still people who don't want me there."

"Who?"

Brent. Mike's mom. Probably Mike as well. "People who don't like me."

"Come on, Sylvie. Are you trying to tell me that you've only ever done what other people like? You and I both know that's not true."

"Yes, but—"

"Why would you let someone's ill-informed ideas stop you from doing what will give you comfort and joy?" He tapped his left eye. "And what will help you stop looking like you're crying all the time."

A buzzer sounded, drawing her away. But Clifford's words kept bubbling through her mind. She knew why he'd said that to her. And while she hoped she didn't smell like pigs, she couldn't deny there'd been times in her life when she'd felt like she'd gotten pretty muddy. That she'd wished she didn't have to live this way. That she was tired and wanting a place to fit in where she belonged. But was God waiting, like a patient father the likes of which she'd never known? Did He actually love her, or had Clifford's "miracle" actually blinded him from the truth? It seemed too far-fetched, impossible. And while Clifford seemed to believe it was a real possibility, she knew hope was only a mirage, something that tantalized, before the scent of a delicious roast meal was proved to be the stench of gone-off cat food.

Bree might've invited her to return, but Sylvie knew she couldn't. Well, she could, but not to stay. Life had taught her that she didn't belong anywhere.

Her phone rang. She glanced at the caller ID on screen, her eyes widening. Mike? But she couldn't answer now. Personal calls weren't allowed during her work hours. But when the call ended with no voice message, she couldn't help but wonder what he wanted. He'd probably heard about her and Ryan. Was calling to warn her to stay away. She shook her head at her selfish thoughts. Maybe it was about Bree. She hoped that Bree and the kids and babies were okay.

GAMES PASSED. Dallas, Minnesota. Concussion protocols had seen him miss the next game after a crunch of a hit from Mitchell Reilly, which Ryan had staggered up from, which had instantly earned him a visit to the club physician, and a mandated day off, before a next-day evaluation by the neuropsychologist saw him cleared to play in time for the Battle of Alberta game against Calgary.

It hadn't been the hit that had caused him to stagger. Both he and Mitch knew there'd been no direct blow to the head. More the slam of his ribs into the boards that had caused him to stumble. But admitting that they still hadn't healed fully wasn't something he could do. He needed to play. Staying at home, even for a day, had shown just how lonely things could be.

Sometimes he liked to imagine what it would be like, if he didn't share his apartment, if he had his own place. If he had a wife to come home to, like Chris and Mike. It was a dangerous game to play, because too often a certain dyed-brunette's face would take the features of this mythical one-day wife, and he'd drift into imagining what life with her could be like, before conviction would squash that thought and he'd remember his vow to stay away.

She was temptation. He was still weak. And while Josiah and the rest of the guys might be praying for her, thinking too much about Sylvie was what had gotten him into this mess in the first place. So, it was best if he just… didn't.

He caught Mike and Franklin when they arrived at the arena, and he was glad to have something else to talk about in the minutes he squeezed in to talk with them.

"Saw the hit. Mitch Reilly is a beast."

"He needs Jesus."

"Truth."

"So you're all good?" Franklin asked.

Ryan presumed he was talking about his head. He'd concentrate on that at least. "I rested, recovered, and the doc said I'm back to my neuro baselines and can play."

Mike winced. "I remember when Woletsky knocked me out in that Florida game a few years back. My ribs hurt more than my head, but I was glad to have time off to recover."

"My ribs took the brunt of it."

"Got a nice bruise?" Franklin asked him.

"Maybe not as good as your nose last year."

Mike smiled as Franklin shook his head. "That wasn't very pretty."

"Yet you're gonna marry her anyway, huh?"

"Can't wait. Hey, that reminds me. You two need to save the date."

"When are you talking?"

"June 22 at the ranch. Cassie says they should be able to work it around the movie that's filming then."

"It still seems surreal to me that your family has its own movie set."

Franklin shrugged. "Can't help these things. Families. What can I say?"

For some reason, that phrase triggered a memory, something Sylvie had once said about families coming first. Why was she so focused on that? Then he remembered. She'd lost her parents. Compassion pushed past the frustration that thoughts of her often provoked. No wonder she'd acted as she had. She just wanted love. He forced himself to refocus.

"Speaking of saving the date, I know it's a little early, but Bree and I hope you two might make it to Ethan's birthday party," Mike said.

"Nothing I like better than to eat kids' party food," Franklin said.

Yeah, he sure looked it. The man had a physique that was ripped. "Just tell me when and where."

"I checked the schedule. First day off after the regular season."

"April 20?" Franklin confirmed, getting a nod. "I'm in."

"I'll be there, too," Ryan said.

"Good."

Franklin was called away, leaving Mike with Ryan. "Have you had anything more to do with Sylvie?"

He choked. "No. Why?" How much did he know?

He shrugged. "Brent mentioned a while ago he'd seen the two of you at a hotel—"

"We were having dinner, that was all."

"I believe you."

"Yeah, well, I broke up with her that night, so there's nothing to see here." He folded his arms.

"Broke up? You were going out?"

He huffed out a breath, looked away. "If you can call it that. We went out a few times, it didn't work out, so we've moved on."

"Have you moved on?"

"Dude, why do you care?"

"Because you haven't seemed like yourself for weeks now. You're avoiding us, and when you've showed up, it's like you're missing in action."

So he obviously hadn't done a great job at hiding his mess. "I haven't known what to say."

"Just say it," Mike said softly.

Ryan exhaled heavily. "She's not a Christian. I thought she was, but I was wrong. And now I feel like an idiot, okay?"

"Hey." Mike placed a hand on Ryan's shoulder. "You're not an idiot."

"I still care about her, but I can't afford to think about her, or even pray for her. I feel messed up. And a little humiliated, if I'm really honest, especially to have Brent there."

"What if Brent was there for a reason?"

"My conscience, huh?"

"Did you need a conscience reminder?"

Yes. He'd known his kisses weren't exactly of the meek and mild variety. He glanced away again.

"Don't answer that question."

"We didn't do anything but kiss."

"Hey, I'm not being Holy Spirit's little helper here. But I am your friend, and your brother in Christ, and I know I've been distracted, but if you want to talk, I hope you know I'm always here for you."

The lump in his throat meant he couldn't speak. Could only nod. He was turning into such a wuss.

Mike half-smiled. "So, you haven't heard from her?"

"No. Why?"

"I tried to call her to invite her to come stay to surprise Bree, but she didn't answer. I hope she's okay."

Ryan frowned. Mom had mentioned that Sylvie had barely spoken to her at work, which made him realize that she probably hadn't admitted the true state of their relationship to Mom either.

He winced. That was something he would probably have to explain when he saw his parents on Friday night. Awesome.

CHAPTER 15

The days passed with Sylvie continuing to put up her hand for extra shifts. More shifts meant more money, meant less time at home filled with regrets, or avoiding the creepy guy next door. And working at Aspen Lodge, even if some of the residents didn't seem to have excellent memories, at least made her feel useful.

Monday saw her back again, tucking in Mrs. Androvsky's quilt, smoothing it flat around the woman's spindly legs. Oh, the challenges of getting old.

Her thoughts turned to her own grandmother. How was she doing? She didn't want to feel sorry for the woman who had spurned her own mom, but maybe she was helpless like this, needing attention like this. "Androvsky is a Ukrainian name, isn't it?"

The elderly woman nodded. "My husband—my second husband, really, after my first died, God rest his soul—was involved in the local association. His father had come out after the war. But he always considered himself Canadian first."

Her chest thudded. Of course. She should have realized

there was likely to be a group like that around here. "My grand-parents were Ukrainian."

"Really? What were their names?"

"Esther and John Melnyk."

"I'm sorry, dear. I don't recall anyone by that name."

Well, it had been worth a try. She'd known not to get her hopes up. Sylvie packed away the dirty plates, then straightened the room and moved to the door. "I'll see you again tomorrow."

"Very well, dear." Mrs. Androvsky paused. "Esther?"

Her name was Sylvie, but whatever. "Yes?"

"Did you say Esther?"

"I did."

"Ah."

Sylvie didn't have time to suddenly develop patience. "I need to go and see—"

"I knew an Esther once."

Hope immediately bobbed, like a life preserver tossed in a lake. Oh, the heart was a funny thing, so desperate to cling to anything that might buoy the spirits. "Really?"

"Yes. But she wasn't married to a John."

Oh. Those fickle hopes plunged straight back down. "It's okay. They've probably died anyway." She winced, as Mrs. Androvsky looked out the window again. Was she allowed to make comments about death here? It seemed insensitive, even if it was true. People didn't get younger, here. This wasn't *Cocoon*.

She pushed her trolley from the room, only to almost bump into Heather. "Oh!"

"Sorry, I didn't mean to startle you. I couldn't help but over-hear you before. Who has died?"

Sylvie shook her head, not able to look Heather in the eye. "Nobody."

"Did I hear the name John?" Heather smiled. "That doesn't sound like a nobody to me."

"Oh, it's just somebody I was trying to find. But it doesn't matter. I need to get to Mr. V's—I mean, Mr. Vettori's room."

Heather studied her for a moment then nodded. "Well, when you get a spare minute, can you come and see me in my office?"

Her stomach tensed. Oh no. She nodded, Heather smiled, and Sylvie's feet slowed as she went to the next room. Surely that meant Ryan had finally told his mom about their breakup. Which meant she was going to fire her. Judging from that smile she'd probably be nice about it, but she was going to have to look for another job.

She attended Mr. Vettori and then slowly moved to Heather's door. Was it bad to wish for an emergency so she didn't have to face her? She rehearsed her lines for the possible conversations Heather might insist on having:

I'm so sorry for hurting you, and for hurting your son even more.

Yes, I tried to seduce him, but I know that was wrong.

I agree, I shouldn't be working here, but I hope you'll still give me a second chance.

She knocked, hoping with all her might that Heather wouldn't answer.

"Come in."

No joy. She pushed open the door.

Heather looked up from her computer, pulled her glasses from her nose, and gestured for Sylvie to take a seat.

"Thank you."

Heather leaned back in her chair. "There's no need to look like that. I won't bite."

Memories flashed of Ryan saying something similar. She pressed her lips together.

"That." Heather pointed to her. "What did you just think now?"

She couldn't admit to what Ryan had said.

"And don't think I don't want to know. I *do* want to know."

Fine. "Ryan." His name sounded foreign spoken aloud after

floating through her head for so long. "Ryan once said something similar."

"That I don't bite?"

Sylvie nodded, lowered her gaze.

"How is he?"

So she truly didn't know they'd broken up? Tension increased.

Heather sighed. "We've barely spoken in recent weeks."

Sylvie blinked back emotion. She knew that feeling too well.

Heather shook her head. "I know that boy loves me, but he's never been the best at communicating. I expect you're finding that out too."

Sylvie offered a half shrug-half nod movement. This was ag-o-ni-zing.

"Anyway, I'm looking forward to seeing him after his game on Friday night."

Great. So she might have her job until Friday.

"We should go up together." Heather smiled. "It'd give us a good chance to talk."

Bless the woman, but this was excruciating. "I, um, I'm not going. I've got other plans." Which probably consisted of painting her nails and avoiding creepy pizza-and-beer dude next door.

"Well, I don't mind saying I admire a woman whose life isn't so entwined around a man's that she feels obliged to watch his every game."

Go the sisterhood.

"But having said that, I miss you coming to watch the games with us—"

No. Heather wasn't going to ask her to join them again, was she? How could Sylvie ever avoid spilling the truth?

"—but looking at the hours you've been doing, I can understand why. You've been doing a lot of shifts, Sylvie."

How to answer? Maybe with a simple, "Yes."

"So, you're enjoying your work here?"

Her shoulders eased a fraction. "The residents are lovely, and the staff are great. Very supportive."

"Well, you've obviously made an impression. I keep hearing good reports about you. I knew we were right to take you on."

She probably wouldn't think that once she found out about why Ryan had broken up with Sylvie. Words floated through her mind: *Tramp. Skank. Whore.* She shook her head.

"No, it's true." Heather obviously misread that shake of the head. "I'm very glad. You being here has lightened the load for others, and they're thankful too. But you're not overdoing things, are you?"

"No. I just like to keep busy." Being busy meant distraction.

"But you are enjoying it here?"

Affection for this kindhearted woman rushed her to say, "I'm truly very thankful for this opportunity. And I want you to know I'm prepared to do anything to stay." There. If—when—Heather learned about the breakup, then she'd hopefully remember that Sylvie still appreciated this opportunity, would remember her words, and somehow keep her on.

"You don't need to prove anything to me." Heather's smile reached her eyes. "I'm even hearing stories about some of the residents wanting to get their own tattoos."

Sylvie's mouth sagged. "I didn't know that. I certainly haven't encouraged that at all."

"You don't need to worry. But I did want to check in with you and make sure you weren't overextending yourself."

"I'm fine." Was that it? She could leave? She slipped forward in her chair. "Is that all?"

"Yes. Oh! I wanted to ask about these people you mentioned before."

"Which ones?"

"John someone?" Heather's face creased into a smile. "I think you might've thought they'd died, perhaps?"

"Oh." She shrugged. "I can't remember if I mentioned before that I had grandparents who lived in Red Deer. They're my mom's parents, and I wanted to find them." To know why they hadn't showed at Mom's funeral last year. What kind of parents ignored their only child's death? Unless they were too sick or ill to travel. Or dead.

"What were their names?"

"John and Esther Melnyk."

Heather nodded, writing down the names. "I'll ask around. I'm sure someone knows something."

"You don't have to. I don't know that they'd want to see me even if I was to find them."

"How can you say that?"

"Because they pretty much cut off my mom, which is why she moved three provinces away and built a life there." Not that it was much of a life.

"I'm so sorry."

Her lips twisted. "I think that's part of what I enjoyed about going to your place, seeing your strong family connections. It's something I haven't experienced in a long time." If ever.

"You know you are very welcome anytime at all."

She shook her head. "Thank you, but it's a little complicated now."

"I know. It's easier when Ryan is there, but you should know that Pete and I want you to feel welcome for your sake as well. Come visit us any time. We could watch a game together, or just have a meal. It would be good to have some more time with you."

It would be good to enjoy another home-cooked meal. She was so over baked beans. "Thank you."

"Let me know when suits. You could come visit this Saturday, if you like. Ryan is playing in Seattle, I think."

Sylvie nodded. He was.

"But of course, you know that." Heather smiled.

Oh, she'd be disappointed when she found out Sylvie had been basically lying.

"And if not this time, then maybe we can go together the next time he's playing in Edmonton. We could make a night of it, have dinner with him afterwards."

Her smile faded. Yeah, that definitely wasn't going to happen.

"I hope we can do something soon."

"That'd be nice."

"Just make sure you're not working too hard."

"I will." She pushed to her feet, smiled, and hurried from the woman whose kindness she would have to avoid. She needed an excuse to stay away from her.

Even if Heather seemed to hold the keys to something that part of Sylvie still craved.

THOUGHTS OF HEATHER'S invitation pursued her home, chased her through sleep, sat with her during her daily breakfast of a Pop-Tart and tea. She'd basically lied to the poor woman. Had basically pretended she and Ryan were still together when they weren't. How terrible a human being was she to have acted like that?

An image of a person swimming with hogs came to mind. She shook it away. She wasn't that bad. Was she?

Her phone rang. Mike. What did he want? After avoiding his last calls, she had to answer. "Hey Mike."

"Sylvie? How are you?"

"Great." Her voice sounded stiff. But the fact he'd been nearly as persistent as his wife in trying to contact her proved he was trying to connect. She had to give him a chance at least.

"Look, I'm sorry for bothering you as I'm sure you're busy, but I wanted to ask you if you want do a favor for Bree."

"For Bree? Sure. If I can."

"Are you free this weekend?"

"Free for what?"

"I wanted to surprise her by taking her out for dinner."

"That's a nice idea. So, you want me to come babysit?"

"Not exactly."

"Aren't your mom and dad around to do that?"

"It's their wedding anniversary, and he's booked them a trip away, and I was hoping we could borrow you for this weekend."

"They won't be there?"

"No."

She sighed, the tug of obligation making it hard to say no. "Bree has asked me to come visit."

"So you'll do it?"

"If I can swap my shifts." Not that that should be a problem, seeing as she'd been saying yes to covering so many others. Some of the other aides owed her big time. And if she visited Bree this weekend, she'd get out of feeling obliged to attend Heather and Pete's and avoid the awkwardness there. "What time and where?"

He didn't know if he was the world's biggest fool, or if this was just fate, but the irony of his dad choosing the very restaurant where Ryan had planned to take Sylvie seemed too much. Then, knowing there'd be questions about her, about them, was filling his heart with fear. This wasn't like with the Bible study guys. He couldn't shrug things away or turn off the screen. His parents were here, in his face, and he'd need to face them with the truth.

But it was way past time he did so. And owning up to his mistakes was like a pimple he needed to pop, get the whole ugly messy truth out there. And pray that they didn't take it out on her. He'd hate to be the reason she lost another job. Again.

"Ryan!" His mom opened her arms and hugged him.

"Good game, Son," his dad said.

"How are you feeling? Are your ribs okay? You looked like you were moving a little stiffly at times."

He winced. If his mom saw that in the stands, what were his coach and trainers seeing? Nobody wanted to advertise their weakness. Opposing teams would watch footage and know they could target him.

"Not good?" his mom asked. "Are you sure you're okay to play?"

"Mom, I wouldn't be playing if the doctors hadn't cleared me."

"But your ribs? How are they?"

"They ache every so often, but that's normal."

His dad smiled. "Come on, let's order. You can continue the interrogation once our food is on its way."

His dad shot him a wink, and he nodded, mouthing a "Thank you."

Their server appeared, they ordered, and conversation centered around the game, the team's upcoming travel to Seattle, and more.

"I asked Sylvie if she would be here tonight," his mom said. "It's such a shame she was busy."

He swallowed. "Yeah." Such a shame. But seriously? Mom still didn't know? Then the thought of what Sylvie would be busy doing snuck in, stealing his relief. Was she on a date? Out clubbing? Red Deer had a few. Although he didn't know many a Goth girl like her would be welcomed at. Or which she'd deign to attend.

"So, how are things with you and Sylvie?"

"Leave the man alone," his dad said.

Ryan shot his father a look. Did Dad know the truth?

"She said that things have been a little complicated. I hope everything is okay."

He downed his water to avoid answering. Oh, he was such a tough guy.

"She mentioned something about her family, too."

He glanced at his mom. "Really?"

"Mm. Something about her missing grandparents."

"They're missing?"

She sighed. "I gathered from what she said that her family life has not been easy. I've always noticed how Sylvie's face tightened when family gets mentioned. What do you know about hers?"

"Not much." There was so much he didn't know about Sylvie. So much he hadn't known. So much he longed to know. But now it was too late. Conscious his parents were watching him, he shrugged. "She never said much, apart from being out here to find and reconnect with her grandparents."

"The ones who are missing," she clarified.

"I guess so."

"Do you mean missing like in some *CSI* way?" Dad asked.

"I don't think we're talking murder. But it was funny, when I looked up their names I couldn't find them, either."

"Were you checking out her story?" Maybe his mom would learn the truth. Like how this woman she apparently would like as a daughter wasn't even a Christian. Despite lying about that too.

"You should talk to her then, honey," Dad said to Mom.

"Poor girl." Mom shook her head.

"Why poor?"

"Oh, it must be so hard for her, having lost both parents, then unable to find what family you still have."

He ducked his head. He'd forgotten that.

"She keeps herself locked tight, that one," Dad said. "Oh good. Here comes our food."

Like his mom was some kind of snake charmer, able to lure thoughts of Sylvie from where they'd been confined, memories of her continued to twist through his meal. What was she doing now? Where were her grandparents? How had her parents died? Sympathy rose, stealing through his emotions, chasing each mouthful of flavorsome steak.

Sylvie was like that, he realized. She flavored his thoughts, his emotions, his heart, his family. His parents loved her. Which meant this pretense couldn't go on any longer.

"Mom, Dad, I need to tell you something."

"What's that, Son?"

He placed his fork and knife on one side of his plate. "We're not together anymore."

"What do you mean? Who isn't?"

"Sylvie and I. We, uh, broke up at Valentine's Day. Actually, the night before."

"What?" His mom blinked at him. "Why are you only telling us now?"

He shrugged. "I didn't know what to say."

"You tell us the truth, that's what you say."

"Why'd you break up, Son?" Dad asked.

Ryan stared at his plate. "She's not a Christian."

"But she said she was."

"I think she was confused about what a real Christian actually is. I think she thought going to church was enough. But it's not."

"No."

"Oh, Ryan. I'm so sorry." His mom clasped his hand and squeezed.

"I didn't want you being upset at her or for her to lose her job."

"What? I'm not about to fire the best aide we've had on the floor in years. I didn't hire her because of you. I hired her because her CV was excellent, and I knew she'd bring a special spark to the place, and she has." She pushed her pasta to one side. "I can't believe you'd think I would make decisions like that based on my son's dating life."

Okay, then.

"So, she needs Jesus, huh?" Dad said.

"Yes." Images of her dressed like she was on that last terrible night danced through his mind. *God, forgive me.* "She really does."

"Then we pray."

"Yeah."

"And we do all we can to show her that she's loved and accepted." Mom picked up her knife and fork. "No wonder the poor girl didn't tell me herself. She must've thought I didn't want her there."

Probably.

She pointed a knife at Ryan. "You need to be careful though, and guard your heart."

"That's what I've been doing, Mom. I can't talk to her. I've struggled to even pray for her, because she's like this vine that's there, sucking away all my good intentions."

"Sounds like you need more Jesus too."

Didn't everyone? "Probably."

"Okay, then." Mom straightened, snapping back into businesslike mode. "So, we pray. And ask God to help her know how much she is loved by Him. By Him first." She eyed Ryan.

"I know, Mom. I don't want her dependent on me, and I especially don't want her faith to be dependent on me."

"And yet how Christians treat non-Christians so often determines how they see God."

He inwardly groaned. So what had Ryan's actions said? What were they saying now?

"I think that woman has faced enough hurt and rejection in her life. And it's time she found God's love and finds a family in Him."

Amen.

"Sylvie!" Bree's arms held such comfort as she hugged Sylvie. "Oh, I can't believe it. Mike said he had a surprise for me, but I never believed it would be this good." Her voice quavered. "Do you know I've prayed for this to happen?"

She had? Now Sylvie was getting teary.

"Oh, my friend, I've missed you. Now come inside." Bree led the way indoors. "It feels like ages since we last saw each other. How are you?"

"All the better for seeing you." It was true. The moment she'd pulled up outside the Vaughan house she'd felt peace settle on her. "You look great, Bree."

Bree sighed. "I've lost some of the baby weight, but I'm afraid I'll never be as slim as I'd like."

"You're alive, Bree. You've got a body that works, that does what it was designed to do, and that's something to be glad about, right?"

"Wow." Bree's purply-gray eyes widened. "Look who's gotten all motivational. What's been happening in Red Deer?"

"Not much."

"Something has," Bree touched Sylvie's hair. "Judging by the new hair color." Her eyebrow lifted. "A new man?"

Sylvie sighed. How much did Bree know? Maybe neither Brent nor Mike had shared as much as she'd thought they would've by now. "It's over."

"What's over? Who? I need details. Sit down. The babies are asleep and I'm making chai. And you're spilling all the tea."

Sylvie sank into her usual place at the kitchen table, but before the kettle switch could be flicked, Ethan was running toward her, screaming her name, little Ellison toddling behind him. "Sylvie!"

She picked him up, blowing a loud raspberry on his neck.

He instantly wriggled and laughed. "Do it again!"

She obliged, then took a long moment to hug the little boy, before a tug at her skirt drew her attention to his little sister. "Hey sweetie."

Ellison lifted her arms, her cue for a hug, and Sylvie drew her close, breathing in the sweetness of the little girl. Her eyes filled, and she tried to hold back the tears, but they insisted on spilling with a loud sob.

"Why is Sylvie crying, Mommy?"

"I don't know, sweetheart," Bree said, before drawing closer, and tucking an arm around Sylvie. "Hey, it's okay."

It wasn't. She didn't know why she was crying either. But something about being back here, back with people who loved her, who missed her, felt so, so good. Like maybe the sewer of her life might somehow get turned upside down and she could find sunshine and roses again.

But when Ethan wrapped his arm around her legs too, and said "Don't cry, Sylvie," her sobs became wails, and she had to hand a startled Ellison to Bree, then sink her face into her arms on the table, tears soaking her sleeves, snot slipping out, as Bree placed a hand on her back and rubbed gently.

She wanted *this*. She wanted family. And it seemed so impossible. Everything she did she messed up. She wanted love. What was wrong with her? Why couldn't she feel peace?

Gradually she became aware that Bree's hand had stilled, and that heat seemed to be flowing through her back. That Ethan's little voice was murmuring, "God, help Sylvie. We loves her."

She turned, wiped her nose, and wrapped him in a hug. "I love you too."

He let her hold him for a while then drew back, placing his little hands on either side of her face, his blue eyes solemn, yet holding light. "And God loves you too, Sylvie."

God. Her heart prickled. "Really?"

He nodded.

"How… how do you know?" she asked him, half-unbelieving she was having this conversation with a four-year-old.

"Because He told me."

A broken chuckle escaped. "Who told you?"

"God."

She peeked at Bree, but she was focused on her son.

"Mommy and Daddy pray every night for our family," Ethan continued. "And you're part of our family, Sylvie."

Her lip wobbled, then she broke down again, her tears blurring her vision as she pressed a kiss to Ethan's head, holding him near. "I'd like to believe that, but…"

"It's true," Bree said softly.

Did Bree really think that? She wiped at her wet eyes, caught Bree's nod, as an almost tangible wave of warmth flowed through her. Maybe she *could* afford to think herself loved.

Ethan wriggled from her grasp. "I missed you."

"I missed you too, little man." She propped her head in one hand, as Ethan clasped the other. Why had she turned her back on this? They might not be related by blood, but this love was what she wanted. Needed. How could she have turned her back on Bree and her family? "I'm sorry for going away. You're right. We *are* family."

"I know," Ethan said, as if he hadn't dropped a bombshell. "And then I was praying for our family, and God said that He loves me, and Mommy, and Daddy, and Ellison, and Maddie and Matthew, and you."

"Me?"

He nodded.

"God said this to you? That He loves me?"

"Yep!" He looked up at Bree. "Hey Mommy, what's that verse that Granny always says?"

"Which one, sweetheart?"

"They did it at Sunday school this week."

"Oh. You mean the one about God loving the whole world —"

"Yeah! That's the one." He turned and patted Sylvie's cheeks. "Your face is wet."

"I know."

"You need a tissue. Your nose is running. Mommy always says I need a tissue when snot comes out."

"I know." She could barely breathe. But it wasn't just from tears clogging her nose. Bree handed her a tissue box, and Sylvie blew her nose, and turned back to Ethan. "Is that better now?"

"Yeah. But your eyes are red. They match your hair." He pulled across a chunk then watched it fall.

"What was it you were going to say before, Ethan? About the whole world…" Bree prompted.

"That's it!" He grabbed Sylvie's hand. "God loved the whole world so much that He gave"—he peered up at Bree. "What did He give, Mommy?"

"His only S—"

"His only Son," Ethan rushed to say, "that everyone who b-believes in Him will not die but will have eternal life." He beamed at her.

"You said that so well, Ethan," Sylvie said, as her heart tumbled and turned.

"Isn't it good? It means that God loves everyone." He flung his arms around her neck. "And God loves you." He emphasized this with a big kiss on her cheek.

God loved everyone. And God loved her.

Loved *her*.

She scarcely dared believe it. "You don't think I have to be good enough?" she asked Ethan.

She didn't know why she kept asking him, but it felt like there was something safe in the little boy's innocence, the way he looked at her so seriously like he was old beyond his years.

"No." He peeked up at Bree then whispered to Sylvie, "I'm not always good, but my mommy and daddy still love me."

"You have good parents, Ethan. You're very lucky."

"Granny says she doesn't believe in luck. She says we're blessed."

"You *are* blessed." So blessed, so fortunate to have a family who cared so much.

"And so are you." He smiled. "Because God loves you, even if you do bad things too."

"Does he?"

Ethan nodded, while Bree moved closer, Ellison in her arms.

"You know he does, Sylvie." Bree winced, and Sylvie quickly took Ellison from her, settling again in her seat with Ellison's head tucked between her chin and shoulder, her little thumb in her mouth.

"You know the next line of that verse says that God did not send His son into the world to condemn the world, but that the world through Him might be saved," Bree said softly. "In other words, God *wants* the world to be saved. He wants *you* to be saved. Because He loves you, Sylvie. God loves you."

"I've messed up so many times."

"But He still loves you."

"I don't feel like I belong."

"Our feelings aren't as reliable as facts. And the fact is that God loves *you*. He wants you as part of His family."

No. It seemed impossible. But Bree and Mike believed. Heather and Pete. Old men like Clifford, too. What if they were all right, and she'd been wrong?

Something kept tugging at her heart, that same heavy presence she'd experienced at the christening service all those weeks ago. "I don't know what to do."

"You don't have to do anything. It's not about your efforts, or how good you are, or about being good enough for God to notice you. He's already noticed you, Sylvie. He already loves you. All you need to do is pray and talk to Him. Ask God to show you His love, help you to know, *really* know, that you are His child. It doesn't matter what your family is like, or what hurts you have suffered, God's love is here for you now, and He wants you to know you're His child."

Like the father who'd waited for his lost son to come home.

What was it that Clifford had said? People focused on the sin more than the potential for a relationship. Maybe it wasn't only Christians who did that.

"God loves you, Sylvie," Bree said softly. "He's waiting for you to come home."

She crumpled again. She knew she wasn't perfect, that she was broken and had broken others, and was filled with regrets. But if God could see past all of that and still love her, then maybe she could take a chance on Him. "What do I need to pray?" she whispered.

Bree drew a chair beside her, wrapped an arm around her, and asked Sylvie to repeat after her. "Lord, thank You that You love me."

She echoed it in a whisper. It was true. She now deeply sensed that God *did* love her.

"And that you sent Jesus to die for me."

He loved so much He'd sacrificed His own son to die in her place.

"So that I can have eternal life."

She sniffled, and prayed this too.

"I believe You, and I want to have this new life."

Oh, new life. New life! Without the stains of the past, without the regrets. Oh, how she *longed* for this.

"And experience Your peace, and a hope, and a future in You."

Peace. Hope. A future.

"And follow Jesus all my days. In Jesus's name, Amen."

"Amen."

Amen. She kept her eyes closed, one second, two seconds. Then a sense of peace rushed through her heart, like a giant fresh, clean wave. Her eyes filled again, but this time with happy tears, as she could see the gunk and pain and all the hogwash she'd believed for years being washed away. She might feel battered and bruised, and as naked and helpless as Bree's babies, but she also knew she was loved. *Knew* she was loved. By her Heavenly Father. The one who waited so patiently, yet had run to meet her and wrap her in His arms of love.

More tears flowed as she turned to Bree, and her friend wrapped her in a hug. "I'm so happy for you. *So*, so happy," Bree murmured. "I've been praying for you for years."

"I think those prayers have kept me alive." Sylvie grabbed another tissue.

Ellison protested, and Bree eased back, taking the little girl in her arms. "Oh, we must look like such big messes, hey, little girl?"

"You need a tissue, Mommy," Ethan said.

Sylvie laughed, then Bree laughed too, then Ethan joined in. "You're funny, Mommy."

"I know, sweetheart. Mommy can't help it."

That kicked off a new cackle of laughter from Sylvie, who

was feeling giddy, wondrously light and free, for the first time in years. Maybe ever. She stroked Ethan's hair. "Thank you, Ethan. You'll never know how much I needed to hear that."

"That Mommy is funny?"

"No." She giggled. "That verse before. Where is it? I'm going to have to look it up."

"It's from the Bible, the book of John, chapter three, verse sixteen," Bree said.

"So, the verse after…?"

"John, chapter three, verse seventeen." Bree smiled.

"Granny says it's the best verse in the Bible," Ethan announced.

"I think your Granny is right." Sylvie glanced up at Bree, and mouthed, "Granny?"

Bree smiled. "Mike's mom."

RYAN PLAYED his game against Seattle, then the next, an at-home against Pittsburgh, before a road trip east took him to Boston, Columbus, Buffalo, then home again. In that time, he worked hard, scored a goal, assisted on two others, spoke to his folks, and prayed a lot, for his family, for himself, and for Sylvie. That God would work in her heart. That he would learn to let her go from his. That she'd find peace and a sense of family. That God would heal both of them.

On his first Tuesday back, his first day off in way too long, he was tempted to go visit his folks, but the thought of yet more travel seemed too much. Besides, he could actually attend the online Bible study, after missing the last couple. Not that he wanted a repeat of last time by any means.

"Missed you, bro," Chris said, when Ryan logged on.

"Road trips will do that."

Luc exhaled. "We just had a killer. I mean, Florida and Texas are sure warmer than The Peg, but man, I'll be really glad when it's summer and I can just relax."

"Summer seems so far away," Jai said.

"Especially when you gotta get through playoffs first." Chris grinned. Vancouver was tracking to make the playoffs top of their zone this year.

"Your boy Zac is playing hot," Franklin said.

"Right? Everyone's wondering what Parotti has been eating lately, because he's on fire. If he keeps playing this well he'll be getting our team's nod for the Richard Trophy."

The award given to the NHL's leading goal scorer and named after Maurice 'Rocket' Richard, who led the NHL goal scoring five times in his eighteen seasons with Montreal, once scoring fifty goals in fifty games. Total legend.

"There's still time for you to get a few more, Chris," Luc joked.

The screen filled with smirks at the thought of the goal-tender getting any goals, let alone forty-plus. Yet it had happened, once or twice.

"I think there's something very wrong with that picture," Josiah said.

The study soon focused on today's topic of patience, and Ryan leaned in, the verses feeding his soul. He needed this encouragement. Needed these guys in his life. He might not like what they had to say all the time, but they did have his best interests at heart.

Brent had reached out a few more times, Mike and Luc had checked in, too, but a few texts weren't the same as this kind of conversation.

They talked, shared, prayed, gave prayer requests, and got updates.

"Mike couldn't be here tonight," Franklin said, "but wanted to say thanks for your prayers. Things have settled down with the kids a lot."

"Awesome."

"Great."

"That's good."

"Oh, and your prayers have worked. Their babysitter, Sylvie, has returned."

Ryan's heart clenched. She had? Why didn't he know? Why hadn't Mom said anything? Why hadn't Mike?

"You okay there, Ryan?" Luc asked, with a big ol' smirk.

"Yeah." He rolled his neck, popped a fake yawn. He didn't need eyes on him. He wanted off this call and onto one with his mom, and find out what had happened. Did Sylvie not work there anymore? Why didn't he know?

"Oh, and before I forget, Hannah and I have set a wedding date, so keep June 22 free if you can."

"We should've wrapped up the Cup by then," Chris said smugly.

"Gotta win it first," Luc jeered.

"Watch this space."

"Yeah, and back to me," Franklin said, earning a few guffaws. "Honestly, we'd really love all of you to be there, so if you can tell your significant others that'd be great." He smiled. "And Luc and Ryan, if you plan to have significant others, then get on with it, as Hannah and my sister, Cassie, are planning things and will need numbers soon."

"Yeah, nothing to see here," Luc said, folding his arms.

"How about you, Ryan?" Jai asked. "Did anything more happen with that lady friend of yours?"

Ryan blinked. "I don't know what you mean," he lied, his voice cracking.

"You know. The bookstore girl." Luc smirked. "I believe her name might be Sylvie, right?"

"Not Mike's Sylvie," Josiah said, with a frown.

"She's not Mike's. Mike has Bree, remember?" Luc winked. "This one is Ryan's. Or was."

"Wait—the babysitter we're praying for to become a Christian? You had a thing with her?" Chris's face held incredulity. "Wow."

The disappointment loading that word pummeled deep inside. He'd been friends with some of these guys for years now, and yeah, he understood their confusion. He'd be as disappointed with any of them who had done what he had, and flung themselves into a relationship with someone who wasn't equally yoked, as the Bible described it. He'd failed them, just like he'd failed himself. And God. And Sylvie.

"I did, and it's over." He folded his arms. "Never to return."

"Except if she becomes a Christian, right?"

He ducked his head, as the tease and chatter ceased, and he clamped his lips together so hard he thought they might bleed. He couldn't afford to think like that. Wouldn't dare to think like that. Sylvie needed God, not him. It was best he left her well alone.

"Dude."

He didn't know who said that, but he couldn't afford to find out, as emotion roared and he shook his head. He could've earned himself a trophy for leading faker in the NHL as he finally lifted his head, faked a smile, and muttered, "I've gotta go."

"No, dude, don't—"

He pressed "Leave Meeting" then sank his face into his hands, as hot moisture burned in his eyes then slipped between his fingers.

His phone started buzzing, and he knew that'd be most of them checking he was okay.

He wasn't. But he couldn't answer. He was clinging to God, but his emotions were hanging by a thread.

"God," he prayed, his voice as raspy as a saw, "I really need some help here."

CHAPTER 17

That first weekend back at Bree's had turned into two, then three, as her shifts allowed for weekends off. She hadn't wanted to go to Heather's church, not feeling an inclination to run into bookstore owner Marie, whom she suspected she owed an apology to. Neither did she want to explain to Heather what she was doing there. Her new faith felt so fragile, like the first tender shoot of a snowdrop, that she wanted to protect it a little longer. And while she knew that Heather could be trusted, the fierceness of the woman intimidated Sylvie, and she knew that as soon as Heather knew, she'd be inviting her to all kinds of things. Who knew? Maybe even pushing her to get back with Ryan. She still couldn't believe that she had her job after Heather had said Ryan had told them. Or that Heather had been so kind about it.

But she couldn't even afford to think about him. She had too much mess to sort out. And Bree was great in listening and offering advice when Sylvie asked. What a difference that was to advice that was given without being asked. Bree had offered to help her with studying the Bible, and on Sundays took her to church in Calgary. Bree had told Mike about Sylvie's new faith, with Sylvie's permission, and Sylvie had begged him not to tell anyone else.

"But why not?" Bree had asked.

"I don't want anyone thinking I'm doing this because of Ryan. And I don't want him thinking that either."

"We won't say anything to anyone until you're ready." Bree had smiled. "I hope you'll let me tell Regina."

Sylvie had shaken her head. "I'd rather keep that a surprise too."

"Just show up at church and take communion?"

"Something like that."

She knew from reading her new study Bible that communion had something to do with believers gathering together, remembering what Jesus had done. But surely she could never forget this wiped clean feeling, like her soul had been dipped in the most powerful bleach, stripping out all stains and shadows. Jesus had died on that cross. For *her*. Even if there had been nobody else on this planet, she knew He would've done exactly the same thing. Because He loved her. That amazing love still overwhelmed her. She knew that a person who could heal the sick and raise the dead could've busted off that cross if He chose. Instead, it was love that kept Him on that cross, not nails. And that immense and overwhelming love sent her to her knees every day. She would never forget, could never forget, God's love.

Bree had also encouraged her to seek out a Christian counselor, and the sessions with the counselor was helping Sylvie deal with the past. A past Bree hadn't known, until one day, during a fierce storm at Bree's house, when Ethan and Ellison had run to hide, Sylvie had comforted them, and admitted she used to run and hide when things were scary too.

"You don't anymore?" Ethan had said.

"I'm trying to be braver now."

He traced her spiderweb behind her ear. "Did that hurt?"

"A little bit. But only at the time."

The storm had passed, and she'd soon tucked them up in bed, before rejoining Bree and Mike downstairs.

"Are the kids okay?"

"They are now."

Mike smiled at her, and she smiled back, glad that the tension from several weeks ago seemed to have gone.

"It's really good to have you back here again," he said.

"It's really good to be back. Even if it is only on weekends."

Bree threaded her fingers through her husband's. "You know I've been grateful for your mom stepping in, but I have to say it's been really nice to have Sylvie here."

"I think Mom and Dad are enjoying getting a little bit of space, too," Mike said.

"Boundaries are good."

Sylvie nodded. Boundaries *were* good. Keeping her focus on God, and on work, and on life-giving friendships that nourished like this, was about all the capacity she had these days. She'd drawn a line in her heart and mind not to think on anyone who might distract her from this. God would have to deal with that for her.

"I don't know why the kids get scared of storms," Bree mused. "I don't remember being that way when I was a kid." She poked Mike. "It must be from your side of the family."

"Must be," the tough defenseman agreed.

Sylvie snorted, which drew Bree's smile.

"So what did you say to them?"

"Just that I used to like to hide when I got scared."

"You don't seem scared of storms now."

"It wasn't storms I was afraid of back then."

Bree straightened, and joined Mike in watching her carefully. "What were you afraid of?"

She swallowed, her hands twisting in her lap. But she was learning that being vulnerable was necessary for healing and going forward. And seeing Bree hadn't judged her last weekend when she'd admitted to her failed seductress tactics on Ryan, she figured this couldn't be any worse.

"You don't have to tell us if you don't want," Mike said kindly. "Or I can leave the room—"

"No, it's fine." She sighed, her stomach knotting. "It's just something I haven't admitted to many people." Except the counselor. And God.

"What is it, Sylvie?"

She straightened her fingers, was tempted to duck her head, but instead looked them in the eyes. These dark truths about her past weren't going to keep her prisoner anymore.

"You know my mom died a year ago."

Bree nodded, her lips flat, brow puckered.

"I don't know if I told you that my real dad went to jail when I was eight."

"Oh my goodness." Bree's eyes were wide. "I didn't know that."

"Why should you? I don't go advertising that to everyone."

"What did he go to jail for?" Mike asked.

"Drugs. He died in there." She shrugged. "My mom was addicted for a while, too, then she got sick. All of that was probably why..." She bit her lip.

"Probably why?" Bree asked softly.

"Probably why she didn't notice when her boyfriends used to act up when I was around."

"Act up?"

Some people were so innocent. "They used to suggest things we could do when Mom wasn't around."

Bree covered her mouth with both hands. "Sylvie."

"It's why I started going out when I was pretty young, looking for guys who could maybe beat some of Mom's boyfriends up." She swallowed. "Mom had one boyfriend who used to beat me when I said no, so I used to go hide in the closet when I knew he was angry with me." Which could be anytime, really. When he was drunk. Or high. Or feeling low. There was no way to know. Her mom sure had set the bar high when it came to relationships.

"Anyway, Mom did her best, but she was struggling with her treatments. Eventually it became one of those things where I'd see what she did and decide not to do the same, but keep failing and do it anyway."

"Oh, like when I decide to diet," Bree said, "then chocolate appears and I can't help myself."

"Yeah, something like that." Not at all like that. She'd much rather have worn the effects of her poor decisions on her hips than on her heart.

"I'm really sorry this happened to you," Mike said.

She shrugged. "Others have had things worse."

"But that doesn't negate the fact that this shouldn't have happened to you," he said, his look as serious as his son's.

No. It shouldn't have.

"Did you report him to the police?"

"There was no point. He died in a car accident soon after that." One of the best days of her life. *Sorry, God.*

"What about other family members who could've helped?"

"Mom's parents lived in Red Deer, and I still remember them rejecting her, looking at Mom and looking at me, calling us tramps."

Bree's breath sucked inwards.

"They didn't even go to her funeral last year. I'd even sent them a letter telling them."

"Oh, Sylvie." Bree moved beside her and hugged her. "I'm so sorry."

"It's in the past."

Although it had shaped her to this very day. Her eyes traced the tattoos on her arm, as a chunk of magenta-dyed hair swung past her cheek. Who would she have been if she hadn't gone through all that? Would she be as sweet and innocent as shocked Bree? Maybe. But maybe going through all of that had helped make her tough. The counselor had helped her recognize that she sometimes used her clothes and tattoos as a shield, a kind of defense system as she figured out that those who rejected her first weren't the ones worth fighting to be friends with. But God kept whispering His love song to her, so maybe it meant she could leave it in the past.

"It *is* in the past," Bree agreed. "And God can redeem anything."

Sylvie nodded, knowing now that was true. "And I'm trying to leave it there, but some things bring it back."

"Like friends who prod." Bree sighed. "I didn't know."

"I know you didn't. But I'm glad you now know. But honestly, looking back, I know I made choices that were wrong, but things could've been worse."

Bree grasped her hand. "If it's any comfort, I've always liked that you are a tough, sassy chick."

"And now I think about it, coming here was a Godsend, although I didn't know it at the time." Another shrug. "I felt so lost when Mom died, that I needed something new to focus on. So to come here, to get a fresh start, was awesome."

Bree and Mike smiled at each other, then Mike's head tilted. "Did you ever tell Ryan any of this?"

"No." His question, the searching way he looked at her, bugged her. She had to know. "Why?"

"I spoke to him not so long ago."

Her heart skittered. "Not about—"

"No. It's up to you when you tell others you're a Christian. But I hope you'll do it soon and put the poor guy out of his misery."

"I'm not strong enough to deal with him yet," she murmured.

He nodded. "I know he regrets a lot of things."

"He's not the only one."

"You don't have to deal with him now," Bree assured. "But when you're ready, he'd probably really benefit from knowing some of why you've done what you did."

Sylvie nodded. "One day."

Just not any day soon.

She drove home Sunday afternoon, thankful to have missed Regina again at church this morning. It seemed Regina preferred the earlier service, which suited Sylvie fine. She was another person Sylvie needed to talk to, and another person she was happy to leave conversation with for another time. She rolled her eyes at herself. Tough chick, that was her.

She pulled in at her dump of an apartment, heart tensing at the sight of Pizza Dude from next door. She didn't like the way he looked at her sometimes, nor the way he beat on the walls in the middle of the night, calling out drunkenly. Still, she was trusting that God would keep her safe. Bree had encouraged Sylvie to pray for a hedge of protection around her, and while it sort of sounded silly, she did feel greater peace believing that God had His angels watching over her, ready to intervene.

"Hey, Sylvie. How you doin'?"

"Fine." The past years had taught her to never exhibit too much emotion or too much interest in guys she didn't want attention from. That's how bad things always began. Too much eye contact. The wrong tone or inflection.

"Wanna watch the game tonight?"

"No, thanks. I've got to get an early night."

"Come on. I know you like hockey."

Because he'd seen her here with Ryan. Fresh regrets massed. "Not so much anymore."

"Then what about football?"

"What about it?" Ah, she might be redeemed but Ms. Snark was still alive. "Night."

She closed the door, and locked it, then double-checked she'd locked it properly.

Night it literally was. Not a good night. Not when he kept complaining loudly, beating on her door. Calling her all kinds of names she'd heard plenty of times before.

But she *wasn't* that girl anymore. The Bible told her so. And words of abuse could remain just words. She didn't need to let them enter her soul.

He kept at it though, annoying other neighbors who told him to shut up, until she wondered if she should call the police. The closet here wasn't big enough for both her and the mice.

She retrieved her Bible and read over the verses Bree had highlighted for her. Romans, chapter five, verse eight: *God demonstrates His own love for us in this: That while we were still sinners, Christ died for us.*

Pizza Dude was just a sinner, who needed God as much as she did.

She flipped to Psalms. Found the bookmark in number ninety-one, and spoke it aloud from verse two. "I will say of the Lord, He is my refuge, and my fortress, my God, in whom I trust. Surely He will save you from the fowler's snare, and from the deadly pestilence. He will cover you with His feathers, and under His wings, you will find refuge; His faithfulness will be your shield and rampart. You will not fear the terror of night, nor the arrow that flies by day."

She huddled on her bed and closed her eyes. "Lord, I don't want to be afraid. I don't want to fear the terror. Keep me safe."

"Sylvie? What's wrong?"

It wasn't any wonder Heather was asking. Sylvie was unsteady on her feet, giddy for all the wrong reasons. "I had a noisy neighbor last night and didn't get much sleep."

Heather's nose wrinkled. "Do you need to take your break early?"

If her break involved a bed and sleep, then absolutely. "I should be okay."

"I don't think so. Go. Have a rest on the couch in my office for ten minutes. I don't want you falling asleep on the job."

She obeyed, thankful for her boss's understanding, and shifted the box of files and curled up on the couch, setting her alarm for ten minutes.

Heather returned, just as the alarm started bleeping. Ten minutes definitely wasn't long enough. "Are you doing okay, sweetie?"

Sylvie nodded.

"I know something is different about you, but I don't feel like I get to see you much these days. You know that offer for dinner is always there."

"Thanks, Heather. But I'm really okay."

"Apart from that noisy neighbor, eh?"

Sylvie shuddered. "Apart from him, yes."

Heather chewed her lip, but Sylvie's next patient waited, so she went to speak with Clifford, Mr. Vettori, then Mrs. Androvsky. By the time her shift ended she was in a zombie-like state of exhaustion.

But Heather was waiting for her again. "Got a spare moment, Sylvie?"

One always had to have a spare moment for their boss, didn't they? "Sure."

Heather closed the door, gestured for Sylvie to take the chair while she sat behind her desk. "Look, this may be me speaking out of turn, but I haven't been able to stop thinking about it. Are you okay? I mean, do you feel safe where you are staying?"

Sylvie pressed her lips together.

"I'm going to guess from that expression that the answer is no." Heather sighed. "Maybe I shouldn't be saying this, but Ryan did mention that your apartment is not exactly the most salu-brious of accommodation."

Salubrious didn't sound like a Ryan word, but what did she know? "It's what I can afford."

"Can you afford to feel unsafe?"

"I don't have any other option."

Heather studied her for a moment. "Yes, you do. Come stay with us."

What? "I…uh, thank you for the offer, but I can't."

"Why not?"

For so many reasons. Not least of which was Heather's son. "It would be, er, awkward, especially as…as Ryan and I aren't together anymore."

"I know that, Sylvie."

"And you still want me to come?"

Heather shrugged. "We have room, and it's not like he's due to come visit any time soon. He's on another road trip, and even when he has his next day off he's unlikely to come visit."

The sadness lacing Heather's voice tugged at her. But she had to remain strong. Heather obviously didn't know all that Sylvie had done. "I don't think you would really want me there."

"Of course we—"

"I tried to seduce him," she blurted.

Heather's eyes widened, and she was quiet for a long moment. "Would you do that again if he were there?"

"No."

"Why not?"

Sylvie licked dry lips. "Because…because I know it was wrong. I knew it was wrong then, but I *really* know it now. I…I became a Christian recently. I thought I was before but now I really understand."

Heather placed a hand on her heart. "You're a Christian?"

Sylvie nodded. "My friend Bree prayed with me. And her son, Ethan." She half-smiled.

"Oh, sweetheart." Heather hurried around the desk and hugged her. "I'm so glad."

The tears in Heather's eyes sparked Sylvie's own. Man, she'd never cried so much since she'd become a Christian. "I am too," she admitted shyly.

"Oh, Sylvie." Heather's smile seemed to have captured sunbeams. "You have no idea how thrilled I am about this."

She was getting some idea.

"That's it. You're definitely staying with us. At least until we can find you a better place to stay."

"But I don't want to upset Ryan."

"Like I said, he's not there. He's not said anything about coming home soon, and even if he does, it's not like you have to stay in his room. We have another spare room."

"I can't."

"You *can*. But you simply can't go back to a place where you feel unsafe. You definitely can't do that. *Please* come. I'd love to hear about your salvation story. It's honestly one of my favorite things to hear. And Pete and I and Ryan have all been praying for you—"

Ryan had? "I thought he hated me."

Heather smiled. "He doesn't hate you. I think he hates himself for what he wanted to do. He hasn't been himself much lately, either."

Sylvie's heart twisted. No. She had to be strong. "I really shouldn't—"

"You really should. We can come with you and get your stuff today, and you don't ever need to be worried about a weird scary neighbor again. And Pete is cooking tonight, so it's guaranteed to be amazing."

"I don't know if his cooking can be better than yours."

"And you won't know unless you come. Please? Say you'll stay."

Sylvie mock-sighed. Sometimes persistent people could be a

very good thing. "Fine. Thank you. But I'll only stay until I can get another place." And she'd be doing all in her power to make that happen as soon as possible.

The hours before sunset saw a flurry of activity between her and Heather's arrival at her apartment, and packing up and removing her items. Pizza Dude scratched himself and watched, but she ignored all his lewd suggestions, as Heather prayed under her breath, and looked about to cross herself at the state of the place.

They drove to Heather's, where Pete soon warmly welcomed Sylvie, hugging her after Heather announced her new Christian status. "Good on you, Sylvie. Best decision ever." He glanced at his wife. "I know someone else who'll be pleased to hear this."

"Please don't tell him," Sylvie rushed to say. "I didn't make this decision because of him, and I don't want him to think that I did."

Heather nodded. "We won't say anything. You do need to talk to him but when it's the right time. And it's not that time yet, is it?"

No. It still wasn't.

Heather refused to let Sylvie use her own bedding, suggesting it should be burned after the vermin-infested state of the apartment she was in. "At least you should wait until it's all been washed and we can make sure any critters have drowned or been spun-dried to death."

"She doesn't like her critters, this one," Pete said proudly.

"We've had too many residents join us at the home who have had issues with, er, pests, so don't take it personally, Sylvie. No, don't use that pillow. We've got another one somewhere."

A moment later she returned with another one. Blue check. "Use this."

It was only much, much later, after Sylvie had enjoyed a meal and shared about her salvation experience, and a little of the story she'd shared with Bree and Mike, which drew both

Heather and Pete's tears, that she was able to shower and change into pajamas and snuggle into a bed that she knew was clean and fresh as anything at Bree's place.

And while she burrowed into the bedding, the Cool Water scent of the pillow drifted to her, and she realized where she'd seen this particular pattern before. On Ryan's bed. Her heart clenched as she imagined him dreaming on this pillow, his face pressed against it, and yearning stole through her again for what would never be.

"Good game, guys. Nice assist, Ryanator." McHale fist-bumped Ryan.

The plaudits continued as he went down the tunnel, the Jets fans a little subdued. Ryan had caught up with Luc for the promised steak at lunch, before a quick pregame nap, then the game, then they'd escape the arena for the two-hour flight home.

It'd be past midnight by the time they arrived, but with their three-game winning streak away, which had led Coach to make tomorrow's team skate optional, he was planning on opting not to.

He liked his teammates, but he needed to get away. Needed time to himself.

Needed time to process what Luc had said at the steakhouse where they'd had lunch.

"You know we care about you, bro. So, stop isolating yourself. Don't think you're in this on your own."

"I just feel so dumb."

"Do you really feel like you're the only one who has ever been sucked in by a pretty face?"

"Have you?"

"No. But then, I am pretty close to superhuman."

"Supersized ego, perhaps."

Luc had tugged Ryan's plate away. "Finished with your meal, huh?"

Ryan tugged it right on back. "Just because my steak was cooked better than yours."

Luc shook his head. "Crazy. You'd think they'd pay attention to wanting to impress their top goal scorer."

"You better advertise that a little more."

Luc laughed. Then got serious again. "Look, you can't keep living in the past. You need something new to focus on. Maybe you and I should take up Mike's offer and go to the Philippines this summer."

Ryan nodded. Focusing on something other than himself had to be good. And focusing on those who were far less fortunate was a helpful way to gain perspective. Mike and Bree had started fundraising for a kids' mission organization based in the Philippines that Mike was the spokesperson for, and some of the Bible study guys had visited the children sponsored by MPFG. Mission Possible for Future Generations helped underprivileged children gain education and other life-enhancing opportunities. Ryan had a couple of sponsor children and it would be good to finally meet them in person. "That could be a good idea."

"Full of good ideas, here," Luc tapped his forehead.

"Full of it, for sure," Ryan teased.

Luc shook his head. "I'm not hearing a lot of gratitude for your amazing steak."

"I am very grateful," Ryan said. "I do appreciate you taking time to eat with the enemy before a game."

"Not an enemy, you're a brother. Which is why I hope that after everything that's gone down that things are cool between us. I don't want you to have hard feelings about what I said before."

He forced himself to meet Luc's brown gaze. "You mean about Sylvie?"

"Look, God has got her on a journey, and you never know, she might get saved one day soon. Franklin mentioned that she's been hanging with Bree and Hannah some weekends recently."

What a turnaround from the last time they'd talked. How did Luc know all this anyway? "For a guy who always complains he doesn't like all the talk about relationships, you sure seem to talk a lot about relationships."

"Look, I'm not opposed to it. Just don't need it for myself. Not until I finish my hockey career anyway."

"So you're not going to go chasing a girl until you're in your mid-thirties, huh?"

"I don't have time for a relationship. I've seen what it does to all of you, and no offense, but I don't plan to get all emotional like I've seen you guys do."

"You know emotions aren't bad. Even Jesus wept."

"Yeah, but he didn't play hockey and have a reputation to uphold now, did he?"

There was no arguing with a guy who clearly thought emotions were a waste of time. "I hope you meet your Miss Right this summer."

"Hope all you like."

"That's it. I'm going to pray really hard that God will bring the right woman to finally turn your bachelor head."

"Yeah, good luck with that." Luc rolled his eyes. "Anyway, back to you. I don't think you should be scared to ask God to give you and Sylvie a second chance. *If* she becomes a Christian first, of course."

"Don't worry. I've learned my lesson. I'm not going there again."

"Even if she does become a Christian?"

He shrugged. The thought seemed impossible, which might not say too much about his faith right now, but he barely dared consider the what-ifs should that miracle happen. What if he stuffed things up again?

"Well, as they say, turnabout's fair play." Luc pointed at Ryan. "If you're threatening to pray for me, then I'll double that in prayers for you that your Miss Right shows up one day soon."

Ryan nodded. Except he didn't want someone new.

He was still thinking about this when they finally returned home, past midnight like he'd expected. But he couldn't sleep. Mats had made no secret about his plans with his girlfriend, and while Ryan didn't want to be a prude, he also didn't want to be exposed to the activities that would be going on in Mats' room soon. He needed to get out of here. And go…where?

A thought crossed his mind, so he grabbed his keys and, ignoring Mats's protests about the late hour, hit the road.

Nighttime was the best time to drive the Lexus. Less traffic, apart from freight trucks, which meant he could push it to top speed. Fortunately, they hadn't had much snow lately, so the road conditions were good and it meant he got to Red Deer faster than he usually did. He slowed as he entered the city limits and drove to his parents' place. The lights were off, and he picked his way around to the back door, where the hall led to his room, the route his usual one when stealing in late. He opened his bedroom door, snuck inside, closed the door and turned on the light. Something was out of place. He couldn't quite put his finger on it, but…Huh. There was only one pillow. That was weird. Nobody used this room except him.

Whatever. As if the sight of his bed reminded him of his exhaustion, he stripped off his clothes and got into it, annoyance about only having one pillow strumming beneath his weariness. He probably should book tomorrow to visit the

Philippines if he was having a hissy fit over something as dumb as this.

He sighed, and closed his eyes, and nearly drifted off, when a noise came from the hall. He tensed. His parents' room was at the other end of the house. Was an intruder here? He pulled on his track pants and picked up an old hockey stick. Bauer boasted about making every shot pop. He sure hoped this stick would prove that.

He crept to the door, stick in hand, conscious he probably looked like a killer from a bad movie. He jerked open the door.

Only to see Sylvie, her eyes wide with fear, before she screamed and raced back down the hall to the spare guest bedroom and slammed the door.

What the—? He blinked, rubbed his eyes. What was going on? Was this even real?

His dad appeared, his own hockey stick in hand, blinking as the hall light turned on. "Ryan? What are you doing here?"

"Uh, surprise."

"Was that you screaming?"

Come on.

"Or was it Sylvie?"

"Sylvie's here?" So he hadn't just dreamed those really cute batwing-decorated PJs?

"Is she okay?" His dad started to the guest room.

"Yeah, Dad, she's fine." He hoped. "I heard a noise, and scared her. I wasn't expecting to see her and she sure as heck didn't expect to see me."

His father pointed at the guest room door. "Do I need to sort this out or do you?"

How could he face her after what had gone down at the hotel? But then, how could he not? Sooner or later he'd need to, and it looked like sooner was right now. Man. Sometimes he really wished he wasn't an adult. "I probably should."

"Yeah. You probably should. I'm gonna have to tell your

mom it was a wild animal." He hugged Ryan then tapped him on the chest. "Put on a shirt, wild animal, and don't scare that girl anymore. Oh, and welcome home."

He obeyed, then moved back to the guest room and lightly tapped on the door. "Sylvie? It's Ryan. Are you okay?"

There was no answer.

Huh. She couldn't have gone to sleep yet. That scare had to involve an hour's worth of adrenaline, at least. "Look, I'm sorry about scaring you," he said softly. No way did he want his mom coming out here to investigate. Dad would already have his work cut out for him to keep her away. "Sylvie? You don't have to open the door, but just tell me you're okay."

Still nothing. Concern ramped up. *Was* she okay?

"Hey, you're starting to worry me now. I'm just gonna open the door." He opened the door slowly, peeking inside.

The bedside lamp was on low, its golden light spilling across the rumpled sheets—and his pillow. Huh. So there it was. Had she taken it? Wanting a souvenir? But the fact she'd run away and not toward him said maybe she didn't still harbor such feelings. His heart wrenched, but he kept looking around. Where *was* she? She couldn't have vanished, and he would've seen if she'd returned to the hallway. Was she under the bed? No. Another peer around the room revealed only one more place.

The closet.

SYLVIE'S TREMBLING was making the clothes above her move. She had to stay still, very still, then he wouldn't find her. A kaleidoscope of memories flashed from the past. The beatings. The whispered words. The threats. The searching hands. She shrank back as the murmured voice came again.

Cover me with Your feathers, Lord. Keep me safe, and—

"Ahh!" Light flooded the closet, and she shut her eyes.

It might not be the past, but the present threatened to cover her with fresh shame. He must be so angry with her still. Would think she was stalking him. Would think her a creeper. And she wasn't! Even if she'd glimpsed his chest and known she'd take that sight to her dreams she hadn't done it intentionally. She *hadn't*. She'd only needed to get to the toilet and now her bladder was really protesting, but she didn't want to move in case he thought she was coming onto him again. Breath escaped in a shudder.

"Sylvie?"

She squeezed shut her eyes more tightly as there came the squeak of hangers being moved.

"Sylvie? What are you doing in here?"

She cracked open an eye. He'd put a shirt on now, which was a shame. Another glimpse might've fueled her with enough energy to pack her things and drive to Bree's right now.

"What are you doing in here?" he repeated.

She inched away from the wall and shifted her cramping legs. She tried to speak. Couldn't. Swallowed, then wet her dry lips. "Isn't it obvious?"

He huffed in disbelief, and shook his head, his gaze intent on hers.

"I'm checking my clothes are hanging correctly."

"Is that so?" His head leaned against the closet door. "Are you staying there all night?"

"Depends if you plan on hitting me with that hockey stick." He hated her. Had been so angry with her. Wouldn't want to see her again.

"Hey, I'm sorry." His face, his voice, softened. "I didn't know it was you."

"And if you had?" God bless her propensity for too-quick words.

"I would never hurt you, Sylvie."

Too late for that.

"Even though I can tell that I have." His head ducked down, then he shook his head, as if frustrated with himself. "Shall I leave you there or do you need a hand?"

She stared at his outstretched hand, then up at him, sensing he was trying to help in more than a simple escape from the closet. Which meant this could be her opportunity to practice some of that forgiveness the Bible seemed to go on about, and take her own steps toward reconciliation.

His fingers twitched, and fearing he would withdraw, she clasped his hand and let him help her up and out. Before the pins and needles in her legs saw her stagger and slump back to the ground. "Ow!"

"Whoa." He instantly bent to help her, drawing her to himself, and she wasn't above taking a delicate sniff of his neck. So much better than the pillow. Then his arm tightened around her shoulders for a fraction, before he froze and dropped his arm and stepped away, like she might be contaminated with Ebola or something.

Mortification writhed within, like a dozen snakes. Oh, how awful. He didn't want her. He *shouldn't* want her. She mightn't have a killer disease but he obviously wanted nothing to do with her. Which was only fair. Now she knew what she knew, if a half-dressed man had tried to entice her to bed, then taken her by surprise dressed in his nightwear, then gone crazy and hidden from her, she'd be right to be concerned. It was actually amazing he remained at all. She would *never* live down that awful moment from Edmonton. And she so shouldn't have sniffed him just then.

By now the pain in her legs had eased, and she staggered to the bed, ignoring his outstretched hand. No way did she want to appear like she still needed his help. She grasped hold of the bed and leaned on the mattress to help her stand. New embarrassment heated her cheeks. She must look as decrepit and frail as the aged folk she cared for, who suffered all matters of indignities due to falls. Shame thickened, deepened, simmering across her skin in heated waves.

"Is that my pillow?"

He was asking about his stupid pillow at this moment? Any hopes of pretending he might care dissolved. "Your mom gave it to me to use. But hey," she picked it up, "take it. And then go away."

"Sylvie."

She held out the pillow, shaking it, as she crossed her other arm across her chest. Why did she have to choose these pajamas to wear on this day of all days? "I don't need it."

He glanced at the bed, his face crossing with a strange emotion, before meeting hers again. She jerked her gaze away. Then tossed the pillow at him.

"Sylvie, please."

"Would you mind leaving? Or are you going to insist on staying there until I do?" She shivered. She had no idea what time it was but she was cold. She tugged the fluffy blanket off the bed and wrapped it around her, still keeping her gaze averted. No way was she going to give the impression she was that loose woman from before. She wasn't now. God had saved her.

"I don't want to upset you—"

"Too late for that," she muttered.

"Fine." From the corner of her eye she saw him bend, pick up his pillow, then leave, before pausing in the doorway. "Sylvie, I'm really sorry—"

"So am I." She hurried to shut the door in his face and raced back to the bed, tears spilling as she began to cry.

She woke at dawn. Resolution had firmed during what sleep she'd snatched in the night. She had to leave. Had to find somewhere else to stay. She couldn't risk seeing him again. It had been enough of a risk sneaking past the door to his room to finally go to the toilet, when her only option had been that or wet the bed. She hadn't heard a peep when she'd tiptoed past—he probably had his door locked and barred—and she'd returned to her room to huddle in her bed. But not to fall asleep easily. Because seeing him, having him so near, only reminded her of what couldn't be, and made her sick with shame and worry. God might cover her with His feathers, but shame had crept under there too.

She slowly eased from the bed, glad it didn't squeak. She didn't want to do anything to wake him up. Then she quickly packed her bags. She would leave. Then the happy family could continue being happy, and she wouldn't have the agony of seeing the man she'd loved toss her away again like all the others. She swiped at her cheeks. Not that he was anything like the others. He'd only used her kisses, not her body. But still. It hurt almost as much. So to leave was the best option for everybody. She'd been so stupid to agree to come here.

But when she made it down the dark hallway it was to see that the kitchen lights were on. Her steps slowed, and she peered into the kitchen, heart beating fast. Oh, thank goodness. It was only Heather, sitting at the table with a mug of coffee and a book.

Heather glanced up, her smile fading as she saw Sylvie's bag. "What are you doing?"

"Thank you for the chance to stay here, but I can't stay any longer. I'll find another place today."

"Why can't you stay?"

Didn't she know? "Ryan returned last night."

"He did? And he didn't tell me? Oh, that son of mine." She shook her head, patted the chair beside her. "Come on. Sit down and tell me about it. I was just reading my Bible. Oh, help yourself to coffee if you need." She gestured to the pot.

"I'm okay."

"Are you sure?" Heather peered at her. "You look like you need a cup or three."

"Fine, then."

As she moved to pour herself a cup of coffee, Heather said, "Sylvie, sweetheart, you don't have to pretend you don't want something just to be polite. Just be honest." She pointed to the nearby chair. "We could do with more honesty around here. I bet that was what Pete went to investigate. He should've told me Ryan had returned."

Sylvie took her seat, sipped her coffee. It sparked instant alertness to her brain.

"Now, tell me what happened."

Sylvie placed the cup on the table, studying the faded pink and yellow roses on the inside of her cup. "It was late, and the only reason I knew was because I had to go to the bathroom and then he heard me and came at me with a hockey stick—"

"What?" Heather's shriek would wake the roosters.

"—and I hid in my room but he came in—"

"Oh, that boy."

"—and I couldn't face him. I still feel so ashamed."

"What did you do?"

"I hid in the closet," she whispered. "I used to have to do that as a kid when I was scared, and…"

Heather grasped her hand. "And you were scared of him?"

She nodded.

"You know he wouldn't harm a flea."

"I know. But in that moment, I had a flashback and was so frightened, and then when I realized it was him I was so embarrassed and ashamed, and now I don't want to be here. I can't face him, Heather. I need to leave."

"Honey, no. You need to face your fears."

"I can't."

"You can." Heather tapped her opened Bible. "I was reading this just now. God hasn't given us a spirit of fear but of love, power, and a sound mind. Fear is just the enemy whispering for you to not trust God. And when you prayed that prayer of salvation, you became a new creation, remember? The old has passed away, the new life has come."

"I don't feel very new right now," she whispered.

"Sometimes our feelings aren't to be trusted. This, however," Heather tapped the book again. "You can always count on God's promises."

She sure hoped so.

Heather's grip tightened. "Can I pray with you?"

Ryan could barely breathe as he watched Sylvie nod, then bow her head, and his mom begin to pray. He kept himself ruthlessly still, not wanting to give away a single movement to alert them to his presence. Maybe he was being a creeper, standing here in the kitchen doorway, nearly out of sight, but when he'd heard her sneak past he'd had to follow, had to try and make things right. Just hadn't realized how much things had already been made right if she truly was a Christian as his mom seemed to believe.

Sylvie followed God now? His heart tumbled over this information. Why hadn't she said something? Why hadn't his mom? Was that why they'd opened their home to her? Did Bree and Mike know? Why didn't he know? Did this mean they might have a chance?

But no. He couldn't afford to feed his heart one scrap of that hope. He had to shut thoughts like that down. Fast. She might be saved, but it didn't mean God thought they should be together. He'd wrecked that, letting lust get in the way of real love.

Regrets kneaded his heart, as sorrow at his actions squeezed within. How could he have ever thought himself immune from the danger of playing with fire? He wasn't nearly as strong as he'd once believed. There was a penalty for love when it came in the wrong season, and he—they—had paid the price. The only good thing was if it had somehow led her to find Christ.

Watching Sylvie now, seeing her brokenness and distress, remembering the way she had backed away from him, barely looked at him, revealed a very different woman to the one he had last encountered in Edmonton. She was a different person, and if she was a Christian, then she was a new creation. As was he.

That thought hit him and made him leave them to their sacred moment and steal back to his room. The shame he'd been feeling since Edmonton was as much of a weight as the fear that came from the enemy. He flicked open his phone's Bible app and tapped in that verse. Yep. Like he thought. It was from second Timothy, the first chapter, verse seven. He read it again. *For God has not given us a spirit of fear, but of power and of love, and of a sound mind.* He tapped on a different translation. *For the Spirit God gave us does not make us timid, but gives us power, love, and self-discipline.*

He winced. Then tapped on another version, which this time gave the last phrase as self-control.

He mightn't be a Bible scholar, but the message was clear. God, who had redeemed him, had placed in him a life-giving spirit that filled him with power. Not his own power, but godly power. Same with love. Same with the ability to exercise wisdom and good judgment. He'd had plenty of moments when he'd been chasing Sylvie before when he'd not exercised those things. But though the shame threatened to swallow him, he didn't have to live there. He could throw off the shackles of sin and shame and not live under the fear that too often in his life had paralyzed him.

He might be quiet by nature, but God called him to not live

timidly. He wasn't a coward. God had redeemed him just as He had redeemed Sylvie, and empowered him, which meant he could own a godly confidence again.

Shame was like fear, a whisper from the evil one who wanted people to shrink back and not trust that God's forgiveness and grace was enough. But he knew he was forgiven. Knew he had been set free. Knew he didn't have to live under this weight. God had set him free.

It was time to start living like it.

He stayed in his room until he heard a vehicle drive away, not because he was afraid, but because he didn't want to cause Sylvie any more embarrassment. When he got to the kitchen, he saw his dad, who half-smiled at him.

"The coast is clear."

Ryan pointed at his dad. "Not clear enough."

"If you wanted it to be completely clear, you should've stayed in Edmonton. What brought you here anyway?"

"I was too hyped after the last game, and Coach made training optional, and I knew this was my only chance to see you guys for a while so I took the chance while I could."

"And didn't expect to find a pretty brunette, huh?"

He sighed, slumped at the table, scrubbed his face with his hands. "What is she doing here?"

His dad chuckled. "Your mom thought you'd be asking that question."

"She knows I'm back?" Duh. Sylvie must've mentioned it.

"She saw you this morning, listening as she was praying."

A wry chuckle escaped. Of course she had. Eyes in the back of her head, his mom.

"Apparently Sylvie was being harassed by some creepy neighbor, so your mom, God bless her, decided to bring her back here." He lifted his coffee mug at Ryan. "None of us expected you to show up."

"I can leave."

"And disappoint your mom? You know she's now planning your favorite supper."

Tempting... but, "I don't want to stay if it makes Sylvie uncomfortable."

"Then you probably need to talk to her about it. Or at least call your mom and ask her opinion." His dad winked. "And we both know she's never short on them."

Whew boy. Good thing he'd just been reminded to be brave.

"So, what are you going to do today?" his dad asked.

Apart from man up enough to talk to his mom, at least? He didn't want to push Sylvie until she was ready. "I thought maybe you might need some company."

"I'm going fishing."

Ryan smiled. "That's what I hoped you'd say."

MOM MIGHT BE the more vocal of his parents, but Ryan could always trust that what his dad said would be worth listening to. For as long as he could remember, people had commented on how Ryan and his dad shared a similar easygoing personality and laconic sense of humor, which meant they could sit for hours saying nothing, but both still be happy. He wondered if he could do that with Sylvie.

When he got home from Sylvan Lake her car was still there. He braced, prayed, then went inside to speak to her, finding her in the kitchen. Sylvie glanced at him, then froze, avoiding his gaze. His heart twisted. Still, he had to say what he needed to say. "Sylvie, I'm sorry for scaring you last night. Please forgive me."

She pressed her lips together, darted a glance at him then

back somewhere over his shoulder. She wet her lip, then finally murmured, "It's okay. I forgive you."

Those last three words sent an effect like crashing dominoes through his chest, as further apologies and questions threatened to burst. He wanted her to stay, so he could make things right, so he could learn about how she'd come to faith, but the way she kept looking at the clock suggested she had somewhere else to be. "Do you need to leave?"

"I, uh, need to go soon to get to Bree's."

"Please don't leave for my sake."

Her lip curled, just for a microsecond, but he saw it. "I'm going for mine."

"I'll be gone tomorrow," he rushed to assure. "I could even leave now if that makes you feel better."

"Away from you makes me feel better."

His heart bent in two. "I'm really sorry, Sylvie. About everything."

She nodded, her gaze still averted. "I'm sorry, too."

HIS APOLOGIES CHASED her to Calgary, and she relived the way he'd seemed nervous, the way she'd dismissed him out of hand. He probably thought she was being rude again, that Miss Snark was back, but it was her only way of keeping herself together, and not crumbling. Heather's words might've helped this morning, but she'd felt fragile all day, and knowing he was there, so close yet so far away, was torture. Hence her brain-wave to go a little earlier, and keep Bree company as Mike played away. Hopefully she would soon find alternative accommodation. Or at least have secured a promise from Ryan that he wouldn't return unexpectedly. It felt a little wrong to expect the man to stay away from his family home, but she wouldn't let him toy with her emotions again. She had to be stronger than that. The verses Heather had shown her reminded her that she *was* stronger than that, because of what God had done.

Her chin tilted, as she saw Calgary's high-rises appear on the horizon. She could do this. Get through the next few days with Bree, who probably would not shy away from asking questions, but at least Bree's was a safe place. Safer than the Guillemettes' would be. For while she'd physically been safe, the fact that their house was filled with Ryan, filled with his life, his dreams, his memories, meant she was better off staying away. It didn't help that she was starting to love Heather as the mother she had never really known. But Heather was Ryan's mom and as such would always be loyal to him. Which was how it *should* be. She hoped she could trust that what she'd said to Heather would be safe and not shared. With Bree, she didn't have to worry about that to the same degree.

She pulled up, her stomach tensing as she recognized a vehicle in the drive belonging to Mike's mom. That was unexpected. But hey, if the Bible could be believed, then Sylvie was a new creation, and she didn't need to worry about what this woman thought of her. Besides, a part of her was grateful for what Regina had imparted to Ethan, which had led to that moment that had changed her life for good.

She pushed back her shoulders, knocked on the door. It was opened by Regina. "Oh!"

Sylvie pushed a smile past the fear. "Hi Mrs. Vaughan. Sylvie, remember?"

"I don't think I could forget."

Awesome. This would go well, then. "Is Bree in?"

"Ah, yes. Come this way."

Sylvie pressed her lips together, not liking the woman's officious ways, but hey, she could now appreciate how Sylvie must've appeared very odd to Regina's worldview.

A missile on little legs ran toward her. "Sylvie!"

She bent and opened her arms, stumbling back a little as Ethan hugged her tight.

"I loves you."

"I loves you back," she murmured in his ear, before blurting a raspberry on his neck which drew his shriek of laughter.

"Hey Miss Popular," Bree called from the lounge, her arms holding two tiny babies.

"Hey yourself, Momma." She gently removed Ethan's clinging hands from her neck, then said to him, "Can you take me to your babies?"

He nodded, grasped her hand, and led her to the lounge while Regina watched, her mouth a tight bud.

But Sylvie didn't need to take on her disapproval. Right now wasn't about this woman but about her daughter-in-law, whose weariness might be masked by a smile, but was apparent, anyway. She gestured for a sleeping baby, and Bree handed her tiny Madeline, and Sylvie cradled her, as Ethan gently patted the baby's face, crooning in a high babyish voice he'd probably copied from his mom or grandma.

"Is that your special sleeping song?" she asked him.

"Mommy does it, and so does Daddy."

Amusement poked out in a smile at the thought of a tough hockey player singing a lullaby to a tiny child. "Maddie seems to like it. It's working."

"I know."

She smothered her laughter, pressed a kiss to her fingers then to his cheek, before mussing his hair. "Where's Ellison?"

"She's coloring."

"Are you going to color too?"

"Want me to draw you a picture?" he asked.

"Yes, please. Can you draw me a dinosaur?"

"Yeah!" He nodded. "Want me to make him big and scary?"

"Yes, please."

"Okay."

With a last pat and a kiss for his tiny sister's head he clambered off the couch and ran to the other room, leaving Sylvie to take a breath as she caught Bree's giggle. "Why do you have such a sweet kid?"

"Um, hello? Sweet mom here." Bree waved a hand, then her face softened. "He's such a good boy, isn't he?"

"It's the legacy of his family and upbringing," Regina said.

Sylvie couldn't look at her, feeling the judgment in those words as she studied the innocent sweet face of a sleeping Maddie. Families did have legacies. She was proof of that. Her grandparents had rejected her mom after her mom's bad choices. Her mom had in her own way rejected Sylvie. Sylvie was only too aware of her own bad choices. But she didn't want to pass that on anymore.

"I'm really grateful for our godly heritage," Bree said softly, as she kissed tiny Matthew. "But I believe God can redeem anyone and anything, and that an ungodly past does not have to influence our future."

"You don't have an ungodly past," Regina said.

"But I do." Sylvie finally looked up at her. "And I think what Bree is trying to say is that I don't need to keep looking back at the past, but need to keep trusting God for the future."

"Trusting God? Are you—?"

Sylvie smiled at Regina's confusion. "Apparently, Ethan's granny has been sharing about certain Bible verses."

"Memory verses," Bree said.

"And when I came here a few weeks ago Ethan basically showed me that God loved me, and wanted me to know Him."

Regina's eyes were wide. "Are you saying you're now a Christian?"

Sylvie nodded. "I prayed with Bree and Ethan, and since then I've been reading the Bible, and praying, and trying to follow God."

Regina placed a hand on her chest. "Oh Sylvie."

Was that a tear glistening in her eye? "Anyway, I'm glad to get the chance to tell you this, and to say thank you."

Why was the woman looking like she might cry? Regina's chin wobbled, then she heaved in a shaky breath and sniffed. "I'm overwhelmed. As a grandparent, you hope that some of the seeds you sow find good ground, but to think that God might've used something that I said in helping someone find Him is so wonderful." She glanced at Bree. "I don't know if anyone has ever gotten saved before because of something I said."

Bree smiled at Sylvie as she caressed her son's head. "We're so glad you did, Regina."

"So glad," Sylvie agreed.

Then Regina stood and did something Sylvie thought she would never ever see, as she opened her arms. "Welcome to the family."

Sylvie's own tears came then—honestly, since becoming a Christian, she'd lost all ability to keep her tears away—and she carefully placed Maddie on the couch and received the woman's hug, finally feeling her acceptance.

"I'm so sorry for giving you a hard time before," Regina murmured as she pulled away. "I was scared about poor Bree and Mike, and everything was happening so fast. I know that you had come to help Bree, but I felt so far away. I thought that us being here could help me feel like I was being useful and still had a part to play in my children's lives."

"Regina," Bree reached out a hand. "You've always had a part to play."

Regina sniffled. "But I probably pushed too hard, and pushed in where I wasn't needed, and I'm sorry. Sorry to both of you." She looked at Sylvie. "I'm sorry if I made you run away."

This was a moment for forgiveness. Just like the one with Ryan before. And after all she had been forgiven by God for, she couldn't hold a grudge anymore. "I forgive you." She found a smile, and carefully resumed her seat next to a still-sleeping child. "And hey, it worked out for good, right? You got what you wanted, a Christian friend of Bree's to care for her kids, even if it took some time."

Regina dabbed under her eyes. "I hate to think how prejudiced I've been."

"I think we can all judge others, wittingly or unwittingly at times."

"So true."

Sylvie glanced at Bree, who was looking at her with a big smile. "What are you smiling about?"

"This." Bree sighed. "This just makes me so happy. I'm so grateful for the wonderful women in my life."

"Aw, you're just saying that." Sylvie stroked Maddie's little pink-clad toes.

"Saying it, and meaning it. Thank you for being my friend."

She met Bree's gaze. "Always."

"Sylvie!" Ethan came running back in. "Look what I drawed for you!"

"Wow." She examined the picture, holding him close so he wouldn't wake his baby sister lying on the couch. "It's beautiful."

"It's not beautiful," he insisted. "It's scary."

"It sure is," she agreed.

Beautiful and scary. Words Ryan had used to describe her once upon a time.

Her heart ached. And she wondered how he was doing.

REGINA STAYED FOR DINNER, and they were joined by Mike's dad, and Hannah Wade, who had a rare night off from her news reporting. The meal passed in conversation about salvations and the reminder about the Easter services over the weekend.

The Vaughans left after cleaning up, Mr. Vaughan declaring he had to watch Dan Walton play in his five hundredth game, leaving Hannah to delve more into Sylvie's salvation, her reporter nose sniffing out more details as they ate in front of Toronto's muted hockey game.

Hannah's excitement was as genuine as Bree's own, but all the attention on her salvation was making Sylvie exhausted, so the first opportunity she had she turned the conversation to Hannah's wedding news.

Hannah shared about her plans. "I hope you'll come, Sylvie."

"Really? You want me there?"

"Of course." Hannah smiled. "I want to see what a Goth girl wears to a wedding."

"Please. I'm not a Goth girl. Not really."

"You can't wear black," Bree warned.

"You want to dress me now, do you?"

Bree's eyes widened. "I'd *love* that."

"Come on. You have enough children you can use as your dolls."

"It's not the same though, especially dressing somebody who has a figure I'll never have again," Bree said. "Please? It would truly make me happy." She sat up higher. "I once helped my friend, Holly, you know, the Olympic—"

"—skater, yes we know," Hannah said, winking at Sylvie, forcing Sylvie to bite back a smile. So she'd heard this a few times, too.

"Anyway," Bree seemed unfazed by the interruption. "She and Brent were still not quite together at that stage. I mean, it wasn't helped by them living so far apart, but anyway, she was going to see him in Montreal, and asked for my advice, and I'm pretty sure it was my clothing selection that made him finally do the deed."

Sylvie blinked. "Um..."

"What deed?" Hannah asked.

Bree's face was comical as it went from a frown to a wide-eyed, "Not *that* deed. I just meant a real kiss." She waved at her cheeks. "Oh my gosh, I'm blushing."

Sylvie smiled, but part of her twisted inside. What she'd give to not have the memories from the past, that she could be as innocent as Bree, the married woman whose children said she was now plenty familiar with that particular marital act. She bit her lip.

The TV footage showed the game, and the camera swung to the stands where a pretty redhead stood cheering, her jersey bearing Dan Walton's number and A for alternate captain.

"That's Sarah, Dan's wife," Bree pointed out. "She writes all these great songs we sing in church."

"I interviewed her and Dan recently," Hannah said.

Of course she had.

"I'm pretty sure Mike said that they'd both be coming to Ethan's birthday party on the twentieth." Bree glanced at Hannah. "Mike and Dan were part of the Original Six online Bible study group."

"Gotcha."

Bree poked Sylvie. "So will you let me help pick out a wedding dress?"

Sylvie jerked a thumb at Hannah. "Pretty sure she's the one needing a wedding dress."

"Oh, I've already got mine," Hannah said. "My mom and Franklin's mom and sisters all came and we had a big day looking at dresses, and I found it then."

"Details?"

Hannah grinned. "You'll see it the same time as Franklin does."

Bree laughed, and Sylvie smiled, as the hockey game continued. "You're still coming to Ethan's party, right Sylvie?"

"Wouldn't miss it."

"Just as well. I'm pretty sure you're his favorite person these days."

She was? Her heart glowed, but no way was she going to let Hannah know that these days she was getting as gushy as Bree could be. "It's not surprising. I am the coolest kid around here."

"Truth." Hannah smiled at her. "Maybe it sounds cheesy, but I've always been impressed by your chutzpah."

Was she serious? "You mean my rudeness."

Hannah laughed. "I mean it. You've got a gutsy attitude and a cool edge I'll never have."

Sylvie pointed to her spider tattoo behind her ear. "Not sure this is a good look for someone on TV."

"It works for you, though."

Huh. Well, there you go. You could never tell what people thought.

Bree motioned Sylvie closer, then murmured, "Speaking of Ethan's party, you know that, ah, a certain someone has said he's coming too."

She'd suspected as much. She shrugged. "I'm an adult. I'll cope." And she'd keep busy in the kitchen avoiding him. Yes, really mature of her.

Hannah studied her, her eyebrows aloft as if they were her antennae for a juicy story.

"Nothing to see here," Sylvie felt like saying, but didn't, knowing that would be like waving a red flag.

"You'll be fine," Bree whispered.

Sylvie nodded. Avoiding Ryan would be the name of the game for as long as it took until he was out of her system.

Toronto scored, and Dan was credited with an assist, which again saw the camera zoom in as the redhead leapt to her feet.

"He's having a good game," Sylvie said.

"Five hundred in a row. The man's a machine."

"They call it an Iron Man streak," Hannah said.

"How many has Mike done?" Sylvie asked.

Bree shrugged. "He's had a few too many injuries and other things to ever get on a streak. I'll be glad when they get a few days off before playoffs begin so he can rest up a bit."

Hannah sighed. "I can't wait for the regular season to be done, so Franklin and I can finally have a chance to settle a few more things about the wedding."

"It must be hard for you both, when your job takes you away from here so often," Bree observed.

"I'm super grateful that I even have a job."

"Not just any job," Bree said. "ESPN."

"I still can't believe it myself. It all happened so quickly."

"You deserve it. You've worked so hard."

Comparison, that terrible beast, raised its ugly head and dared her to wonder what right she had to sit here with these women when she was just a broken mess. But, she reminded herself fiercely, she wasn't broken, not anymore. As Bree, Heather, and her counselor regularly reminded her, God was in the business of healing her, and making her whole. She might still feel patched together, but she was healing because she was being stitched together by God's love.

"What are you thinking about so seriously?" Bree poked her with a cheese-loaded cracker which Sylvie took and chewed.

"Just what a miracle it is to be here with you."

Bree clasped her hand. "That's one of the things I love about God. He's into miracles, and hasn't finished with any of us yet."

CHAPTER 20

$\mathcal{E}$aster slid by, bookended by games against Anaheim
and St Louis. Ryan was grateful for a day to relax, to be
game-free, even if it had meant catching an early morning flight
on game day. He'd spent the day with his folks and Jake, after
they'd watched the game the previous night, but part of him
kept wondering how Sylvie was doing. This, her first Easter as a
Christian, had to be a significant time. It always was for him, at
least. But she'd kept on with her silence, ignoring his text, even
though it had been innocuous, simply saying *Happy Easter*. It
seemed she really didn't want anything more to do with him.

He regretted everything so much, but kept hoping God
would open the door if they were to have a second chance. God
could do miracles, after all.

During his visit home he came to an agreement with his
mom to let her know when he planned to visit Red Deer again,
as she insisted on keeping a room for Sylvie. "Because it's not
just a room that girl needs. She needs to feel loved and wanted.
And you making things hard for her by being here is tanta-
mount to saying she doesn't matter."

"Careful, Mom," Jake said. "It sounds like you're saying Ryan doesn't matter."

"Yeah, I'm your actual son here, Mom."

"And she's a girl you actually still care about, am I right?"

Dad smiled, Jake smirked, and Ryan sighed. His mom knew him too well. Yes, he cared about her. Yes, he still dared hope for a future.

"All I'm asking is that you let us know when you plan to drop in."

"I won't have much of a chance," he admitted. "I've got too many away games and a few back-to-backs to make it to Red Deer any time soon."

"In that case, we should be okay." She sighed. "The poor girl. Can you imagine what it would be like to have no family?"

"Sometimes," Jake said with a mischievous grin.

"You didn't have any luck finding her relatives?"

"It's the strangest thing. It's truly like they've disappeared, which we all know isn't really possible in this day and age."

"Has anyone checked death records?"

His mom nodded. "I did that with her a few days ago. There was nothing under the names she gave me."

"What if they changed their names and deliberately disappeared?" Ryan suggested.

"Come on, bro. This isn't *CSI*. Aren't they supposed to be old?"

He shrugged. "People change their names when they marry." Sylvie Guillemette. He half-smiled. It had a nice ring to it.

"I bet I know what you're thinking," Jake said, with another of those annoying smirks.

"Maybe that's a possibility," his mom mused.

He mentally scrambled. Was she talking about Sylvie and him or her grandparents?

"I think we'll do more digging and see what we can find."

He nodded, glancing away through the window at a budding

tree. Soon it would hold blossoms. It was just a matter of being patient, of waiting for the right time, the right season, the day when everything would align for it to bloom. It had survived the depths of winter, but it was now spring. He'd pray that that would hold true for him and Sylvie, too.

THE NEXT TIME he played Mike, he took the chance to meet with Mike and Bree at their house after the game. With both him and Mike having days off the next day, and Sylvie staying in Red Deer, it seemed a good chance to finally present his side of the story to them. They knew both him and Sylvie, and might be able to offer advice about what he should do. And he was trying to be more open, trying to not shut people out, so he explained about the hotel, then about Brent, and finally that encounter when he'd surprised her at his parents' house.

"...and I didn't know where she was. Eventually, I found her hiding in the closet."

Bree's eyes widened, then took on a fierceness he'd never seen before. "What did you do?"

"What do you mean?"

"She only hides when she's scared. You must've scared her."

He threw up his hands. "She scared me. So I had a hockey stick, and—"

"You went after her with a hockey stick?" Bree's mouth sagged. "Ryan!"

"Babe, I don't think he meant like that," Mike calmed her, before cocking an eyebrow at him.

"What? No! I'd never do anything like that. I'd never hurt her, or anyone." He rubbed his jaw. "Then the next morning I found out she is a Christian, and now I don't know what to do."

"What do you mean?" Bree asked.

"I have so many regrets. You don't know how much I wish I could do a redo of everything."

She studied him for a moment, glanced at her husband and had a silent conversation, then looked back at him. "Maybe you can."

"What do you mean?"

"Have a redo. You know she's a Christian now. What's stopping you from picking up the phone and calling her?"

"She wants space."

"You might find she wants less space than you think."

"But you won't know if you don't talk to her," Mike said.

True. As was the fact that God hadn't given him a spirit of fear. He needed to talk to her, empowered with God's love, knowing the Spirit within would give him self-control.

SPRING BLOOMS in windowsills had a way of brightening everyone's day. And Sylvie agreed with Mrs. Androvsky, daffodils had to be the happiest flowers. They certainly went a long way to making her heart feel a little lighter, anyway.

"There you go." Sylvie collected Mrs. Androvsky's teacup. "Now, is there anything else I can help you with?"

"Esther Melnyk."

Sylvie blinked at the abrupt change of conversation. "Yes?"

"I remember now. I had a friend at the place I was at before I came here, and she remembered a woman called Esther who used to live there. My friend told me this funny story about how Esther was married to one man, and then he died, and she married again."

"Are you saying John died?" Her heart squeezed. Her grandfather was dead?

"It stands to reason that not every grandparent will make it to my ripe old age."

"Do you remember anything else? What was the name of this friend? And where did this happen?"

"The Golden Pines. I can't remember my friend's name. I only remember the story because it was similar to what I experienced."

"Thank you very much for sharing this with me."

Later, when she was in Heather's office, Sylvie said, "I don't understand why you haven't been able to find a death certificate for John."

"Perhaps he died overseas."

"Maybe." Sylvie frowned. "But wouldn't there need to be evidence of that here in order for Esther to remarry?"

"I don't know."

"I wish there was a way of finding out."

"Melnyk, did you say?" Heather asked.

She nodded. "That's the Ukrainian legacy on my mother's side. On my dad's side we have total loser."

"You really have nothing to do with his side of the family?"

"When he went to jail that was it. They had nothing more to do with us after he died. Last we heard they died too."

Heather's face softened. "So much suffering."

"It's okay, Heather. None of this is news to me."

"I just wish your life had been easier."

"But if it had been easier, I probably wouldn't be here today, would I? And I might not have gotten to know Jesus, so I guess that's not such a bad thing."

Heather dabbed at her eyes. "I'm so impressed with how far you've come in such a short while."

"I think the counseling is helping," she admitted. "And the fact I've been around Bree and Mike means I might have heard some of this before, but not really realized how it applied to me until now."

Heather studied her, until Sylvie was forced to ask, "What is it?"

"I know this is none of my business, but do you ever think you and Ryan would—?"

"Nope. That ship has sailed. And I appreciate that you care, and that you have done so much to take me in and look after me, but I can't risk that again."

"Are you not wanting to risk it because of fear?"

"Maybe. Probably. To be honest, I don't trust myself. I don't know how to do relationships without all that...other stuff." Her cheeks grew hot. Maybe she was becoming more like Bree than she realized.

"But surely you can work at being friends again." Heather hooked a brow. "I'm guessing you can manage friendships without physical elements getting in the way of things."

"Of course." Now her cheeks were blazing hot. Good thing Ryan wasn't here to hear this.

"Well, how will you ever learn to be friends with a man if you don't ever talk to one?"

"I talk to plenty of men."

"I'm not talking men like Clifford or Mr. Vettori. One day you'll meet a man that you might want to build a family with."

Too late. She'd already met him.

"And he'll only know that you want a family if you can talk with him."

She pressed her lips together, studied the bright green tape dispenser on Heather's desk. The thought of having her own family both teased her with longing and terrified her. "I'm not exactly mom material."

"Who says?"

"My family. My family history. How I've always been."

"Except you're a new creation now, Sylvie. You're not your mother. You're not your father. You're not the woman who started working here two months ago. You're a child of God, you are part of His family now, and you know that all things are possible with Him."

Maybe they were. But likely not possible with Ryan. And talking about him in this way with his mother seemed slightly wrong and weird. "Heather, I do appreciate your concern, but I don't want to talk about Ryan anymore, if you don't mind." Look at her, putting boundaries in. She mentally high-fived herself.

"I'm still praying for you," Heather warned her.

"Go for it. I need all the prayers I can get."

"Good." Heather grinned. "Because I'm also praying for him."

"MELNYK?" Mr. Vettori's brow wrinkled. "I knew a Melnyk once."

"What?"

"I don't remember, rightly. I heard that Androvsky woman say something about him recently, then remembered that his wife ran off with another man."

Sylvie felt her eyes widen. "Are you serious?" No way would her grandmother ever do something like that. Especially not after how she'd scorned Sylvie's mom for basically doing the same.

"Oh yes. He was devastated and left the country."

"Who? My grandfather?"

He nodded. "Then she remarried. To some Polish fellow I think. I don't rightly recall all the details."

"Do you remember *any* of the details?" she pressed.

He frowned, and she had to dig deep for patience. "His name might be Polensky, maybe?"

She took this new detail to Heather, and Heather accessed the public database. Privacy laws meant that not everything was accessible, but she did come across a couple of women who might be the right ones. Heather said she'd ask in the local Ukrainian association, and put a couple of questions in their Facebook group. Which left Sylvie with a couple of choices. She could either let the past be in the past, and ignore these people who had rejected her and her mom all those years ago. Or she could do what she could to extend an olive branch. And from what she was learning, from what the counselor had said, it was good to put into place what God had said, that as far as it depended on her to live at peace with others. Like she had reconciled with Mike's mom. Like she'd reconciled with Brent. Like she'd now apologized to Marie. Marie might've just sniffed and turned away but that was on her. Sylvie knew she'd done what God wanted. So if God now wanted her to reconcile with her grandparents, then she'd try. It might mean a reunion, joyous or otherwise, or it might not, but reaching out would at least bring closure to a chapter of her life, and stop the endless wondering.

"So you'll contact these women?" Bree asked, when she met with her and Mike that following weekend.

"I'll call them, and we'll see."

"Do you have addresses for them?" Mike asked.

"No. So I'm not pinning my hopes on anything. It seems impossible that after all this time there might finally be closure."

"Either way, you know God's got this, right?" Bree said.

Sylvie nodded, exhaling slowly. "I'm hoping for the best, but trying to trust Him regardless."

"You know that doesn't just work with your grandparents," Mike said.

"What do you mean?"

"You can probably afford to think like that with some of your other relationships."

Sylvie swallowed. "Are you talking about Ryan?"

"He'll be at Ethan's party next weekend," Mike said. "And from what he's said I think he'd really appreciate the chance to talk."

"We've talked."

He straightened. "You have?"

Not with very many words. But him saying sorry counted as talking, right? Although that was probably not what these two lovebirds meant. "Look, I'm coming to Ethan's party for Ethan's sake. Whoever else happens to be there is extraneous to that. I'm prepared to have conversations with people, but I'm a little scared that he'll just see me as who I was, and not who I'm trying to be now."

"You can't control how others think about you," Bree said.

"And I think you'd find that he's as remorseful as you are," Mike added.

"He's said he's sorry. And I'm pretty sure I said that too. But I don't know if it's healthy for me to try to jump back into a relationship with him. I still have a lot of work to do to deal with some of this stuff."

"You're still seeing a counselor, right?"

She nodded. One of the benefits of not paying rent was she could afford counseling.

"Then how about concentrating on building a friendship with the man. Just take it easy, talk a bit, smile and laugh a bit. You have more in common now than you did."

"We do?"

Mike smiled. "You now both have God."

CHAPTER 21

The party was in full swing by the time Ryan arrived. For a kid's birthday party this seemed more like something geared toward the adults, but he was totally okay with that. He stroked his newly shaven chin, which matched the jaws of all the playoff contenders here. Brent and Holly Karlsson were there again with their little tykes. Chris and Diana weren't, but Jai and Allie Mullins were, with their child. Beau Nash was dripping southern charm while his Quebecois-born wife was talking French with Luc, their son Noah talking to Ethan. Dan and Sarah Walton were chatting with Franklin James and Hannah Wade, the Aussie redhead's wide-eyed enthusiasm as bright as Bree's own.

And now, thanks to an unseasonably warm day, seated outside on the deck, listening to Mike's teammate Tom Chavez was Sylvie, her Goth look amped up with black eyeliner, fishnet stockings, Doc Martens, and new blue hair.

Ryan's eyes kept straying to her, even as he tried to look like he was engaged in the conversations around him. She was like a flame, and although her look was dramatically different to everyone else here, he sensed a new poise to her, a warmth and ease he hadn't seen before. A warmth and ease shared with everyone except him.

The moment their eyes had met she'd stilled, then nodded slightly, then veered away, moving to help Mike's mom in the kitchen with serving things. She was always doing that, just like she had at that first party. Helping others, looking for ways in which to serve. She might appear all tough but she had a heart of gold. And now he knew she was following Jesus, he knew that heart could be available to him. If he pursued her. If she trusted him. If he trusted himself with her.

Luc moved closer and muttered, "Stop looking at her and start talking, okay?"

"I haven't given up hoping you find your woman this summer."

"Good luck with that."

"Don't need luck, just need God."

"Huh. Look who's talking all brave. Just not doing it."

"Fine! I'll go talk to her."

"Yeah, hurry up, man," Mike said. "Everyone is sick and tired of waiting."

"What do you mean?"

Mike gestured to the crowd, who had all stopped talking and were watching an oblivious Sylvie and Tom.

Bree's smothered giggle finally caught Sylvie's attention and she turned, just as Franklin called, "Hey, Tom, come and tell Kurt about who you think is gonna win the Cup."

Wow. Obvious much? Ryan shook his head at his friends, but Luc's not-so-gentle push propelled him onto the deck. He wondered if he needed a drink, or a cupcake to offer her, or anything to help break the ice.

Then the birthday boy himself arrived, stealing the place beside Sylvie.

Wow. Outmaneuvered by a five-year-old.

"Gotta work on your moves, dude," Luc whispered, as he passed by, tossing him a no sugar cola.

"Says the man who likes to pretend he doesn't want a girlfriend."

"Don't make me fight you."

"Luc?" Ethan frowned up at him. "No fighting at my party."

"Yeah, Luc," Ryan murmured, catching Sylvie's quick glance at him, before she looked away.

"Ryan, come sit here," Ethan demanded, catching his hand.

"Gotta do what the party boy wants, right?"

Sylvie's lips—a vivid slash of red—compressed, before she moved. "Ethan, I'm going to see if your mom needs help in the kitchen."

"Don't go, Sylvie," Ethan begged. "I was talking to you."

"And you have to do what the party boy wants, right?" Ryan murmured.

She peeked at him, then she resettled herself, but a little further away. But that wasn't stopping Ethan, who insisted on crawling onto her lap, and counting her bracelets, before tracing her tattoos on her arm.

He bet the kid had done it plenty of times before, but for him to watch felt strangely significant. And mesmerizing. Her skin was so pale that the dark blue and black ink was vivid in contrast. He watched as Ethan kept on with his kiddy talk, not all of which Ryan understood, but he listened anyway, lifting his gaze to see Sylvie look back before her gaze swerved away.

His heart stuttered, but he kept watching, waiting, willing for her to look at him again. He no longer cared if this made him look like a stalker or creepy or whatever. She needed to look at him. Finally, her gaze lifted, her dark eyes sinking deep into him.

And he smiled, and he caught her uncertainty as she nibbled her lip, then glanced down as Ethan demanded her attention. "Sylvie, you're not listening to me."

She blinked, and bit her lip, then Brent called, "Hey Ethan, you ready to open presents soon?"

"Presents? Yeah!"

Ethan scrambled up, and Ryan caught Brent's wink, then the whole party seemed to shift their attention back to the little boy. Except for him. And Sylvie.

She moved again, and he murmured, "Don't leave."

"But Ethan will want me there."

"I'm kind of getting the feeling that even if he did, then there'll be a dozen people throwing me at you again."

Her nose wrinkled. "They're not even trying to be subtle."

"Right? So embarrassing."

She snorted. "For them."

He laughed, and the whole party went quiet again. Then conscious he was on show, he leaned back on his hands, feigning nonchalance, as he waited for the chatter to resume.

When it did, he leaned forward, keeping his eyes on the pink blossom trees, near the pool. "I've missed you."

She didn't say anything, and he didn't want to look across at her, not wanting to scare her into moving away.

When she still didn't say anything, he tried again. "I really wish we could be friends."

He winced. Those words seemed too loaded, even if they were God's honest truth.

Still no answer. He really should've practiced this before coming here, but had counted on his prayers and friends making things easier. And while his friends had made the opportunity to talk to her easier, it didn't mean the actual talking was any smoother. He'd try one more time.

"You'll never know how glad I was to hear about your salvation."

Nothing. Silence. Then she sighed.

He'd take that as a win. But before he could open his mouth

to say anything, she murmured, "Why don't you tell me how glad you are, then?"

He turned to face her, saw how she'd stilled, as if scared he might jump her, or hurt her or something. "Sylvie, I won't hurt you."

"I know."

Knots in his heart released. "I regret so much for hurting you, for getting carried away so easily. I should've put a stop to things but I didn't. And I will always regret the fact that my actions caused so much pain."

"I forgive you, Ryan. And like I said, I'm sorry too." She drew up her knees. "I, uh, might've grown up with different values and, um, experiences, but I knew I was trying to get you to do something you weren't comfortable with. But I've changed now."

"I know. Mom told me. And I, uh, overheard you talking with her. And praying."

She closed her eyes, shook her head. "How much did you hear?"

"Not much more than that."

She sighed again, but didn't say anything for a long time. Then, "Your mom has been so good to me."

"Once you're in with her, you're in. And you are in."

She half-smiled. "I get that impression."

"In fact, you're so in, that I've basically been kicked out, according to my brother."

"Well, good."

"What?"

"It's not safe when you're roaming around at night with a hockey stick."

"Hey, you know that was an accident."

"Seemed pretty deliberate to me."

Her little smirk took the edge off her words, and he calmed. She seemed more relaxed too, putting her hand on the edge of the deck, which dared him to place his hand near there too.

"Why did you hide in the closet?" he asked.

Her breath hitched, and he instantly regretted asking that. "I'm sorry. You don't have to tell me."

She sighed, shaking her head. "Didn't your mom ever tell you?"

"I figured you were scared, but I didn't figure I could scare you that much."

"Have you seen yourself without a shirt on?"

He looked down at his t-shirted chest, then back up as her huff of amusement caught him by surprise. She wanted to play now, did she? "You didn't like it?" he dared.

She met his gaze. "I didn't say that."

Warmth traveled through his body, heating his blood, and he broke the connection. Whoa. This was why he needed to be cautious. It was too easy to get snared by desire again.

"Sorry, I shouldn't have said that."

"It's okay. I don't mind that you like my chest."

Her lips twitched again, as behind them, the party continued with more excited cheers, and Luc's call of "Now that's a sick car, dude. Am I right, or am I right?"

"You're right, Luc," Ethan said. "Thank you. I loves it!"

Sylvie smiled, and he joined in, and they stared at each other. Then he moved his hand right next to hers, their little fingers only an inch away.

She drew in a breath, then exhaled. "I used to hide in the closet when one of my mom's boyfriends used to come looking for me," she said matter-of-factly.

He tried to hide his shock, but wasn't sure how good a job he did of it as her lips pressed together and she dropped her gaze. "Looking for you? For what?"

She stilled, her gaze swerving to face the tree, her shoulders slumped. "He assaulted me, Ryan."

"What?" No. She didn't mean—

"I was thirteen, and he sexually assaulted me."

Heat banded his chest. He clenched his hands and jaw. How could—? *Lord?* Poor Sylvie. *Lord, heal her.* Grief for her washed over him. "Did you press charges?"

"I was a kid. It was my mom's boyfriend. She didn't believe me. Nobody would."

He didn't dare pursue that. Had nothing he could say. He could only pray, and murmur, "I'm so incredibly sorry you experienced that."

She nodded, eyes fixed on the pink petals of the blossom tree. "He's dead now. Died not too long after that."

Was it bad that he was glad? Then a savage thought rushed him to say, "But you didn't think I was—"

"No. Not at all." Again, she gave a snort of amusement. Or pain. Maybe that was simply the sound of awkwardness. "I trust you Ryan."

"Do you?"

He slid off the deck in a sudden move he figured would count as Brent Karlsson-slick, turning to face her. Standing here on the ground now put her at face height. "I want you to trust me. I want to be worthy of your trust. And I know I've done some things that have hurt you, but I want to be your friend, Sylvie. Please, give me a second chance."

Sylvie studied him for a long moment, then leaned in. His pulse raced as, for a desperate second, he wished she'd complete the move and kiss him. Then she pulled back, and his hopes sank in disappointment.

She closed her eyes. Shook her head. "See? I can't be friends with you."

"Why not?"

"I just want to kiss you."

She did? His heart beat a victory parade. "Then clearly we need some boundaries."

"Boundaries?"

He nodded. "No gazing at each other for longer than three seconds. No touching unless it's accidental. And we have to talk about things. About everything. Anything. I want to be your friend. I've missed you so much. Please."

She studied him for a second, two, then ducked her head. "Like that?" she asked.

He laughed. "Like that." He moved to grab her hand, then stopped.

"Like that, huh?"

"Can we amend it so we can hold hands?"

"Sorry, mister. This is a trial only. You'll need to prove to yourself and me that we can actually make this friends thing work."

"And how long will this trial be for?"

"I don't know."

"Next weekend?" he asked hopefully.

"What about Hannah's wedding?"

"That long?"

"Come on. It's only a couple of months."

"Way too long," he said firmly. "How about the next time we see each other we can hold hands?"

"Only holding hands."

"So when can I see you? Tomorrow?"

"Don't you have to get ready for your playoffs?"

Yes. But reconciliation felt as important as any Cup. "Will you come watch me in game one on Monday?"

"Would a friend do that?"

"Absolutely. And a friend would definitely hug them if they won."

"That's *only* if they won."

"Whoa. Did I hear a challenge there?"

"A challenge to keep your hands to yourself," she countered, then smirked. "At least until I see you again."

He smiled. "Challenge accepted."

~

"Ah, Sylvie." Mrs. Androvsky's face lit. "How are you doing today?"

So much better since Saturday. "Pretty good, thanks, Mrs. A."

"I can tell."

"What is it that gives it away?" She touched her earrings. "The zebras?"

"Oh, I just love zebras. And giraffes. And elephants."

That's it. From now on, Sylvie would be wearing her collection of animal earrings to work.

"I always wished I could go on one of those African safaris, but I never could."

Yep. Definitely wearing them. Sylvie moved to fluff her pillows. "Does this mean you're a fan of zoos?"

"Oh, yes."

"Have you visited Edmonton's or Calgary's?"

"Oh, I loved seeing the penguins in Calgary. Such funny creatures."

"A long way away from home, too."

Mrs. Androvsky sighed wistfully. "I remember when we used to do field trips there."

"You haven't recently?"

"Not for several years."

"I'll suggest it to Heather. I think she'd be down for that, especially now the weather is warming." There were probably a lot of older people here who would love an excuse to escape the same walls they saw every day. And Sylvie wouldn't mind an excursion.

"Oh, that would be good. Thank you."

Mrs. Androvsky continued to watch her. Sylvie smiled. "What is it?"

"I don't know. You just seem to have a special glow about you, that's all."

She chewed her smile back to non-*Joker* standards. Nobody wanted to be scaring anyone into a heart attack with random bursts of happiness.

"No, don't try to hide it. It's wonderful to see. Did you finally make contact with your grandmother?"

Ah, that. "I planned to try that this afternoon." When she'd have a solid distraction in case the names suggested in the Facebook group weren't the right ones.

"I hope that goes well, dear. So, if that's not responsible for the glow, then I wonder what is?"

Sylvie shook her head. "Has anyone ever told you you're nosy?"

"Many times, dear. But it's one of the advantages of getting old. People are so much more willing to overlook impertinence."

"Good to know."

"Now, what did you do on the weekend?"

Wow. Terrier with a bone, this one. "A bit of this and that."

"Oh, come on, Sylvie. You can do better than that. You know I like to hear the details about people with more interesting lives than me."

"Fine. I went to Calgary. Saw my friend Bree. It was her son's birthday party."

"A child's party doesn't normally bring about that kind of happy glow. Did you see a special friend? A special friend called Ryan, perhaps?"

She bit her lip to stop a grin. "Maybe."

"Sylvie!"

"But he's just a friend, Mrs. A. We're working on being

friends first." Even if there'd been those moments when she'd desperately wanted to kiss him—and from the way he'd looked at her, he'd wanted to kiss her, too. And the fact he'd sent her a couple of *almost* flirty messages since. Then last night's phone call letting her know he'd put a ticket aside with her name on it for tonight's first playoff game, saying she could come with his family or not, he didn't mind. But she figured he did. That he'd like to see her there with them. And it'd be nice to watch the game, feeling comfortable, not judged or excluded like the last time she'd been. Although she didn't know how she'd cope if they won. Especially in front of his family. Had he been serious about wanting a hug? She could almost combust just thinking about it.

The thought trailed her through the rest of her shift, and later, buoyed her as she finally couraged up in the Guillemettes' kitchen, and made the calls to the two Esthers that the Facebook group had found. Their numbers had been a matter of cross-matching names in the Yellow Pages and via Canada 411.

"You can do this," Heather encouraged. "And I don't have to stay if you don't want."

"No, I want you here." Call her a wuss, but it was good to have someone near who Sylvie felt like was on her side.

"I'll be praying."

"Thanks, Heather." She pressed the numbers and waited, eyes closed, hoping she'd recognize her grandmother's voice.

"Hello?"

Her eyes sprung open. "Hello. My name is Sylvie Miles, and I'm sorry to bother you, but I wanted to know if you knew an Esther and John Melnyk."

"Who?"

"Esther and John Melnyk."

There was a pause, then, "I'm sorry dear. I don't know anyone by that name."

"Are you sure?"

"If you're asking if I'm Esther Melnyk, then the answer is no. I'm Esther Polensky. How did you get this number, anyway?"

"I recently put up a post in the local Ukrainian Facebook group, and I got a couple of comments, and your name was one of them."

"Facebook? Oh, I never check that. Who has time for all these newfangled things?"

Not people living their best lives instead of posting there all the time.

"Why did you want to know, dear?"

"I, er, wondered if you were my grandmother."

"What is your name again?"

It wasn't her. The voice was wrong. "Sylvie. Sylvie Miles. Esther and John had a daughter, my mother, and I haven't seen them for years."

"I'm sorry to hear that, my dear. Families can be complicated, can't they?"

"For sure."

"What was your mother's name?"

"Janet."

"And your name?"

"Sylvie. Sylvie Miles."

"I'll be sure to ask around my friends in that community, and see if anyone knows anything. Give me your number so I can call you if I find out anything."

"Thank you." Oh, how kind were some strangers? "I really appreciate it."

"Good luck, dear."

"Thank you."

She ended the call, gratitude blossoming within.

"No luck?"

"She's going to make inquiries with her friends."

"That's good," Heather encouraged.

She nodded. "Now onto call two."

But when she called that number there was no response, and no capacity to leave a message. Strike two. She shrugged at Heather, who was watching her from the other side of the kitchen counter. "No answer, so I'll try again another day."

"It's tricky, isn't it, between privacy laws and so many women of that generation not using their names in public spaces."

"There weren't any John Melnyks I could find online, not in this region anyway."

"Do you think he might've moved?"

"I don't know. Maybe? Maybe he did go back to Ukraine. Or died, like Mrs. A said."

"What was your grandmother's middle name? Maybe she's going by that now."

"I don't know." Her lips turned wry. "My mother wasn't the best at keeping records."

"Hmm. Well, let's not worry about that now. We need to get on the road to Edmonton if we're going to get a meal before the game."

The game.

She nodded, and went to change. This was exactly why she'd chosen to call today, so that thoughts of Ryan and his game could consume her, instead of this nagging disappointment she now felt. How could they be so hard to find? People didn't just disappear. She'd track them down, even if they didn't want anything to do with her.

The trip north was fun, the conversation between proud parents and Jake proving sufficient distraction as they talked about Edmonton's chances against Seattle. Edmonton had home ice advantage because their regular season wins gave them higher ranking in their western conference zone. That meant tonight was the first of two games at home before they'd fly to Seattle and play there for two more, then return.

"Seattle don't stand a chance," Pete said confidently. "We've got McHale, Malenski and Hansen, and they've got who?"

"An Art Ross winner?" Jake suggested.

"Please. Kyle Tinker won that years ago."

"I think you're forgetting something, Jakey," Heather said.

"What?"

"Your brother has extra incentive to play well."

Jake turned to smirk at Sylvie, but she willed her cheeks to not heat, to feign coolness she didn't feel. Heather didn't know about the agreement Sylvie and Ryan had reached, did she? She might have eyes in the back of her head, but she didn't know everything. Sylvie hadn't even told Ryan she was definitely coming. Even if it was an obvious yes. And while it was nice he was thinking about her in the pointy end of the season she wasn't about to demand his attention. They were friends. That was all.

But later, as she cheered and clapped as Edmonton crushed Seattle four zip, and joined the cheering masses in waving orange tinsel pom-poms, and she met Ashley, Jason McHale's girlfriend, later in the family and friends' suite, she was conscious of eyes on her. Not least because Ashley had commented on the fact she hadn't seen Sylvie since that game back in February.

"Where have you been?"

Someone had noticed she hadn't been around? Another brick in her wall of defensiveness fell. "I've had work stuff and, uh, some things." Like the fact she and Ryan had broken up. That counted as "things" right? Not that it mattered now.

"Well, it's good to see you again. You'll have to come to the party at our house when we win this series."

Sylvie blinked. "Me?"

"You're with Ryan, right? All the wives and girlfriends go."

"Oh, but..." Who knew what their status would be if—no,

when—that happened? She was prevented from having to answer as a cheer went up and the players entered the room.

The crowd surged and she moved to a white wall, holding back as the players were inundated with hugs and cheers. Her eyes searched for Ryan, and then she found him, being hugged by his mom and dad, Jake not far behind. Ryan grinned, then bent his head and said something to his mom. Heather smiled and turned, peering through the crowds as if looking for someone. Then Ryan saw her, his gaze connecting with her, the energy pulsing between them as clear as if nobody else was in the room.

She stayed where she was, Doc Martens boot propped against the wall, and he appeared, sweaty and helmet-marked and tall and big with his shoulder pads on. And so very, very handsome, especially with that facial scruff that the playoffs would soon see grow into a beard.

"Congrats."

"Thanks."

He studied her, she studied him, as attraction arced between them. One second, two seconds, then she lowered her gaze. Then back up for one second, two seconds, before she needed to break the connection again.

How she wanted to hug him, kiss him, like what was going on around them. Instead, she held out her hand.

He glanced at it, his hand automatically grasping it, his warm, firm fingers wrapping around her smaller, cool ones. "Is that all I get?" he asked in a low voice.

"We're friends, right?"

"Friends who hug when one of them wins a game."

She shook her head. "I don't know that I agreed to that."

"I think you did."

But hugging him would only make her imagination go back to where it shouldn't. "I'm really proud of you, but I don't think I can do that right now."

He visibly deflated. She hated herself for doing that to him. "We're just friends, remember?"

"No, we're not," he said. "You and I both know we're a lot more than that."

She angled her face to look up as he drew closer. "We only just agreed to be friends, Ryan. I need more time."

He exhaled. "Another game?"

"Win the next one, and a hug is yours."

"Promise?"

She nodded, saw his eyes dip to her lips, then meet her gaze again as his grip tightened. "I'm holding you to it."

"Good." She smiled. "So hurry up and win again."

CHAPTER 22

Frustration filled the next week. An overtime loss in game two then two wins played away had kept the team focused on this next game. They needed to win. For all kinds of reasons. Win, and they'd close out the series and move to the next playoff round. Lose, and he'd have to play away and likely have to wait even longer for a hug. He might've been playing well, getting assists in the last two games, but Sylvie hadn't gone to the Seattle games, although his folks had. When he'd called her, she'd explained she couldn't due to work and a counseling appointment she couldn't miss, and while he'd told her he understood, he didn't really. It sounded like an excuse, like she didn't want to see him. She could get his mom to change her shifts, couldn't she? Or rearrange her counseling?

But while part of him was frustrated, another part admired her for this stand. Prioritizing these commitments over seeing him proved that she really had changed, and was doing better than him at keeping things in the friend zone, even in their conversations and texts. They talked after each game, about her work, her ongoing quest to find her grandparents. He offered to go visit with her if she found them, which she seemed touched by, not realizing he'd do anything to be in her company.

She watched his games, complimenting and encouraging him depending on how he did, reminding him of what God said about success and trust in Him. She was good for him. He loved lying on his bed talking to her via FaceTime, enjoying the animated glow that sparkled in her eyes and spilled out in her laughter and sly tease. Yet he wanted more, and was growing hungrier for her hug, hungrier for her kiss. He really hoped the go-slow could change tonight.

SECOND PERIOD. They were trailing by three goals. Not ideal for a team playing in front of passionate fans. But they were resilient and not gonna quit.

Ryan watched the action from the bench, adrenaline pumping, as he gulped his energy drink. Viktor had the puck and sent it in a stretch pass to McHale, who skated into the left circle and scored on a wrist shot that went under the right arm of Seattle's goalie. Yes! As the arena erupted he joined his teammates in cheers, fist pumps, and tapping their sticks on the ice, as his teammates skated in.

He backslapped them then clambered over the boards, ready for his next shift. Focus, drive, awareness of the puck. The clock was ticking down, he was protecting Will Santana, as Seattle's Kyle Tinker powered toward him. Ryan skated, reached across and stole the puck, sending it to McHale who scored.

Awesome. Amid the back pats and congratulations, Ryan was reminded he was now on a three-game point streak. Ten seconds remained in the period, then the buzzer sounded, and they went back down the tunnel to rest, refuel, and talk strategy.

In the second minute of the third period, Viktor scored,

tying the game, but despite the momentum swings, nobody could break the deadlock, sending them into overtime again.

Coach talked strategy in the break, before reminding them that in overtime, it was never a bad play to just fire pucks at the net.

Ten minutes in, McHale sent a stretch pass to Mats, who shot through heavy traffic and found the back of the net, sending everyone wild.

The music and lights and deafening cheers flooded through the building as Ryan and the team spilled onto the ice and huddled around McHale in back thumps, hugs, and cheers. A little later, as the team skated with upraised sticks, thanking the fans, Ryan looked up in the stands where the team's family suite was. He glimpsed Sylvie and pointed to her.

She smiled, pointed to herself as if to say "me?" and he nodded.

That woman now owed him a hug.

It was much later by the time he was released, the media wanting to do interviews with him for once. Hannah Wade had gone easy on him, and he appreciated that, knowing he was a little rough around the edges with such things. He wasn't as polished as McHale, that was for sure.

He joined the party in the family room, which was wild, amped up on excitement, music, and exhilarated players, family, and friends. Then he saw her, propped up against the wall in what he was coming to think of as her usual spot, then, after quick hugs with his parents, he moved to her, eyes intent on her, as he opened his arms wide.

She smiled, but didn't move until he was only two feet away. Then she propelled herself from the wall into his arms.

"Congratulations," she murmured, against his cheek.

He savored the closeness. After so long apart, it felt so good to have her near. To feel her breath against his skin from where her face was tucked against his neck, to feel like a relationship with her might have a chance. A real chance. A *good* chance. Which meant being good and putting to rest any desires hugging her for longer might induce.

He pulled back reluctantly. "I missed you."

"We spoke last night and texted earlier today."

"It's not the same."

She sighed. "No."

He grabbed her hand. Hugging might be dangerous, but he figured hand-holding was okay. "Can you come to the party at McHale's?"

"Um, maybe."

Disappointment arrowed through his soul. "Maybe?"

"I came with your parents, and I have work tomorrow, and if I stay I don't know how I'd get home."

"I'll take you."

Her eyes widened. "All the way back to Red Deer?"

"We'll probably get a few days off, as the Vancouver-San Jose games look like they're going to game seven."

"I'm glad you closed this in five."

"Me too."

He leaned close, trying to figure out if she was okay with another hug. She leaned away. He'd take that as a no, then. Man. While he appreciated her self-control, he really wished—

"Are you two coming tonight?" Jason interrupted, his girlfriend at his side.

"Are we?" Ryan asked Sylvie.

"You better be," Ashley said. "It's so good to see Ryan with a girlfriend, so we need to know all the gossip."

That they did not. He arched a brow at Sylvie, not wanting to push her. He was trying to learn self-control too, and needed to be wise.

"Are you sure about taking me home afterwards?" she asked him.

"He'll have plenty of time to take you home," McHale said. "Coach just confirmed we've got two days off, thanks to San Jose tying the series tonight."

"Two days, huh?" Ryan smiled at Sylvie. "See? Plenty of time."

"But you'll be so tired."

The adrenaline coursing through his body said otherwise. "I'll be fine. And hey, I'll get the chance to drive another hour or two with you."

"Hour or two?" Ashley's heavily mascaraed eyes widened. "Aren't you going to take her back to your apartment?"

He met her questioning gaze squarely. "No. Back to her place in Red Deer."

Sylvie's lips turned up, catching his reference. Yeah, her place was with his family, with him. Just not *with* him, until she wore two rings on her left hand's ring finger.

"Red Deer?" McHale dropped a mild cuss word. "Are you insane?"

"Nope."

"I have work tomorrow," Sylvie explained, which seemed to appease them.

But it was time to let his captain and his girlfriend know it was more than that with him. "We're Christians. And not doing any of *that* until we're married."

He caught McHale's dropped jaw, Ashley's gasp, and the way Sylvie glanced at him wide-eyed.

"Wait—are you two getting—?"

"No." But maybe one day. "We just don't want all that to complicate things and get in the way of building a real relation-ship. Know what I mean?"

McHale frowned slightly. "I don't know that I get it, but okay. You do you."

"Thanks." Like he needed his captain's approval.

"I think that's actually kind of sweet," Ashley said, tucking her head on Jason's shoulder.

And that comment felt a little patronizing, but whatever.

"And I knew you were a Christian," Ashley said. "I really liked that thing you and your friends did to support Hannah Wade."

"It's important to stand up for what's right."

McHale nodded, eyeing him curiously, then offered Ryan a fist bump and Sylvie a rare smile as he was called away.

Ryan glanced at Sylvie. "And we're doing this right, aren't we, Sylvie?"

Her smile layered fresh joy across his heart. "Yes. We finally are."

ESCAPING the chaos of downtown's fans in the Ice District fan park was one thing. Entering the sleek domain of Jason McHale's luxury condo was another. Sylvie grasped Ryan's hand tightly as he led her inside, and she smiled and pretended ease as she was introduced to a host of people.

"Jason and Ashley often host team events here," he said, pointing to the sleek gray kitchen with its huge island and dining table that looked like it could seat twenty.

A giant designer dog padded out to meet them. "This is Rex." Ryan rubbed the furry dog's head. "Rex, say hi."

Rex put out a paw and Sylvie shook it. "Hey Rex. Aren't you a cutie?" She glanced up at Ryan. "I think he knows it, too."

"One hundred percent. I'm pretty sure that dog eats better than I do."

She laughed, but only really understood what he meant when he took her to the basement area, and pointed out the neon-lit sign that read "Rex's Palace."

"Wow. That's, uh…" She shook her head.

"Next level," he suggested.

"That's one way to describe it."

He snickered, and they joined the others in sharing food and continuing the celebrations.

Later, as the party grew more raucous, she was glad to have given him the excuse to leave early, even though his announcement that they needed to leave was met with knowing winks and jeers. "Don't do anything I would do," Mats said.

"You can count on it," Ryan said, to Sylvie's muffled laughter.

Finally, they escaped, and he opened her door to his car—such a gentleman—and they drove home. Home to Red Deer. His parents' home.

"Are you doing okay?" she asked him.

He held her hand. "I am now."

They didn't need to speak much. So much had been said in recent days. It was enough to be with him, to hold his hand, to wish they were going home to their place together, like Jason and Ashley, and—

No! *Lord, forgive me.* She didn't need to imagine that. See? This was exactly why she couldn't get caught in his hugs or anything physical and stir up feelings that she knew had to be tamped. She had to change the focus of her thoughts. Start a conversation.

"So, what are you going to do for the next few days?"

He glanced at her. "I know what I'd like to do."

Her pulse raced. "You know I only do hugs after you win a game, so it sounds like you'll have to wait a little longer."

"Aw, come on. Surely a playoff series win deserves at least another hug."

At least? Was he suggesting he wanted a kiss? No way could she afford to even *think* about that yet. "I'm just trying to be careful here, Ryan."

He exhaled heavily. "I know."

The headlights of his Lexus flashed on the road marker to Red Deer. Only twenty kilometers to go.

"Hey." His voice had brightened. "But the fact you weren't there for our wins in Seattle has got to mean you still owe me two more hugs, right?"

"I'm getting the impression you really want me to hug you."

"I'm glad you're getting that impression, Sylvie, because it's true."

Oh, she loved their banter. Loved the fact he could tease, and accept her mockery, and it seemed to knit their friendship stronger. Their phone calls and messages were drawing them closer than before, when it had been the kissing and surface conversations that had contributed to the headiness of infatuation. Now, the fact she shared his faith made everything feel richer, more meaningful, like there was an assurance in his pursuit of her that meant this relationship finally had the depth to last. That finally she had found the man who mightn't leave her. That his comment about not having sex with her until they were married might mean one day she'd wear a wedding ring. She would never jeopardize that. Especially now she knew how easily she could. But no. They were friends. And she wouldn't get ahead of herself. She *wouldn't*. Her hand tightened in his.

"You're being quiet."

"Just thinking."

"What about?"

"You."

He smiled. "Ditto."

See? This was how easy it was to tip back into heady attraction. She exhaled. "So, back to my question. What are you going to do for the next two days?"

He yawned. "Sleep in."

"You deserve it."

He glanced at her. "Spend time with you."

Her nose wrinkled. "I have work tomorrow." She yawned. "Actually, today. In eight hours."

"Then tomorrow—tonight, then, we'll have a date."

"Better keep it easy. I'll probably be so tired that I won't be up for much."

"You'd seriously like to stay home and watch a game?"

"I didn't say watch a game, but yeah. It'd be fun to see how some of your other friends are doing in the playoffs."

"You're like the perfect woman."

"Like?"

He laughed, squeezing her hand as his car ate up the miles. "So, tell me more about where things are up to with the missing Esthers. Have you had any more word?"

She sobered. Way to kill the mood. "I've tried that other number a few times now, with no luck. Then the first lady got back to me and said there was a woman in the Ukrainian group who recognized that name."

"Really?" He glanced at her quickly. "Why didn't you say anything?"

"Because I didn't want to distract you, and there's nothing much to say. There was no phone number, just an address."

"Are you going to go see her?"

"Not tomorrow. I'd wondered about the next day, when I have a day off, but seeing you're back—"

"I'll come with you."

"You don't have to. You need to rest, see your family. Not get caught in what is probably just another wild goose chase."

"I want to chase wild geese with you, Sylvie. I want to do everything with you."

Again, his words held a meaning she needed to harness her mind from chasing. Friends. Just friends. Who might hug sometimes. Even if there had been that moment before when he'd looked at her and said things about marriage that made her wonder—

No. She could *not* afford to think like that. She forced herself to focus. "Well, if you want to come, then that's what I hoped to do on Thursday."

"I want to come." He squeezed her hand as the lights of Red Deer appeared on the horizon. "I mean it. I'm in this with you."

Oh, this man. What was she going to do with him? If he wasn't careful, then these feelings of tenderness and respect and extreme affection might finally tip into what Bree called love.

She knew now what love was. It wasn't what she'd felt before. That had been lust, and selfish. This wanted his best. That had been impatient, based in fear. This was prepared to wait. She had learned a lot about what real love looked like, thanks to understanding more about how God loved her. And knowing how much God loved her meant she was prepared to trust Him with her future, and sorting out whatever may come.

CHAPTER 23

*R*yan clenched the wheel as he drove the Lexus along the long empty road. New-planted wheat was growing either side, ready to make the most of the spring and summer sunshine. The road sign indicated that they were nearing the small hamlet of Trumbo, where the mysterious Esther person lived.

Today might change Sylvie's world.

If she found her grandmother, then she might want Sylvie to move out here nearer her, which would be great for Sylvie but potentially make life trickier for her and him. If she didn't find her, then her questions might remain, might always remain, which meant any future would be impacted by her questions over identity. *Lord, help her feel Your peace whatever happens, and to know she's Your child.*

He glanced across at her. "How are you feeling?"

She inhaled then exhaled slowly. The heavy makeup, skulls, and fishnets were gone today, her tattoos hidden by long sleeves, her long flowered skirt like something Bree Karlsson might wear. Even her hair was pulled back into a modest bun. Anyone who didn't know her would think she could be auditioning for *As The Heart Draws*, the TV series starring Ainsley Beckett that had filmed a few episodes on Franklin's family property, Three Creek Ranch. Except for the blue hair. "To be honest, I'm a bit nervous."

"It'll be okay." He squeezed her hand. "Whatever happens, you know we're here for you. And God is, too."

She nodded, her shoulders dropping slightly. "I keep reminding myself of that. But it's one thing to know it, and it's another to actually own it in the middle of circumstances, isn't it?"

"Yeah." His heart swelled at her insight, a maturity he'd not known long himself, despite growing up as a believer. She was amazing, full of spunk and fire but also depth and compassion. If he wasn't driving right now he'd tell her he loved her.

He jerked the wheel. Whoa.

"Are you okay?" She slid him a concerned look.

"Yep. Just got distracted for a moment."

"If you're too tired, I can drive." She smiled. "I suspect someone shouldn't have waited up so late watching a certain hockey game."

Toronto knocking out Detroit in their first-round playoffs clash. The group chat had been fun, his friends making predictions then most being confounded when Brent's swagger was silenced by Dan's teammate Matt Reynolds, who sent Toronto's arena into virtual meltdown. He smiled. He now knew what that was like.

"It was a good game, huh?"

"Your dad was so funny to watch."

"He's got some pride. He's really happy to see some Canadian teams getting through to the second round."

"And then Vancouver play tonight."

"Can't wait." Chris had gone into rare radio silence for a time, which showed just how important the final battle between Vancouver and San Jose was. Either way, he'd have a friend progressing. And Coach had said they'd all better be watching the game tonight, as the winner would be who Edmonton took on in the second round. "And hey, just for the record, I'm happy if you want to drive anytime."

"You mean it?"

"I trust you."

He meant that. This woman was like a safe pair of gloves, ready to catch him, to pick up on his moods, when he needed encouragement or confidence; she somehow always knew the right thing to say. And now, having spent more time with her that wasn't just about physical affection, he was recognizing all kinds of other qualities that checked the mental list of attributes he'd long prayed for in a relationship. She was patient. She was kind. She had snap and sass, but he realized now it was her natural personality, now the walls were mostly down. She was still cautious, and he knew that if they were to one day progress into serious, permanent territory, that he'd probably need to attend some of her counseling sessions too, to learn some hard truths about this woman who had long fascinated him. But that was okay. He'd do that. He'd do anything to make her feel secure and that she could trust him.

"Well, just for the record, I'm happy for you to continue to be a gentleman and drive me."

"A gentleman, huh?"

"Yep." He peeked across. Her gaze was out the windshield. "I trust you."

Okay, maybe he should just pull over, because anything else she said like that might just make his heart explode. He exhaled.

"What is it?"

See? Kindly concerned about him. He loved this woman. He blinked, oversteered.

"Are you sure you're okay?"

"Never better." He pointed to the sign that said they were getting close. "Look, only five kilometers to go."

She clenched and unclenched her hands, so he reached across and held them, then prayed aloud. "Hey God, thank You for being with Sylvie. Thank You that You love her, and whatever happens today, You remain large and in charge of her life and the plans You have for her. So thank You that we can trust You, all the time, every day. Amen."

"Amen," she whispered.

When he next glanced across he caught her blinking back tears. "What's wrong?"

She took in a shaky breath. "What's wrong? Nothing is wrong. You're so good to me."

"Yes, I am."

As hoped for, she chuckled, but it didn't take long before her tension became obvious again. "Sylvie?"

"No, I'm okay. Everything is good."

"It'll be fine, you'll see."

She sighed. "I don't want to sound like a pessimist, because that's not who I'm trying to be anymore. I want to live by faith, I really do. But I can't help feeling this sense of dread that this won't work out."

"God doesn't promise a life without hardship, but He does promise to always be with us."

"I know."

By now he slowed, and they started watching the mailbox numbers. Google Maps had said it was the eighth property on the right, number 3095, so he counted aloud. "3086, that one's 3088, so it's on your side."

"There it is, 3095."

He slowed then stopped the car. Parked here on the main road through town, his red Lexus stood out like a sore thumb. But he hadn't wanted to drive hers and risk a possible breakdown, and these days he liked to travel in comfort. "Okay, so you're doing okay?"

She nodded. "We've got this. Actually, God's got this."

"Amen." He picked up her hand and kissed it. Then at her indrawn breath realized what he'd done. "Sorry."

"You don't make it easy, do you?"

"We don't do easy."

"Not anymore," she said, then smirked.

He laughed. "You must be feeling okay if you can make jokes like that."

"I'm not joking. No matter what my grandmother might've once said, I'm not like my mother, and I'm not easy in that way now."

"I know you're not." Respect for her grew, and he was tempted to finally spill his heart and say—

"Come on, let's do this while I still feel brave."

He followed her to the door and she knocked, then they stood there waiting, while the sun beat down, and a few neighbors poked their heads out over the fences.

He managed a wave, wondering if anyone would expect to see someone like him in a place like this only two days after a playoff game. He figured not.

He glanced at Sylvie, gnawing her lip, and tugged her close.

"Are you trying for a sneaky hug?"

"I'm simply doing what a friend would do. Side hug, see?"

She chuckled, her throat white and begging to be kissed. He chained his thoughts. Nope. No kissing. Not even on hands, it seemed.

She knocked, but again there was no response. "Want me to try?"

"Be my guest."

He banged harder, loud enough that anyone with a hearing aid might hopefully hear and respond. Still nothing.

Sylvie's brow furrowed, her face falling. "Looks like nobody's home."

He could complain about chasing wild geese, even though this had provided the best excuse to spend time with her, and now this was done they could spend quality time together. Or he could be the bigger man and say, "Maybe one of the neighbors knows something."

"Good idea."

They stepped off the porch when a sound from inside halted their step. She turned to him, wide-eyed, then smoothed her hair, and grabbed his hand.

He held it tight, as the door shuddered, then opened with a creak. A woman, her hair gray and pulled up in a fat bun not unlike Sylvie's, peered out from a dim hallway. "Yes?"

Sylvie opened her mouth, then closed it, then peeked up at him as if to say "Please help."

He nodded, cleared his throat, and smiled. "Good morning. My name is Ryan, and this is my friend Sylvie, and we were hoping we might speak with Esther, who we believe lives at this house."

The woman's gaze, which had fallen to their joined hands at the word "friend" then swiveled to Sylvie when he said her name, jerked back to him. "Why?"

He peeked at Sylvie, raising an eyebrow, as he mouthed, "Is she...?"

She nodded, squared her shoulders, and he began to pray.

"Gran."

Her grandmother's eyes widened, then she began to shut the door.

No. *No, no.* Sylvie's gaze swung to Ryan and he instantly put a hand on the door, stopping it from closing any further. "Please, Gran. I just want to talk."

"Don't call me that name again."

"But you are my grandmother. And—"

"And I thought I made my position very clear. I want nothing to do with you, or your mother."

Sylvie's mouth dropped open. Did she not know? "Did you not hear what happened?"

"If it concerns your wretch of a mother, then no."

Emotion quivered, then roared. "She died, Gran. She died last year."

Nothing. Not even a flicker of an eyelash.

"I've told you not to call me that name."

"But you're my family. You're all the family I have." Although, "Where's Granddad?"

Her grandmother blinked. So that had struck a nerve.

Sylvie straightened. "Well?"

"He, ah, died."

Sorrow panged, but anger soon overrode it. How could this woman deny her own daughter of this knowledge? "Where? When? Why didn't you tell me or Mom?"

"Because I couldn't."

"Why not?"

"I, er, didn't know where you lived."

"We hadn't moved for years. You could've sent a note if you didn't want to speak to us. Why didn't you want to speak to us?" Her voice caught.

Ryan stepped closer, his hand on her back, his presence solid and reassuring. A determined protector. Oh, he lived up to his family's name.

"I told your mother when she was last here. I didn't want anything more to do with her, thanks to her wickedness."

"She was trying—"

"Trying isn't good enough. And it didn't matter how hard she tried, she always fell back on another man, didn't she?" Her gaze flicked up and down Sylvie, like she could see past the good-girl clothes to the pain once tattooed beneath. "And you were never much better."

Sylvie gasped, then clamped her jaw. Ryan's hand dropped from her back.

"Look at you here, dressed up like you're heading to church, when I remember all your tattoos and prostitute clothes."

"That's not fair," Ryan said.

"Don't you dare speak to me, young man, when you're obviously just her latest conquest."

"He's not—"

"I'm not her latest," Ryan said firmly. "I'm her last."

Sylvie's gaze swiveled up, and she caught the throbbing in his jaw, before he met her gaze, his hazel eyes offering reassurance. He was really talking futures? He liked her that much? "That's right. Obviously I've been saving the best until last."

His mouth quirked, and she realized what she said. But in this moment of rawness she had to own her past choices. She turned to her grandmother. "And just so you know, we haven't had sex."

Her grandmother sniffed. "I can't believe a word you say."

"Then you probably won't believe that I'm a Christian now, and I go to church. Although usually," she drew out her skirt, "I don't wear clothes like this. They're far more understanding about things like that where I attend."

"That's what's wrong with the world today. People don't have standards. They let anyone into so-called churches these days."

"Isn't that the point? Jesus was a friend of tax collectors, and was known to hang out with prostitutes and drunkards. Or haven't you read that in the Bible?"

Her grandmother shook her head. "You're either good or you're not. There is no in-between."

"Don't you believe in second chances? That's what Jesus was all about. *Is* all about." Sylvie tapped her chest. "That's why I can call myself a child of God, because of what Jesus did on that cross. He died for sinners, Gran. For people like me. And Mom."

Her grandmother eyed her, gaze unflinching. Was there no getting through to this woman?

"What are you even doing out here in the sticks? What happened to the nice house near Red Deer?"

Her grandmother glanced away.

Sylvie peeked up at Ryan. His frown eased as he smiled reassurance, and she nodded, and fixed her gaze back on her grandmother. "Well? I've come all this way. The least you can do is tell me where Granddad is buried."

"I don't know where he is."

"You don't know where Granddad is? You said he died."

"He did. In Ukraine."

She exhaled, her heart deflating, sore. So it was just as they'd suspected. "When?"

Her grandmother shrugged. "Not long after your last visit."

"So why didn't you say anything? How did he die?"

"I don't know."

"Weren't you there?"

Her grandmother pressed her lips together. From her time at the aged care home Sylvie recognized fatigue. "Gran, can we come in? You look like you need to sit down."

"No."

She was stubborn, this one. But Sylvie had inherited one thing from her at least. She was stubborner. "So, you don't know where he is buried?"

Her grandmother cleared her throat. "I believe the war there destroyed records."

It had destroyed so many things. "But that still doesn't explain what you're doing living out here."

A voice called from within. Her grandmother flinched.

"Who's that?"

"Nobody."

"No, that's definitely someone." Was it her grandfather? Had her grandmother lied? Maybe he wasn't dead, and there was still hope—

"Who is it, Esther?" Then an elderly figure appeared behind her grandmother.

Sylvie sagged, and Ryan wrapped his arm around her. "Mr. Thompson? It's Sylvie, remember?"

He blinked at her from behind silver-rimmed glasses. Her grandmother's neighbor. From back in Red Deer.

Her mind was awhirl, pieces from her past, vague recollections, her mother's murmurs, comments from Mrs. A and the others at Aspen Lodge, drawing up like a whirlwind, sucking up the scattered fragments of her past in a giant kaleidoscope of images she could now see with adult understanding.

"You." She pointed to her grandfather's betrayer. "You and her." She pointed to her grandmother.

"It's not what you think," her grandmother began.

"It *is* what I think." Sylvie eyed Mr. Thompson. "Where's your wife?"

He wrapped his arm around her grandmother. "Right here."

"You're married?"

"Well, not exactly in the eyes of the law, but we're married in our hearts."

Sylvie's gasp sent her grandmother's gaze to the floor, her cheeks tinting pink.

"I don't mean my grandmother. I mean the woman I remember being married to you, back when my grandfather was married to her." She pointed to her grandmother.

"You don't have to say anything," her grandmother murmured.

"Actually, I suspect I do." The geniality in his face departed as he eyed Sylvie soberly. "Marjorie left me when she found out. Then John left soon too."

Poor Granddad. "Let me get this straight. You two had an affair, broke up two marriages, and the reason you haven't wanted anything to do with us is because you're ashamed of what *you* have done?"

"That's not it at all," her grandmother snapped.

"Actually," Mr. Thompson murmured, before her grandmother's hard nudge in his ribs shut him up.

"Actually what?" Sylvie persisted, her gaze narrowing as she studied him.

His shoulders slumped. "It isn't too far from the truth."

No. How could they? Sylvie grasped Ryan's hand, his hand infusing so much strength into her, she could feel it permeating her blood, as she faced her grandmother again. "How dare you judge my mother and me when your actions are so despicable? You might say you're married in your hearts, but your actions have had consequences that have affected so many more people than just you. You don't know where my grandfather died, do you?" Clarity came to her. "In fact, I bet you're not even sure he is dead, and that's why you haven't married, because you can't get a death certificate, and until you do, then you'd be considered a bigamist."

"Sylvie—"

"No. Don't try and justify yourself to me. I don't understand how you can dare sit in your glass house and throw stones at me and Mom, when what you've done is so much worse."

Ryan nudged her with his shoulder, and the peak of her anger subsided, allowing her to hear a gentle whisper that echoed the words before. This woman, who thought people were either good or not, who didn't believe in second chances— although she'd obviously taken a second chance with this man— she needed Jesus. Not more condemnation. She needed *Jesus*. And forgiveness. Just like Sylvie.

But saying those words felt impossible, anger rippling beneath her skin preventing her from speaking with any grace. *Lord, I need You.*

She sucked in a breath. Ryan squeezed her hand. The flames

of indignation eased enough to allow her to say, "Gran, I don't think I'll ever understand why you cut off me and Mom. But I'm going to ask God to help me to forgive you. You're all the family I have left in this world, and I don't know if you care about that, but as far as it depends on me, I'm willing to keep the door open."

Her grandmother's cold stare could freeze a house fire. "I'm not willing." Her grandmother stepped back inside the house. "Goodbye."

Then she turned and slammed the door.

CHAPTER 24

Ryan caught Sylvie as she swayed, sagging into him, before her head fell against his chest, her arms slipped around his torso, and she murmured a broken, "Ryan."

He wrapped his arms around her, holding her tight, offering what comfort he could, while praying furiously for God's peace to fill her. That had been horrific, more emotionally grueling than any playoff game. They needed to get out of here. Although it wouldn't hurt for Esther to know how much her actions had hurt her only relative.

But even with Sylvie's pain and grief, he was so proud of her. *So* proud. She'd spoken the truth, been honest and real, and though the answer wasn't what she'd wanted, her courage inspired him. His admiration and affection only deepened.

"I don't understand why she cut us off," Sylvie murmured, "why she cut me off, when all I ever wanted was to feel loved."

"You are loved. You know that God loves you. You know Mom and Dad do too, Bree. Ethan. Me. We all do."

Her face was wet, pressed into the crook of his neck. "You do?"

"I do." He squeezed her tighter. "I really do."

She relaxed against him, and he closed his eyes, wondering if she could feel his heart pounding away. But this moment wasn't about rekindling passion, it was about her recognizing her worth in God's eyes. She needed to know that, even in this moment that felt shaky. God was with her, God's love remained sure.

And just like God's love could always be counted on, so Ryan's love was also a promise for the future. He loved this woman. Loved her. And she would always have a place within his heart. "Come on. Let's get you back home."

Home. It was where she belonged. With him. With his family. Where she was loved.

He loved her, and while she still hadn't said the words yet, not since their reconciliation, anyway, he was getting the impression from the way she looked at him, talked to him, prayed for him, that it would only be a matter of time. They were good together, and today's incident, awful as it had been, only reinforced the depth of their bonds. And while he knew both of them staying in his family's house might get a little trickier in the off-season, he planned to be away in the Philippines for part of that, and she could always stay with Bree sometimes, or he could have her visit him in Edmonton, and they could bike rides or picnic in River Valley. Although he wondered whether a girl like her rode bikes…

The journey back to Red Deer was quiet, his silent prayers filling the car as she held his hand, and he drove. He didn't want to go home just yet, and suspected neither of them had emotional fortitude enough to face his mother. Nor did he want to run the risk of fans intruding on their time together.

"Hey, I don't know about you, but would you mind if we stop somewhere and get food? I'm hungry."

"You're always hungry," she murmured.

"I'm high-maintenance."

Her lips curved, but her usual animation wasn't there.

"Is drive-through okay?" Best way to avoid any fans.

"I don't mind where you go."

"If you're tired, close your eyes and have a rest."

"I might just do that."

He drove to the place his mom had mentioned as having reasonable coffee, his car standing out as he joined the line. He might regret this. He never ate fast food during the season, but today's drama had sucked so much energy from them both it had to be worth a few extra thousand calories, at least.

Scanning the options on the board, he gently nudged Sylvie awake. "Hey, what do you feel like eating? Chicken or beef burger? Coffee? Shake? Fries? Water?"

"I don't care."

Okay, then. He'd get a wide selection of options, then. Healthy-ish for him, or her if she'd prefer, and a few items that might be considered comfort foods. And if she didn't want that Biscoff-flavored shake, then he'd be totally okay with helping out.

He ordered, paid, then they got to the window. A guy inside handed him the first bag of food, which meant Ryan had to nudge Sylvie awake. "Hey, Sylvie, can you hold this for me?"

She stirred, stretched, and smiled at him. "Sure."

The dude in the window handed out the second bag, then did a double take.

Ryan braced. Here came the fandom.

"Sylvie?"

Huh?

A peek at her showed her glance at the guy, her eyes widening. "Dave."

"You know this guy?" Ryan asked.

"I, um, yeah." She winced, adding in a lower voice. "I might've worked here in my 'hospitality' phase."

Pieces clicked into place. The job his mom had rescued her

from. That might be why he remembered the name. The coffee here had better be really good, then.

"Wait, are you Ryan Guillemette?" Dave asked, as he handed out the cardboard drinks tray.

Ryan nodded, passing it to Sylvie who balanced it on her lap.

"And you're here with her?"

Ryan turned to Sylvie, just in time to catch the wash of rejection steal over Sylvie's features, as if she knew others would have the same doubts about their relationship as this idiot did.

Ryan picked up her hand, kissed it. "Sure am."

She smiled at him, and he knew he'd do anything to keep that expression there. He loved her. He wanted what was best for her.

He glanced back up at the guy. "I'm a lucky man."

He left the man and his gobsmacked expression and drove to the park in the center of the city. They took their food to a seat near the Norwegian House, its grassy roof plain to see now the snows had gone. They ate in silence in the sunshine, him wearing his cap and sunglasses, happy to avoid being recognized within his hometown, she with her sleeves pushed up, her tattoos on display, so once he finished eating, he could trace them with his finger.

She tucked her head on his shoulder, and he held her hand, tracing her skin, in a movement that felt both intimate and yet comforting. It was like touching her in this way proved a point of deeper connection, soothing the agitation of earlier, as they watched children play while springtime blossoms drifted on the slight breeze. If this had been a movie, an orchestral string section would be building up the romantic music about now.

A little boy, maybe around Ethan's age, kicked a soccer ball that rolled near, and he shifted to flick-kick it back, in a move Mats had taught him during their pregame warm-ups.

"Thanks, Mister," the kid called.

"You're welcome."

She snuggled closer, her arm around his torso. "Do you want kids?"

"One day. You?"

"Yes. Especially if I knew they'd turn out to be like Ethan."

"That's probably got a lot to do with his parents, right?"

She nodded, and he tucked her closer.

"I think you'd make a great mom."

She stiffened. "I don't know. I can't help but think I'd just mess things up. There's such dysfunction in my family, and I wouldn't want to pass that along."

"But you wouldn't be," he gently objected. "You'd be passing on the goodness and grace of God. And what child wouldn't want to grow up knowing that? And who could share about that better than someone who has experienced it firsthand?"

She peeled away from his side, and looked up at him, shifting his sunglasses so he could read her eyes. "Do you mean that?"

"I do."

She bit her lip. "Do you think that you could overlook my past and see…?"

His heart leapt at what remained unsaid. "And see a future with you? Absolutely."

They stared at each other, for far longer than three seconds, then she smiled. "I love you, Ryan."

Sunbeams filled his chest. And he didn't care that the park was filled with people and he might be seen. There was only one thing to do in this moment. So he leaned closer, angling his head…

Then she pulled away.

"What?" Had the pickles on that greasy burger flavored his breath that fast? He knew he'd regret going to that restaurant.

"I don't want to kiss you. I mean, I do, but I don't."

"You'll need to help me out in understanding that one."

"We're going slow, remember?"

He sighed, and resumed his position from before, and she tucked in beside him. "How long do I have to wait?"

"The wedding?"

Whose wedding? Theirs? Had she grown so modest she didn't want to kiss until their wedding day? He might need to propose right now if that was the case. "That long?"

"It's only six weeks away."

Oh. Franklin and Hannah's.

"Whose did you think I meant?"

"Never mind."

She chuckled softly. "You're funny."

"I am."

She squeezed him. "I love funny."

"And I love you."

~

Six weeks later
Calgary

"Oh, Sylvie."

Sylvie glanced up from Bree's guest room's full-length mirror, and caught her friend's expression, the way her mouth had parted, and her hand was at her throat, and the doubts abated. "You think it's okay?"

"You look stunning. You're going to melt Ryan's eyeballs."

She laughed, but tugged at her neckline. This dress was making the most of the girls today. "You don't think it's too much?"

"You look fantastic. I wish I had your curves and not all these extra ones."

"You have curves born from love, with all those gorgeous kids of yours." Part of the reason she'd stayed here last night, so she could help Bree get her tribe ready for Hannah's wedding.

Bree joined her, and hugged her. "You're so sweet. Even though I'm pretty sure they result from my love of food."

Sweet was a word she'd never heard about herself before. But she'd take it. She swiveled and eyed the low back, the halter neck style which revealed her tattoos, the designs etched on her arms on full display. "You don't think it's too revealing?"

"Of your curves? Not at all. Everything is covered that needs to be. You don't need to dress like the Amish to be following Jesus. And if you're worried about your tattoos, then don't be. That's why we picked this dress, remember? You shouldn't hide them away. They are part of who you are." Bree stroked her upper arm. "They don't make you who you are, but you don't need to hide who you are, either. You have a unique style and distinctive expression of your identity, and it's part of what makes you *you*, and why we love you."

Sylvie blinked rapidly. "Don't make me cry. At least not until Ryan sees this."

"So you're happy we opted for this and not that Victorian lace disaster?"

Sylvie smiled at the reflection. The subtle shimmer on the navy-blue chiffon was something she'd never normally pick out, but the convertible neckline options meant she should get more wears from it. She looked good. Actually, she looked the best she ever had, especially with her hair and makeup done. Her chin lifted. She could probably even rival Ashley in the hotness stakes today.

"Go on. You can admit it. You like what you see."

"You did well. But I gotta say, the other dress's matching parasol was cute."

"From what Hannah and Cassie have said, there might well be a few parasols ready today, so I don't think you're missing out."

A tap came from downstairs, and Sylvie peered from her window, recognizing that red sports car.

"Is it him?" Bree asked.

She nodded, her mouth suddenly dry.

"Then go. Kids are all dressed and ready, thanks to you, and Holly and Brent can help us get them in the car. You've got a date, Cinderella."

A date. With her prince. And after all this time she wasn't waiting until midnight for their next first kiss.

She collected her bag, and a light wrap, in case it got cool—or too many raised eyebrows meant she needed to hide—and, one hand on the banister, descended the stairs to where Mike and Holly were chatting, supervising the kids, while Brent had answered the door.

Mike whistled, and Ethan gasped, and cried, "Sylvie! You're so beautiful. Like a princess!"

She bent and straightened his bow tie. "Are you going to be my prince?"

"No. That's Ryan."

Holly grinned. "You look amazing, Sylvie."

"Thanks." She gestured to the Aussie's green satin gown. "You look beautiful yourself. And yes, you look handsome too, Mike."

"Dressed by Bree."

Holly poked a spangled sandal out from under her long skirts. "I think we all have been today, right?"

"I've got a reputation to uphold now," Bree said from behind them. "Sylvie, go. We'll be fine."

"See you there, then."

She moved to the entryway, where Brent and Ryan were talking, then their conversation ceased. Brent's lips twisted to a smirk, then he said, "I can see I'm not needed here."

"Not at all," Ryan muttered, his gaze fixed on her.

"You look good, Sylvie," Brent said, then sauntered away.

"Thanks." She didn't look at him, though she was glad they'd made their peace. Ryan, dressed in a navy suit, pink shirt and brown brogues, demanded all her attention.

And she was demanding all of his, apparently. His mouth parted. "Sylvie."

"Are they kissing yet?" Bree said loudly from behind them.

"They're such children," Sylvie said, taking his arm. "Come on. We better get going."

They exited, and only then, away from prying eyes, did he take her in his arms. "You look so beautiful. Like a dream."

"All Bree."

"All you. You're the one wearing this. It's not wearing you."

She smiled at him, her heels putting him at eye height, and he lowered his head. "Can I kiss you now?"

"Not yet, not here," she murmured.

"But today?" he pleaded.

She shivered. "Absolutely."

THE WHITE CHAPEL at Three Creek Ranch, Franklin's family farm, was everything as gorgeous and vintage as one would expect from a place that had played host to various heritage-themed TV shows and movies. Cassie, Franklin's oldest younger sister, was the movie set's manager, and Sylvie had met her at Bree's a few times before. "It all looks so beautiful," Sylvie said.

"We've gone for rustic chic."

"And did I hear *As The Heart Draws* was filming here recently?"

Cassie's face blanked. "Yes. It's been exciting."

Strange. She didn't look excited. "And Harrison Woods is staying here?"

Another strange expression crossed Cassie's face. "Mm-hmm."

But there was no time to further pursue this, as Cassie's attention was needed elsewhere.

The ceremony was as beautiful as the stained glass and oiled wooden chapel, the precious promises between Franklin and Hannah stirring Sylvie to pray that their marriage would be blessed. Then the happy couple were pronounced husband and wife and they kissed, to great cheers and applause. She and Ryan joined the other guests—family, teammates, Hannah's workmates, friends—as they paused on the chapel's front steps for a photo, then they all traipsed up the western town's dusty main street toward a huge white marquee. Her heels demanded she hold Ryan's arm, which neither of them minded, as it meant they could walk slow, hold each other close, and enjoy the happiness buzzing around them.

The sky was blue and clear, necessitating those parasols that Bree had mentioned before, which took pride of place in several more photographs while they waited for the meal to be served. Sylvie leaned against Ryan, his arm wrapped around her waist, as they watched the photos being taken of the families: Hannah and her mom, with Franklin; Hannah swallowed up in the much larger Franklin family. Then it was more photos, of Franklin and his teammates, from both his former team, Boston, and Calgary, then Ryan joined the other guys in the Bible studies. Dan Walton had sent his apologies, as his wife Sarah wasn't well, but Chris, from the newly crowned Cup champs, after the wunderkind Zac Parotti had a hat trick of goals in the deciding game, was more than making up for it. Vancouver had knocked out Edmonton, Ryan admitting the only comfort in being knocked out in the second round in four games was that it was at the hands of the current champs.

"Now let's get the wives."

Sylvie watched, as the Bible study's wives gathered around Hannah. Then Hannah glanced at her. "And the girlfriends. Come on." She gestured for Sylvie to join in. "You know you have to do what the bride says. Come on, you're part of the family now."

Moisture heated the backs of her eyes as she stood between Holly and Bree, Allie, Diana. Finally she was fitting in. It didn't matter what she looked like, or what she wore on her skin, or what had happened in her past. This group of believers was as much a family as Bree's own, as Ryan's own, all of whom had opened their arms and welcomed and accepted her. Like Bree said, she was an individual, unique, but God had made her that way, and here, she was part of God's family too. For a girl who'd been looking for a family for so long, she was almost overwhelmed by the love embracing her now.

Then another photo, this time with the guys and the girls, and Ryan wrapped her in his arms, her back to his front, as they smiled at the camera, and she relaxed in the arms of her determined protector.

By the time photos were done it was time to eat, so they moved inside the big marquee. The meal was delicious, filled with laughter, and friendship, and tease. She and Ryan sat at a large round table with Luc, Chris and Diana, the Karlssons, Mike and Bree, and their kids. It was fun to witness the dynamics, the joshing between the men, the easy conversation between the women. Ryan and Luc shared about the Philippines. Then Chris asked Ryan about his new place, and he told the others about his new apartment, having told Mats he wouldn't continue sharing during the next season. Ryan's recent trip overseas meant he hadn't moved in yet, but was looking forward to it soon. He'd mentioned picnics and fishing and bike rides to Sylvie, and she couldn't wait for him to teach her how to ride a bike. Not that she'd told him that yet.

Franklin and Hannah cut the cake, and the dancing began. After the bridal waltz, Brent dared Holly to dance, and Mike took Bree's hand, and both couples joined in.

Ryan arched a brow, but before she could reply, Ethan came up and touched her hand.

"Are you having fun, sweetheart?" she asked him.

He nodded, then turned to Ryan. "Hello, Prince Ryan."

Aw, bless him.

Ryan grinned up at her, then bowed his head. "Good afternoon, Prince Ethan."

"I'm a boy, not a prince," Ethan said solemnly.

"Ah. I see. But I'm a prince because Sylvie is my princess?"

"Yes."

"You're right," Ryan said, pressing a kiss to the back of her hand. "She is."

He arched a brow, and she knew what that brow was saying, and she shook her head. "Not yet."

"You *are* a princess, Sylvie," Ethan said. "And you should be dancing."

"Oh, I love that boy," she murmured, a short time later, as Ryan held her close as the music slowed.

Ryan's hand touched her bare back, and she shivered. "I'm a big fan of his, too."

She laughed, and tucked her head next to his jaw, happiness swathing her as she studied the people around her.

Hannah and Franklin kissing. Franklin's teammate, Tom Chavez, chatting with Cassie's sisters, Poppy and Jessica. One was a dancer, the other a vet, and both seemed cut from the Cassie mold of determination and sweet tease. She glanced back at their table, where Diana's head was under Chris's chin, while Chris talked with Luc, who looked uncomfortable in his suit, tugging at the collar like it was too tight. They'd already heard him tell plenty of people that no one would ever catch him dancing, saying he didn't want to squash any poor woman's toes.

Ryan chuckled softly. "I'm praying Luc meets his Miss Right soon."

"Good luck to her. The man's got plenty of opinions."

"For sure." Ryan tipped her chin up. "Speaking of Miss Right, can I kiss you now?"

Not here in front of all these people. She smiled. "Not yet."

Later, when the sky dimmed, and the first of the stars appeared, Ryan took her outside, wrapping her up in a hug that drew her close to him, past the point of friendly, but still not too close. Several strings of twinkling lights created a romantic, fairytale feel, and he bent his head, and murmured, "How about now?"

She stared into his eyes, way longer than three seconds, and murmured, "Yes, please."

He drew nearer, three inches, two, one, and she tilted her mouth to meet his.

His lips brushed hers in a chaste kiss. A kiss that promised there would be more. One of friendship, grace, and love. Real love. The kind that came from above.

He drew back. Eyes alight. "I love you."

"I love you."

Her heart was dancing, then it danced some more as he leaned close and slanted his mouth across hers again, in another not-quite-so-tame kiss, that seared her lips with passion and sent her soul tingling.

She wrapped her arms around him, as the laughter and music continued to fill the evening air. And she knew that here, loved by God, loved by others, in the middle of this huge group of people who treated each other like family, who had welcomed her into their midst with open arms, was where she finally fit in, and that she *finally* belonged.

The End

Make sure you check out the next book in the Northwest Ice series, and discover whether Luc can dance in *Pointe, Shoots, and Scores*

Thank you for reading *The Love Penalty,* the second book in the Northwest Ice romance series. I was thrilled so many readers enjoyed the Original Six series, so it was fun to establish a new Christian romance series set in some of the hockey cities of the north and west Canada and USA. I've been lucky enough to visit some of these places, and you can find pics on my website at www.carolynmillerauthor.com

I'd like to give a shout out to the reader who first suggested that Sylvie (from *The Breakup Project*) needed her own story. I love a good redemption arc, so I hope you enjoyed! While the characters and institutions mentioned in this book are fictional, some of the scenarios are based on truth. I'd like to thank Jeannie Madden for the story about her father, Clifford Howe, and the true miracle of his eyes. I also want to acknowledge David Hocking, a friend for many years, who is proof that a man of God can be in a nursing home and still be touching lives for the Kingdom.

The ranch near Calgary boasting its own movie set is real, and forms the basis for my new romance series based on Franklin's three sisters from the Three Creek Ranch. Find out more about Cassie's path to romance in *A Cameo for a Cowgirl*.

Mission Possible for Future Generations is a real missions organization run by friends of mine that helps sponsor children in the Philippines. Find out more here. And you can listen to the Northwest Ice playlist on Spotify here.

～

Reviews help other readers find new-to-them authors, so if you can spare a moment to write a quick review at Goodreads / your place of purchase, I'd be very grateful.

Make sure you check out Luc's story in the next book in the Northwest Ice romance series, *Pointe, Shoots, and Scores*.

If you enjoy Christian contemporary romance you may want to check out the books in the Original Six hockey romance series, a sweet & swoony, slightly sporty Christian contemporary romance series.

The Breakup Project
Love on Ice
Checked Impressions
Hearts and Goals
Big Apple Atonement
Muskoka Blue

Romance fans who enjoy small town life may also enjoy reading the Muskoka Romance series, that starts with *Muskoka Shores*.

I'd love for you to check out my other books and to sign up for my newsletter at www.carolynmillerauthor.com where you can be the first to learn all my book and contest news, and discover more behind-the-book details and photos. Newsletter subscribers can also get an exclusive bonus book free, so grab your copy of *Originally Yours* here.

ABOUT THE AUTHOR

Carolyn Miller lives in the beautiful Southern Highlands of New South Wales, Australia, with her husband and four children. A long-time lover of romance, especially that of Jane Austen, Georgette Heyer and LM Montgomery, Carolyn loves to write contemporary and historical romance that draws readers into fictional worlds that show the truth of God's grace in our lives.

To find out more about Carolyn's books, and to subscribe to her newsletter, please visit www.carolynmillerauthor.com

You can also connect with her at

ALSO BY CAROLYN MILLER

<u>The Original Six hockey series</u>
The Breakup Project

Love on Ice

Checked Impressions

Hearts and Goals

Big Apple Atonement

Muskoka Blue

<u>Muskoka Romance series</u>
Muskoka Shores

Muskoka Christmas

Muskoka Hearts

Muskoka Spotlight

Muskoka Holiday Morsels

Muskoka Promise

<u>Northwest Ice hockey series</u>
Fire and Ice

The Love Penalty

Pointe, Shoots, and Scores

<u>Three Creeks Ranch Romance series</u>
A Cameo for a Cowgirl

<u>Trinity Lakes collection</u>
Love Somebody Like You

Tangled Up in Love

Only You Can Love Me

<u>The Independence Islands series</u>

Restoring Fairhaven

Regaining Mercy

Reclaiming Hope

Rebuilding Hearts

Refining Josie

Historical:

<u>Regency Wallflowers</u>

Dusk's Darkest Shores

Midnight's Budding Morrow

Dawn's Untrodden Green

<u>Regency Brides: Legacy of Grace</u>

The Elusive Miss Ellison

The Captivating Lady Charlotte

The Dishonorable Miss DeLancey

<u>Regency Brides: Promise of Hope</u>

Winning Miss Winthrop

Miss Serena's Secret

The Making of Mrs Hale

<u>Regency Brides: Daughters of Aynsley</u>

A Hero for Miss Hatherleigh

Underestimating Miss Cecilia

Misleading Miss Verity

'Heaven and Nature Sing' from the Joy to the World Christmas
novella collection

'More than Gold' from

the Across the Shores novella collection